I0558860

Love

Immortal

Linnea Hall

This is a work of fiction. Names, characters, places, and incidents are products of the author's imagination or are used fictitiously and are not to be construed as real. Any resemblance to actual events, locales, organizations, or persons, living or dead, is entirely coincidental.

KTJ Publishing
8928 Swinnea Road
Southaven, MS 38671

Copyright © 2009 by Linnea Hall
ISBN: 978-0-98325350-1
ISBN-10: 0-98325350-1
www.KTJPublishing.com

First KTJ paperback printing: January 2010

Printed in the U.S.A.

Cover art by Tom Konrath
maninthewood.com

To my Jewell, my inspiration and to the man that put up with me for the months, that stretched into years while I wrote this. And to all of the people that helped me edit and rewrite this book to help me get it "write."

Love
Immortal

CHAPTER 1

The man had been in full cardiac arrest for over a minute, but he was still screaming. His screams filled the emergency room with blood curdling intensity and reverberated throughout the rest of the hospital. Jewell McKean looked at the monitors. He *was* dead; his heart had stopped beating. She leaned against the door to the room where they worked on him and watched as the doctors and more experienced nurses worked to save the man's life. While they worked, she tried to imagine how his screams could be described to someone who wasn't here to witness his pain; blood curdling, certainly. Anguished? Tortured? Otherworldly? She contemplated the eerie sounds emanating from the body that lay in the room. His screams sounded inhuman, like a banshee's wail echoing across the Irish countryside heralding death. The hollow scream foretelling of the man's imminent demise: terrifying in their torment, frightening in their volume.

She felt a connection to this man; something other than pity, other than sorrow. She was drawn to him, belonged with him. Maybe because he looked so young; it was tragic that his life had taken this turn. He should still have his whole life ahead of him. She thought about his family; how would his parents cope with the loss of their son; no parent expects to outlive their children. She wondered if he had brothers and sisters that would miss him; whether he had a girlfriend.

Working in triage, Jewell was one of the first to see the man. He was the victim of a drunk driver, just like her mother. Seeing him, brought back all of the memories of her mother's death so many years before. The blood, the broken bones, the pain so apparent on his face reminded her of the last time she saw her mother's broken body.

It had been nearly two minutes since the last futile beat of the man's heart when his screaming abruptly stopped.

Jewell watched as the doctors tried desperately to bring life back to the man's empty, now soulless body. They worked feverishly for another several minutes before finally calling the time of death: 11:26 p.m. She stared as the doctors and nurses slowly filed out of the room, covered in blood and gore evidencing their ineffectual attempt to save the man's life. Their faces drawn with their efforts, their lips pressed tight together against the unspoken question that was on everyone's mind: Why?

Jewell stepped silently into the room. The machines that only moments ago were beeping and moving, indication of hope, were now woefully silent. The flat green line split the EKG monitor in half, evidencing the absence of life.

The man's lifeless body lay silent on the gurney that had carried him into this room; the room where he would take his last breath. His body was covered with a plain white sheet; a shroud covering the remains of what had once been his life. Jewell didn't know why she entered the room to take one last look at the man: why it seemed so important to her. And yet, at the same time, she knew unquestionably that she had to look upon him one last time.

She carefully pulled the sheet away from his face, her eyes averted, perhaps fearing what she might see. After folding the sheet back to reveal his face and upper chest, she returned her eyes to his body. His right collarbone was crushed, his shoulder twisted at an awkward angle. His torso, what she could see of it, was covered with bruises. An incision had been made on his right side, evidencing the doctors' efforts to drain his lungs of blood that was seeping into them maliciously working to take him into the cold embrace of death.

There were red marks on either side of his chest where the paddles of the defibrillator had been placed in an effort to start his silent heart beating, to carry precious blood throughout his body, to keep his body alive if only for a short while longer, until his family had the chance to say good-bye. On his right side, just above the sternum, there was an unnatural depression, suggesting that some of his ribs must be broken, crushed beyond repair.

The man's screams echoed in her mind again – he shouldn't have been able to draw enough breath to produce the deafening scream that resonated through her head. With his injuries, he shouldn't have been able to manage a whisper. Then she reminded herself that he was screaming even after his heart had stopped.

Jewell finally braced herself and forced her eyes up the line of his sternum and into the small hollow at the base of his neck. Her eyes moved further up, to trace the line of his jaw. It was strong, angular. It reminded her of carved marble, chiseled to perfection by the artist's tools and vision. And yet, the hard line was softened ever so slightly by his youth. He had a small dimple in the center of his chin, not a flaw, but character in an otherwise perfect face.

The man's mouth was peaceful; beautiful when it wasn't stretched wide in a dying, agonized scream. His lips were full, conveying just the hint of a pout. They were nearly white in death, but she imagined in life they would be the deep red of garnets caught in sunlight. His nose had been broken in the crash, and now curved on his face at an eerie angle. Somehow, even distorted as it was, she could see that his nose was in perfect proportion to the rest of his features. His right cheek was crushed, flattened by the force of whatever had damaged the rest of his right side. His right eye was swollen, bruised.

His left side had suffered little damage in the crash. Jewell reached across his body to grab a four by four gauze pad from the tray of instruments on the other side of the bed. She saturated the pad with alcohol and gently wiped the dried, caked blood from the left side of his face and forehead. Despite the pallor of his skin, she still had a sense of how his rosy cheeks would glow through his sun-kissed skin when he smiled. His cheekbones were pronounced, high on his face and well-proportioned but, like his chin, the strong line softened by youth.

She tried to imagine the color of his eyes. His heredity seemed to be Anglo, with sandy colored hair and light skin. His eyes would probably be blue, the color of sapphires, or a clear winter sky. She longed to look into those eyes, to see life reflected back in them. His sandy hair was matted with dried blood, an ugly gash cut through his hair, from the crown of his skull to the middle of his forehead. At certain angles, the wound sparkled as if it was filled with diamonds. She leaned closer, noticing glass embedded in the injury, not attended to because death took him before the wound could be cleaned and sutured.

She stared down at his peaceful, beautiful face, which such a short time before had been drawn tight with pain. She consoled herself with the thought that at least he was no longer suffering. At least he would never again feel pain: or love, or joy, she appended sadly to her thought.

She was surprised when a small drop of water splashed onto his face. Her eyes turned to the ceiling where she searched for the source of the leak. There was no sign of any water on the ceiling. She lowered her head, once again gazing into his battered and broken face. She tasted the salt of tears on her lips, and only then realized that she was crying.

Beep. The sound pulled Jewell from her reverie, reminding her that she had responsibilities. She glanced at her watch and realized that she had been sitting with the man for over ten minutes. She was certain that people were wondering where she had wandered off to. Though, they may have thought that she needed some time to recover from the shock of seeing someone die. It was expected of the new nurses, that they wouldn't be able to handle death easily. They were not yet jaded to the realities of the ER. She was assured, each time she saw someone die, that it would get easier. While the pain would still linger, the ability to handle it would improve with time.

Jewell slowly pulled the sheet back over the man's peaceful face, trying to imagine that he was only sleeping, though his injuries betrayed the truth. She stood for a minute looking over his shrouded corpse feeling as if she should have known him. That somehow, he was a part of her, their lives meant to be a part of one another's. She felt that somehow, losing him was like losing a part of herself.

Beep. It was the same sound that she had heard before. She turned, looking for the source of the sound and heard only silence. After standing completely motionless straining to hear that sound again, and hearing nothing but the beating of her own heart, she decided it must have come from the hallway, or her imagination. As she turned to leave the room, she heard the sound again: *beep.* But this time, she saw the flat, thin green line on the EKG monitor spike.

*   *   *

It took a few seconds for Jewell's brain to register what her eyes were seeing. Could it be possible? Could he still be alive? "Code blue!" She screamed into the hallway, yanking the sheet from his shrouded body. *Beep.* Her training kicked in and she immediately started checking for other signs of life. Her hand wrapped around his wrist, her finger on his pulse while her other hand rested lightly on his crushed chest. She leaned her ear close to his mouth to see if he was breathing; she felt a gentle exhale of air, and felt his chest rise, perhaps a fraction of an inch. It was impossible, but he *was* alive.

As she leaned over his broken body, a single nurse sauntered in to see what the commotion was. When she saw the strong, if somewhat irregular heartbeat on the EKG monitor, she ran out of the room for a crash cart, screaming code blue as she ran.

Seconds later, doctors and nurses poured into the room. As doctors ran to the man's side, nurses frantically tore open sterile packs, readying instruments for the doctors' use. Instead of stepping back as she had done in most critical situations since she had started working here, Jewell stayed close to the man's side, ensuring that the doctors were doing everything they could to save his life…again. Refusing to release his hand, Jewell continued to monitor his pulse despite what she could see on the heart monitor.

It had only been about fifteen minutes when the doctors pronounced him stable enough to move upstairs for surgery. It was critical that certain injuries be stabilized to improve his chances, amazingly he seemed stable enough to endure it.

CHAPTER 2

These late night calls were brutal. Sheriff Hugh Payne was annoyed that he had to cut his date short for a call. *What a mess* he thought, stepping from his cruiser. Hummer versus…well the car was barely recognizable. The force of the impact had ripped two of the tires from the car and propelled them across the road where they came to rest next to the curb of a convenience store. The top of the car which had once been a convertible, flapped lazily in the light southern breeze blowing in from the gulf. The only undamaged piece of the car that attested to the former identity of this twisted horror was the small cobra snake emblem lying on the ground next to the car's shapeless mound. The miserable remains of a Shelby GT 500 Mustang.

Sheriff Payne wandered from the mangled car to the ambulance that held one of the victims, probably the Mustang's driver considering his condition. The young man in the ambulance did not look like he was going to make it. He listened as the EMT worked to communicate the young man's vital signs to University Hospital.

As he suspected, one of the drivers was drunk. In another ambulance the paramedics were *attempting* to administer to the driver of the Hummer while the police restrained him. The driver's outbursts signaled to Sheriff Payne that the driver was drunk; drunk drivers tended to be combative. Well, maybe he could get a few statements from the driver while the memories were still fresh. Sheriff Payne inhaled deeply as he approached; but within ten feet of the driver, he could smell the stale alcohol on the driver's breath. It was clear that the driver was in no condition to respond to questions, or to give any coherent answers as to the sequence of the night's events. He would deal with it tomorrow.

* * *

Early the next morning, Sheriff Payne laid the MVA file in his "In" box to work on later rubbing his eyes to clear his head. The hospital had called just after midnight to let him know that the Mustang's driver had died. That would mean there would be a charge of vehicular manslaughter, which would mean the District Attorney's office would be contacting him. The message light on his phone was blinking an angry red, probably the DA, but he wasn't ready to speak with anyone. He still needed to speak to the witnesses, and he wanted to speak to the Hummer's driver first, now that he was sober.

* * *

At the hospital, Sheriff Payne leaned on the receptionist's desk. "Morning ma'am." Sheriff Payne smiled a tired smile at the hospital's receptionist. "Where is he?"

She turned to the computer, ready to pull up the information he was seeking, smiling sweetly as she asked "Which one did you want to see first Sheriff?"

This brought him up short. He was tired, and in no mood for games. "The one that's still alive – I would assume that the dead one is rotting in the morgue." He answered tersely.

She glanced up from the computer with a questioning look on her face, "Didn't anyone call you? The Mustang's driver survived. He's in intensive care. The driver of the Hummer is in room 387."

Sheriff Payne blinked, trying to assimilate the information he had just heard. In an MVA, the hospital never calls until after a victim is pronounced dead. Sheriff Payne stared at the receptionist with his jaw hanging open. When he finally had the sense to close it again, he was at a loss for words.

CHAPTER 3

Jewell arrived at the hospital at about 5:30 that evening, almost twelve hours since she had left the hospital early this morning at the end of last night's shift. As she pulled into the parking garage, she saw the police cars. The gate, which was usually up, was down blocking the entrance to the garage. She stopped at the attendant's booth and waved at Tom, who worked in the parking garage during the day. "What's going on?" She asked.

"Seems that guy they brought in last night is a bit of a celebrity."

"What, you mean he's someone famous?" She asked, incredulous. She hadn't recognized him, but then, his injuries had been pretty severe, and it wasn't unusual to see famous people in New Orleans.

"No." Tom waved his hand to indicate that she had misunderstood. "Somehow it got out that this guy died and came back to life. The local news wants to get the story."

"Poor guy. What's with the police?"

"Patient privacy mostly. Doc Babineaux is up there giving a press conference, explaining how this sometimes happens and it's not that unusual. Sheriff Payne is up there with him, making sure that the press leaves this guy alone."

"That's good. I'd hate to wake up after an accident like that just to have a bunch of reporters in my face. I won't see you until this weekend; this is my last night this week."

Tom smiled and waved as he closed the gate behind Jewell's car. At the doors to the hospital, a small stage had been set up with a podium set in the middle. Jewell could hear Doc Babineaux's explanation making the incidents of last night sound as if this was as common as humidity in New Orleans; not rain in Death Valley.

Edgar Durand was among the reporters clamoring for information, even though he wasn't a reporter. His interest had a far more important purpose. He was only half listening to the doctor's explanation as his mind wandered to the possibilities of this event. If this particular patient was what Edgar thought he was, the patient would not only wake up, but walk out of the hospital within weeks, to live a long, long life unless he was punished for his crimes.

Edgar Durand was not an ugly man, but he was not remarkable either. Edgar was the type of man that a person could meet, and then forget within minutes after leaving his presence. It was seldom that someone remembered meeting him if he happened upon him a second or even third time.

Edgar was born twenty-eight years ago in an unremarkable house, in an unremarkable town, to unremarkable parents. He was however, a devoutly religious man.

It wasn't until college that his life became interesting. As a requirement, he had to take a class on early European history. Edgar enjoyed this class. His professor spoke of fascinating events, but what Edgar enjoyed the most, the lecture that changed his life, was the passionate lecture given on the subject of the Crusades and the Templar knights. Edgar remembered that lecture well. But what he remembered most were the stories claiming that the Templar Knights were allowed to meet on the Temple Mount. It was here, on the Temple Mount, that it was rumored that the Templar Knights unearthed the Holy Grail and its secrets of immortality. This was how the lecture ended.

Edgar eagerly attended his next class, hoping for more information about the Holy Grail and the secrets it held. However, the next lecture detailed the disbanding of the Knights Templar, and the creation of new orders with similar purpose, the Teutonic Knights and the Knights Hospitaller. The professor never again spoke of the Holy Grail. This spurred in Edgar an interest so fierce, so overwhelming that it consumed his life from that moment onward.

His personal quest for the Holy Grail began with his professor. His professor was a wealth of information. He explained that the myths of the Grail have been romanticized since the publication of Le Morte d'Arthur. He also explained that besides the Teutonic Knights and the Knights Hospitaller, a third order existed, the Obsidian Knights who sought to right the wrong that transpired so many centuries past, to kill the unjust that stole the secret of the Grail, and reclaim what once belonged to the rightful.

It was only a chosen few who were invited to join the Obsidian Knights. They were hand selected and initiated into the Order only after it was ascertained that they could be trusted to carry on the search for the Grail while maintaining the secrets of the Obsidian Knights. It was three years before the Order was convinced that Edgar was of the caliber of individual they were seeking for their yet unfulfilled task.

Upon initiation into the Order, secrets were shared teaching the true nature of the Holy Grail and the gifts that it endowed upon those that drank from it. There were people that not only knew of the Grail's existence, but drank from the Grail and gained its gift of immortality. These were the thieves of God's gifts to the faithful, the enemies of the righteous. The mission of the Obsidian Knights was to identify these infidels, and to swiftly mete out justice through beheading, without trial or mercy.

It was one of these infidels that Edgar sought now.

CHAPTER 4

Jewell walked into the women's locker room at the hospital. In the locker room, she was immediately the center of attention. The other nurses clamored around her, asking their excited questions at once. "They said you were there, when he came back to life!" This question was from Megan, another new recruit to the hospital. Jewell had met her during orientation.

"Um, yeah." Jewell pulled her scrub top over her head.

"Was he really dead for an hour?" Jeannie asked this.

"No, it wasn't like that. It was only a few minutes." It was all Jewell could do to get dressed while being bombarded with questions from the other nurses. As quickly as she could, she left the locker room and went to report to her supervisor. She wanted to go see the man before she started work. She could not stop thinking about him, and was certain that it was just her concern for his well-being. Once she saw that he was doing well, she would be able to let it go.

Nurse Carla Yohanan, the ER nurse supervisor, had a stern bearing about her. Most of the other nurses that worked with Jewell in the ER hated Nurse Yohanan; they thought she was insensitive, but Jewell liked the woman.

Jewell found Nurse Yohanan talking to one of the doctors but didn't remember the doctor's name. When Nurse Yohanan finished with the doctor and noticed Jewell standing behind her, she turned with that tight lipped smile she always wore; it almost looked like a grimace. Some of the other nurses said that Nurse Yohanan didn't know how to smile. Jewell knew differently. She had watched Nurse Yohanan with some of the patients. She had more compassion, and more caring than most of the other nurses combined. Nurse Yohanan reminded Jewell of her mother who was also a nurse before she died.

"Good evening Jewell. Are you ready to start? You're a little early." She started flipping pages on the clipboard she held, looking for an appropriate assignment.

"Actually Nurse Yohanan, I was hoping that I could take a few minutes to see the man that they brought in last night. I just wanted to see how he was doing."

Nurse Yohanan's face hardened. Jewell could see that Nurse Yohanan was thinking that another one of her nurses wanted to gawk at the freak, as if he was some sort of circus side show. It was clear that Nurse Yohanan was getting tired of hearing the story of last night's raising of the dead. After a minute though, the corners of her lips turned up in what Jewell could only guess was a smile. "That's right. You were one of the nurses who took care of him last night, weren't you?"

"Yes ma'am."

"Well, I think that would be very appropriate. He's in ICU, but seems to be stable."

Jewell sighed in relief. She had been worried about the young man's fate, afraid that his heart had restarted, only to fail again. "Thank you Nurse Yohanan. I won't be long." Jewell didn't wait for Nurse Yohanan's reply.

Although she wasn't exactly running, she was moving as fast as she could towards the ICU. Something inside her made her want to see him again, a need, and a burning desire. She could feel her heart speed at the thought of seeing him again; her hands started trembling at the excitement of seeing this man she had only glimpsed briefly the night before.

As Jewell rounded the corner, she saw Carol sitting at the nurses' station in front of the ER. Jewell liked Carol. She was an older woman, with graying hair and a pleasant smile.

Carol's face lit up when she saw Jewell nearly running down the hall. "Slow down honey, or you're going to end up in ICU when you trip and land on your face. Trust me, he's going to be here a while." She smiled, knowingly.

Jewell slowed her pace, embarrassed that someone had seen her in her excitement to reach the ICU; to see him. "I know," she answered. "I was just…concerned."

Jewell signed the log at the desk before moving to the entrance of the ICU. She paused before the door, trying to catch her breath. Suddenly, she found it very difficult to breathe, her breath coming in short gasps. Her heart was racing. It felt as if her heart was going to punch through her chest and go bouncing along the floor. She choked back a laugh at the thought and turned to look at Carol, certain that Carol could hear her heart thudding against her ribs, but Carol just smiled her reassurance.

Jewell reached for the doors, and pushed through. The man was in the first bed on the left. He had been cleaned up, so he looked better than he had the night before. His hair was a soft sandy color where she could see it sticking out in short spikes from beneath the bandages that covered his head. She knew that the gash underneath the bandages had been cleaned and sutured, his head partially shaved to administer to the wound. She grieved for the loss of his perfect hair, even if it was only temporary. Both of his legs were in casts, but on his left leg, the cast only went up to his knee. His right leg had a cast that covered his entire leg. Two metal pins stuck out of the side of this cast near his knee. His chest was bandaged, but no longer sunken as it had been last night, though she knew this was only because his ribs had been set. His collarbones were no longer disfigured. He wore a figure–of–8 brace to hold them in place.

Her knees felt weak as she gazed at the man's face. It looked so familiar. It was like looking into the face of someone she had known her whole life. Someone she was meant to know for the rest of her life. Someone she should have met a long time ago, but didn't due to cruel circumstance. Her hand started moving of its own accord toward his face. When she realized what she was about to do, she snatched her hand back just before her fingers could brush along his perfect cheekbone. She longed to touch his face, to hold his hand, to look into his eyes.

She reached for the man's chart on the wall next to his bed. She flipped it open. His name had been filled in on the chart; Collin Sykes. She looked at his birth date next to his name. She was surprised to see that he was older than her by two years. He looked so young. She glanced through the rest of the chart. She was shocked by the extent of his injuries. He must have been with the surgeons for most of the day to correct everything that was cracked, broken, and bruised.

When she had satisfied herself that he was going to live through the night, she walked slowly from the room. She didn't want to leave. She wanted to stay there, to sit with him until he woke. She wanted to be the first thing he saw when he opened his eyes.

She scolded herself knowing that these feelings, these longings were unfounded. She didn't know who the man was, she had no connection to him, and the professional thing to do would be to never see him again. She was probably feeling this way because she had helped to save his life. Once she left, it would be easier. There would be no reason to see him again as she rarely had reason to leave the ER, and she definitely had no reason to go upstairs to the patients' rooms so after she left, she would never see him again. As she left, she silently vowed to forget that Collin Sykes ever existed.

She smiled at Carol as she walked past the ICU desk. "Well, I need to get to work or Nurse Yohanan is going to hunt me down."

"Do you want me to let you know when they move him upstairs?" Carol asked.

Jewell paused for a minute, remembering the face she so desperately longed for. "No. No I don't," she responded a little too abruptly as she turned and strode back toward the ER.

CHAPTER 5

Percy Knighton sat in his car outside the hospital watching as news reporters clamored for information about the victim of a car accident that had occurred the night before. They were seeking sensationalist headlines, something to sell papers. A rumor had been leaked that one of the drivers of the previous night's collision had died, but was then brought back to life after medical knowledge shouldn't have been able to revive him.

Although Percy couldn't hear what was being said, he could imagine. It probably played out like a headline in the Weekly World News; *Man Rises from the Dead after Car Accident*, or *Zombie Driver Terrorizes Hospital Staff*. It wasn't a completely impossible occurrence. It had happened before; children falling through the ice and pronounced clinically dead, only to be revived after thirty minutes when the body temperature begins to rise. Once in a while news stories were published about people that were taken to the morgue or even buried, only to be found alive hours later – these stories though usually originated in third world countries, not in the United States. He knew that the story of this young man's survival, his nephew's survival, would be the topic of news stories for weeks to come. He also knew that this meant it was time to run.

Percy had been taking care of Collin since Collin was only three months old. This wouldn't bother Percy if he wasn't a hunted man, forcing him to run from place to place to protect his identity, his secrets. He hated forcing Collin into this lifestyle. He hoped, when Collin was born, that Collin would live a normal life with his parents, but Collin's parents had been murdered. The details of that particular murder had been in the news for months, the murder having been particularly…gruesome. Percy felt a pain in his chest at this unexpected memory. He also regretted the realization that what made him a hunted man, now made Collin hunted as well.

After a time, the media representatives dissipated. The doctor and the sheriff had retreated back into the hospital, denying entrance to the reporters. Percy waited for another half hour, just to be safe – he didn't want to have to answer any questions - and walked to the hospital. He told the young woman at the desk who he was, and who he had come to see. She didn't need to look Collin up in the computer; she knew who he was, and where he was. After confirming Percy's ID, she told Percy that he would need to speak first with Dr. Babineaux, head of the ICU. Dr. Babineaux liked to prepare the family member for what they were about to see; to prepare the family for the emotional shock.

A young man escorted Percy down the hall and ushered Percy into a large office where Dr. Babineaux, who was sitting behind the large desk, stood and gestured for Percy to have a seat in one of the chairs facing the desk. The office was tastefully decorated, expensive looking, but not ostentatious. There was a large mahogany desk on the right, facing a large window on the left wall. Behind the desk was a bookshelf covering the whole wall, front to back, top to bottom which was completely filled with medical texts and references. In front of the desk were two large, comfortable looking leather chairs.

After Percy had settled into one of the chairs, Dr. Babineaux sat with his hands folded on his desk, scrutinizing Percy. The intense stare, coupled with the curiosity in the doctor's eyes made Percy nervous; it seemed that the doctor knew, or suspected something out of the ordinary. The doctor sat silent for a long moment. Percy was unsure whether the doctor was waiting for Percy to speak first, or if he was simply gathering his thoughts. This was a rather unique situation, after all. Percy was a man of interminable patience, so he waited for the doctor to speak first.

The doctor began by clearing his throat. He looked at Percy again, with that strange and curious stare, before speaking. "My name is Dr. Nicholas Babineaux, head of ICU. I generally like to speak to a patient's family before allowing them to see the patient, typically to prepare them for what they might see. As you can imagine, it can be…difficult."

"Nicholas Babineaux, the researcher?"

"Yes, I have published some articles."

"I've read some of your work. You're interested in…" Percy didn't want to reveal too much. Babineaux's research indicated an interest in his kind, but it in no way revealed on what side his interests lay. "…in the effects of certain enzymes on wound healing and life span."

"Yes, yes, exactly. Are you familiar with my research?"

"I too am a doctor and researcher. I'm interested in the area though I've never published. I seek to disable the enzyme where I understand you seek to enable it."

"Interesting. And is your interest personal or medical?"

Percy didn't answer, but simply watched the doctor intently.

"Yes. I see where that question might be a little…personal."

Percy didn't say anything, only nodded.

"Your nephew was involved in a very serious car accident. His injuries were quite extensive. When he arrived in the ER last night, we had reason to believe that he wouldn't survive." The doctor paused for a moment, apparently waiting for Percy's reaction. Percy gave none.

The doctor continued. "He…we," the doctor seemed to change the direction of his thoughts, "were able to…revive him…" the doctor seemed uncomfortable with his explanation. Percy knew why. If Babineaux's research interest was what Percy thought it was, then Babineaux knew the exact reason for the unusual events of the previous night. The doctor probably wondered if Percy knew but would want to confirm his understanding of the situation. "He was in surgery for most of the day, but he is stable, in ICU. We expect to move him to a room sometime tomorrow, despite the extent of his injuries. He seems to be…responding well to treatment." It was clear to Percy that this man was not frequently at a loss for words, but in this case, the words did not flow easily.

Percy remained silent, waiting for the doctor to continue; to explain the strange occurrence of the previous night before Percy had the opportunity to read it in tomorrow's headlines.

Instead, the doctor said something unexpected. "I would like to include Sheriff Payne in our conversation. He saw the accident site shortly after the accident occurred."

Percy took a moment to consider the Doctor's comment. He was on edge; he did not know if he had just walked into his hunter's snare, or if this was simply standard procedure, or if, against all odds, he had found a sympathizer. Perhaps because the injuries occurred as the result of an automobile accident, the sheriff would want to speak to the family. Percy was uncomfortable being questioned; there was much that he could not disclose.

"If that's necessary," he replied carefully, in an even tone. He tried not to reveal his reluctance in his response; in his experience, refusing to answer questions generally only made things worse.

"I believe it is." The doctor pushed himself up using his desk for support. He glanced again at Percy and walked to the door to his office.

The doctor's inquisitive looks were beginning to make Percy increasingly uneasy. Percy folded his hands carefully in his lap, and casually crossed his legs. He had practice at looking at ease, even when he was not.

When the doctor returned, he had the sheriff with him. Percy stood as the sheriff walked toward him. The sheriff's uniform was neatly pressed, and the name tag on his left breast pocket read "Payne." The sheriff extended his hand in greeting. He was smiling, but the smile was cautious and did not reach his eyes. He looked at Percy with the same intense, curious gaze as the doctor.

The sheriff took Percy's hand and looked into Percy's eyes as if he were trying to look into the depths of Percy's soul. As he firmly shook Percy's hand, maintaining contact longer than was customary, he resolutely introduced himself to Percy giving his full name. "Hugh Payne."

Percy showed no reaction to the sheriff's introduction, but at the sound of the name his heart skipped a beat. He looked at the man shaking his hand, "Interesting," he responded cautiously. "Hugh Payne? Were you aware that one of the original Templars had the same name? Are you perhaps related?"

"No, not related. I was lucky to have the surname. My father though, was a great admirer of Hughes De Paynes."

"I see. Perhaps his life has had as much of an effect on your life as it has on mine?"

"Have you led a penitent's life?" Sheriff Payne asked the verifying question.

"I have, but all has not been forgiven." Percy replied in the standard response, carefully looking at each man individually.

"No my *friend*," Dr. Babineaux responded, placing special emphasis on the word 'friend.' "Indeed it has not."

All three men grinned as the doctor gave Percy a friendly slap on the back. Percy was almost giddy with relief. Perhaps, he and Collin wouldn't need to leave after all. The men standing before him had sworn to protect his and Collin's lives with their own.

CHAPTER 6

Jewell was glad she was back at work. Nurse Yohanan would keep her busy. She had spent the past three days trying to occupy her time. Time and again she found her thoughts turning back to the man, Collin, in the ICU. On Friday, she accidentally took the Mandeville exit heading towards the hospital. Having the pond between her and Collin seemed to make it a bit easier to resist her yearning to see him. It didn't however, ease her thoughts.

At night, she would dream about him. The dream never changed. It took place in an expansive home that looked like the inside of one of the plantation homes she had toured with her father on the Natchez Trace last summer. Jewell was in a room, with *him* and several other people she didn't know. They were arguing. She couldn't understand what they were saying, but somehow, she knew that she was the topic of the argument.

The dreams were the worst because she couldn't stop them. They were a manifestation of her subconscious, an indication of her deepest desires – or fears. At least during the day, if she tried hard enough, she could distract herself, think of something else. Even so, her thoughts always strayed back to him.

When she walked through the doors of the hospital, her body trembled as she thought about how close he was. When Nurse Yohanan asked her to take some paperwork to Carol early in Jewell's shift, she hesitated only a second before snatching the folder out of Nurse Yohanan's hands, anxious to complete her task. Of course, Nurse Yohanan was used to Jewell's enthusiasm, so she didn't notice the excitement in Jewell's eyes as she turned to walk toward the ICU.

When Carol saw Jewell coming, she smiled. Jewell walked casually up to the desk and handed Carol the folder. "Nurse Yohanan asked me to bring this paperwork to you." Jewell said as casually as she could, though she could hear the excited quiver in her voice. She wondered if Carol could hear it as well.

"Thank you, sweetheart. Tell Nurse Yohanan I appreciate her sending it to me so promptly. It wasn't urgent. I could have waited if there were other things she needed you to do."

"Oh, no!" When Carol's eyebrows drew down over her eyes at Jewell's outburst, Jewell casually waved her hand and added "We aren't that busy down there right now. I was happy to bring them."

"Well, thank you dear."

"Um…Are all of patients doing well?"

"I guess as well as can be expected." Carol responded, a hint of sadness in her voice. "Yesterday they brought in a woman who suffered a heart attack. She's so young, only twenty-six, and a newborn baby at home too. I've been praying for her."

"Wow. That's really sad." Jewell paused.

"Are you concerned about anyone in particular?" Carol wasn't dense. She had a lifetime's experience to learn to read people's faces.

Jewell casually dragged her finger along the edge of Carol's desk. "No, not really." She knew as soon as she said it that she didn't sound convincing at all. Even to her ears, the lie was as obvious as if it had been tattooed across her forehead.

"He came out of his coma about an hour after you came by to see him. When he remained conscious, they moved him into a private room upstairs."

"Who?" Jewell winced as she said the single word that betrayed her longing for news about Collin. She could see that Carol was not the least bit convinced that she didn't know who they were talking about.

Carol grinned. "I would've told you, but you said you didn't want to know when they moved him."

"I didn't. I don't. I guess I just kind of wanted to know if he was going to make it and all." Jewell turned and nearly bolted down the hall. She could feel the warmth of the blush in her face as she walked briskly away.

At lunch - even though it was just after one in the morning, most of the night duty nurses still considered this lunch - Jewell sat at a table in the corner of the cafeteria with Ashley. Jewell had met Ashley a couple of days after she started working at University. Ashley worked in obstetrics. When they met, they took an instant liking to each other and had been best friends ever since.

Jewell enjoyed having such a close friend. Throughout her childhood she had watched the other children play, or whisper together at the lunch tables, and longed for that kind of relationship, to be "one of the girls." She had that with Ashley. They ate lunch together whenever they were working the same shift, and on their days off they would always find something to do together. Yesterday, they had gone for pedicures when Jewell told Ashley she needed to do something to help her relax.

"How do you do it?" Ashley asked abruptly as she set her lunch tray on the table.

"Do what?"

"How do you deal with the death, the suffering, day after day? Isn't it depressing? Or do you just sort of get used to it?"

Jewell finished chewing the food she had just placed in her mouth. She thought seriously about Ashley's question, trying to think of how best to explain it. "No, you don't get used to it. It's more of an understanding, an acceptance. After all, what's life without death? If everyone lived forever, they would never feel the need to accomplish anything, there would be no pressure, no ending. It's kind of like buying presents for Christmas. In June, you don't really think about it because there's so much time, but on December 15th, all of a sudden, all of your shopping gets done. Does that make sense?"

"Well, I guess I see what you are saying, but I much prefer to bring life into the world than see it leave." She frowned as she thought about what her friend had to deal with day after day, and tried to imagine what it would be like. She tried to imagine herself in the same circumstances. She knew that people had to die, it was a part of life, but she was happier not to be reminded of it every day. "But what if we could have life without death, or what if *you* had the opportunity to live forever? Would you take it?"

Jewell slowly shook her head. "I don't think I would want it. Imagine living every day knowing that you would have to watch everyone you love die. Could you imagine the pain in that? Seeing it happen, over and over again, with no end?"

"But couldn't you love them, knowing that they would have you for the rest of their life? Wouldn't that bring you some level of happiness?"

"I guess, but how would you feel if you loved someone who was going to live forever, but you knew you wouldn't. Would you want them to have to suffer that for you? Wouldn't that be selfish?"

"Well then, what if everyone could live forever? Then you would never have to watch anyone die."

"That wouldn't work either. Whether you believe in God, or the big bang, or Darwin, or whatever, there has to be balance in everything; black and white, night and day, good and bad. If no one died, there would need to be something else to balance that. Perhaps, no one would ever be born. You would understand that Ash. Think about the joy that someone feels in holding a baby, even if it's not their own. Think about how you feel when you carry a baby in to its mother. What if that was the balance, giving up that joy?"

"Well, what if like…maybe everyone lived until they were 200 or something?"

"So what then, you know you are going to die on your 200th birthday? How do you act at the end? Are you depressed? Do you give up? Do you try harder, hoping to accomplish just one more thing? How would you live your last days Ash?"

"Jeez Jewell, you are so depressing sometimes! I think working down there is getting to you. I personally think it would be cool. Think about all the stuff you could do."

"Can I ask you something Ashley?" Jewell asked pushing her spaghetti around on her plate.

"Sure."

"Have you ever met a guy, I mean saw him only once, but then you just couldn't stop thinking about him?"

"Yeah, I met this hunk at Padre Island during my senior spring break. I haven't stopped thinking about that sun tanned hottie since!" Ashley laughed.

Jewell smiled. Then her eyebrows drew down over her eyes as she tried to think of another way explain. "I mean someone that you don't really know, but somehow you know that the two of you are meant to be together." Jewell stared at the patterns in her pasta as she waited for her friend to answer.

"Do you mean like love at first sight?" Ashley asked, a little more serious now.

"Yeah, but he doesn't know who you are. But you still know that if he could just see you, that he would feel the same way. That there was some sort of bond between you, making your lives inseparable."

"Well," Ashley paused, giving serious consideration to her friend's question. "I've never experienced it, personally. But I had a friend in high school. One day, this guy walked in to our English class, a transfer from another school. He didn't even look at us, but she passed me a note that said he was the man she was going to marry." Ashley took a bite of her salad, and chewed, thinking about the details. "She would follow him around sometimes. She knew his whole class schedule, and somehow even got his locker combination. She would clean out his locker sometimes, but he never knew who did it."

"So what happened?"

"We were at Senior Prom. That was two years after he had walked into that classroom. He had brought a date. His date was gorgeous; long blonde hair, beautiful huge blue eyes, figure of a super-model. We had come with our own dates too. She came with a guy she had been dating for a few weeks, and I brought a friend who, like me, didn't have a date." She made a face.

Jewell was surprised. Ashley was beautiful, in Jewell's opinion. Ashley was tall, and slim. She had thick black hair, and beautiful chocolate eyes. And she *always* looked good in the latest fashions. Jewell assumed that the boys in high school would have been clamoring to ask her out. "So what happened?"

"They met at the punch bowl. Their eyes locked and the rest is history. They both went to the same college – they made sure of that, but I guess they couldn't wait to get married so they eloped last year in Vegas. I still keep in touch with her. Their relationship is perfect. Not just like teenage love, there's something deeper. You can see it in their eyes when they look at each other."

"Wow, that's really cool."

"So I guess yeah, I do believe in love at first sight. Why? Did you have someone in mind?" She looked at Jewell and winked, raising her eyebrows suggestively.

"I don't know, not really."

"Well, who is it? Don't leave me hangin'! I'm your best friend, you *have* to tell me. It's a rule."

"Do you swear you won't tell anyone?" Jewell asked in a conspiratorial tone, lowering her voice to make sure no one else heard.

"Of course!"

"That guy who came into the ER the other day. The one who…died."

"Whoa! Creepy. Do you think it might be some nurse thing, falling in love with your patient or something?"

"That's what I thought too, but it's not. It's more. I just know it." Jewell sighed.

"So what are you going to do about it?"

"Nothing. They moved him out of ICU so I don't have any reason to see him."

"Girl! You cannot just let it go like that! You need to play your part. Be the nurse, go in there and look at his chart or something. See if you can get him to see you. I mean really *see* you!" Ashley said excitedly, a plan clearly hatching in her mind.

"I don't know. I guess I'll think about it."

"Well, let me know when you're finished *thinking* about it and ready to do something!" She smiled at Jewell as they both got up to clear their trays and head back to their respective jobs.

*   *   *

When Jewell got back to the nurses' station, no one was there. She looked at the charts on the desk to see if anything needed to be done. She knew the supplies were all stocked; she had checked that before she went to lunch. There was a little boy in a room with a broken arm, but there was already a doctor and two nurses in the room. She had some notes she had to type into the computer; she thought she should probably get that done while she waited for Nurse Yohanan. Nurse Yohanan hated it when she had to remind her charges to put their notes into the computer.

Jewell sat down at the terminal and grabbed her notes entering the information. When she finished, her mind started to wander. She could use the computer to look up what room he was in, maybe just walk by to see how he was doing…no, probably not a good idea. Ashley was right when she called her infatuation "creepy." In her opinion, that was the best term to label her freakish obsession.

She opened the internet browser and checked her email. Nothing except the hundreds of spam emails she received every day. She glanced over the computer's desktop and noticed the desktop icon for the application for looking up patient room numbers. She quickly went to Google and tried to think of something that she needed to research. Nothing. At this point, her mind was only on one thing. She opened the application and quickly typed in his last name "Sykes."

While she sat staring at the screen, she was so lost in her thoughts that she didn't hear Ashley walk up behind her.

"Looking something up, are we?" Ashley grinned.

"Um, no. Just checking on some things." Jewell said as she quickly closed the open window. Jewell could feel her face burning at being caught. "What are you doing here?" She asked, trying desperately to pretend that she wasn't doing exactly what Ashley had suggested she do.

"You forgot this," she said handing over Jewell's small leather wallet with a smirk before walking away.

CHAPTER 7

At the end of her shift, Jewell was just reaching for the handle on her car's door, when her thoughts turned back to Collin. She hesitated, before turning back to the hospital.

"Did you forget something?" Nurse Yohanan was on her way out as Jewell walked past her.

Jewell tried to sound casual as she answered. "I just thought I'd check on that MVA they brought in the other night. I heard he's doing a lot better and they've moved him into a room. I thought I'd go up and see how he's feeling."

"That's sweet Jewell. Don't stay too long, you'll need to be back to work before you know it."

"Yes, Ma'am, I promise not to stay long."

Jewell walked slowly to the elevators. As she pushed the up arrow, she had the sudden urge to bolt; the urge to run, not away, but toward him. She looked at the numbers above the elevator doors. Both elevators were near the top floor and not moving. In her urgency, she decided to take the stairs not even considering that she would need to ascend six long flights.

She turned towards the stairs, glanced back at the elevator, and pushed through the fire doors into the stairwell. And then she ran. She took the steps two at a time up the first two flights and then taking them one at a time as she tired but continuing as fast as she could. When she reached the sixth floor, she stopped, winded. She was surprised that she felt a little dizzy from her exertion so she sat down on the top step with her head between her knees, and concentrated on long slow breaths; in and out.

When she felt like she could stand, she walked through the door into the hallway. Collin's room was on the opposite side of the floor from where she had come up. As she rounded the second corner, into the hallway with the private rooms, she wondered if she might be a little crazy. *After all*, she thought, *what was she doing here stalking some poor injured patient?* She looked silently down the hall towards his room. *Perhaps*, she reflected, *it would be better if I just turned around now.* She was tired anyway; she really didn't have time for crazy adventures. Her father was home too, and he would be expecting her. By the time she decided that she should probably head home, she realized that she was standing in front of the door to his room. She didn't even remember walking down the hall.

She looked at the name card on the side of the door; Collin Sykes. This was definitely the right room. She gently pushed the door open, hoping not to disturb him if he was still sleeping; it was still quite early in the morning.

The walls were painted a cheerful blue. It reminded her of a spring day after months of winter, when the sun first comes up in the morning. It wasn't a hospital color at all. There was a large vinyl reclining chair on one side, a television set mounted to the ceiling. The television set was silent, but turned on. It looked like it might be tuned to CNN or some other news channel. There was also a rolling table that was pushed away from the bed, but within easy reach. There was a tray on the table with a half-eaten breakfast. It looked like

Collin had chosen eggs for breakfast, scrambled. There was a half-finished glass of orange juice, and a fruit cup with everything eaten but the pineapple chunks. She also noticed something missing. It took her a moment to realize there were no cards, no flowers, no balloons; nothing to wish him well.

As she stepped into the room, he was lying on the bed facing away from the door, either sleeping, or looking out the window at the city beyond. There wasn't much of a view here. She tried to close the door soundlessly, but it made a small click as she let it close.

"Please," he moaned. "No more. I feel fine. I swear. I don't need anyone poking me with needles or taking my temperature. Just go away." His voice washed over her, making her feel faint. He had a tenor voice with a muddled possibly European accent, though she couldn't place the country. She thought that it sounded a bit British, but some of the words seemed to have more of a Mediterranean accent; perhaps French, or Italian, definitely not Cajun. It was subtle, not pronounced, but enough to give his voice an alluring, exotic quality.

"Um, hi," Jewell said timidly by way of introduction. "I'm not one of your attending nurses. My name is Jewell; I work downstairs in the ER. I was there when you came in the other night."

He was silent for a long time. She thought that maybe he wasn't interested in visitors so she turned to leave. She knew this was a stupid idea anyway. Her heart sank, but in her head, she knew this was for the best. She was acting like some infatuated teenager. She reached for the door to leave.

"Wait." His plea made her heart flutter and her knees go weak. "It was you that came to see me in ICU." It was a statement, not a question.

She swallowed against the lump in her throat. How could he possibly know that? He was in a coma when she saw him last. "Well, yes, but I'm sure that a lot of nurses came to see you when you were in ICU."

"Yes, but you…" he paused, looking for the right word. "You *felt* different. I can feel you that way now."

"You *felt* me?" She had turned back towards him, but his back was still to her, still looking out the window.

"Maybe felt isn't the right word. Have you ever been sitting in a room with your back to the door, and all of a sudden you know that someone is right behind you, even though you didn't hear them come in? It was like that, sort of. Well, that's still not exactly it, but it's the same now. You only came in one time. I could feel you watching me. Not like you were checking my injuries, but like you were looking at *me*."

Jewell was taken aback by his words. How could he know what she was doing when she came to see him in ICU? How did he know it was her, and not someone else?

"In the emergency room too. I felt you, your eyes, looking at me. I know it was you. You sat with me, you were crying. Why?"

Jewell didn't know how to answer that question. In fact, she was unsure of a lot of things right now. She felt like a deer caught in a car's headlights, knowing that it needs to run to save itself, but not being able to move, staring at the car that would soon end its life.

He turned then, to look at her. His eyes were nothing like what she had expected. They weren't blue at all, as she imagined they would be, but gray, almost black, like clouds just before a thunderstorm. And now those eyes were focused on her, trapping her in his intense stare. He didn't say anything else; he simply waited, expecting her to respond to his question.

She couldn't remember the question. She couldn't remember her name, or what she was doing here. Her heart was racing so fast she was certain she was going to faint. Her knees started trembling, and her hand was pushing against the wall, bracing her, keeping her from falling. Then she realized she wasn't breathing. She concentrated, and was able to draw a deep, gasping breath.

Swallowing hard, she took another deep breath before trying to speak. When she finally felt she could say something, she asked "Excuse me? What did you say?" But her voice was only a whisper, and she wasn't sure that he heard what she had said from across the room.

"I said, why were you crying?"

"How…how do you know that? How can you know when you were…?" Her voice trailed off, unable to say *dead*, unable to convince herself that his death had really happened, that he had defied death and was now speaking to her.

"I don't know," he whispered, "it was like I was dreaming, but it was more…real. I knew even before I turned around what you would look like, because I saw you then, in the emergency room." His voice was measured, even. She realized then that he was probably as confused as she was. "Would you like to sit with me? I don't get many visitors. At least, none that don't want to poke me with something."

Jewell stepped away from the door, testing her legs. She wasn't sure that they were solid enough to support her weight. When she was certain that she wouldn't collapse if she let go of the wall, she walked carefully across the room toward the recliner on the other side of his bed. He watched her attentively as she moved around the room. When she reached the recliner, she put her hands on the arms of the chair and carefully eased herself down. She was relieved to be sitting, she wasn't sure she would have been able to stand much longer.

"You still haven't answered my question." He grinned, his smile lopsided because of the injuries to his face.

"I'm sorry; I don't remember what you asked."

"Why were you crying?"

"Well, I guess because it's sad when someone…" She was about to say "dies" but thought better of it "well, when someone gets injured because someone else was doing something stupid. My mother was killed by a drunk driver; I guess the situation just reminded me of her."

"Oh." He sounded disappointed as he looked away from her.

Was he expecting something else? What was the answer that he wanted to hear? That she was crying because she thought she had lost her soul mate? Because she wouldn't meet someone she should have met? Because fate had ripped from her the one person who would complete her life? Was that what he was waiting for? Was that how he felt too? Could she find the courage to tell him that?

When he didn't say anything for several minutes, she pushed herself up from the chair. "Well, I guess I had better go. My father will be expecting me. I'm...well, I'm glad to see that you are doing so well."

"Thanks," he muttered without turning to look at her as she left.

When he heard the door close behind Jewell, he rolled over to stare at the door hoping that she would come back to tell him the she felt about him the way he felt about her. It was crazy, but when he looked into her eyes, he felt like she was the only thing that mattered in his life. There was nothing else in the world, just her. When she was in the room, all of his pain disappeared; all of his thoughts were about hope and beauty and her.

She was the woman that he had been looking for his whole life without even knowing that he was looking. He had dated before, in high school, in college, but nothing could have prepared him for this. The electricity between them was palpable. He was certain that she must feel it too. For a moment, when she first walked in, he believed that she could feel it, like he did, the inexorable draw, pulling them together like two magnets.

But then, it was gone. The look in her eyes that made him think, maybe...just maybe; but when he asked her why, her answer was one of concern; simple, professional concern. Then he understood. She was a nurse, concerned for her patient, checking on his well-being, nothing more.

But he could not bring himself ignore that she did not feel about him the way that he felt about her. He would convince her. He would make her see the possibilities of what they could be, together. He tried to go to sleep. He was tired. He hadn't had a good night's sleep since his accident. Every couple of hours someone came in to give him a shot, or to check his injuries, or to measure his pulse, or to shine a light into his pupils to make sure that they were dilating correctly, to ensure he hadn't suffered an injury to his brain.

He hadn't, he was sure of it. In fact, he felt fine. The self-administered morphine that hung from a bag next to his bed and attached to a tube in his arm, remained untouched. He hurt, but not enough to suffer the disorientation brought on by the drug. He asked the nurse for an aspirin now and again drawing confused looks and sometimes a reminder about the morphine.

The nurses always seemed surprised he wasn't in more pain but he wasn't. When he was five he climbed a tree in front of his house that was tall, but spindly. It was very young, and not strong enough to support the weight of a young boy. When one of the branches broke he plummeted towards the ground landing with his arm twisted under his body. His arm broke in three places. The doctor told his uncle that Collin would likely be in a cast for at least six weeks, more likely eight. His uncle, who was a doctor, had removed the cast only two weeks after it had been put on. Collin's arm was fine. His uncle didn't seem pleased. In fact, he almost seemed despondent that Collin had healed so quickly. Collin was thrilled to be climbing trees again so soon after his disastrous mishap. So the fact that Collin now felt fine, with the exception of some lingering pain where the injuries were particularly bad, did not surprise Collin.

Now, lying in a hospital bed after a near fatal crash, he was grateful for his quick healing. His body ached. Sometimes, when he was sleeping, he would turn onto his right side and the pain from his injuries would jolt him awake, pain stabbing through his entire body. When he was awake however, he was able to maneuver so as to minimize the pain. It had been almost five days since the accident. He knew that he shouldn't feel this good, not that he really felt all that good, but he was glad that he did.

But now, there was a new pain. Something in his chest, stabbing, throbbing, and sending a conspicuous ache throughout his body from his head to his toes that he was unable to ignore. He glanced at the morphine. He knew the morphine was there to help curtail the physical pain of his injuries, but he knew that the euphoric effects produced by the drug may help to ease the psychological pain he was feeling now. He pressed the button on the morphine drip; the audible beep of the machine indicating that the measured dose was being administered. He felt the medicine start to take effect as it moved through his body. At first, there was just a slight dizziness, but as he maxed out his dose, he felt oblivion creeping in to cloak his mind and relieve him from his heartache.

CHAPTER 8

When Jewell started to leave the house two hours before her shift started at the hospital, her father was curious.

"Isn't it a little early to be leaving for work? I haven't heard anything about traffic on the causeway, what's the rush?

"There's something I need to do dad, at the hospital, before my shift. I need to look in on a patient." That was the truth, but not all of it. She found that she had been leaving out a lot of information in her explanations of late.

Her dad, always curious about her job and how she spent her days, pressed for details. "I didn't realize they expected you to do that. Shouldn't they let you do that during your shift, rather than making you come to work early? Your shift is already twelve hours. This morning, you stayed almost an hour late, and today you're headed in almost two hours early. Doesn't seem quite fair, the way I see it."

Jewell could tell by the tone in his voice that he thought she was up to something. She had never been able to hide anything from him. He tried so hard to treat her like an adult, but he still thought of her as twelve years old. She knew that he would never ask her directly about what she was doing, but his tone, his curiosity, were not any less direct than if he had come straight out and asked her what she was up to.

"I've just sort of been following that MVA that came in a couple of days ago. Checking on his progress to make sure he's doing okay." There it was again, half of the truth. She had always been able to tell her father everything, why couldn't she open up to him now?

"Really?" He dragged the word out just a little too long, his tone a bit more than curious. Even though Jewell had never heard this tone in her father's voice before, she knew *exactly* what he was asking. "You haven't been this interested in any of the other patients you've treated in the ER. What makes this one so special that he has you running off to work two hours early and coming home an hour late?" Her father's voice was almost teasing.

"Ugh! Dad!" She was a bit embarrassed that she had been caught. "His case is just really interesting. It's not often someone dies and comes back to life again. It's just professional curiosity, I swear!"

"Is he cute?"

"Oh my God, dad! What is wrong with you? Stop, please?" She could feel the blush heating her face, telling her father everything that he wanted to know, betraying her secrets.

Her father crossed his arms over his chest and smiled. "Have a nice time at work."

"Whatever." She stomped out the door, slamming it loudly as she left, acting like the teenager her father thought of her as, rather than the adult she was.

She didn't go straight to his room when she arrived at the hospital. She went to the locker room first, and put her tote into her locker. She dallied a bit, trying to calm her excitement. First she dug around in her bag for a hairbrush.

She walked over to the mirror and brushed her hair until the static caused it to stick out on the sides. She went to the sink for some water to brush out the static. Then she parted her hair on the right side. She usually wore the part in the middle, because that's where it naturally fell, but she thought that made her head look pointy. The part on the right didn't look very good, it accentuated a cowlick she had on that side of her head. She tried parting it on the left side. That looked better, but she couldn't keep the hair from falling into her eyes. She ran her fingers back through her hair and let the part fall naturally in the middle again. Maybe if she teased the back a bit. She rummaged in her bag for a comb and wandered back to the mirror. She pulled up a section of hair and started back-combing to give it a little lift. By the time she was finished, it looked like a colony of rats had decided to take up residence on the top of her head. She combed it back down, working out the tangles she had created with her failed attempt at hair styling. It was then that Ashley walked in.

"Hey ugly. Whatcha up to?" She grinned as she started unpacking a curling iron, along with various cosmetics.

"What are you doing here?" Jewell asked, incredulous. She looked at the clock; it was still an hour and forty-five minutes until their shift started.

"Your dad called. He said he thought you might need a little help and asked me if I would mind coming in early to give you a hand."

"Oh, for the love of…" Her voice trailed off. It was impossible to hate her dad, but sometimes she wished he was just a little more obtuse.

As Ashley plugged in the curling iron and started laying out the cosmetics, Jewell asked herself what she was doing here. It was obvious that her feelings for Collin must be the result of the nurse – patient relationship. Or maybe it was that longing for something that you can't have. He was really handsome, but obviously he wouldn't have any interest in someone like her; for heaven's sake, she still lived with her father! She knew that guys just weren't interested in her. Even the boys that she had grown up with, the ones that *didn't* tease her, the ones that actually defended her, treated her more like a sister. They never liked her *that* way.

When Ashley had finished setting up her make-shift beauty salon, she dragged a chair over and placed it with the back to the mirror. "You can't see until I'm finished."

It didn't take Ashley long to finish her makeover. Curling Jewell's hair took the longest, but as Ashley dusted the mineral powder base on Jewell's skin, she commented about how pretty Jewell could be if she just made a little effort. She dusted on the blush, and used a gray eye shadow "To bring out the blue in your eyes, and give you a sultry look," she had said.

"Okay…look!" Ashley told Jewell turning her chair toward the mirror. What Jewell saw was astonishing. It wasn't that she had magically transformed into a super model, but she really didn't look quite so plain. It was an interesting revelation. When she turned around, Ashley held up a blouse apparently expecting Jewell to change out of her Tinker Bell t-shirt before heading upstairs. When Ashley finally pronounced her acceptable, Jewell headed for the elevators.

Jewell didn't want to take the stairs today. In fact, she almost hoped that the elevators had stopped working to give her an excuse not to go see him. But it seemed like it had been only seconds when she heard the elevator ding, and saw the doors open beckoning her inside. She pushed the button for the sixth floor and watched the doors close, trapping her into her decision. As the elevator moved slowly past each floor, all she could do was wait, and think. Maybe the electricity would go out while she was in the elevator. Maybe she would be trapped inside for hours, unable to escape. She wasn't sure which idea frightened her more; the idea of being trapped in the elevator, or the idea of facing Collin only to find that he was truly uninterested.

When the elevator doors opened, she left the elevator and walked slowly to his room almost without conscious effort. Again, she stood in front of the door, too frightened to go in, too frightened to run away. She took a deep breath and pushed the door open. He was sleeping, with his back to her again, on his left side. It made sense that he was always facing away from the door when she entered, it was probably more comfortable to lie on the side that had suffered less injury.

As Jewell stood in the doorway, Collin was dreaming. In his dream, Collin was suddenly standing at the house in South Carolina where he lived when he first arrived in the states a couple of years ago; the fragrant flowering vines winding along the long fence enclosing the property. The smell was intoxicating, enchantingly sweet, inviting. The smell was fresh, almost fruity in its fragrance with a subtle hint of spice. It was alluringly feminine, enticingly romantic. That was when he saw her, standing by the gate, waiting for him. But as with many dreams, the closer he came to her, the further away she seemed, forever out of reach. As he thought about the bouquet, trying to remember the name of the flower so abundant at that home, the delicate scent of the small flowers slowly drew him from his dream. That was when he realized that the smell was in his room. He slowly rolled to his back, careful of his injuries, to see where the aroma was coming from.

Collin watched her standing in the door. Honeysuckle, that was the name of the vine, the smell in his room; it fit her, he thought. When he saw her this morning, she smelled of antiseptic soap and alcohol. As he thought about it, he realized that he had smelled the honeysuckle this morning, but not as strongly. This scent, this fragrance was her. This was how she was supposed to smell; of freshness and beauty, not sterility and medicine. He looked into her eyes. She was anxious, unsure of what he felt. He tried to smile, to reassure her, but knew when he felt the lopsided turn of his lips that his effort would be futile.

"You look better today than you did yesterday." He grimaced. The medicine was definitely not helping his ability to charm her with his smooth vocabulary. "I mean, you're not in your scrubs. Your hair looks nice when it's down. Aren't you working?"

"Well, no. I got to work a little early so I thought I'd come by and see how you were feeling." She didn't move further into the room, she felt awkward and uncomfortable; still unsure of his feelings.

"Can you sit down? Do you have some time to stay?" He was afraid that like before, she had only come by out of professional concern for his wellbeing, that upon seeing his improving condition, she would leave again to check on other patients or ready herself for her shift.

"I'd like to, if you don't mind." She walked timidly into the room and sat carefully on the edge of the recliner next to his bed.

"I was hoping that you would come by again. I know you don't need to come up here, that I'm not part of your duties anymore."

"Really? You wanted to see me again?" Ugh, too eager. Maybe he just liked having someone to talk to. It seemed obvious that no one came to visit, and most nurses didn't spend a lot of time socializing with their patients; not because they were unkind, but because they were usually very busy and responsible for many patients.

"Yes, I *really* wanted to see you again." He tried his lopsided smile again, hoping that it wasn't too hideous. He had scrupulously avoided mirrors since arriving. He moved his good hand to the edge of the bed, palm up, an invitation.

When his hand moved to the edge of the bed, Jewell felt a flash of hope move through her and the butterflies turned into bats. Did he want her to hold his hand? She slowly moved her hand towards his, hesitant, but eager. She gently brushed the tips of her fingers against his and was shocked at the sudden searing heat that surged through her body and turned to a smoldering burn. Collin carefully curled his fingers, pulling her hand into his.

She was overjoyed when his hand curled around hers, holding her, unwilling to let go. His touch was warm, like hot chocolate on a winter day. It warmed her hand the warmth flowed through her, engulfing her in his touch

They sat like this, without speaking, until Jewell had to leave for her shift. It wasn't an uncomfortable silence. That it felt so normal made it that much better. Jewell didn't want to leave, almost couldn't leave, but she had to. He looked at her as she stood up and released his hand. "Will you come to visit again?"

"Of course."

*   *   *

At the end of her shift, Jewell couldn't move fast enough to change. She slipped out of her scrubs, and back into the outfit she had been wearing the night before. Instead of waiting for the elevator, she ran up the stairs. She arrived on the sixth floor, breathless. She took several deep breaths as she walked towards his room. When she stood before his door this time, there was no fear, no hesitation. She pushed the door open slowly, it was still early in the morning and she didn't want to wake him if he was sleeping.

He was waiting, lying on his back, looking at the door. "Honeysuckle," he said when she came to sit in the blue vinyl recliner next to his bed. He was smiling, only half of his face, but she knew that if it could, it would light up his whole face.

"What?" It was a strange greeting, and confused her.

"That's what you smell like; honeysuckle. It was really strong last night when you came in, but it's more subtle now; hidden a bit under the antiseptic soap smell." He wrinkled his face in disgust.

"Yeah, the antiseptic soap doesn't smell really great does it? The honeysuckle is from my yard at home. It's pretty much taken over and choked out anything else that had been trying to grow. My mother planted it, so my dad refuses to dig it up – though I don't think it would hurt to trim it back a bit now and then." She smiled, thinking of the summer that she almost gave her father a heart attack when he came home and found her pulling it up by the handful. "I like to collect it when it blooms and make potpourri with it."

"The smell suits you. I remember it from the last spring my uncle and I were living in South Carolina. It grew on the fences there. The fragrance when it first blossomed was overwhelming. It was almost enough to make you dizzy. It bloomed all summer, but the smell wasn't as strong as in the spring. I would sometimes walk along the fence so I could breathe in its fragrance, it made me feel...content. I wasn't sure why; it reminded me of something, but I never figured out what it was. Have you ever had that happen, you hear something, or smell something that you've experienced before, but no matter how hard you try, you just can't remember what it was?"

"I do, all the time. I think that's because I have a bad memory though." They both laughed. Then they sat silently, neither of them knowing what to say.

Finally, Collin looked at her, "Now I know what it was. I was remembering you; I just didn't know it yet." His gaze moved from her face to look past her, out the window at the buildings beyond, almost as if he was suddenly shy.

Jewell felt a single tear roll down her cheek. It was the same way she felt looking at him in the ER, they were supposed to have met before, but something kept their paths from crossing.

Jewell couldn't stay long. She still had to work. She brushed her hand along his arm as she left, feeling his hard muscles underneath the flesh. Where her hand touched his arm, Collin felt a ribbon of fire.

The next morning, Jewell came to sit with Collin again. "You said you moved here from South Carolina? Did you live there a long time?" Jewell had never been outside a one hundred mile radius of her home town.

"No. We lived there when we first came back to the states. We, my uncle and I, had been living in the UK, but before that we lived in Italy."

"Wow." His life was so much more exciting than hers. "Is your uncle in the military?"

"Well, no. Not really. We just move around a lot. I guess my uncle has a severe case of wanderlust." He didn't want to tell her that his uncle was running from something, for Collin's whole life, they had been hiding from some unnamed, unseen enemy.

"So it's just you and your uncle then? What about your parents?"

"Both of my parents died when I was very young. They were murdered." He shrugged a little, as if he were trying to shrug off the pain.

"I'm sorry. My mom died when I was ten, so I know what it's like."

"Well, I never knew them, but somehow, it still hurts. I miss the parents I wish I had, if that makes sense. My uncle has been taking care of me ever since, and I love him, but somehow it's not the same." He paused for a minute.

"Yeah, I guess I can see what you mean. I've always had my dad, and I had my mom for ten years. I really miss her though. She's the reason I became a nurse." She swallowed the lump that rose into her throat thinking about her mother. Even after all these years, it's still like she died yesterday.

Jewell reached for Collin's hand suddenly needing the comfort. "So, you've lived in Italy?" Jewell asked when she felt like she could speak again without her voice breaking.

"Yeah, overseas we lived in Italy, Romania, France and the UK. Here, we've lived in Montana, South Carolina, and now Louisiana. We usually stay someplace for a few years and then move."

"So you have a lot of family?"

"No, not really; they're not really my aunts and uncles. Just close friends of my uncle. He's been travelling for several years and has met a lot of people. Everyone we stay with has known my uncle for years."

"So, are you staying with someone here? Your 'family' I mean?" She made little air quotes with her fingers when she said the word family.

"No, it's just us this time. We have a house a ways out of town."

"I guess that's why you said you don't get many visitors. Just your uncle, huh?"

"I wish! I've been here for what, a week now? And he hasn't stopped in once!" The irritation in his voice was obvious.

"Well, I do know he came to see you in ICU. Carol at the desk said that he checked in on you. He's a doctor or something?"

"Well, it would be nice if he would acknowledge the fact that I'm stuck in this place, and come by to say hello or something! But that's Uncle Percy. He's never been one for a lot of emotion. Things just are what they are with him. He'll probably send a cab to pick me up when I get released!"

Jewell didn't know how to respond to that. It seemed strange to her that Collin's only family wouldn't come by for a visit. With most patients, you had to practically drag them out when visiting hours were over. She felt bad for Collin, but despite his irritation, she could hear the affection he held for his uncle in his voice. She could tell that he knew his uncle really did care about his well-being, even if he didn't come to visit. She glanced at her watch. She wanted to stay all day, but she had to work the night shift and still needed to go home to get some sleep. She said good-bye and promised to stop by at the start of her next shift.

CHAPTER 9

Edgar tried to move into the hospital after the doctor had announced that the press conference was over. His explanation, that the victim had not actually been "clinically" dead, and therefore had not actually been "brought back to life," did not sway Edgar in his convictions. Joey, a friend of Edgar's and an orderly in the hospital, had told Edgar what had really happened. The man had been clinically dead, his heart had stopped beating and the doctors had called the time of death. The dead body, Edgar knew he had been dead, had been in the room for more than ten minutes after the doctors had called it. Unfortunately for Edgar, his friend had been a bit tardy in removing the body, so it didn't go unnoticed when the body had come back to life. This upset Edgar. If the body had come back to life in the morgue, Joey would have been the only one to know about it, and could have discretely removed the now living body from the hospital. Bodies went missing from time to time.

This person was an infidel, a defiler of the Grail. There had been other suspected infidels, but this was the first Edgar identified. Some truly were infidels; some were simply in the wrong place at the wrong time. Without a trial, it's difficult to really know for sure. Just so, people disappeared all the time, and despite the crime shows on television that showed week after week how a single hair at a murder investigation could lead to the murderer, Edgar knew that most police departments were neither that sophisticated, nor capable of solving a well-executed murder.

Immediately following the press conference the sheriff didn't let anyone into the hospital. Edgar tried again later that afternoon to enter through the main entrance. He walked casually past the front desk and was on his way to the elevators when he was stopped by security and escorted from the hospital.

After midnight, Edgar returned to the hospital, this time entering through the ER. He first tried to make it to the elevators, but was told he needed to check in at the desk. Edgar checked in, giving a false name and stating that he was having chest pains. He was put in a curtained off area in the emergency ward.

When the nurse left, Edgar got out of his chair walked towards the elevators. He was just about to push one of the buttons when another security guard asked him where he was going. He told the security guard that he was confused, that he didn't know where he was. He was escorted back to the nurses' station and then escorted back to the where he had been before. This time when the nurse left, Edgar left the hospital.

This, he realized, was going to be more difficult than he thought. Edgar would either need to be sick or injured to be admitted. And then, he would need to be sick enough, or injured badly enough, to warrant an overnight stay in the hospital, hopefully on the same floor as the infidel.

Edgar started considering injuries that might be sufficient to get him admitted to the hospital. A gunshot wound, but that might raise too many questions. A knife wound, but that would be painful, he might not make the wound deep enough, and he might make it too deep or hit a major organ. Yet another consideration was being admitted to the psych ward, if the investigators thought he was suicidal.

This was far more difficult than Edgar could imagine. He had to be admitted, but he definitely did *not* want to die. That was crucial to the plan. Edgar finally determined that a car accident would be the easiest way to get admitted to the hospital. Even if his injuries were minor, the hospital would surely want to keep him overnight for observation.

Actually planning the car accident was a little more difficult. A single car crash always raised suspicions, unless there were circumstances to suggest that the driver may have lost control. Involving another vehicle in the crash was unacceptable. Edgar finally decided that spilled coffee, especially when it was hot, could definitely cause a driver to lose control.

A few days later, Edgar drove through the McDonald's drive-through and purchased a cup of plain black coffee, large. He drove around the corner and poured the cup of coffee into his lap, quickly accelerated, and drove his car down the embankment.

As the car started to roll, Edgar leaned into the fall. When his car suddenly flipped onto its side, Edgar, to his horror, realized he had not fastened his seatbelt. *Now that was stupid*, he thought as his head smacked into the passenger side door.

Edgar wasn't sure if the car stopped rolling before or after he fell unconscious. He was in a lot of pain. His head was where most of the pain was focused, at the moment, but as he looked down to see his leg bent in a rather unnatural direction, the pain in his head lost precedence to the pain in his leg. He wasn't sure how badly he was injured, there were parts of him he could not feel at all to his immense concern. When he heard the grating sound on the door above his head he looked up, trying to focus, and saw a fireman trying to pry the car door open.

He remembered the fireman yelling into his car, trying to get his attention. Edgar tried to respond, but the world quickly swam out of focus and he lost consciousness again.

CHAPTER 10

Jewell found it difficult to concentrate on assigned tasks, and had difficulty remembering the simplest things. She was relieved that she wasn't assigned to triage. Even though she thought her training would kick in during an emergency, she couldn't be certain, and she didn't want to test her theory when someone's life was at risk.

Jewell was in a room with a worried mother and her sick toddler taking a history. It didn't seem serious, probably strep or a bad cold. She never told the patients what she thought, it wasn't her place to diagnose illness, but she did reassure the mother with a kind smile, and reassuring pat to her hand.

As Jewell walked out of the examination area, she heard a commotion as a stretcher was unloaded from an ambulance. She stood against the wall while a man was whisked past her into a room. He didn't look good, but his injuries didn't look too serious. He was conscious, his eyes darting between the people surrounding him. As he passed her, his eyes found hers. His stare made her uncomfortable. She tried to look away, but was unable to until a paramedic stepped in front of her, breaking the line of sight. Something about that man sent a shiver down her spine making the hairs on the back of her neck prickle.

Jewell walked toward the nurses' station to record her notes on the toddler she had just seen. As she walked, she looked back toward the man. Even though she couldn't see him anymore, her stomach tightened at the thought of being in the same room with him. She hoped she wouldn't be asked to help in his care.

At the nurses' station, Madelyn was sitting at one of the computers typing in notes. Maddie was always a wealth of information. She kept her ears open and never missed a detail. The problem was that she was usually anxious to share those details with anyone who would listen.

"What do you know about the guy who just came in?" Jewell asked Maddie in the most casual tone she could muster. Jewell was still a little creeped out by that man's stare

Maddie grinned and her eyes lit at the opportunity to share some gossip. "Well," she started, as if the information was so juicy it was just oozing out of her, "it was a one car MVA; the idiot spilled coffee in his lap and drove off the road. What a schmuck!"

Jewell sighed; Maddie could be a bit judgmental as well. Jewell didn't dislike Maddie, but sometimes, Jewell found her a bit irritating. Jewell gave her a slight nod and forced a bit of a smile in appreciation for the information.

"They'll probably just keep him overnight for observation because he has a concussion, and then send him home in the morning. Idiot! Coffee! Can you believe it? What a moron!"

Jewell looked at her notes as she rolled her eyes, shut her folder and stood up. She smiled, "Thanks Maddie. I'll probably see you later."

"Sure Jewell, see you around." Jewell heard Maddie giggle quietly to herself and mutter the word "idiot" under her breath as Jewell walked away.

Jewell turned her thoughts back to Collin. She glanced at her watch and was chagrinned to see that it was only ten o'clock. Eight hours until she could see Collin again. She knew he was probably asleep and wished she could sleep away the next eight hours as well. On a positive note, there was a full moon tonight. That meant the ER would be interesting at least.

She was right, not a dull moment from the drunk stumbling in to let everyone know he had been poisoned, to the man who had been bitten by an alligator while he was noodling; a southern tradition of catching a catfish by sticking your arm into a dark murky hole hoping to find a catfish.

Jewell's stomach knotted with anticipation as she watched the hands on the clock slowly creeping towards six a.m. She was tired, dead on her feet, and could barely lift her arms; it had been a busy night. But Jewell knew that Collin's presence would melt away any physical and mental fatigue she felt. As six approached, she hoped that there wouldn't be one last case that she would need to attend before leaving. She had finished her last case half an hour ago, and if nothing new came in, she could leave right at six. As the hands moved ever closer, she heard the screams of a siren approaching. Her heart sank. She hoped that the case wouldn't be assigned to her. *Please, please, please*, she thought as an elderly woman was wheeled into the ER.

The woman was in her eighties. She had suffered a heart attack. Her husband was by her side holding her hand as she was wheeled back to a room, whispering that he would never leave her. It made her think of Collin. Would they grow old together? Would she someday be holding Collin's hand as one of them passed from this life to the next? Surprisingly, the thought didn't make her sad, but instead, gave her hope that perhaps this is what her future held, a long and happy life with someone she loved. And she did love Collin; as crazy as it seemed, she knew that it was love and she would sacrifice everything to be with him.

Fortunately, Jewell was not assigned to this case, so she quickly ran to the locker rooms. She took a cold shower not waiting for the water to warm, partly to wake her up after her long shift, but also because she knew that Collin didn't like the smell of the antiseptic soap. It prolonged the wait to see him, but it was for him, she wanted to make him happy. Besides, he needed his rest. She hated to wake him so early in the morning. After she had showered, she changed into fresh clothes that she had brought specifically for this. She had also put one of her honeysuckle sachets in her bag to help keep her clothes smelling fresh as they sat for twelve hours in her locker.

She pulled on a pair of faded jeans that made her legs look good. Then she pulled her royal blue polo over her head. She had chosen this shirt because Ashley told her it made her eyes look amazing and it was one of the few shirts that actually fit her right; it wasn't so oversized that it hung off her body. She quickly brushed her face with mineral powder and dusted her cheeks with a little blush. Then she very carefully applied the eye shadow Ashley had given her just as she had been instructed. She pulled a brush through her hair and stepped back from the mirror to assess how she looked. She knew Ashley would be proud of her. As an afterthought, she rubbed the sachet of honeysuckle over her hair, and threw everything in her locker.

She waited impatiently for the elevator and when the doors finally opened she rushed in, pounding the button for the sixth floor repeatedly as if it would make the elevator move faster. After what seemed an eternity, the doors opened releasing her from her temporary prison and she ran to Collin's room.

Fearing that he would still be asleep, she very slowly opened the door and peeked in. As was usual, he was lying on his side, facing away from the door. "Honeysuckle" she heard him say, and she could hear the smile in his voice. She laughed as she pushed through the door and quickly crossed the room to sit in the ugly vinyl recliner next to the bed.

Collin smiled and reached for her hand. She took it quickly, reveling in his warm touch. She looked into his stormy gray eyes and lost herself.

"Has your uncle come by to visit yet?" Jewell asked, breaking the silence.

"No, but like I said, that's Uncle Percy. He probably figures that if the hospital hasn't called to tell him I'm dead, everything must be fine. Plus, I keep leaving messages on his phone. I'm assuming I sound better than I did a few days ago, so that gives him even less excuse to stop by." He shrugged like it didn't matter, but Jewell could tell that it hurt him. "At least I have you to look forward to every day. It gives me an incentive to get better." He grinned. Jewell noticed that his smile wasn't quite as lopsided as it had been. The right side of his face was starting to regain some of its mobility. This was a great sign; it meant that there might not be any serious nerve damage. Too, even though he seemed lucid enough, it was another indication that there was no brain damage.

"Your smile looks better. It's not as one sided as it was. Does it hurt when you smile?"

"Yeah, everything hurts, but honestly, it's not too bad. I don't even use the morphine. And I've figured out what hurts the most when I move; so I don't move that way."

Jewell was sure that he was trying to play down the true extent of his pain for her sake. She appreciated the effort, but she knew that the pain must be excruciating. She thought that he was sweet though, trying to spare her feelings that way.

"You look tired. You should probably go get some rest." Concern creased his face. He was right though, she hadn't been getting enough sleep lately. Not only had she been spending extra time at the hospital, but her dreams had been troubled, and her excitement to see him had made it more difficult to not only fall asleep, but to stay asleep as well.

"I'm not tired," she lied. But she could tell by the look in his eyes that he knew.

"If you are going to have to drive all the way home, I don't want you doing it half asleep. I'd rather not have you in the room next door." He smiled. "What's more, I really don't feel very well today. I think I need some time to rest."

Jewell knew that he was lying, trying to give her an excuse to leave, other than her own needs, but he was right. If she stayed too much longer, she wouldn't be able to drive home safely. She needed to sleep, and she needed to sleep in her own bed.

"Besides, I'll see you tonight when you come back into work, right? You need to get some sleep so you can handle your long nights."

"I'm not working tonight, it's my day off. I'm on a four this week; two on, two off."

"So, I won't see you tonight?" He tried to keep the pain from his voice, but he could feel the lump forming at the thought of missing any time with her.

"I was thinking…" Jewell began, "even though I'm not working, I can come by anyway."

"You don't have to come in on your day off. That seems like too much to ask." Collin replied.

"I *want* to. I could stay for a couple of hours, maybe bring you some real food?" She couldn't imagine being away from him for two days.

"That sounds nice. The stuff in here is horrible." He made a face. "So, I'll see you tonight then?"

"Absolutely. I might be a little later tonight, maybe around six or so. Is that okay?"

"Sure, it's not like I have any place to go." He laughed at his joke, but for some reason his words made her suddenly nervous. Apparently he caught her apprehension because he asked, "What's wrong?"

"Huh? Oh, nothing. I guess I just really need to get some sleep." She smiled as she stood up to leave. She didn't want to, but he was right, she could barely keep her eyes open. She needed to get home before she fell asleep. "Rest well," she said, as she turned at the door.

She heard him whisper something about dreaming of her as the door closed. She didn't see the eyes watching her from the other side of the nurses' station as she left.

* * *

Edgar sat in a seating area with a window overlooking the dirty city below, but his interest was drawn by what he saw taking place near the nurses' station. The young nurse who had passed him in the ER the night before was leaving one of the rooms. She wasn't wearing her scrubs, but instead, a tight pair of jeans, heeled shoes and a blue polo and she didn't look like she had been working. Edgar made a mental note to find out about the young nurse as he wheeled himself back to his room.

CHAPTER 11

"Well kid, it looks like you got yourself into a bit of a pickle." Percy said with a grin, striding into the room. Percy was Collin's uncle with whom Collin had lived as long as he could remember.

"Hey, Uncle Percy. It's about time you bothered to stop by. I hope I didn't inconvenience you. I've been practically dying for a week and this is the first you've bothered to check on me. You didn't even answer my calls." Collin was a little heated. Uncle Percy was the only family he had and he felt abandoned when his uncle hadn't come to visit.

"You called? I must've been busy." Uncle Percy pursed his lips as he looked at Collin. Considering his injuries, Collin looked pretty good. There were still some areas that had the yellow hint of a healing bruise, and his broken bones were rebuilding themselves at a remarkable rate but they would need some more time to heal completely. Of course, Percy wasn't surprised; a little distressed, but not surprised.

Percy knew that he would need to get Collin out of the hospital soon. He could not only take better care of Collin than the hospital could, but there were certain things better kept secret that would become apparent if Collin were to remain here for much longer. The doctors were already marveling at Collin's rapid recovery. Of course, the hospital had no idea what Collin was, except for Dr. Babineaux, but there was only so much the doctor could do to defer notice of this unusual person. If Collin remained too long, the news crews would be back en masse.

Collin didn't even know what he was. It was bad enough that Collin had had the near death experience; it wouldn't help matters if certain people were to find out how fast he healed. Percy wasn't really concerned about the media, Dr. Babineaux and Sheriff Payne had made it seem unremarkable so the article was buried in the Local section, and quickly forgotten. The whole article was two short paragraphs describing a car accident. One driver, his nephew, was in critical condition. The other driver would be charged with DUI. There was no follow up on the condition of the driver in ICU. Thanks to the help of some friends, the media was the least of his problems, though Percy knew that even with the help he had, that could change quickly.

"Actually kid, I was in here the day after you came in. I saw you after they moved you to ICU. When I saw you were going to be okay and that they were taking good care of you, I left to take care of some things." As Percy turned to pour Collin a glass of water, he muttered under his breath, "Besides, you weren't practically dying."

Collin wasn't sure if he was meant to hear the last part of his uncle's comment but he responded anyway. "What do you mean I wasn't practically dying? I've heard the nurses whispering around here. They seem to think I'm lucky to be alive."

"Let's just say that my superior medical knowledge and skill led me to believe that you weren't in as bad a shape as they thought you were." He forced a grin, but his eyes were hard, staring at Collin as if he knew something about Collin's injuries that he didn't want to share.

Uncle Percy had gone to medical school before Collin knew him. Sometimes, when they stayed in one place for a while, his uncle would find work in a hospital or clinic. Uncle Percy said it was to earn money to keep them going, but Collin doubted they needed the money.

"So how've they been treating you in here?" His uncle said, trying to lighten the mood as he took a drink from the glass of water he had poured for Collin before placing it on the tray next to the bed.

"It's been Hell," Collin replied. "It seems like every fifteen minutes someone comes in to give me a shot, or check my blood pressure, or change my bed linens. I swear I can't get a moments peace. Even though I've been in bed for a week, I'm so tired I can't think straight."

His uncle laughed.

"I cringe every time I hear someone coming through the door," he continued, then paused wondering how much he wanted to share with his uncle, or more specifically, how much he wanted to share about Jewell. He decided a little bit of information wouldn't hurt. "But there is one nurse. Her name is Jewell. She comes and sits with me every day. I really look forward to her visits."

His uncle made a small grunt as he assessed Collin's eyes. He knew the look, he'd had it himself once. It was a look of longing, of unconditional love. "Let's see what I can do about getting you out of here," he said as he pushed himself up from the only chair in Collin's room. He was out the door before Collin could reply.

In about an hour, his uncle came back in, grinning like a Cheshire Cat. "It's all taken care of. An ambulance will be here in a bit to take you to a small, private continuing care center where you can heal. It wasn't too hard to convince them to let me take you, Dr. Babineaux was a big help."

"How long?"

"How long what? Until you can leave? Don't get your knickers in a bunch. The ambulance should be here in a couple of hours and then we'll be on our way."

Collin glanced at the clock. It was just before one in the afternoon. It would be several hours until Jewell had promised to come by. He had to see her before he left. He had to let her know that he would be back for her. Collin didn't even know Jewell's phone number, or where she lived. "Can we wait until after six?"

"What, is the food so good here that you want to stay for another meal?"

"No. I really wanted to say good-bye to Jewell. She's been so nice; I just wouldn't feel right leaving without saying something to her." He could feel his throat tighten at the thought of not seeing her again.

His uncle assessed the emotion in his nephew's voice, appraised the look in his eyes. He hated what he was doing, hated to hurt his nephew like this, but he knew it was better this way; for both of them, Collin and Jewell. Before they got too close, before their feelings could really grow. This was a relationship that wouldn't work. "Sorry kid. We have to leave when the ambulance gets here. I'm going to go check on the arrangements."

Collin watched his uncle leave. He could feel the tears building. He was embarrassed that he was acting like this, crying over some girl he had just met. He rubbed angrily at his eyes. But Jewell was different. Somehow, he felt as if he'd known her forever. It was like waking up one day and realizing that you're in love with the girl next door. The girl you grew up with, that you ate mud pies with, that you threw rocks at, the one that you chased around the playground at school making kissing noises, your best friend.

After a while his uncle returned with a couple of orderlies. They transferred him to a gurney and pushed him through the hospital towards the exit. Even though Collin knew there was no chance that he would see her, his eyes searched anyway. If he could just see her one more time, let her know that he loved her. He didn't care if she didn't feel the same way about him; he just had to let her know.

The orderlies loaded the gurney into the ambulance, his uncle climbing in behind. He was facing the wrong way to look out the door, but he could hear the doors on the ambulance slam, closing the doors shut on any possible future he might have had with Jewell.

*   *   *

Jewell's father was home when she came in; he wasn't working today. He was watching something on the television, probably golf – how he could watch that game was beyond her. "Jewell, is that you?"

"No dad, it's armed robbers, come to kill you and steal your twelve inch tube TV."

Her father laughed. He didn't watch a lot of TV so he didn't see any reason to buy anything bigger. As far as he was concerned, this TV was perfect. He was more likely to be out with the guys from his Krewe, playing softball at the fire house, or reading a book. He used to tell Jewell that the quality of television had diminished in direct proportion to the number of channels available, so he didn't see any reason to get a bigger TV – or cable. He saw no desire in watching the prolific stupidity of reality shows on a larger screen or in higher definition.

"Dinner from last night is in the fridge," her father called as Jewell started into the hall.

Jewell poked her head into the refrigerator as she called to her dad, "you know dad, you could at least get cable. You know, you're going to have to if you want to keep watching TV after the digital switch."

"The what?" He had no clue. Jewell wasn't surprised. Technology and Tommy McKean mixed about as well as oil and water.

"Never mind dad. What're you watching?"

"I don't know. Good Morning America I think. I don't even know why I have this on. I should probably go to the bookstore, I need a new book."

"Why don't you do that dad? I'm going to bed anyway. I'll see you when I get up."

He grunted an acknowledgement. He liked to be home when Jewell was home and awake. Sometimes he felt that he didn't spend enough time with her.

Jewell ate a salad while watching an interview with some sports guy. When she was finished, she took her bowl into the kitchen, rinsed it out, and put it in the dishwasher. She walked into the living room and stood in front of her dad, blocking the TV. He looked up at her. "I really love you dad. Thanks for everything you do for me."

Her dad reached out and pulled her into his lap. She was an adult in so many ways, but felt a child in so many more. She sat on her dad's lap for a few minutes, her arms circling his neck, just content to be in his arms. Then she turned, kissed him on the forehead and gave him a quick hug. "I'll see you when I wake up dad. Don't worry about dinner. I don't have to work tonight so I'll fix something nice." She used the arm of the chair to lever herself off her father's lap and walked slowly to her room.

When she woke, she looked at the clock and was surprised at how long she had slept. It was nearly six. She got out of bed and walked to the kitchen. She had promised both Collin and her dad a good dinner but it was already six and it would take her a half an hour to get to the hospital. She opened the refrigerator, leaning on the door to see if there was something she could heat up. She found some seafood gumbo that her dad probably picked up at Morton's so she threw some of that in a Gladware container with some rice that was left over from Chinese her father had brought home, and popped it in the microwave to heat. Her dad wasn't home; he was probably out with some of the guys or playing softball at the firehouse. She wrote him a quick note:

"Dad: had to run to the hospital for a while. Didn't have time to make dinner. Saw some Gumbo in there. Thought you could eat that. Sorry. Love you. Jewell"

She ran into her room and threw on some clothes. She tried to choose clothes that Ashley would pick out. She grabbed a pair of khaki pants, and a pink blouse. She had a pink, western style belt that she threaded through the belt loops quickly and then threw on a pair of white and pink Skechers with pink laces. She checked herself in the mirror and thought that she looked like she was thirteen, but she didn't want to take the time to change. She ran to the kitchen, grabbed the gumbo from the microwave and her keys from the table and ran out the door.

On the causeway, she was pushing it. She knew that she couldn't afford to pay for a ticket, but she couldn't seem to ease up on the accelerator. She also knew that any extra time she gained by speeding would be lost if she was pulled over. She scanned the bridge, looking for police cars parked in the crossovers scanning for speeders. Fortunately, in the whole twenty-four miles she did not encounter a single officer. She had to slow down once she got into town, but the distance from the bridge to the hospital was the shortest part of the trip.

She parked in the visitors' lot and went in through the front door; this being the shortest distance to his room. These elevators let out on the same hallway as Collin's room. When she exited the elevator, she walked quickly to his room and paused just before her hand pushed the door open. The nametag in the placard next to the door was gone. She pushed the door open and saw that the room had been cleaned; the bed was made, and...empty. Did they move him? Why would they put him in another room? Had something happened? Did they need to move him back down to ICU? The questions bombarded her brain like hail.

Jewell let the door close and walked to the nurses' station. Out of the corner of her eye, she noticed a patient in a wheelchair sitting at the end of the hall looking out the window. She didn't pay any attention to him; it wasn't Collin so it didn't matter. Kelly was sitting at the desk. Jewell didn't know Kelly very well, but remembered her name because when Ashley introduced them she said, "Just remember that Cheers song that Woody sang: 'Kelly, Kelly, Kelly, Kelly, Kelly...'"

"Kelly, do you know what happened to Collin?"

"Who?"

"Collin Sykes. The patient in room 637?" Jewell's voice was bordering on panic.

"Oh, I remember him. I just came in about fifteen minutes ago so I'm not sure. Give me a sec and I'll see what I can find out." She spun her chair from the desk over to the computer on the other side. Jewell watched impatiently as Kelly pushed keys quickly, eliciting pages of information which she deftly moved through, looking for the information she wanted. "It looks like he was transferred this afternoon."

"Transferred? Transferred where? On whose authority?" Jewell knew that she was nearly screaming, and felt bad taking her anxiety out on Kelly. It wasn't Kelly's fault that Collin wasn't in his room. She took a couple of deep breaths trying to calm her nerves.

"It looks like Dr. Babineaux signed the release papers. A Dr. Percival Knighton requested the transfer. It looks like he was taken to a continuing care center in Lake Charles."

"Does it say which one? Does it give the address, or a phone number?"

"What's with the interest Jewell? It's no big deal; patients get transferred every day."

"Yeah, but this patient was special. I...I, well, I sort of liked him." She felt a blush shading her face. She wasn't surprised. She hadn't really wanted to tell anyone about her and Collin, but it was bound to get out sooner or later. Ashley was discrete, but who knows who else took notice of Jewell's visits to his room.

"I don't see anything here Jewell. Do you want me to pull his file? There may be something in there that wasn't put in the computer."

"Yeah Kelly, that would be so great. Thanks."

Kelly left the desk to look at the patient files on the other side of the divider. She emerged a minute later carrying an open file in her hands. She laid the file on the desk so that Jewell could read it. "I'm not really supposed to give you this but...just promise not to tell anyone I gave it to you, okay?"

Jewell nodded as she grabbed a pad of paper and started transferring the information to the notepad. When she was finished, she ripped off the page and handed the pad back to Kelly and left the hospital.

CHAPTER 12

Collin didn't remember most of the ride in the ambulance. Even though Collin hated the way that the painkillers made him feel, his uncle insisted on a morphine drip. His uncle was adamant that it was necessary, and because Percy had a medical degree while Collin didn't, Collin wasn't able to convince his uncle that he would be better off without it. His uncle also gave Collin an additional oral sedative; as if the morphine didn't do a good enough job alone.

When Collin finally awoke, still groggy from the effects of the medication his uncle had given him, he realized that he was home. He had assumed that this was where his uncle was bringing him, but with his uncle, he never knew.

He scanned his surroundings. He was at home, on a hospital style bed instead of his own, and he was in the parlor off the front hall instead of his room. A morphine drip with the familiar red button hung by his left arm, and his uncle had placed a small table next to the left side of the bed along with a plastic cup of water and a small silver bell. Curiosity overcame him as he reached for the bell. It made a sweet tinkling sound as he shook it back and forth. He set the bell down, and picked up the glass of water. It was still difficult to raise his head, and his bed didn't have the mechanical features of the one in the hospital that allowed him to raise himself into a sitting position.

As he struggled to raise his head and bring the water to his mouth, the French doors at the entrance of the parlor burst open as his uncle came striding quickly toward his bed. "What is it Collin? Can I get you anything? Are you in pain? Are you hungry?"

Aha, so that was what the bell was for. In lieu of the button on his bed to summon a nurse, he now had this pretty little silver bell with the merry tinkling ring. The summoning button for the nurses had been silent in the room, but sometimes he could hear the grating buzz it made at the nurses' station. He had tried not to use it. It seemed the other patients on the floor kept the nurses busy enough, and aside from that, he knew that if he waited for five minutes, someone would come in to poke him with something anyway. He had to admit, it was nice to be away from that sterile, unfriendly place.

"No Uncle Percy. I don't need anything. I just saw the bell and didn't know what it was for." Collin grinned mischievously, "Now I guess I know. It seems you are at my constant beck and call until I can get up on my own."

"Well, not really. I've called in reinforcements. Gladys is here. I'll pick up Dorothy and Carl at the airport in a couple of hours, and Kendryck said he may drive in sometime this week if he can."

"Are you kidding me? Why? Did you call everyone we know?"

Each of these people loved Collin, and they were all an integral part of his life, often sending cards, or presents when he was young. Most of them stopped sending presents after he was fifteen, but some, like Aunt Gladys, still insisted on sending him a present on his birthday. Usually something well suited for a ten year old; although, this year Gladys had sent him a remote controlled Ferrari. Collin really enjoyed this gift, especially since he would probably never own a Ferrari. His uncle indulged his preference for sports cars, but refused to buy him anything that would "draw attention" to them. That meant Ferrari, Porsche, Lamborghini, and his favorite, the Saleen S7 were definitely out of the question. Instead he settled for more practical cars, Fords, Chevys, and Hondas. The GT500 he had just totaled was a real loss.

"Gee Uncle Percy, are you too old and feeble to take care of one little invalid? How difficult do you think I'm going to be?" Collin smiled angelically at his uncle.

"You, I'm not worried about. I just hate being in this big house all alone. Gladys came to keep me company while you were in the hospital, and the others were just concerned about you."

"Actually, now that I think about it, can you bring me some pillows for my back to prop me up a bit? You can't imagine how hard it is to pour water into the side my mouth without soaking the pillow."

"Sorry about the bed. It was the best I could do on short notice. I can prop it up in the back if you want, or I can bring you the pillows; whichever you think would be easier. I put the remote control..." Percy glanced at the table next to Collin's bed. Not seeing the remote, he frowned and looked around the room. "Oh, here," Percy said grabbing the remote off the credenza under the 65 inch flat screen. "This'll give you something to do while you're laid up."

"Can I have a phone? And a phone book?"

"Why? Were you planning on ordering a pizza?"

"No, I just really wanted to call the hospital and talk to that nurse that was so nice to me. I wanted to thank her for everything she did for me." He knew his uncle would probably say no. His uncle was adamant that Collin not encourage relationships outside of his circle of friends. That was fine, but there really weren't any that were his age. There had been a girl, Sophie, in France who they stayed with for a while. She seemed to be about the same age as Collin and she was absolutely gorgeous, but even though Collin liked her, he didn't *like* her. But Jewell was his other half, his true soul mate.

"I'm sure she has better things to do than talk to some patient. I think it's best if you just let her get on with her life."

"But Uncle Percy, I kind of liked her, and I think maybe she liked me too."

"Florence Nightingale Syndrome," his Uncle said, dismissively. "You'll forget about her in a couple of days."

"What kind of syndrome," Collin asked, now completely confused, and a little upset that his uncle wasn't taking him seriously.

"Florence Nightingale. She was a nurse, quite a talented woman actually." He sighed. "She was so beautiful...." He stopped, embarrassed and cleared his throat. "She was a nurse during the Crimean War. Amazing woman." His uncle sighed again, a faraway look in his eyes.

"What in the world are you talking about? I know who Florence Nightingale was. I mean jeez Uncle Percy; I *did* study History at Oxford. They taught me a thing or two." Collin had no idea what his uncle was talking about. Sometimes when he talked about things in the past, he talked like he had been there. He was very unusual in that respect. "What I wanted to know was what does Florence Nightingale have to do with me?"

"Oh, sorry kid." His uncle suddenly looked at Collin as if he had forgotten where he was. Pulled back into the present, Percy answered Collin's question. "Florence Nightingale Syndrome: it's when a patient falls in love with his caregiver. It's very common. It's not really love though, just misplaced appreciation for their caregiver's efforts. We learned about it in med school. More common when the nurse is pretty." Percy winked at his nephew.

"This is *not* Florence Nightingale Syndrome. She's not even my nurse. She's a trauma nurse down in the ER."

"Well, I don't think that's what you should be thinking about right now. You need to concentrate on getting better." His uncle adjusted Collin's bed so that Collin was closer to a reclining seated position, instead of lying down, and walked over to switch on the TV. "You get some rest. I'll bring you dinner before I head off to the airport. Don't worry, Gladys is cooking, not me." He smiled.

Collin let the matter of Jewell drop. He knew that his uncle wouldn't change his mind. Instead, he smiled gratefully at his uncle. Even though his uncle was a pretty good cook, Collin liked to tease him about his cooking skills. "Thank goodness for that. If you were cooking, I think I'd ask to go back to the hospital for dinner!"

His uncle playfully threw the remote control at Collin as he left the parlor.

Collin flipped through the channels on the television looking for something interesting. He stopped on a history show about trebuchets that seemed promising, but his thoughts kept drifting back to Jewell. He was still a bit groggy from his uncle's ministrations for the ride to the house so he turned off the television, closed his eyes, and drifted into a dreamless sleep.

When his uncle returned a couple of hours later with a steaming bowl of red beans and rice, Collin was feeling a bit better. He had slept off some of the medicine, and was thinking more clearly. He took the bowl from his uncle and inhaled the scintillating aroma of spices and Andouille sausage causing his stomach to growl.

His uncle laughed. "Guess they didn't feed you really well in the hospital, huh?"

"Sure they did Uncle Percy; I absolutely loved the red Jell-O and rubbery eggs." He took a bite of his food. It was still too hot to swallow so he sucked air in through his teeth to try to cool the hot rice. When he was finally able to swallow, he savored the strong spices. He picked out a piece of sausage and chewed it slowly savoring the spicy heat. It was unbelievable; even though Aunt Gladys was from Montana, she could make a mean red beans and rice.

"I've got to go to the airport. I'll be back in about two hours. If you need anything, just ring the bell and Gladys will get you whatever you need."

After he heard the front door to the old plantation house close and the sound of his uncle's car disappear down the long driveway, he picked up the little silver bell and rang it gently. Gladys appeared so quickly that he was certain she must have been standing right outside the door waiting for his call.

"What can I get for you, sweetie?" She reached to ruffle his hair, a habit she just couldn't give up, but pulled her hand back at the sight of the bandage still enveloping most of his head. She started to pinch his cheek, but thought better of that as well. Finally, she bent and gently kissed his forehead.

It was amazing. Collin had known Gladys for most of his life. He and his uncle had moved in with her shortly after his parents were killed. When he looked at her though, she didn't look any older than she had when he lived with her twenty years ago. She didn't look much older than him, maybe early to mid-thirties. He knew she must be at least fifty. He wondered why she wasn't married.

He briefly thought about asking Gladys for his phone and a phone book, but he knew that she would spill the beans to his uncle as soon as Percy returned from the airport. Invalid or not, Percy did not like to be disobeyed, and would not temper his yelling at Collin for circumventing his wishes.

"Well, I haven't seen you in a while, I thought we could talk."

Gladys's face lit like a thousand stars. Collin was certain that he was her favorite nephew, even if he wasn't really her nephew.

"What do you want to talk about?" Gladys pulled a cushioned arm chair from the corner of the room and placed it so that it was facing Collin's bed. After she had made herself comfortable, she folded her hands in her lap.

"So, how's Montana?" Collin began.

Gladys laughed. "Oh sweetie, I haven't lived in Montana for close to seventeen years now. Shortly after you and Percy left, I moved to Greenland, then the Ivory Coast, and now I'm hanging out in the Bahamas!"

"Why do you move around so much? You sound like Uncle Percy."

"Maybe that's why we get along so well!" She laughed. "How do you feel dear? I just hate to see you looking like this." She asked, smoothly changing the topic of the conversation.

Collin didn't miss the evasion. He had learned when he was young that when his 'family' didn't want to talk about something, it didn't matter what you did, the matter would not be discussed. "Well, I guess I don't feel all that bad. My chest hurts a bit still when I breathe. I think this bandage on my head bothers me more than the cut underneath. It doesn't hurt to smile anymore, but it does hurt to laugh – both my chest and my face." Collin grimaced. He liked to laugh and his Uncle Percy usually had him rolling on the floor. He appreciated his uncle's restraint today. "It would be nice to be able to move my legs."

"Sweetie, I'm sure you'll be up and around sooner than you can imagine. You always were a quick healer and your Uncle Percy is a great doctor, even if he doesn't practice much. I keep telling him that he really should spend more time working as a doctor." She spoke fondly, with the same emotion of a sister discussing her wayward brother.

"I suppose. I'm just so sick of being cooped up like this. I guess some of Percy's wanderlust has worn off on even me."

"Percy has a wheelchair. I could put you in that and take you around the grounds; maybe down to the bayou? If we hurry, we can see the sunset. It should be really pretty." She grinned at him.

"You know Aunt Gladys; I think that's just what I need."

* * *

Percy filled Dot and Carl in on the ride home. He described Collin's accident and shared that one of the doctors in the hospital, and one of the Orleans Parish sheriffs were members of the Templar group. He had been told there were others, but had not yet been introduced.

"Thanks to Dr. Babineaux's influence, I was able to move Collin home, before suspicions began to rise. He and the other Templars will work with us, but we need to think of the *Family* first."

CHAPTER 13

Ashley was watching American Idol when the phone rang. She looked at the caller ID and saw that it was Jewell calling from her cell phone. Ashley grabbed the phone "Hey chickie baby, what's up?"

Jewell tried to answer through the tears but the words wouldn't come. She tried again, but nothing came out but her choking gasps as she tried to breathe between racking sobs.

"Jewell, honey? What's wrong?" Ashley asked, panicked. "Where are you?"

Jewell managed to choke out the word "hospital" before her weeping overtook her again.

"What is it? Your dad? Is Tommy hurt? Are you hurt? What honey? I can't help you if you can't tell me what's wrong!" Ashley tried to think. As a nurse, she knew that she should be able to handle the situation, but hearing the devastation in her friend's voice made her unable to think.

Ashley grabbed her cell phone from the charger as she spoke on the cordless house phone. "Sweetie, stay put. I'm coming to get you. I'll call you from my cell in one minute. Hang up, and I promise, I'll call you right back." Ashley waited for the click that indicated the connection had been terminated. She quickly punched the three button and send to call Jewell's cell phone. Jewell didn't pick up the phone. When Ashley heard the voicemail pick up, she hit the end button, immediately followed by the send button. She pulled open the car door, slid into the driver's seat, and jammed the keys into the ignition. She heard Jewell's voice mail pick up again. She quickly tried again while turning the key. Her car chugged, trying to turn over, but it wouldn't start.

"Come on!" Ashley screamed, pumping the gas pedal of her 1980 Toyota Corolla; she really needed to get a new car now that she had a job. She turned the key again, praying that the car would start. It whirred twice again, before she finally heard the engine roar to life. She jammed the car into reverse, and floored the gas pedal. As she backed into the street, she slammed on her brakes as she heard the long scream of a horn announcing that she was about to crash into a passing car.

Ashley took a deep breath, trying to calm her racing heart. She wasn't going to do Jewell any good if she was dead. She carefully looked behind her as she pulled out into the main road. She turned towards the Causeway and picked up the phone to call Jewell again. This time, Ashley was relieved when Jewell picked up the phone.

"Ashley?" Jewell was still crying, but she seemed to have calmed down a bit.

"Jewell, thank God. What's going on? What's happened? Is it your dad?" Ashley tried to probe Jewell for more details.

"No, not my dad." Jewell started crying uncontrollably again.

"Jewell, take a deep breath." She heard Jewell suck in a large breath of air. "Okay, now let it out slowly." She listened as Jewell slowly released the breath. "And again." Jewell did as Ashley instructed. When it sounded to

Ashley like Jewell was in control of her voice, she tried once more. "What happened?"

"Oh Ashley, he's gone!" She sobbed into the phone.

"Who's gone? What are you talking about?"

"Collin. He's gone."

"Oh God Jewell; I'm so sorry." Ashley knew that Jewell had developed some strong feelings for Collin in the short time that she had known him. "But it's really amazing that he survived as long as he did. He should have died that first night. Sometimes, there's just nothing you can do." She grieved for her friend's loss.

"No Ash; he's not dead. He's gone. They've taken him out of the hospital."

Ashley didn't know what to say at first. She was relieved, but it took her a minute to figure out what her friend was saying. "Well, that's not so bad. Do you know where they took him?"

"Yeah; his uncle took him to a private care center. I've got the name, and a phone number and address. It's in Lake Charles."

"Well, call him then. What's the big deal? Why are you so upset?"

"I tried. I got an invalid phone number message. Ash, I don't know what to do. I have to see him."

"Okay Jewell, sit tight. I'm on the Causeway now. I'll call you when I get to the city. We can figure out what to do then."

"Thanks Ash. I know this is crazy, but thanks for understanding."

"Don't worry about it hon. Are you going to be okay until I get there?"

"Yeah. I'm in the parking garage. I'm just going to wait for you here in my car. I can't drive right now." Jewell clicked the end button on her phone and set it on the seat beside her. She had only known Collin for a little over a week. Really, she'd only known him for three days; since the first time she'd actually spoken to him. She leaned her head against the seat trying to think about what she wanted to do. Suddenly, she heard her phone ring. She glanced at the clock; nearly twenty minutes had passed, she must have dozed off. She looked at the phone and saw that it was Ashley calling. "Hey Ash."

"Hey. I'm just coming into the garage, where are you?"

"Third floor, near the elevators." As she hung up the phone, she could hear the engine in Ashley's car approaching. Jewell was surprised Ashley was willing to drive that death trap across the Causeway every day. Jewell opened the driver's door and eased out, testing her legs. They seemed sturdy enough so she got out and walked around to the back of the car to wait for Ashley. Just as she leaned against her car she saw Ashley's car chugging around the corner.

Ashley saw Jewell standing behind her brand new Ford Focus. Ashley thought to herself that she *really* needed to get a new car. She pulled into the spot next to Jewell and got out gathering Jewell into her arms. Jewell clung to Ashley like she was about to fall off a cliff. After a minute, Ashley moved her hands to Jewell's shoulders and gently pushed her away so that she could look at Jewell's face. Even in the dim lights of the parking garage she could see that

Jewell's eyes were red and swollen. A stream of tears flowed from Jewell's eyes and her body shook with convulsive sobs, though she made no sound.

"Girl, you've got it bad," Ashley commented shaking her head.

Jewell didn't trust her voice so she just looked down at her pink and white shoes.

"So do you have a plan? What do you want to do?"

Jewell shrugged in response, not having the ability to respond around the lump in her throat.

"You have an address?" Jewell nodded. "Do you want to go see if you can find him?" Jewell shrugged again. When Ashley took her chin and gently pulled Jewell's head up so that she was looking into Ashley's eyes, Jewell gave a slight nod. Ashley sighed. This was absolutely nuts, but Jewell was by far her best friend and Ashley would do anything for her.

"Well," Ashley said glancing at her watch, "it's ten forty five. Lake Charles is what, like three hours away? If we left now, we wouldn't get there until two a.m. and there's no way they would let us in that late. Plus, even if we have the address, we have no idea how to find this place. Why don't we go back to my place, we can map it to find where he's staying. I'm not working tomorrow," she glanced at Jewell to see if she had been scheduled. Jewell shook her head. "Cool. We'll get some sleep; then we can get you some decent clothes," Ashley grimaced looking at Jewell's outfit. "You look like something that eats rainbows and poops butterflies!" Ashley quoted from Horton Hears a Who; one of her favorite movies. "We can get an early start and be there by ten. Does that sound like a plan?"

Jewell nodded. "Good," Ashley replied, handing Jewell her phone. "Call your dad, let him know you're staying at my place tonight and tell him we have plans for tomorrow. That way he won't be worried."

Jewell called her dad, then gave her keys to Ashley so that Ashley could drive them home. "I'm not going to be stranded in your car somewhere in Louisiana."

"Yeah, I really do need a new car." Ashley said, sliding into the driver's seat of Jewell's car.

CHAPTER 14

Edgar listened to the blonde nurse he had seen leaving Collin's room as she spoke to the nurse at the nurses' station. He had been in his room when he heard a commotion outside his room. Usually he wouldn't be interested, but the nurses' station was right outside his room and when the name Collin Sykes drifted through his door, he decided that this was a conversation he did not want to miss.

He carefully edged out of bed and tested his weight on his casted leg. It didn't hurt too much so he thought that he could make it out of his room with the help of his crutches rather than the wheelchair. He used the crutches to limp to the door, carefully cracking it open so he could hear part of the discussion.

"Collin Sykes. The patient in room 637?" The blonde nurse that he saw leaving the Sykes' room earlier sounded agitated, nervous.

"Oh, I remember him. I just came in about fifteen minutes ago so I'm not sure. Give me a sec and I'll see what I can find out." The other nurse, the one with the darker hair responded. Her hair reminded him of the color of mud. Looking at the beautiful nurse beside this one made her look all the more beautiful. Her hair glistened like sunshine, and her skin glowed, her cheeks were the color of roses. The nurse on call on the other hand, had skin the color of paste, her hair was the color of mud, and her eyes were as dull as graphite.

When the nurse at the station turned away from him to use the computer, Edgar carefully eased out of the door to his room and limped the few feet down the hall to the seating area in front of the nurses' station. He actually liked it here, sort of. There were large picture windows that looked out into the city. Although it wasn't the best view during the day, the city was so dirty; he had to admit that the city had its own beauty at night, with all the lights, sparkling like stars throughout the city.

Although any passing nurse, patient or doctor would think that he was simply resting outside his room, admiring the city stretched below, in truth he was listening intently to the conversation between the two nurses.

The blonde nurse seemed particularly interested in the whereabouts of Collin Sykes. Did she, like him, know what he was? Why was she so agitated that he had been taken from the hospital? What information did she have that he didn't?

After he watched the blonde nurse leave, he carefully hobbled over to the nurses' station. "Can I get you something Mr. Durand?" The nurse's voice was short, clipped. None of the nurses liked Edgar; he didn't know why.

"I need a pad of paper and a pencil." She grabbed the same pad the blonde nurse had used and slapped it on the ledge in front of him along with the pen sitting next to it.

"No, I said a *pencil*." He said this slowly, as if talking to a slow witted child, putting special emphasis on the word pencil.

The nurse with the mud colored hair looked at him for several moments as if trying to understand. Edgar remained silent, staring at the woman, fuming internally at the nurse's slow response. Finally, she huffed, pushed the chair back and walked to a cup at the other end of the desk. Picking it up, she tipped it toward her face, squinting and peering in trying to locate a pencil among the many pens, highlighters, and markers also filling the cup. Finally, she shook the cup a little and reached two fingers into the bottom. She pulled out a small orange stub. With a smirk, she walked back and set the pencil lightly on the desk. She looked at Edgar as if daring him to complain about her effort. He should have, but he didn't; this pencil would work.

Edgar gave the nurse his most charming smile, reclined his head in a slight nod, picked up the paper and pencil, and hobbled back to his room. Using the crutches while carrying the paper and the pencil was not easy; he struggled as he tried to hold on to his items and still keep the weight off his injured leg. As he turned his back to the door of his room so that he could push the door open with his back, he saw the nurse watching him from the nurses' station, her arms crossed under breasts, snickering at his efforts. He smiled again, and pushed backward into his room.

With the pad of paper and pencil in his hand he sat on the bed and raised the back so that he was in a sitting position. He reached to pull the tray toward him to create a table upon which he could work.

First he picked up the pad of paper and turned it towards the light. He tilted it back and forth trying to see if an impression of the previously written words were still embedded in the paper. As he tilted the pad toward him, he saw what he was looking for. He laid the paper on the table and started gently moving the pencil back and forth across the middle of the page. He was patient, careful in his work. As the white paper began to turn silver gray, he was rewarded for his efforts when words began to slowly appear in a slightly lighter color.

The pad had been used often. There were many words from which he had to derive the information he sought. He could make out the word Jaffa across the top of the page. His heart quickened at his discovery. The Knights Templar had transported pilgrims from Jaffa to Jerusalem. The Knights Templar found the Holy Grail in Jerusalem in the ruins of the Temple of Solomon. It was an exciting coincidence linking Collin Sykes to the Holy Grail.

Below that, he could make out what looked like an address. It was difficult to read. He could make out Bor du Lac Drive, but the number was difficult to discern. This didn't bother Edgar. He could drive to Lake Charles, find the street, and ask for directions to the Jaffa Continuing Care Center as soon as he checked out.

CHAPTER 15

Collin heard the front door open, and heard the laughter of his uncle along with the voices of two people he recognized vaguely. Of course he knew it would be Uncle Carl and Aunt Dot. He had spoken to them on the phone, usually to thank them for Christmas or birthday gifts, but it had been years since he had had any contact with them. He had never met them in person.

He saw one of the French doors leading into the parlor crack slightly and his uncle's face appeared in the opening. "I'm awake," Collin called, knowing that his uncle was anxious to introduce his guests to the "nephew" they had never met.

His uncle entered first, followed by a young couple holding hands. They were perhaps a little older than him, probably mid to late twenties. Collin was startled by how young they were considering that he had known them for several years. The man approached boldly, arms held out as if to embrace Collin's bedridden body. The woman behind him was a bit more timid. She waited silently by the door until her husband had finished greeting his heretofore unmet family.

"Collin! Wow! It's great to finally meet you. It seems like you have grown up so fast! How old are you now, twenty-five, twenty-six?"

"Twenty-three," Collin responded, smiling, infected by his 'Uncle Carl's' contagious grin and untamed energy. He took an immediate liking to this man that he felt he would soon consider his friend.

"This is Dot!" He gestured to the petite, pixie like woman standing by the door. She had short, very straight, dark hair, cut short in the back and tapered so that it was slightly longer in the front. She had very light skin, and beautiful green eyes. "Come on Dot," Carl called to her. "The boy's not going to get up and come over to meet you!" He smiled warmly at his other half, holding out his hand encouraging her to move into the room.

Dot walked into the room, a little more boldly than Collin expected based on her initial behavior, and took Carl's hand. She smiled warmly into Carl's eyes before looking down at Collin. "You know, you look just like your mother," she said wistfully.

"How do you know I look like my mother?" Collin asked, curious.

Dot hesitated, looking at Carl before answering. "I've seen pictures. She was lovely. It's so wonderful to finally meet you." She leaned over Collin, giving him a careful squeeze and a kiss on his cheek.

"He doesn't look too bad, does he?" Carl asked looking at Dorothy.

"Not at all."

"To hear Percy tell it, we were expecting to see a mangled bloody mess lying in the bed. Heard about the Mustang too. Tough break! I'll make sure your uncle replaces it with something appropriate!" Carl winked at Collin.

"Let's let the boy rest," Percy gently nudged his two friends toward the door. "We have some things to talk about."

"You're right Percy. The more rest he gets, the sooner he'll heal." Dot took Carl's hand and they walked to the door. Percy and Carl held the door to wait for Dorothy to pass through, and then followed, Percy closing the door behind. The door opened a crack, and Collin saw Dorothy's face poke back in to throw him a quick kiss.

As the doors clicked closed Collin considered turning on the television. He looked to the table next to him to find the remote, when he started to hear the conversation in the other room. Under normal circumstances he wouldn't eavesdrop, but he heard his name mentioned twice.

"…need to tell Collin." That was Carl's voice.

"…doesn't need…know yet." Uncle Percy.

"His safety…" From Dorothy

"Is not a concern right now!" Percy's voice had risen so that Collin heard the whole sentence.

"…think about…" Carl.

"When it's right! He's my responsibility. I have kept him safe for twenty-three years; I will keep him safe as long as I have to!"

"Percy…will find out." Carl again.

"Your…is not being fair." Dorothy's voice was strained with concern.

"I will tell him when I am ready to tell him, and not a moment before. If you cannot respect my decision on how to raise my nephew, then you can get back on your plane and go home. Or you can walk for all I care!" Collin heard his uncle storming up the stairs.

"He's scared." Gladys had joined the conversation. "Percy hoped that Collin would be a skip. He hasn't prepared himself for this eventuality." Her voice was clearer and easier to understand. Collin figured she was standing in the hallway outside his door.

"What was he going to do if he was a skip? Just leave him?" Dorothy's voice had increased in volume now as well. It seemed the conversation was making everyone agitated and as a result, raising the volume of their voices.

"He's done it before. People die. It would hurt Collin, but it wouldn't be unexpected." Gladys was speaking emotionally. Collin could hear tears choking her voice.

"…needs to tell him soon." Carl's hushed voice floated through the door.

"…he's ready. …knows…to be soon."

Collin heard Gladys' footsteps as she walked down the hall toward the kitchen. He heard plates and cups clinking and shortly smelled the aroma of coffee drifting down the hall. There would be no more discussion tonight.

Collin closed his eyes and dreamt of a beautiful blonde nurse with clear sky blue eyes and a heart as big as the ocean.

CHAPTER 16

At Hugh Payne's house, the Louisiana Chapter of the Knights Templar sat in the living room, some on couches, others on chairs, and some on chairs brought in from the dining room. Hugh Payne stood in the center of the circle with Nicholas Babineaux. While meetings of the Inner Circle occurred every month, this was a special meeting.

The group consisted of nine members, one each to represent the original nine members of the sect. The knights upheld the overall function of the Templar Knights, to serve the community, and to protect those in need. However, there were individuals that required special protection. These people, the Infinitas, when identified, became the primary responsibility of the Templar Knights.

This tradition began in the twelfth century with one of their own. In 1138, Peredur Kilkenny, one of the Knights Templar was seriously injured while guarding a group of pilgrims. His wounds were fatal. He was carried to the Temple where the Knights witnessed a miracle. The knight, thought dead, began showing signs of life. The Templars enlisted the aid of healers to help the young knight recover. They believed that this was truly a miracle from God; a testament to their cause.

The young knight fully recovered. He continued his purpose as a Knight but as the original knights aged, the young knight did not. For nearly two hundred years, he carried on his duties as one of the Templar Knights. Many believed that his longevity was proof that the Holy Grail existed, and that it was in the possession of the Templar Knights

When the Templars were accused of heresy in 1305, another sect, the Obsidian Knights, stepped forward to testify against the Templars. They proclaimed their purpose was to correct the wrong, kill the unjust, and reclaim what once was lost. To seek out those that had stolen eternal life from the Holy Grail, and mete out justice without mercy or trial. Since then, a religious war has raged between these two sects.

When the Templars were gathered Hugh Payne, the Grand Master of the group, looked each in the eye, testing their commitment to their duty. "Gentlemen, an Infinitas has been identified."

The group gave a collective gasp. The Infinitas were rare, and seldom discovered. To protect their lives, the Infinitas took great pains to remain unidentified.

Nicholas Babineaux went on to describe the situation occurring with Collin Sykes. "Apparently, Collin has been living with his Infinitas uncle, Percy Knighton, but does not yet know that he is Infinitas. It is also likely that Collin does not know what the Infinitas are.

"Dr. Knighton has been reluctant to give his nephew too much information, concerned for his nephew's safety. Dr. Knighton had seen signs that his nephew carried the trait, but after Collin's accident, it is certain.

"Understandably, Dr. Knighton did not want to reveal where he's staying, but he did specify that more Infinitas may be joining him in the coming weeks. At this time, they don't want to leave the area but they're ready to move at a moment's notice." Dr. Babineaux paused to pass around several pictures.

"These are photos of Dr. Knighton and his nephew. Dr. Knighton provided us with the picture of his nephew prior to the accident. He said that the picture is about two years old, though my observations in treating Collin show that his appearance has not changed in those two years."

He paused while the pictures were passed from person to person. Each man carefully studied the photographs to ensure that they would be able to recognize both people. While it was unlikely that the Infinitas would have reason to come in contact with the group, should they see either person or believe that they were in apparent trouble, the Templars were to act immediately. The loss of a single Infinitas was considered a failure to the Templars.

After the pictures had been returned to Nicholas Babineaux, he sat down to give Hugh Payne an opportunity to speak. "Among us, we have three firefighters, two sheriffs, a doctor, and three police officers in different precincts. We should be able to provide the protection required. Should any of you hear or see anything suspicious, it is your sacred duty to use whatever resources are necessary to protect the Infinitas from harm until they are able to leave the area." He paused to look around the room. "Does everyone understand?"

"Yes, Grand Master," came the unified response from the group.

There was a solemn silence as the group replaced displaced furniture and slowly left for their cars. They all were aware of the import of the task that lay before them.

CHAPTER 17

Jewell had been to Ashley's apartment before. It was a nice, two bedroom apartment in a gated apartment community in Mandeville. Although the walls were standard Apartment White, she decorated her apartment the way that she picked out her clothes; with style and class. Her taste was impeccable.

Ashley used the second bedroom as a guestroom/office. She had a double bed in the room, along with a bookshelf, a desk, and a computer. Jewell walked straight to the room and turned on the computer. As she waited for the computer to boot up, she dug the small piece of paper out of her pocket.

Jaffa Continuing Care Center
1135 Bor du Lac Drive, Lake Charles
337-555-8410

When Windows had finished booting she opened the internet and quickly navigated to Google. First she typed in the name of the private care center, trying to get more information. She scanned through the results and found nothing. Next she tried Google Maps. The exact address couldn't be found, but Bor du Lac drive was a short road on the banks of Lake Charles. She quickly typed in Ashley's address to get driving directions and printed them. She laid the papers on the desk as carefully and gently as if they were an original copy of the Declaration of Independence.

Ashley called from the kitchen where she was heating up some leftovers. "Did you find anything?"

"Nothing about the care center specifically, but I did find the street on Google Maps. It's a short street so finding the care center shouldn't be difficult. I printed the directions."

"Great. Hungry?"

Jewell thought for a minute. She hadn't eaten anything since this morning when she came home from work. She had heated the gumbo to take to Collin, but hadn't eaten any herself. She wasn't sure what she had done with that. She probably left it at the nurses' station at the hospital. "Yeah, I guess. Now that I know where he is, I feel like I could eat something."

Ashley set two paper plates on the table and went back to the kitchen for forks. Jewell took a tentative bite and realized she was famished. With everything that had been going on today, she hadn't had time to think about her building hunger.

When they had finished eating, Ashley gave Jewell a pair of sweatpants and a t-shirt. She also gave her an unopened pack of underwear. "I bought it yesterday, guess it'll come in handy. Go ahead and try to get some sleep. I'll wake you up at about eight. If we leave by nine, we can be there at noon."

Jewell turned towards the guest room with her borrowed clothes, "thanks Ash." Ashley just smiled and went into her own room to get some sleep.

Jewell sat on the edge of her bed. She was certain she wouldn't be able to sleep. She thought about going to the computer, but she couldn't think of anything she wanted to look up. Instead, she turned off the lights, and laid her head on the pillow. Before she knew it, she was asleep, dreaming of a sandy blonde man with stormy gray eyes.

It felt like only moments before she became aware of Ashley gently shaking her shoulder. "Come on sleepy head. If you want to take this road trip, we need to get started so we won't be too late getting home. I've already had my shower. I left a towel in there for you. Get your hair dry and we'll fix your face and figure out what you are going to wear today."

Jewell dragged herself out of bed and wandered sleepily into the shower. The warm water felt good and seemed to wash away all of the stress and worry she had felt over the last twenty four hours. She quickly washed her hair and got out of the shower; wrapping the huge bath sheet around herself and drying her hair. She hadn't taken out her contact lenses the night before so she searched Ashley's cabinets for some solution to clean her lenses. After drying her hair and cleaning and replacing her contact lenses, she walked out of the bathroom with the towel wrapped around her.

Ashley was in her room, her closet door open and three drawers pulled open in her dresser. She had laid out several shirts, pants and skirts on the bed and was swapping tops with bottoms looking for the right combination. Jewell sighed and walked up next to Ashley. Ashley glanced over at her, and went back to her study. Jewell looked around her room, peering into Ashley's closet. She was overwhelmed by the selection of clothes owned by her friend.

When Jewell saw Ashley at the hospital, she was always in scrubs. The hospital had a dress code which didn't allow Ashley to fully express herself. When they went out on their days off, Ashley usually wore jeans and a t-shirt. Granted her t-shirts were much more stylish than what Jewell wore, Jewell couldn't begin to fathom the extent of Ashley's fetish with style. Well, Jewell thought, at least she'd look good today.

"Got it! This is the one!" Ashley suddenly shouted. She turned, holding a violet wrap shirt which she held up to Jewell's shoulders. "Oh yes, definitely. This is it!"

Jewell shrugged out of her towel and started getting dressed. She had some difficulty trying to figure out how to make the shirt work, but with a little help from Ashley, she had it on and expertly tied. She had to admit, Ashley knew what she was talking about. Ashley also gave her a pair of pleated front black capris, and a pair of black strappy sandals with heels. Ashley dragged Jewell into the bathroom, added a few loose curls to the bottom of Jewell's long blonde hair and sprayed it with hairspray. Finally, Ashley fixed Jewell's makeup to give her a bright summer glow.

When Ashley was finished, she took Jewell to the full length mirror in Ashley's room and asked Jewell what she thought. Just as before, Jewell was shocked. She had no idea she could look this good. Ashley was a miracle worker.

Ashley told Jewell to go grab the directions while she grabbed two Cokes out of the fridge and they started out on their trip. As they started out, Jewell's dad called, obviously worried about his daughter. Jewell assured him that she and Ashley were just going to hang out, and Ashley promised that they wouldn't be late. When Jewell finished talking to her father, she turned off her phone and stuck it in the center console. She didn't want to answer any more questions from her dad; he knew her too well to hide things from him. The less she spoke to him, the better it would be.

By twelve thirty, they had found Bor du Lac drive, but they had no luck finding the care facility. The road wasn't long, so they drove the length of it three times before finally giving up. They drove to a gas station and Ashley got out asking the attendant if she had ever heard of the Jaffa Critical Care Center. The attendant shook her head as she apologized. "No, not in town. I know for sure that it wouldn't be on Bor du Lac drive. There's only one building on that street and it's definitely not health care. You might want to check with the hospital. They may know something. St. Patrick Hospital is just down the road," she quickly jotted down some directions. "I'm sure they would know if there was a private patient care facility somewhere in town."

"Thanks." Ashley smiled at the clerk and took the paper out to the car. "The clerk inside said we should ask at this hospital. They might be able to give us some more information."

Jewell nodded her head. She knew that the hospital wouldn't have any more information. Jaffa Critical Care Center didn't exist. What she wanted to know was why Collin's uncle would take him out of the hospital and lie about where he was taking him. She also wondered why Dr. Babineaux would release a patient to move to a facility that didn't exist.

"Let's go home. There's something weird going on here. Dr. Babineaux wouldn't release a patient to a facility that didn't exist unless he knew something. I'm going to ask him if he knows anything. Plus, I might be able to get Collin's home address from his file."

"Jewell, you know Doc Babineaux isn't going to tell you anything, and if you get caught looking in a patient's file, you could get fired. Maybe you should let it go."

"I know Ashley. I can't. I don't know why, I just need to see him again."

They stopped for lunch at a Burger King on the way out of town. As they ate, they didn't say anything. Jewell didn't trust herself to speak, and Ashley didn't know what to say, to either talk her friend out of her crazy quest, or to make her feel better about her futile search. Really, there wasn't anything she could say.

When they had finished eating, they threw their trash in the bin and started walking out the door. In the parking lot, Jewell saw a man that she thought she recognized. As she got into her car, she watched as the man pulled a leg with a cast out of the car. Instantly, Jewell knew where she had seen him before. He was the guy they brought in that had the car accident, the one who had spilled coffee on his lap; the one with the really creepy eyes. She shuddered.

Ashley noticed Jewell staring and looked over her shoulder to see what she was looking at. She saw a man getting out of his car, and then she noticed Jewell shudder. "What's up?"

"I know him. He came into the hospital a couple of days ago. When they brought him into the hospital, he stared at me and it really gave me the creeps."

"Do you think he's following you?"

"No, I don't even think he saw me. It's probably just a coincidence."

"Probably. You ready to go home?"

"Yeah. Let's go."

*   *   *

When Edgar was released from the hospital, he borrowed a car to drive to Lake Charles to find the care facility where the infidel had been taken. When he took the Ryan Street exit in Lake Charles heading towards downtown, he realized that he hadn't had breakfast. As he drove down Ryan Street, he saw a Burger King. He pulled in and was just about to get out of his car when he saw the blonde nurse from the hospital leaving with another woman.

He sat in his car, watching the women as they left the restaurant. He wondered if they were in town for the same reason he was. He couldn't be one hundred percent positive, but considering the conversation he overheard the day before, he was relatively certain that they were here looking for the infidel as well. From the look on the blonde's face, it didn't look like their search had been successful. As the women got into their car, he opened the door to get out. Out of the corner of his eye, he noticed the blonde looking at him. He wondered if she recognized him. He limped into the restaurant without looking back.

CHAPTER 18

They drove to Ashley's apartment. As Ashley got out of the car, she leaned in the passenger side door assessing Jewell's face. She had the same deadpan expression that she when she first found out Collin was gone. Her eyes were devoid of hope, and her face was drawn and pale. "Are you going to be okay?"

"What?" Jewell looked at Ashley as if she didn't realize she wasn't alone.

"I said are you going to be okay?"

"Yeah, fine." Jewell's voice caught in her throat.

"Maybe we can drive to work together tonight."

"I don't know Ash. I just...I don't know if I'm going to work tonight."

Ashley's face creased with worry. Something had to change. What could she say to give her friend a little hope? She couldn't stay home alone tonight; it wouldn't help her at all.

"What about his file? Didn't you say you might see if you can find his address?" Ashley tried to sound hopeful. "I could help. I go into the records room all the time. I doubt anyone would notice if I took a quick peek in the wrong file...accidentally, of course." She winked at Jewell and gave her a half smile.

"Yeah, I guess."

Ashley stood up and closed the door. She watched until Jewell drove through the gates of the apartment complex then picked up her phone and dialed Jewell's home number. She didn't know if Jewell's dad was home today, but she had to try.

Tommy picked up on the second ring. "Hello?"

"Hey Tommy, this is Ashley. I'm glad you're home. We've got a problem."

"I knew last night wasn't about a girl's night out. What happened?" Tommy sat at the kitchen table and rubbed his temple. He sensed that something was very wrong.

"It's Collin. What do you know about him?"

"Is Collin that guy at the hospital that Jewell took a liking to?"

"Yeah. Apparently, she *really* took a liking to him. She was visiting him every day before and after work. There was something, I don't know how to explain it. It's like, after she met him, she was whole. Like there had been a piece of her missing, but we had just never noticed it before."

"I know." Tommy sighed heavily. He was quiet for a minute. *Every person has one true soul mate.* That was what he used to tell Jewell all the time. Tommy saw it in her eyes the first time she spoke of Collin. This was her soul mate. He could only hope that she hadn't lost hers the way he had lost his. "What happened?" Tommy knew that if he was her *true* soul mate, the feeling would be mutual. He wouldn't have turned her away. But if he wasn't, if this was just the infatuation of a first crush, then she would just need to get beyond the first couple of days of heartbreak.

"They discharged him. His uncle is a doctor and he supposedly took him to some private care facility. Jewell managed to get the address in Lake Charles. We went there today but there was no private care facility. The information was deliberately falsified."

So he hadn't necessarily left her by his own choice. If he was her soul mate, he would find his way back to her, but would it be too late? "I'm assuming she didn't take it well."

"No, she's worse than she was before. She said she wasn't going to go in to work today. I think I convinced her to go, but…Tommy, I'm worried about her. Really worried. I think she needs someone to be there, just in case…" She let the thought trail off.

"That's not a problem. I've got some vacation time saved up at work. I'll call in a few favors and take a couple of days off. Is she on her way home?"

"Yeah, she left maybe five minutes ago. Just before I called you."

Tommy checked his watch. She should be home in the next ten minutes. "Don't worry Ashley. I'll take care of her. Thanks for looking after her and being a good friend."

"You're welcome Tommy; I just hope it's enough."

After what seemed like an eternity, he saw Jewell's blue Focus driving down the street. He sat down in his favorite recliner and grabbed the book he was reading. When Jewell came in the door, he set down the book. "Hey honey. Did you have a good time with Ashley?" She shrugged in response and walked into her room and shut the door.

At five o'clock, Tommy knocked on Jewell's door. "Do you want something to eat before work?" He waited for a response. When she didn't answer, he cracked the door to look in on her. The shades were drawn; the room was completely dark. Jewell sat in the middle of her bed, hugging her knees to her chest. Tommy eased his way into the room and over to the bed. He sat on the edge, placing his hand on Jewell's back. "It's time to get going if you want to get to work on time."

Jewell looked at him, or more accurately, looked through him. She got up, went to her dresser to get her scrubs and then walked to the other side of her room to get her shoes from the closet. Her movements were stiff; she looked like one of the zombies from Dawn of the Dead.

"Why don't I call Ashley? She can give you a ride to work." Tommy worried that Jewell would be unable to safely drive to work in her condition. When Jewell didn't answer, Tommy left the room and called Ashley. Ashley told him she had already thought of that and was on her way.

When Ashley pulled into the driveway, Jewell was sitting on the couch in the living room, blank eyes staring at nothing. Tommy opened the door stepping back so that Ashley could come inside. Ashley walked to the couch, took Jewell's hand and coaxed her out the door. As she left, she gave Tommy a reassuring look. She would take care of Jewell.

At work, Ashley checked on Jewell a couple of times during the night. Although she wasn't her normal, cheerful self, she seemed to be functioning relatively normally. She was speaking to patients and other nurses and doctors.

To someone who didn't know Jewell as well as Ashley did, they might just think that she was a little tired or out of sorts, but Ashley doubted anyone would notice more than that.

As promised, Ashley managed to find Collin's file and jot down his address. It was in Lacombe, just about twenty miles from Covington. Maybe when Jewell had this information, she would perk up a bit. Ashley went to the cafeteria at eleven thirty, when they usually met for lunch. Jewell wasn't there. Ashley grabbed an apple and went looking for her. By the time Ashley's break was over, she still hadn't found Jewell. She felt better at the end of her shift when Jewell was out in the parking lot waiting by Ashley's car.

"Rough night?"

Jewell didn't answer.

"Okay then...Hey, I found Collin's address. It's in Lacombe. You want to head over there tomorrow?" She handed the piece of paper to Jewell. Jewell took the offered paper and looked at it. Her expression didn't change. She opened the car door and sat down in the passenger seat, looking at nothing out the front window. Ashley got into the car, and drove Jewell home. Neither said anything for the entire trip.

At Jewell's house, Ashley opened her door and stood up shaking her head at Tommy to indicate that there had been no change. Tommy waited at the door for his daughter to walk up the front walk. He put his arm around her shoulders as he waved thanks to Ashley and led Jewell inside.

Tommy watched as his daughter went into her bedroom and shut the door. He checked on her several times that day while she slept. When she didn't wake up for dinner, he went into her room and sat on the edge of her bed, resting his hand on her shoulder. He breathed a sigh of relief as he felt her arm slowly rise and lower with her steady breathing. It was no wonder she was still sleeping. She hadn't slept in over twenty four hours. He left, carefully closing the door behind him.

Tommy slept in his recliner in the living room. He wanted to be there when Jewell finally woke up. He was surprised when he woke up to find the sun shining in through the front window. He got up and walked to Jewell's room. He cracked the door, and saw her sitting on her bed, brushing her hair. "Morning. Do you want some breakfast?"

"I'll get it dad. I think I'm just going to have some cereal. I have some errands to run."

"If you're sure. Do you want some company?"

"No dad. I'm good. I'll be back in a couple hours." She grabbed her cell phone, and walked out the door.

Even though she knew this address was going to be just as bogus as the address for the clinic, she had to check. She drove down I-10 toward Lacombe. It was a short drive, only about twenty minutes. She had mapped the directions and drove directly to the location. She pulled into a parking lot and looked at the number above the door; 29230. The sign in front of the building said "Tropical Interiors." She wasn't surprised.

As Jewell pulled away, the tears started to run down her face. She didn't have the energy to keep trying to fool her friends and family. How long would it be before she finally gave up?

CHAPTER 19

Collin lay in bed looking at the TV. It was a soap opera, he didn't know which one. He picked up the remote and flipped through the channels. He switched to a crime show then turned off the television and threw the remote on the floor. This was insane. He felt fine, and yet, his uncle insisted he get his "rest." He reached his hand up to run it through his hair but felt only peach fuzz, reminding him of why he was in this situation in the first place. He rubbed his head, feeling the healed scar that ran along his scalp. It itched a little, but was healed for the most part. A light pink scar ran through his peach fuzz hair.

His uncle had removed the figure-of-8-brace when they arrived home the week before. He removed the bandages on Collin's head the next day. Two days later, he had taken off the cast on his left leg. The only remaining evidence of the accident was the cast that extended from his right hip all the way down to his toes. His knee itched. He tried not to think about it, but then his ankle started to itch; then his shin and his thigh. Before long, he was convinced that his cast was filled with little ants crawling up and down his legs. He looked around for the yardstick his uncle had left for just this purpose. When he didn't see it immediately, he sat up and looked around his bed. He saw it on the floor, under his bed, just out of reach. Unfortunately, even though he could get off the bed, because the cast also immobilized his hip, he was unable to reach the yardstick.

He looked at the doors to the parlor and started to hobble toward them. His right leg didn't hurt when he put weight on it, but it was extremely difficult to move it forward. He stepped forward with his left foot, and then dragged the right leg to meet the left. By repeating this process, he was able to make slow, if inexorable progress across the room.

When he reached the doors, he pulled them open, catching one of them on his right leg. This situation was really becoming impossible. He looked toward the front door, he thought that sitting on the porch might be nice, but then he heard voices coming from the kitchen. He could use something to eat so he started moving in that direction: thump, scraaaape, thump, scraaaape, down the hall. When he was within a few feet of the kitchen, his uncle came out to stand in the doorway, hands on his hips.

"I was wondering how long it was going to take you to get out of that bed boy." Uncle Percy winked and grinned wickedly. Then he turned towards the voices in the kitchen and remarked "Look, Frankenstein's monster. HE LIVES!" Collin heard a collective chuckle emanating from the kitchen.

"Well, are you going to give me a little help, or just stand there and watch?"

"Thought I'd just stand and watch. It's really interesting the way you move that right leg."

"Ha ha," Collin remarked sardonically. "I thought I'd see if I could find a butcher knife big enough to cut this thing off. It's making me crazy! I swear there are ants in there crawling around."

Percy moved to the side as Collin dragged himself into the kitchen. Finally making his way to the counter and propping himself against it, Collin looked at the gathered faces. Gladys, Kendryck, Carl and Dorothy all sat at the table eating sandwiches. Gladys grabbed the plate of sandwiches in the middle of the table and handed it toward Collin. He took a sandwich off the top and took a bite. "So you guys decided to throw a party but didn't invite me?"

"Actually," Percy responded, "we were just discussing taking you to get your leg x-rayed. I think that cast is about ready to come off, but since it was such a bad break, I wanted to be sure. Seeing as how you're walking on it now, it seems I was correct. Still, better safe than sorry. Do you feel like going for a ride?"

"Oh yeah, definitely." Collin breathed a sigh of relief.

Carl, hating to see Collin struggling, got up and put his shoulder under Collin's right arm to help him to the door and down the stairs on the front porch. Percy had a nice, big, SUV. This made it easy for Collin to push himself into the seat and turn himself toward the front. "At least there's plenty of legroom," Collin joked, as Percy got into the driver's seat.

The drive was short. Percy pulled into the parking lot of an orthopedic clinic. Dr. Babineaux greeted them at the door. "I remember you from the hospital," Collin remarked. "I thought you were a trauma surgeon, not orthopedics."

"I am. This clinic belongs to one of my friends from med school. He sometimes lets me use his X-ray machine for extracurricular pursuits. I love it! State of the art, all digital." Dr. Babineaux smiled as he held the door open for Percy and Collin.

After several X-rays, and much consultation between Percy and Dr. Babineaux about the condition of Collin's leg, they finally agreed that his leg was healed enough to remove the cast. Because of the pins, the process took longer than removing the cast from his left leg. When it was finally off, Collin reached down with both hands and scrubbed his leg from top to bottom with his nails, sighing contentedly at being able to rid himself of the crawling ant feeling.

Percy wanted to test the weight on Collin's legs slowly. He gave Collin a pair of crutches and encouraged him to stand up. After Collin had gained his balance, Percy told him to slowly start transferring weight to the leg. It hurt, quite a bit actually, but the pain was not unbearable. Finally, Collin had transferred all of his weight to his newly freed leg, using the crutches for support.

"Amazing. Absolutely remarkable." Dr. Babineaux marveled. His eyes sparkled as his mind started processing the medical implications of what he had just seen. "And you're all like this?" He asked, turning his attention to Percy.

Collin looked at Percy who gave a barely noticeable shake of his head, looking subtly towards Collin. It was clear that Percy was discouraging Dr. Babineaux from speaking in front of Collin about something. What did he mean when he asked if they were *all* like this? Collin's thoughts were interrupted when his leg suddenly started to collapse beneath him. He was glad that he still had the crutches under his arms.

"Humph," Percy grunted. "Maybe I rushed things a bit."

"No, no Uncle Percy. It's great. I just need to get used to putting weight on it. It feels really good."

Percy turned to Dr. Babineaux and said something. Dr. Babineaux left the room and came back in a couple of minutes with a simple cane. "Try this," he said, handing Collin the cane. Collin put down the crutches and tested his leg using only the cane. It seemed that he could put most of his weight on his leg without too much pain. He walked across the room and back, and then grinned triumphantly at his uncle.

"Alright then! Nicholas." He shook Dr. Babineaux's hand. "Let's go home kid." He patted his nephew on the back and they headed slowly toward the door. Dr. Babineaux held the door as Percy and Collin left. Collin walked out in front of his uncle and he heard Dr. Babineaux ask Percy if they could talk later. "Later." Percy replied. It was clear to Collin that there was something that Percy did not want Collin to know, and Collin had an uneasy feeling that it had to do with him.

When Collin had settled himself into his seat and Percy had started the car, Collin asked his uncle, "What were you talking about back there with Dr. Babineaux?"

"Oh, just doctor stuff; medical babble and the like. Now, when we get home, I want you to exercise that leg, but if it starts bothering you, I want you to give it a rest. I want to check it later and make sure that it's not swelling. If it hurts, we can give you some pain killers and ice it tonight."

Collin sighed. He was obviously not going to get the answers he was looking for today. "Sure Uncle Percy, whatever you say."

At home, Collin did exactly as Percy asked. Instead of going inside, he walked along the path that skirted the edge of the bayou. He passed a vine covered tree. "Honeysuckle," he thought. He sighed. He wondered if he was going to be able to get away from his uncle to see Jewell again. He wondered if Jewell would want to see him again. He sat down on a fallen tree and shut his eyes, inhaling the sweet, spicy smell of the flowers. He imagined a beautiful girl, with golden blonde hair and sparkling blue eyes. He had memorized every feature of her face. He imagined her, sitting next to him, her warm hand in his, her musical voice.

He didn't know how long he sat there, thinking of her. When his Uncle Percy tapped him on the shoulder, he noticed that the sun was low in the sky. He had been there for several hours. Maybe he fell asleep. His uncle supported him under his arm, and they slowly walked together, back down the path to the house.

That night, Collin was finally able to sleep in his own bed, in his own room on the second floor. He imagined showing Jewell his room. It was beautiful. The 1800's plantation home was decorated in period furniture. The huge canopied bed in the middle of the room faced a fireplace on the far wall. Paintings of southern landscapes decorated the walls. To the right of the bed stood French doors that opened onto the second floor balcony that ran around the entire second floor, a mirror to the porch below. Although it was too hot right now, in the fall, when the weather changed, he could open the doors, the smell of the clematis and pine would drift through the room. He wanted to share this with Jewell. As he thought of Jewell, Collin slipped into a deep sleep.

Collin spent the next day practicing moving around the house. By early afternoon, he was walking smoothly with only a slight limp. Tonight, he thought, he would go to the hospital and wait for her. He didn't know if she would be working but he knew her shift started at six o'clock. If he arrived at five, and waited, if she was working, he might be able to speak to her before she went in to work.

"Hey, Uncle Percy, I was thinking..." Collin started.

"That's dangerous." Percy winked at Collin.

"I'm so tired of being cooped up in this house. I thought I might go downtown, maybe get a po'boy at Felix's then hang at Pat O's for a bit." He tried to sound nonchalant, casual, and indecisive in his plans.

"Sounds like fun! Let's do it!"

"Um, Uncle Percy, not to be rude, but..."

"Yeah I get it. You don't need some old guy hanging on you to cramp your style." He got up from the table and walked over to the counter. He pulled open the drawer and pulled out a set of keys and threw them to Collin. "I figured I couldn't keep you penned up in here for long. I took the liberty of acquiring a new ride for you."

Collin caught the keys and looked at them. Chevrolet. He looked at his uncle "Vette?"

"Of course. I didn't think you'd drive an Aveo."

"ZR1?" Collin asked hopefully.

"Try 2LT. Nice try kid."

Collin sighed dramatically. "I guess it'll have to do." Collin got up and started limping to the door.

"Don't stay out too late. You're still not 100%. And if you end up having a good time at Pat O's, call me, I'll bring Carl; we'll come get you and the car." He eyed Collin seriously, making sure that he understood.

"Absolutely Uncle Percy. No drinking and driving. Got it! I won't be home late."

Collin drove to Felix's for that po'boy. He had a little time before he had to be at the hospital though he had no intention of going to Pat O's. He had other plans. After he had eaten, it was about four-thirty. He drove directly to the hospital, parking near the top of the parking garage; fewer cars, fewer people to see him. At the employee's entrance to the ER, he found a shadowed area next to the doors where he could stand, unseen unless someone looked directly at him. In his black jeans and black t-shirt, he was nearly invisible in the shadows.

He leaned against the wall, resting most of his weight on his good leg. He was hoping that he would be able to stand here until she came in. He glanced at his watch; five fifteen. He knew that her shifts started at six. Was he here early enough? Had he missed her? Was she already inside? Was she even scheduled tonight? He glanced around the corner through the glass door. He briefly thought about going inside to ask if she was scheduled to work but thought better of it. Would she get in trouble if they saw him here? The longer he waited, the more questions he had, the more worried he became.

After about ten minutes, the flow of employees into the building began to increase. He carefully watched each group as it passed, looking for the golden blonde hair that was unique to her; pure sunlight, captured in golden strands. As the procession of employees slowed to a trickle, he began to lose hope. He had just decided that he would leave and try again tomorrow when he felt his eyes pulled towards the rear of the group where he caught a glimpse of her hair, behind the crowd, set apart, walking more slowly. He watched her as she approached. Her eyes were sunken, black circles shaded the creases below her eyes. Her skin appeared to be paler than he remembered and the glow to her cheeks was gone. Beside her, a woman with dark hair had her arm around her back. She looked worried; concern creased her forehead.

Immediately, Collin knew that something was wrong. Jewell was sick, she shouldn't be at work. She needed to be home, resting. Did she have the flu? Would it be safe for her to work around sick patients? Somebody needed to help her; *he* needed to help her.

Collin stepped from the shadow beside the door. He walked slowly, two steps toward the advancing pair. There were no other employees in the parking lot behind them. Most of the employees in front of them had already entered the hospital. He looked at her, his eyes asking what she needed, but he could not find the words. His worry kept him from speaking.

The pair stopped as he stepped in front of them, blocking their entrance to the building without meaning to. He didn't want to appear threatening. The dark haired woman grasped Jewell's arm, holding her, as Jewell slowly surveyed him, standing in front of her. She reached her hand out, tentatively, slowly reaching her hand toward him as if she wanted to touch him to ensure that he was real. Suddenly, something in her eyes changed, a spark, a slight glow returned to her face as she started to collapse.

Collin took two long quick strides toward her, catching her under the arms as she fell. When he caught her, she looked up into his eyes. "Collin?" Her gaze made his hands tremble. The fact that she recognized him made his stomach turn in knots. Was she happy to see him?

Like a bolt of lightning, realization struck. He should not be standing here. He should be in a hospital bed for, how long? He didn't even know. And after that, how many months of physical therapy to return him to the condition he was in now? Was it fear he saw in her eyes? He glanced over to the woman that had walked in with Jewell. The look on her face was one of both fear and relief. A smile tugged at the corner of her lips as she started inching towards the entrance to the building. It was at that moment that he realized his being here was a good thing. *He* was what Jewell needed.

"Collin," she whispered. He picked her up so her feet were no longer touching the ground and held her in his strong arms. "Honeysuckle" he whispered as he held her close and buried his face in her hair. Her body quivered, as she felt the heat of him melting into her. She wrapped her arms around his neck and held tight, luxuriating in the feel of his warm body.

Something about him, the way he smelled, made her feel comfortable, safe. She inhaled deeply, trying to identify the smell. Suddenly, she had a flash of memory. He smelled like her grandma's house. Like cedar and rain and laurel in the spring. She buried her face in his neck, breathing in his scent. Too soon, he let go and set her back on her feet.

Softly, she heard Ashley whisper "I'll see you later Jewell." Jewell had forgotten that Ashley was standing there. Jewell didn't respond. She didn't look towards her friend as she walked away. All she could do was to stare into Collin's eyes, memorizing their color, the same color as the clouds darkening today's sky, his full ruby lips, his strong jaw. She drank in his every feature.

"Collin...how? What are you doing here? How are you here? Where have you been?" The words tumbled out in an excited flood.

He responded, the deep symphony of his voice sending ripples of fire through her. "In order, how – I drove, what – I came to see you, where - well, that's a long story."

Jewell was too light headed to think. She started to feel dizzy and lose her balance when she felt Collin pull her into his arms again. She wished that she could stay like that with him, forever. She shook her head, trying to clear her thoughts. She tried to remember the days since he had first arrived at the hospital. How many days had it been? About two weeks, maybe a little more? It was impossible. There was no way that he could be healed enough to be standing here in front of her, supporting her, holding her.

She slowly pushed herself away from him. She looked again, up into his storm gray eyes. He was taller than she had thought he would be. Of course, she had only seen him lying down. His sandy blonde hair was cut short, slightly shorter than a crew cut. It was probably cut that way because of the injury on the top of his head. This was certainly better than a reverse Mohawk.

Jewell tried to think of all the injuries he had when he arrived in the emergency room, surveying each as she moved down his body. The cut on his head, she couldn't see that without asking him to bend down. His right cheekbone had been crushed, his eye swollen completely shut. She carefully reached up to touch his face, trailing her fingers lightly along the bone. She saw his eyes close at her touch. She moved her fingers to his nose, straight and beautiful. Her hands trailed across his lips which were slightly parted. A small moan escaped his lips as she touched them. Her inspection continued, down to his collarbones, across his ribs. She moved her hands to his arms, gliding them down to his hands. She entwined her fingers in his, lifting his arms carefully, turning them over. Then she slowly, reluctantly dropped his hands so that she could step back and gaze down at his legs; neither had a cast nor a brace.

Collin watched her as she began surveying each of his injuries one at a time. The touch of her fingers sent fire shooting through his body. Where her fingers touched him, it left a trail of heat and pleasure. He closed his eyes, feeling the light touch of her hands as they moved across his face, touching his lips, and moving down to his chest and along his arms. His fingers wrapped around hers as she entwined them in his. For a moment, he wondered if she was going to bend down and run her hands down his legs as well. When she released his hands and he felt the warmth from her body move away, he opened his eyes. He saw her, staring at his legs, her mouth hanging partway open. He waited silently for the questions he knew were about to come; the questions for which he had no answers.

"Collin, this is...it's impossible. Your injuries; there's no way that you can be standing here. It's medically impossible." As Jewell said the words, she almost expected this apparition standing in front of her to fade, to leave her once again, standing alone and despondent.

"I've always been a quick healer." Collin said lightly, knowing that this answer would not be enough.

"But...how?"

"Honestly Jewell, I don't know. I don't know why I'm able to stand here, to hold you in my arms. A part of me wants to believe that it's because I couldn't stand to be away from you, and this was the only way I would be able to see you again before I died of loneliness."

"I thought you were gone. I thought..."

Collin laid a finger on her lips to silence her thought. "I will never leave you Jewell. It is physically impossible for me to be away from you. This last week, you're all I've thought about, every moment I was awake, every moment I was asleep. I would wake with your name on my lips thinking, hoping, believing that you would be there. The emptiness I felt when I realized I was only dreaming made me feel like I was a ghost, like I no longer existed, like I had no substance without you."

"Collin, I've missed you so much. I don't ever want to be away from you again." She stepped toward him, wanting him to fold her in his arms, wishing that they could melt together into one person.

Collin held her, breathing in her honeysuckle scent, memorizing how she felt in his arms. "I have to go," he laid his hand on her lips as she began to protest. "You need to work, and I need to get back home before my uncle comes looking for me. I'll be back in the morning waiting for you, right here, at six-thirty." He gently lifted her chin and lowered his face to hers. She felt his lips brush against hers, not a kiss, but a promise. His breath tasted of honey and almonds. His lips trailed along the line of her jaw and up to her ear. The warm breath of his whisper sent fire through her body "I will be back for you, always."

He let her go, and walked swiftly away. Before Jewell could react, he had disappeared once again into the shadows

When Jewell walked into the locker room, she walked right into Ashley who was waiting for her by the door. Jewell yelped in surprise. "What are you doing here? Aren't you supposed to be upstairs working or something?" Jewell pushed her way past into the locker room so she could get changed glancing at her watch and realizing that she only had five minutes to get ready.

"Duh! What happened out there? Did you think I didn't notice? Wasn't that *Collin?*" She said his name with a teasing tone in her voice.

"Ash, I've got to get to work. I don't know about *your* supervisor, but Nurse Yohanan will be heated if I haven't checked in on time." Jewell pulled her scrub shirt over her head, grabbed her shoes and slammed her locker shut. She started walking briskly toward the locker room door, carrying her shoes.

Ashley followed behind her, obviously waiting for *any* crumb that Jewell might accidentally drop. Just outside the door, Jewell threw her shoes to the floor and shoved her feet in as she ran towards the ER.

Ashley stood at the locker room door, completely dumbfounded. She couldn't believe that her *best* friend would dis her on such an important matter. Couldn't she at least share the tiniest bit of information? Was it good? Were they going to see each other again? She turned to walk toward the elevators. It wasn't until she was standing in the elevator, rising toward her job in obstetrics that it occurred to her that Collin shouldn't have been able to stand there and talk to Jewell. He shouldn't even be able to stand. Ashley pulled her phone out and hit the message key. U O me the 411! TTYL or LS! She hit the send key on her phone and tucked it back in her pocket.

Feeling her phone vibrate, Jewell knew it was Ashley asking for information. She knew it wouldn't be Collin, he didn't have her number. She would have to remedy that the next time she saw him; if there *was* a next time. She felt giddy, anxious, worried, and excited all at the same time. She knew her face was flushed. She walked towards the file room with a pile of folders that Nurse Yohanan had given her to put away. Usually the nurses didn't do the filing, there was a high school girl who did the filing during the day but she had been sick for the past week and Nurse Yohanan hated disorganization.

When Jewell reached the file room, out of Nurse Yohanan's sight, she pulled out her cell phone and replied to Ashley...*k*. She figured she would have to tell her everything. What was everything? What would she tell Ashley? She put the last file on the shelf and walked back out to the nurses' station. Things were crazy. Apparently, while she was brooding over her situation, there was an accident where six people were injured. None of the wounds were life threatening, but there was plenty to do. Whatever she thought about Collin would have to wait.

Things finally slowed down just after midnight. Jewell ducked into a treatment room to send a quick text to Ashley. *Can u eat?* She didn't even have time to put her phone back into her pocket when Ashley replied: *mEt me inda cafe 10 mins.*

It was almost twenty minutes before Jewell made her way down to the cafeteria. Ashley was waiting, leaning against a wall, tapping her foot impatiently. When she saw Jewell walking down the hallway, she stood up and strode to meet her. "It's about time! This has been absolutely killing me! So what did he say?"

Jewell looked around at the other people in line. "Let's get our food and sit down first."

"OMG! I swear you are doing this just to irritate the heck out of me."

Ashley didn't even look at what she was taking, but filled her tray quickly and moved to the register. Jewell chose a little more carefully, choosing a Cobb salad, even though she wasn't even sure that she could keep that down, the way her stomach was knotted like a fist.

After they paid, Ashley made a bee line to the first available table she saw. Jewell walked past her and found a table that was a little more private. The cafeteria was busy, but not so much so that they couldn't put a few tables between them and the other diners.

Ashley set her tray on the table and sat. She put her elbows on the table resting her chin in her hands, staring intently at Jewell, obviously waiting. Jewell took her time, wickedly enjoying her friend's impatience and frustration. She carefully removed the plastic cover from her salad, and placed it next to herself like a bowl. Next, she opened her packet of dressing and squeezed it into the upturned salad lid, making sure that she had squeezed out every last drop. Next, she picked up her napkin, unfolded it, and flipped it out to lay it gently in her lap.

"For the love of all that's holy! Get on with it!" Ashley practically exploded with pent up frustration.

"Fine." Jewell finally conceded. "As you probably guessed, that was Collin. What did you think?"

"Hot. Very, very hot. What else?"

"Well...he said he missed me." Jewell grinned, a little embarrassed. "And...I said I missed him. And then he said he would meet me after work."

"That's it?" Ashley flung her hands out indicating that she had expected more, and much juicier details. "Did he kiss you? Did you kiss him? What was it like when he was holding you after you nearly passed out? Details, girl, I need details!"

"There aren't really any details. I don't know. I felt so safe in his arms, it felt right. It felt like our bodies and souls were two pieces of a puzzle that fit together perfectly. He smelled good. He felt, oh man, he felt...so good; his muscles, his arms squeezing me, holding me like he didn't want to let me go." Jewell stopped for a moment, taking a bite of her Cobb salad, trying to think of what else her friend might like to hear, trying to catch her breath after replaying the episode with Collin in her head.

"He didn't kiss me. I mean, he did, but not really. It was like, his lips just brushed against mine and they were so soft, and his breath was so warm. And then he whispered to me that he would see me after my shift."

"Wow. That is so cool! So, you think he'll really be there, waiting for you?" Ashley hesitated then answered her own questions "Yeah! Duh! You should have seen the way he looked at you!"

"Really? Like how?"

"I don't know. It was like Romeo looking at Juliet."

Jewell blushed and stared down at her salad, pushing it around idly.

Ashley watched her for a minute. "There is one thing though..." She let the thought trail off.

"What?"

"Jewell, you know as well as I do that he should still be in a hospital somewhere. Don't you think that's a little...I don't know, weird? Does it bother you?"

"I don't know. I haven't really thought about it yet. I guess it does, sort of. I asked him about it, he says he doesn't understand either."

"Well, I guess we'll find out sooner or later. Maybe he's with a travelling circus or something. Come see the amazing healing man. Break his arm and watch it mend before your eyes!"

"Yeah maybe."

*   *   *

The time between "lunch" and quitting time seemed to drag on forever. Though the ER had been busy, Jewell's thoughts were elsewhere. She thought, not only of the perfect line of his jaw, his beautiful, hypnotic eyes, his chiseled muscles beneath his tight black t-shirt, but she also contemplated his curious recovery.

She was definitely in love with him. She knew that without a doubt. It was exactly what her father had described he felt when he found his wife, her mother; the perfect fit of two souls, two hearts, merging into one; two halves of a puzzle, the picture unclear and incomplete without the other half. She knew it when she was with him, but more unmistakably, she knew it when she was without him.

But there was a part of her that was scared. Frightened of what this meant, how this would change her life. But even more so, she was terrified of the implications of his incredible propensity to heal. Medically, what she had seen was unnatural; inhuman. What *was* he? He looked human. He most definitely *felt* human, but he was something more. What that was is what troubled her. When she found out, would she be able to make the right choice? Would she be able to run if that was what she needed to do? What if running was the only answer, but she couldn't? What if her feelings for him kept her from thinking clearly?

These thoughts floated through her mind amidst the broken bones, the crying children, the soaring fevers. The question ultimately came down to, "could she pull the plug?" How many times had she seen families agonizing over that decision? Was the decision selfish if they decided to pull the plug, or selfish if they didn't? And after it was done, it could not be undone; there was no turning back. Perhaps in this case, it would be best if she let go, if she just...pulled the plug.

Finally, she saw the day shift milling around the nurses' station. It was a relief to know that she would soon see Collin again, but she agonized over what she would do when she confronted him. Would she follow her heart, or follow her head?

As Jewell finished changing, Ashley shoved everything into her bag, shoved Jewell's clothes into her tote, grabbed both bags and pulled Jewell toward the door. Jewell allowed herself to be pulled along behind Ashley until they reached the doors to exit the hospital. Jewell jerked her arm out of Ashley's hand and did her best to glare at her.

"Excuse me, but this would be *my* date…if he's even here." She felt a knot develop in the pit of her stomach at the thought of Collin not showing up as he had promised.

"He'll be here, and fine; just hurry up!" Jewell was a bit overwhelmed by Ashley's excitement, and it was beginning to make her nauseous. Jewell paused and put her head down between her knees, taking several long slow breaths. When she felt composed enough to face Collin, she steadfastly walked out the door, Ashley following.

He wasn't waiting next to the door as he had been when they came in. Jewell's heart skipped a beat as she quickly scanned the parking lot. When her eyes found him, leaning casually against one of the pillars to the parking garage, her heart leapt into her throat. She gasped, and grabbed on to Ashley for support.

Ashley put her arm around Jewell's waist as she started to lead Jewell in Collin's direction. Collin didn't move, but his eyes followed her, capturing every nuance of her movements, memorizing her walk, her face, her hair.

"Hey," was all he said. That one single word was enough to make Jewell's knees weak.

"Hey. I didn't know if you would be here."

"I promised I will *always* come for you."

"You did."

"So what now?" Ashley's voice cut into their conversation like a knife. They both turned to look at Ashley. Ashley shrugged.

"Well," Collin said, "Are you working tonight?"

"Yes," Jewell replied forlornly.

"Maybe we could spend a few hours together? I promise I'll get you home before lunch. Will that give you enough sleep before work?"

Ashley answered. "Of course it will!"

Jewell and Collin both glared at her. Ashley crossed her arms defiantly.

"Actually, Ashley and I rode together…" Jewell shrugged.

Collin turned to Ashley, "Would it be okay if I brought her home? I promise to take good care of her." Collin winked at Jewell.

Ashley didn't answer this time, wanting to find out if that was what Jewell really wanted. After all, Jewell *had* been the one to drive them to work. If she didn't want to go with Collin, she could just tell him that she had to drive Ashley home. This was Jewell's call to make.

Jewell thought for a moment. She wanted to go with Collin, but what did she really know about him. She was absolutely and irrevocably in love with him, she knew that. She also knew that there was something about him that was not…human? She knew his uncle was a doctor and that he had lived, or so he said, in several different places over the years. Not a very promising profile. Her head said she should take Ashley home and tell Collin that maybe they could double with Ashley and her date on their day off. Her heart told her to let Ashley drive herself home. She looked at the keys in her hand and resolutely handed them to Ashley.

"I'll call my dad to let him know I'll be home before lunch."

Ashley looked at Jewell, trying to give her an "are you sure" look. Jewell could see that Ashley had some reservations as well. Jewell smiled, and nodded at Ashley. You can pick me up tonight at five. Don't wreck my car!"

Ashley gave Jewell a sarcastic grin, "Oh yeah! I'm going to go out and spin some tires in your smokin' Ford Focus."

"Focus, huh?" Collin asked. "Very practical car; inexpensive, great gas mileage, and as cute as you are." He smiled.

"Well, I guess I'll see you at five then. Don't stay out too late!" Ashley turned to walk toward where they had parked the car earlier.

After Ashley was out of hearing range, Collin asked, "Are you sure you want to do this? You look a little…apprehensive. Maybe another day would be better? I don't want you to do anything you don't feel comfortable with."

Jewell smiled. "I am *very* comfortable with this."

"Well, I thought we could start with beignets and coffee, if that's all right with you?" He held out his hand, offering to let her take it.

She looked at his hand a moment, and then settled hers into his warm grasp. She had almost forgotten how safe she felt just holding his hand. They walked slowly to his car, Collin staring at Jewell, Jewell staring at her feet.

"Well, this is me," Collin said, pressing the unlock button on his key chain.

"Wow, 'Vette. Very nice. Is this the LT?"

"2LT. You know your cars." He opened the passenger door so she could get in, and walked around to the driver's side.

Jewell waited for Collin to start the car before answering. "Yeah, my dad always liked sports cars; everything from muscle to performance. He has a '72 Mustang". They talked cars until Collin pulled into a lot near the river. It was gated, and had an attendant. Figured. Jewell couldn't imagine parking this car on the street.

"I hope Café du Monde is okay with you. It's a little touristy, but they have the best beignets in town as far as I'm concerned."

"Sounds good."

They ordered beignets and café au lait and sat at one of the tables where they could watch the carriages roll by. A man playing a saxophone sat right next to the café playing a soulful blues melody.

After breakfast, they walked, hand in hand to Artillery Park. Jewell always marveled at being able to look *up* at the boats as they passed by. Because New Orleans was below sea level, the river was actually above them. It was still early, so there were very few people, and a light fog drifted above the river. They could still hear the haunting melody of the saxophonist playing near Café du Monde.

Collin walked over to a grassy area under a tree, and sat down, leaning his back against the trunk. Jewell sat next to him. They hadn't really said anything at all since the car ride here. At breakfast they had laughed about the powdered sugar, but for the most part, they both seemed to be comfortable just sitting in each other's company.

Jewell sat down in the grass beside Collin. He adjusted his position a bit so that she could lean back against him. He sucked in a long fragrant breath of her hair as he wrapped his arms around her waist and she snuggled into his lap.

"What are you thinking?" She asked.

"I don't know. I guess I was just thinking about what it's like to be here, with you."

Jewell smiled and closed her eyes. "That's exactly what I was thinking." It was so hard to think about anything else when she was with him, especially with his arms around her. She assumed the tingling fire she felt throughout her body would fade after being with him for a while, but it hadn't. She felt lighter than air when she was with him.

"Jewell." She heard her name. It sounded like it was coming from far away. "Jewell." She felt warm lips touch her cheeks. Her eyes slowly came open; his arms will still wrapped around her waist. She moved her hands to cover his. She turned and slowly, reluctantly, sat up. "You fell asleep."

"I'm sorry. What do you want to do now? We could walk by the St. Louis Cathedral or...."

"It's time to take you home. You have to work tonight, remember. And I think you really need to get some sleep."

Jewell hadn't realized how tired she really was. Watching the sun dance hypnotically off the endless waters of Lake Pontchartrain as Collin drove her home added a weight to her eyelids that she was having trouble lifting. She listened to the song playing softly on the radio "Please allow me to introduce myself: I'm a man of wealth and taste: I've been around for a long, long year stolen many a man's soul and faith." She rolled the words around in her head, thinking of Collin, as she continued to stare out at the brown, endless water.

"Okay," Collin said, "I need help from here."

Jewell opened her eyes and looked out the window trying to get her bearings on where they were. They had just left the Causeway and were headed north. "Okay, um, just keep following this road to East Boston and head west. Then follow along on 21st. I'll tell you when to turn. She watched as the landscape slipped away behind her. "Left here. I'm down on the right. The blue house."

"Cute. Is this the house you grew up in?"

"Yeah. It's the house my mom and dad bought when they first got married. I've lived here my whole life. Dad talked about moving some after mom died, but I think there was too much of her here to leave."

Collin stared at the house wistfully. "I've never had a place to call home. My memories go with me wherever I go. That's all I ever take with me."

Jewell didn't know how to respond. She watched him, his face introspective. Finally, he looked at her. He leaned across the seat and kissed her cheek.

"Will I see you again?" Jewell asked. This whole morning had been like a dream, something ephemeral that would disappear the moment he left.

"Tomorrow morning? Or would you rather I wait for you outside the hospital before your shift?"

"Tomorrow morning I guess. I think I can last that long."

He got out of the car and walked around to open Jewell's door. He held out his hand to help her out. As she turned toward him, he took her hand in both of his, and then pulled it to his face. Turning her hand, palm up he gently kissed the inside of her wrist. Instant fire flamed up her arm and through the rest of her body. "Tomorrow morning then," he whispered looking into her eyes, his lips inches from her wrist.

She turned, reluctantly, and walked toward the house. She didn't look back. She was afraid that if she did, he would be gone, validating her fear that it had all been nothing more than a dream.

Jewell was glad that her father wasn't home. She was tired, and even though she had told him about Collin, she didn't want to *explain* Collin. She wasn't ready to explain her relationship to her father. This was the first time she had ever really had a boyfriend, if that's what Collin was – somehow, she wasn't quite sure about what her relationship with him was, and she just didn't feel like she could talk to her father about boys. She felt a sudden stab of pain; she should be talking about this with her mother.

She crawled into bed and fell quickly asleep. Again, she had the same dream; there was a large house, several people sat in a room painted pink. They were arguing, but this time, both she and Collin were there. Again, she knew that the conversation involved her, but this time, the conversation was not about just her, but her and Collin; no, her being *with* Collin. *"She's not one of us."* Her alarm buzzed loudly, waking her from her dream.

She pulled herself from her dream, thinking of the only part of the conversation that she could understand, "She's not one of us." What was that supposed to mean? Was she just dreaming, or subconsciously questioning her feelings about Collin?

As she sat up and rubbed the sleep from her eyes, she smelled hamburgers. She smiled to herself. Her dad must be cooking dinner. She shook her head, the corners of her mouth pulling into a smile. It was funny; she used to always know her dad's schedule. She always knew exactly when he would be working at the firehouse, and when he would be home. But in these last couple of...couple of what? Days? Or had it been weeks? She hadn't really thought about anything but Collin.

Jewell joined her father in the kitchen where he was making dinner. He set a plate with a hamburger and French fries on the table in front of her. Then he set his own plate on the table across from Jewell and sat down facing her. He took a big bite of his hamburger and chewed it slowly, watching his daughter, almost as if he was measuring something in her face. He finally swallowed and picked up a French fry. He held it in his hand for a moment, "So, how was your date with Collin this morning?"

"Dad, it wasn't really a date. We just went out for coffee."

"So, what exactly is your relationship with this boy?" He asked, this time probing, grilling her about Collin's intentions.

A horn sounded from the driveway outside. Jewell grabbed her tote and flung it over her shoulder. She shoved the hamburger into her mouth and grabbed a handful of French fries and a Coke from the refrigerator. "Gotta go Dad. I'll see you later," she said as the door slammed behind her.

Watching his daughter leave, Thomas McKean idly wondered exactly when that would be.

Jewell grabbed the door handle to her Focus and slid into the driver's seat as Ashley moved into the passenger seat. "Ash, your timing couldn't have been better." Jewell shifted the car into reverse and pulled onto the street.

"Dad asking questions about Collin?"

"Yeah, how'd you know?"

"He called me yesterday after you called him and asked me for the 411 on Collin."

"What'd you tell him?" Jewell's voice was worried. She trusted Ashley implicitly, but she didn't know how much she wanted her father to know about Collin yet.

"Let's see…I told him that he's about 6'2" with beautiful blonde hair, and eyes that have the power to hypnotize. That it was clear that his intentions toward you were indecent, and you are planning to run away with him to Vegas to get married." She looked at Jewell smugly.

"Oh God Ash! Really? Did you really tell him that?" The anxiety in Jewell's voice was palpable.

"Of course not! Do you really think that I would tell him that?" Ashley tried to sound indignant. "I told him that he seemed like a really nice guy. That he was polite, and very respectable."

"Anything else?"

"Not really. I mean, what was I supposed to say? Oh, and he died, came back to life, and healed from injuries that should have killed in him in less time than it takes a skinned knee to heal?"

"No, I'm sorry. I guess I'm just a little nervous. I mean, not only that, but I really think I love him Ash. Does that sound weird? He's the first guy I've ever really liked, and I feel like I would die without him. You've had lots of boyfriends, is this normal?"

"Gee, thanks. You make it sound like I date a different guy every week."

"You know what I mean. It's like, when he holds me, the whole world stops. Nothing around us matters, just him and me."

"Wow. You really have it bad. Honestly Jewell, I don't know. I can't really think of a time when I felt that into a guy. I mean, there were guys that I really liked, but it's not like I couldn't live without them or anything. They were fun, and I enjoyed spending time with them, but I couldn't see spending the rest of my life with them or anything. But maybe it's just because I haven't met the right guy. Who knows, maybe you just got lucky and hit the jackpot on your first try."

"Maybe."

"When are you going to see him again?"

"He's supposed to come by the hospital tomorrow. You don't mind taking my car home again, do you?"

"Nope. It's a nicer ride than mine."

"Thanks." It was obvious that Jewell's thoughts were elsewhere. Ashley let Jewell be alone with her thoughts.

When they drove into the parking garage at the hospital, Jewell suddenly looked at Ashley. Her eyes were bright and her cheeks were flushed. "He's here."

"Who's here?"

Jewell hit Ashley jokingly in the arm. "Collin, duh!"

"I thought he wasn't coming until tomorrow."

"I didn't either, but he's here, I know it." Jewell jumped out of the car and started running for the door. Ashley reached into the back seat and grabbed their bags and started walking quickly towards the hospital. She wanted to be there for Jewell in case Collin wasn't there. As she reached the door, she saw Jewell, snuggled in Collin's arms. She smiled, and walked past her into the hospital.

"I told you not to come until tomorrow! I hate that you drove all the way out here just to see me for five minutes." Jewell could hear her voice cracking with excitement.

"I couldn't go to sleep tonight without hearing you tell me good night." He smiled.

"Well, then, good night. Sweet dreams." Her voice was almost a whisper.

"My dreams are always sweet when I dream of you." He bent down and pressed his cheek against hers. His skin a fire against hers that she was sure he must feel as well. He turned his head and gently kissed her cheek. Then he drew back, taking her hand, and kissed her on the inside of her wrist. "Until tomorrow, Honeysuckle." He smiled and turned towards the garage. Jewell watched him until he disappeared into the shadows.

CHAPTER 20

Collin didn't feel like going home. He had been spending too much time at home. It also seemed a little crowded for his taste. He was used to being alone with his uncle; having so many people in the house seemed a little weird. The house was big enough. It was a large sugar cane plantation home built in the 1800's. It had parlors and grand ballrooms along with fourteen bedrooms for residents and guests.

Collin had taken one of the rooms, Dot and Carl had one, Ann and John had one, Gladys had taken one, and Percy had one. That left nine available bedrooms, and yet, the house still felt crowded.

Collin spent a lot of time in his room, ostensibly to read, but it was more to avoid some of the weirdness that seemed to be going on in the house. He also felt like the rest of the *family* was having conversations which they did not want him to be party to. He felt uninvited in his own house. After all, he and Percy had been there first. The others were their guests as far as he was concerned.

Collin eventually chose to move out to the servants' quarters. Besides being bigger than his room and having its own kitchen and bath, it provided a level of privacy he didn't feel in his room. In his room, he could still hear the whispers.

Because of this discomfort, instead of going home, he drove downtown. At Pat O'Brian's he ordered a Hurricane and sat at the piano bar in hopes that he might be able to think about his feelings for Jewell.

There was something about Jewell that was different from anyone he had ever met before. He had had other relationships, dated other girls. They were all nice, but none of them were anything more than a temporary reprieve from whatever happened to be going on in his life at the time. He had written to some for a while after leaving, but soon, the time between letters increased, and before long, both had moved on to other things.

But Jewell was different in so many ways. To begin with, when he was away from her his heart hurt. Not in an abstract way, but really hurt. The pain in his chest was real. When he thought of her, his heart sang. Every time he smelled honeysuckle, he couldn't help but think of her. He was completely unable to think of his future without her. Tonight was a perfect example. He really truly intended to stay home tonight, to let Jewell have a little space, to come in the morning as she had asked. But he couldn't. He *had* to see her, and judging by the way she greeted him, he felt certain the feeling was mutual.

He thought about what he should do. His uncle always admonished him about forming relationships. He knew that in a couple of years his uncle would want to move on. Would Collin stay with Jewell? Would Jewell go with them? Could he ask Jewell to give up everything, leave the only life she's known, for him? Could he give up everything he's ever known for her? Would his uncle let him make his own decisions? The house belonged to him, sort of. They could just live there. Collin was an adult now, it was time he started making his own choices.

The piano player left for his third break. Collin looked down at his watch. It was ten o'clock. He left his untouched drink and a ten dollar bill on the table and walked out.

He turned towards the Mississippi and started walking not sure where he was going, though he knew where he wasn't going. Collin pulled his cell phone from his pocket and dialed his uncle.

"Collin? Need a ride kid?"

"Nah. Listen, I think I'm just going to stay in the city tonight. I'll get a room at the Omni or something. Is that okay with you?"

"Okay kid. I guess we'll see you sometime tomorrow then."

"Thanks Uncle Percy. I knew you'd understand. I should be home by lunch."

"No problem. Have fun."

He checked in at the Omni, and walked up to his room. He flipped on the television and stripped down to his underwear. He could buy a new outfit tomorrow. He lay down on the bed and set his alarm for five thirty, he wanted to be at the hospital when Jewell got off work, and went to sleep.

Collin was waiting outside the hospital when Jewell and Ashley left from work. Ashley didn't bother to ask Jewell if she was going with her or Collin. She took Jewell's bag from her, gave her a brief hug, and walked to Jewell's car to head for home.

Collin held out his hand and Jewell took it happily, ready for the tingle in her stomach that she got every time she touched him. They walked hand in hand to his car. As before, the perfect gentleman, he opened her door, waited for her to get in, and shut the door with a smile. Then he walked around to the driver's side and got in.

"Ummm…I don't want to be rude or weird or anything, but…isn't that the same thing that you were wearing last night?" Jewell asked timidly.

"Not rude – true. I didn't go home last night. I thought we'd start the morning out with some shopping. How's that sound?"

"Um, fine, I guess. I'm not a really big shopper."

"Neither am I" he said excitedly. "This should be fun."

"Well, the stores aren't going to open for…" he glanced at his watch, "about three more hours. How does breakfast sound?"

"Sounds good. Beignets and coffee?"

"Of course." He turned and smiled at her. His smile sent a pleasant shiver through her body.

They drove to the Omni hotel, where Collin parked his car. "Why are we here?" Jewell asked, a little nervous about being at a hotel with a man.

"This is where I stayed last night, which is why I need some clothes. I didn't feel like going home, so I just stayed in town."

"Oh, I see."

He got out of the car and walked around to the passenger door. He opened it, and held out his hand to help her out. She took it hesitantly. They walked through the lobby and onto the street towards Café du Monde.

After breakfast, they started walking towards Canal. By the time they reached Canal Street, the stores were just starting to open. Jewell stared. She was definitely out of her element. As a general rule, she shopped at Wal-Mart or Target if she was looking for something really nice.

They started at Banana Republic where Collin bought himself a gray t-shirt, a pair of jeans, socks, and underwear. He didn't bother to try anything on. After he had paid, he took her over to the women's clothes where he picked out four tops, two pairs of slacks, a pair of jeans, and a pair of strappy flat sandals.

"Oh, I…um, I can't afford these." She told him, a little embarrassed.

"Don't worry about it. It's on me."

"I…can't."

"You can, and you will." He bought her everything. Next, he took her to Francesca's Collections. There he bought her three shirts and a pair of pants. He tried to take her into Ann Taylor, but Jewell refused.

"Collin, this is really nice, but…well, you hardly know me."

"I know your soul, and I know that our souls belong together." He took her hands. "I've never felt like this about anyone Jewell. I'm so worried I'm going to lose you."

"You won't, not if I can help it."

He gave her a quick hug, and took her hand. They walked back to the hotel. "Hey, I've got to shower and change out of these clothes. You're welcome to come up with me, or you can wait down here if you prefer. I don't want to make you feel pressured or anything."

Jewell looked at the comfortable chairs in the hotel lobby. She would be comfortable there, that would probably be the best thing to do. Her father would kill her if he found out she had gone up to a hotel room with a guy. Even worse, he would probably kill Collin despite her being twenty-one. She paused for only a moment, and then followed him to the elevator.

In his room, she stood uncomfortably in the doorway.

"Don't worry, I promise, you are perfectly safe." He took her hand and led her over to a chair and gently sat her down. He grabbed the remote for the TV and flipped it on, then handed her the remote. He took his Banana Republic bag into the bathroom and shut the door.

Jewell sat, uncomfortably, on the edge of the chair. She flipped through the channels once, and finally settled on The Powerpuff Girls. She heard the shower turn on in the bathroom. She tried not to think about what he looked like standing in the shower.

After about fifteen minutes, Collin emerged, freshly shaven, wearing his new outfit. He looked stunning. He ran his hand over his head like he was pushing his hair away from his face, as if from habit, then grabbed the towel and rubbed his close cut hair dry.

After he was finished, he brushed his teeth and turned to look at Jewell. "I guess it's about time to get you home. You look like you're about to fall asleep in that chair."

"No, I'm fine." She tried to stifle a yawn.

"No, I need to get you home, and I probably better check in with my uncle." He walked over to the chair where she was sitting. He held out his hands and pulled her up. He wrapped his arms around her and held her, gently against his body. Her head only came up to his chest. She turned her head and laid it on his chest, listening to the steady beat of his heart.

Too soon, he let go. He placed his hand under her chin and looked into her eyes. "Would it...I mean, well, would it be okay if I kissed you?"

She couldn't answer. She only nodded her head, barely able to move it against his hand under her chin. He slowly bent down, watching her eyes as he lowered his lips to hers. At first, the kiss was gentle, hesitant. His lips gently pushed against hers, their soft warmth radiating through her. He let his lips leave hers, but kept his mouth so close that she could still feel his breath as it came in quick pulls.

She could barely breathe. She wanted more, it wasn't enough. She had to feel more of him. As if hearing her thoughts, he pushed his lips against hers again, this time, harder, with more certainty. She pushed herself against him hungrily. Her mouth, moving with his was so natural, so perfect. His hand moved down her body, pulling her hard against him. Before she knew it, she was laying on her back, on the bed, his fingers moving down her hips, her hands tangled in his hair, pulling him closer.

Suddenly, he stopped. He stood up quickly, wiping his lips with the back of his hand. "I'm sorry." He turned from her, unable to face her. "I'm so sorry. I should...I really think I need to take you home now." He walked toward the door and opened it, waiting for her to follow.

Jewell pushed herself up on her elbows on the bed and looked at Collin standing in the open door. He wouldn't look at her; he kept his eyes focused in her direction, but not on her. She stood up. "Did I do something wrong?" She asked hesitantly.

"No, I just can't. I can't get too close, I...C'mon. I'll take you home."

Jewell walked slowly past him as she walked out the door. She felt the heat of his body, radiating toward her. She felt the pull of his body against hers. She turned, moving her hand up to touch his face. He grabbed her wrist. "No," he said. "You don't understand."

"Then explain it to me."

"I can't. I don't understand either."

He closed the door and turned his back on her as he started walking down the hall.

Collin was silent, the whole ride home. At first, Jewell tried to ask questions, to try to find out what was wrong. She gave up when he refused to answer; his brooding face looking only at the road ahead.

At Jewell's house, ever the gentleman, Collin got out of the car and walked around to open Jewell's door. She took his hand, held it, not wanting to let go. "I will see you again." It wasn't a question, it was a statement that she thought, if she said it out loud might make it true.

Collin pulled his hand to her lips, turned it palm up, and kissed her wrist. He dropped her hand and walked around the car, got in and drove away without answering.

CHAPTER 21

Jewell walked into her bedroom. She sat down on her bed, her back against the wall. What had just happened? It seemed to be something about the kiss that bothered him. She had liked it. In fact, she had *really* liked it. She had kissed guys before, but she had never imagined that it could feel like that. The fire that she felt when he touched her, the fire that burned and tingled throughout her body, was intensified. The difference was like comparing a single match to the fireworks display at the White House. The feelings that she had for him, the longing was so strong at that moment, when his lips were on hers that she couldn't concentrate on anything else. It was total bliss. It was what she thought heaven must feel like.

But what had gone wrong? Did she do something she shouldn't have? She didn't have a lot of experience in this type of thing; maybe something she did wasn't right. Maybe what she felt wasn't the same as what he felt. Maybe when he kissed her, he realized that his feelings for her weren't as strong as he had first thought. She closed her eyes, resting her head on her knees, trying to imagine what went wrong.

She awoke to voices. She hadn't even realized that she had fallen asleep. She lifted her head and felt a shooting pain race through her neck and down her back because of the position in which she had slept. She slowly stretched out her legs, feeling her knees pop. She stood up, arching her back, and rolling her head, while she tried to hear the voices on the other side of the door. It was two men; probably her dad and one of his buddies from the firehouse. She glanced at the clock. It was almost nine. She was shocked that she had slept for that long, she really was tired. She guessed that there had been a game on TV or something, or maybe some of the guys came over for a game of poker.

She sat back down on her bed and picked up a book she had been reading. *Twilight*. It was the typical story about star crossed lovers and unrequited love. A hundred year old vampire had fallen in love with a human girl. Jewell wondered if at the end, the girl would choose to become a vampire, to live with her love forever. She read a couple of chapters and set the book down. Could she give up everything, for someone she loved?

It didn't sound like her dad's friends would be leaving anytime soon, and she was hungry, so she figured she would just have to go out there. She didn't like hanging around when her dad's friends were there. They always, talked about things she had no interest in, and tried to include her in the conversation to be polite. Oh well, maybe she'd just make a sandwich and come back to her room.

When she opened the door, she paused. She recognized both voices. The first was her dad, but the second voice was unexpected. She cocked her head to listen, to make sure she wasn't mistaken. She walked back into her room and looked out the window. As she suspected, in the driveway sat a silver corvette. She went back to the door and opened it, trying to hear the conversation going on in the kitchen.

"Yes sir. We've been living in Louisiana for about two years now. Our house is south of New Orleans, near Houma."

"So what do you do?" Her father was obviously making sure that the man she brought home wasn't a slacker. Her father didn't trust anyone who wasn't willing to work.

"Well sir, I recently completed my bachelor's degree at Oxford University in England. I was considering continuing my education, perhaps pursuing my PhD and finding a position as a professor at a University."

"That's impressive. What does your father do?"

"'Well, he's a dual M.D., PhD. He practices some, but for the most part he performs research. He's interested in cures for genetic mutations and anomalies."

Jewell heard her father grunt. She knew this meant that he was impressed, but not yet convinced.

"And what are your intentions with my daughter?" This was what Jewell had been waiting for. She knew it was coming, but she had hoped she had missed it. She quickly walked to the kitchen to interrupt the conversation.

"Morning dad." She was looking at Collin. His eyes met hers, but then he looked at his hands, folded neatly on the kitchen table in front of him. "I see you've met Collin."

"Yes. He came by to see you, but since you were asleep, I didn't want to wake you. I invited Collin in to wait until you woke up. He's only been here about forty-five minutes. We've had a nice conversation." He looked markedly at Collin. Jewell briefly wondered what her father had said to him before she had started her eavesdropping. From the flush in Collin's cheeks, she assumed it hadn't been mere pleasantries.

"Well," her father said, pushing himself up from the table. "I guess I'll leave you kids alone." He looked at Jewell pointedly. "I'll be right here in the living room, on the couch, reading."

"Okay dad." Jewell understood exactly what her father was saying. The couch offered a clear view of the kitchen, and it was close enough that he could hear all but the quietest whispers. She also knew that he wouldn't be "reading" but listening very carefully to every word they said.

Jewell watched her dad leave the kitchen, then pulled out the chair opposite Collin and sat down. She didn't say anything, she just sat, looking at him, and waited.

"I brought your clothes," he pointed to the shopping bags on the floor next to his chair.

"Thanks."

"I didn't mean...It's just that," he stopped and looked out into the living room where Jewell's dad sat, the newspaper open, and his eyes peering at them over the top. "Do you want to go out and get some dinner?"

Jewell glanced at her dad; he just shrugged. "I guess that would be okay." She looked at the bags on the floor, then down at her jeans and t-shirt. "I'll just go get changed." She picked up the bags and took them to her room. She rifled through the bags and picked out an outfit that she thought would be appropriate for any situation; a nice pair of slacks, and a blue blouse. She also put on the sandals he had bought her that morning. She brushed her hair and then walked back out to the living room.

Collin was standing by the door, waiting. Her father looked at her, and then glared at Collin. "Dad, please?"

"Fine. Have a nice time. You," he looked straight at Collin, "I have a lot of friends on the police force and in the Sheriff's department."

"Yes sir, I understand. I'll take good care of her. I'll have her home before midnight."

"You look really nice sweetie." Jewell's father gave her a hug, turned and gave Collin one more glare for good measure, and then watched them walk out the door.

They left and walked to the car. Jewell could see her father watching them out the window.

Collin led Jewell to the passenger door, one hand placed lightly on the small of her back. He opened the door, let her get in, closed the door and walked over to the driver's side. He could feel Jewell's father's eyes watching him, but he was careful not to look toward the house as he got into the car and pulled out of the driveway.

"It's nine thirty. If I'm supposed to have you home by midnight, that doesn't give us time for me to take you to one of my regular haunts. What do you suggest on this side of the pond?"

Jewell thought for a moment. She wanted something nice, but not fancy. Upscale, but still casual. "There's Morton's in Madisonville if you like seafood."

"Sounds perfect. Just tell me how to get there."

It took about fifteen minutes to reach the restaurant nestled on the banks of the Tchefuncte River. It was crowded, but then, Morton's usually was.

"This is perfect, shall we?" Collin held her hand as they walked up the ramp to the door of the restaurant. As Collin reached for the door, Jewell stopped him.

"Collin, are you going to tell me what happened today?"

"I will. I owe you at least that." She gave him a single nod as they entered the restaurant.

The hostess led them to a table overlooking the river. Collin held Jewell's chair for her, and then sat in the chair opposite, facing her. The hostess put two menus on the table. When the waitress came to take their orders, Collin ordered for both of them.

"Would you like an appetizer? Oysters on the half shell are half price tonight." The waitress gave Collin a wink. Oysters were thought to be an aphrodisiac. Jewell turned her head, as if searching for someplace to hide.

"No, I think just the dinner. Thank you."

After the waitress left, Jewell glanced at Collin and quickly looked away. Collin reached across the table to take Jewell's hand. "I guess I owe you an explanation for this afternoon."

Jewell turned to look at Collin's hand holding hers; her hand tingling. She thought of how his lips felt on hers when he kissed her.

"I guess I need to explain a little bit about my life first. I was born in England. When I was a little more than three months old, someone broke into our house. I was asleep. My parents were both beheaded and the house set afire. A neighbor saw the smoke and was able to save me.

"The police investigated the murder, but the perpetrator was never found. The killing was an execution but the police don't know why.

"I was temporarily put into foster homes until my Uncle showed up to claim me. The courts, satisfied with whatever evidence there was of the relationship, granted him custody. We immediately left the country and moved to live with Gladys who had a home in Montana.

"We lived in the states until I was five, when we moved to Romania. When I was eight, we moved to France. At twelve, we moved to Denmark, and at fifteen, we moved again to Italy. When I was seventeen, I applied to Oxford University where I majored in History. After I graduated, we moved to South Carolina. We stayed there for almost a year, and then moved here about two years ago. Most of the time we stay with *family* or in houses that belong to the *family*," he paused, allowing Jewell to digest the information. While he was waiting, to see if Jewell had any questions, the waitress brought their food to the table.

Jewell took a bite of her salad. As she swallowed, she looked up at Collin. "Are you gypsies, or...what are they called? Travelers? Roma?" Jewell had heard stories of wandering families who move from location to location. They had a bad reputation, but she knew that many of them were upstanding, law abiding citizens.

"I guess you could call us that. According to my uncle, there are a little more than one hundred of us in our *family*. You have to understand too, that when I say *family*, I don't mean brothers and sisters. These are others like us; travelers I guess would be the best term, but not necessarily blood relations.

"Anyway, we don't usually stay in one place for very long. I guess that, because we are constantly moving, my uncle has always discouraged me from developing relationships. He thinks that, because of the way we are, it would be hard for us to change for someone who isn't like us, and it wouldn't be fair to ask someone else to change for what we are.

"I think some of it too is that my uncle lost a wife. It still haunts him and I think that he's trying to spare me the same pain."

"What happened to her?"

"Well, he doesn't talk about it much, but the way I understand it is that she decided to leave her family, to take up his life of travelling, and it was too much for her. She couldn't handle it. Eventually, she got sick and died. Uncle Percy thinks it was a combination of the hard lifestyle, the constant change in climate, along with the grief she felt at losing her family."

Jewell looked at him, trying to read what was in his eyes. They looked pained. "So what, he wants you to marry another Traveler?"

"Pretty much, yeah, but I think it's more than that. Lately, since the accident, it's like he's been keeping something from me. Somehow, I think that whatever this secret is has something to do with his attitude towards my relationships, has something to do with the *family*."

"So you don't think he would approve of me?"

"Think of it like a devout Catholic deciding to fall in love with an atheist." Collin laughed a little as he reached out and took Jewell's hand across the table.

"He doesn't know about me then?" For some reason, this bothered her. It made her feel like their relationship was dishonorable somehow. As if she didn't have the right to have these feelings about him.

"No. And for now, I don't intend to tell him. I'm not sure how he would react. He's my only blood family. I can't lose him. But I can't lose you either. Do you understand?"

"But, you'll have to tell him sometime, right? I mean if we…" Her thought trailed off.

Collin could sense her apprehension. "This morning, when I kissed you, I was afraid I wouldn't be able to stop. I wanted you so bad at that moment. I thought…I thought that if I stopped then, if I took you home and never saw you again…But I couldn't stop thinking of you. I need you Jewell. I'm being selfish, but I can't help myself. It's like when I'm with you, my world is whole."

Jewell felt her heart racing. Suddenly, she felt faint, the room started to close in around her.

Collin watched her with concern. Her face had gone from red, to a shade of green, to pasty white. He moved to her side, worried that she was going to faint. She grasped his arm to support herself. "I…I have to get out of here. I have to leave, now."

Collin pulled fifty dollars out of his wallet and placed it on the table. He gently helped Jewell up from her chair and started to walk towards the door, supporting her weight with an arm around her waist. The waitress saw them leaving, but then saw how ill Jewell looked. She hurried over. "Is she okay? Should I call an ambulance?"

"No, I think she'll be okay once she gets some fresh air." The waitress wrung her hands nervously and watched Collin lead Jewell from the restaurant. Once they were outside, Collin scooped Jewell up into his arms, cradling her like a child. She put her arm around him and buried her face in his neck, breathing in his scent. He carried her to a tree near the river and set her down gently in the grass. "Are you okay?" He asked, fear weighing in his eyes.

"I don't know. I…just give me a few minutes. I need to think." Collin started to walk towards the drawbridge just down from the restaurant. "No, don't leave, just…" She couldn't finish her thought. He settled himself in the grass near her. Close enough that she could reach him if she needed to, but far enough away that he felt like he was giving her the space she needed.

"What are you thinking?" Collin finally asked after Jewell hadn't looked at him for several minutes.

When she turned her head toward him, he could see tears running down her face. "I don't know what I'm thinking. I'm scared, I'm happy, I'm nervous"

He moved closer and held her. "I'm scared too. I'm afraid of what my *family* will think, of how I will tell them. Jewell, I'm afraid that I won't be able to live without you. I'm scared that you don't feel the same way that I do. I know that what I should do right now is walk away, before it's too late."

She spoke into his ear. He could feel her warm, sweet breath as she whispered four simple words, "It's already too late."

*   *   *

The next day Collin picked Jewell up just before lunch and took her to the Fountainbleu State Park. He parked and they started with a hike along one of the trails that started at the sugar mill. When they were done hiking, they went back to the car where Collin pulled a picnic basket from his trunk.

Jewell took his hand and they walked to a picnic table that stood in the shade under an immense live oak with Spanish moss hanging delicately from its branches. From here, they could see the beach on Lake Pontchartrain where several families were enjoying the warm, sunny afternoon. On the lake, the many colored sailboats that drifted in the light breeze looked like so many spring flowers in a meadow yet to turn green.

Collin set the picnic basket on the bench next to the table and opened it to reveal that is was well packed and filled with the most delicious aromas.

They ate in comfortable silence, Jewell savoring every bite. After they were finished eating, Collin started packing everything back into the picnic basket. "Was it okay?"

"Okay? It was unbelievable. Did you make all that?" Jewell was astounded at his seemingly limitless talents.

"Well, no. Actually, my Aunt Gladys cooked all of this. I started to make sandwiches, pimento cheese, but she insisted that if I was going to have a picnic I should probably pack food you could actually eat." He looked appropriately ashamed at his lack of skills, or imagination for that matter.

"So, I guess Gladys knows about us. If she made us this picnic, I would guess she approves." Somehow that made Jewell feel a little better considering their conversation of the night before.

"Well, Aunt Gladys isn't as strict as Uncle Percy. She's more of a free spirit, and a bit of a romantic. But Percy still doesn't know. Gladys promised not to say anything until I was ready. She did seem to have some of her own reservations though."

They put the picnic basket back in the trunk and walked down to the beach where they sat watching the sail boats.

"I've been thinking," Jewell said after a while.

"Don't hurt yourself." Collin said sarcastically.

"Ha ha. Seriously. I've been thinking about what you said about your uncle having a secret."

"Yeah, and what were your thoughts?"

"Well, do you think that it has something to do with the way you healed so fast? I mean, it's been what? Maybe three weeks since the crash, and you barely have a limp. You just went on a four mile hike and it didn't even faze you. You should be dead…sorry…but really, you should at least still be in a hospital bed, and normal people with your injuries would need years of physical therapy. You said your uncle is a doctor. Maybe that's it. Maybe he knows something about why you heal so fast."

"I never thought of that. What do you think it might be?"

"I don't know. Maybe I can look in your file. I don't get much access to the file room, but I can see if there's something in there. It might give us some clues."

"No Jewell, don't do that. You could get in really big trouble for looking at files you're not supposed to be looking at. I would hate it if you got fired on my account." Collin worried.

"It's not just about you Collin." She said quietly.

"What do you mean?"

"I love you Collin, I know that. But I'm also scared of you. I don't know what you are."

"What do you mean, 'what I am'?" Collin asked, suddenly anxious. "Maybe that's what my uncle meant when he said that I shouldn't get close to someone. Maybe you're right. Maybe he's right," he whispered.

Jewell took his hand. She held it in both of hers. "I'm not saying that it would change anything. It's just something that…well, I'm just scared. You're different and it's not just that you're a really great guy."

Collin leaned over and kissed her cheek. She was crying. Jewell noticed that she'd been doing that an awful lot since Collin came into her life, which worried her too. She moved over so that she was leaning against him. "Let's not change anything until we know something else." Jewell said into his shoulder. Collin nodded.

"Are you ready to go home?" The sun was setting and almost all of the other visitors had left.

"I'm sorry Collin. I ruined such a wonderful day. That wasn't fair."

"No," Collin said. "I've actually been wondering about it myself a lot. I told you, I shouldn't have come back to the hospital after I left. It would have been better that way."

"No, we'll figure this out. It'll be okay. This is true love…you think this happens every day?"

"Princess Bride?"

"Very good."

"Death cannot stop true love. All it can do is delay it for a while."

"Good point." Jewell gave a short laugh.

"Let's go. We can decide if it's worth talking about tomorrow." He stood up and then reached down to help Jewell from the pier. They walked slowly. Collin had his hand around Jewell's waist and Jewell's head leaned against his side. "I love you Collin Sykes, come what may."

"I love you too, Jewell McKean, come what may."

CHAPTER 22

"Well, if you don't have any plans for the day, I'm going to go play softball with the guys. Can I trust you two here alone?" He glared at Collin.

"Yes sir. I can assure you that my intentions with your daughter are nothing but honorable." Collin answered formally.

"They better be. You never know when I'll be back. I can be gone for three hours…or I may just decide to drive around the block and come right back."

"Dad!" Jewell's face was turning red as her father continued his lighthearted intimidation.

Tommy McKean chuckled as he picked up his mitt and a bat. He stood in front of Collin, swinging the bat, testing the heft of it.

"Dad! He gets it!" Jewell buried her face in her hands, embarrassed by her father's display. Collin was a big guy, but her dad outweighed him by a good twenty pounds and despite his age, most of it was muscle. The firefighters spent a lot of time training. Collin hadn't missed that fact. Collin also hadn't missed the fact that Thomas McKean didn't just have size, he had experience. Regardless, Collin's uncle had raised him with old fashioned values. He had no intention of doing anything more with Jewell than a little kissing.

Tommy finally decided to leave. When Jewell was sure he was gone, she turned to Collin. "Let's do something really bad!" She grinned wickedly.

"What did you have in mind?" He asked, intrigued.

"Let's jump on the couch and then play catch in the living room!"

Collin laughed out loud. "I knew there was something I liked about you."

They sat on the couch, Jewell leaning against Collin, his arm wrapped around her. "Tell me about you." She said.

"What do you want to know?"

"I don't know. Tell me about your Uncle Percy. What's he like?"

Collin shrugged, shifting a little so that Jewell was settled comfortably against his side. "Percy is Percy. He's kind of a strange old coot." He laughed a little. "He never seems to take things seriously, but he's really serious about everything, if that makes any sense. Every single thing that happens, he notices, and it means something."

"Why do you think that is?"

"I don't know. I guess he's had a rough life. He lost his wife before I was born. I guess he's about what, fifty five or so. Jeez, I never thought about it, but I don't really even know how old he is. It seems like he's always been old, my whole life. But I guess that's just because when you're five, someone who's thirty seems to have one foot in the grave!"

"How'd she die? Percy's wife, I mean?"

"All I know is that she was really sick. Uncle Percy brought in every doctor he could find, but no one could do anything to help her. I think that's why he went to med school."

"Wow. They must've been really young when she died then."

"Why's that?"

"Well, you said that Percy was a doctor before your parents died, and his wife died before that. I guess it's just the math and all. It must have been pretty tough on him."

"You know, I never really thought of that."

"So, was your dad Percy's brother, or was your mom his sister?"

"It wasn't like that. They were like cousins or second cousins or something, but they were close and kept in touch. His relationship was with my mom, but from the way he talks, he really loved my dad too."

"Do you think that's why he moves you around so much? He's lost so much that he cares for, that he doesn't want you to get too attached to anything you might lose?" Jewell had stretched out on the couch. Her legs draped over the end and her head rested in his lap. She was looking up into his eyes as he gently brushed her hair back from her forehead absently.

Collin brushed his hand back over his head. Jewell thought that it looked like a habit he must have developed when his hair was longer, before the accident. He looked like he was pushing his hair back from his face. "Yeah, but not completely. That's not all of it. I've felt like that before, but since the accident, I've overheard him talking to people and some of the things he says...I think Dr. Babineaux at the hospital, he knows too."

Jewell sat up and looked at him. "Do you think it has to do with the accident? Maybe something happened, an injury that they aren't telling you about." She tried to think. "I've only been working for a few months. I only just graduated. I don't know enough to even guess at what..."

"I guess that could be it, but I don't think so. I think it was something from before, something that Dr. Babineaux found out because of the accident."

"Like what?"

"I don't know. That's the problem. Look, can we talk about something else. I can't think about this. Every time I try to ask him, he changes the subject, and the rest of my *family* won't tell me anything."

"Yeah." Jewell laid back down resting her head in his lap again. She had to work tonight. She would pull his file and see what she could find out. Whether Collin wanted to know or not, she had to know.

"So what was it like, living in Europe?"

"I don't know. I guess a lot like living here. In most of the places, there were more markets instead of grocery stores; places where you could buy really fresh food. We shopped almost daily, instead of weekly like here. The languages were different, but otherwise, it was pretty much the same."

"I wish I could go somewhere. I've never been outside of Louisiana, except once. I went to the Stennis Space Center in Mississippi on a field trip." She grimaced.

"That doesn't sound so bad. At least you didn't have to learn a new language every three years."

"I took Spanish in high school. Hola, como estas?"

He laughed. "That's one I missed. I've got Ciao, come lei e? – That's Italian. Bonjour, comment ca va? That would be French. Det, hvordan har du?

That would be Danish, and Alo, ce mai faci? Romanian. Oh, and don't forget Latin: Abyssus, quam es vos?"

"I would have loved to know Latin in nursing school." Jewell sighed. "I still get a lot of the medical terminology confused."

"Speaking of which," Collin said, glancing at his watch. "What time do you have to work tonight?"

"I start at 6:00. I should probably call Ashley and see if she wants a ride." She grinned up at him, "just in case." She got up from the couch and walked into the kitchen. She picked up the phone and dialed Ashley as she watched Collin walk lithely into the kitchen. His graceful movements made her breath catch in her throat.

"Hello?" She heard Ashley answer her phone.

"Hey…" Jewell stopped to catch her breath. "Hey, do you want me to pick you up tonight?" Jewell was leaning against the counter, and Collin moved in front of her, placing his hands on the counter on either side of her waist. Jewell could feel his breath as he bent his head down to gently brush his lips against her neck.

Collin heard Ashley's answer through the phone, "Do I have a choice?"

"No." Jewell was barely able to choke out the word.

"Let me guess," Ashley said, sarcasm dripping from her voice. "You have a guest?"

"Um hm," Jewell mumbled.

Jewell heard Ashley sigh on the other end of the line. "I figured that's what's been keeping you too busy to call me." Her tone was sharp, but Jewell could tell that Ashley was teasing her. "Pick me up at five." Ashley hung up before Jewell had the opportunity to answer, not that she could have if she'd tried.

Collin took the phone from her hand, and hung it on the hook. He moved his hands from the counter to her hips, and gently pulled her close to him. Jewell turned her face up to his as he bent down. His lips brushed hers, and then moved to her cheek where he gave her a gentle kiss; then to her forehead, where he kissed her again. He pulled his head back just enough so that he could look into her eyes, his lips even with hers. She could taste his breath as he whispered, "I should let you get some sleep. You have a long night ahead of you."

Without thinking, she reached up, wrapping her hands around his head, pulling it down to hers. Her lips touched his and fire shot through her body. She felt his hands move to her back, pulling her closer to him. His mouth sought hers hungrily. She felt his tongue, moving over the inside of her mouth. It was so soft and warm. He lifted her up, sitting her on the counter so that her head was level with his. He leaned between her legs, and she wrapped her legs around him wanting to feel his body against hers.

Her breath started coming faster and she could feel him, pushing himself against her. She tightened her grip on his neck, pulling his lips tighter against hers. His hands moved across her back, moving lower. Jewell felt the back of her head hit the cabinet as he pushed himself against her. His hands found the bottom of her shirt, and slipped inside, his warm hands, moving against the skin of her back. She took one of her hands from his neck and placed it on his chest, feeling his muscles beneath the smooth cotton of his shirt pulsing as he moved.

Suddenly, she heard the grating of the front door as it was pushed open. She pushed hard against Collin and he stumbled back, tripping over a chair and just barely catching himself on the table. Off balance, he fell into the chair he had tripped on. Jewell's father walked into the kitchen and examined the tableau laid out before him. He looked first to his daughter. He could read the guilt written on her face as clearly as he read the newspaper. Collin, his face bright red, looked, if not guilty, at least embarrassed. He could only imagine what he had walked in on.

Collin and Jewell watched Jewell's dad as his eyes scanned from one to the other and back again. They watched his face as it turned a subtle shade of red and his lips pressed shut. Jewell's father tried to remind himself that his daughter was an adult, but it was so much easier to remember that she was still his little girl. Collin cleared his throat, "so, like I was about to say, since you need to work tonight, I should really go…now."

"Yes, that would be a good idea," answered Jewell's father, his arms crossed against his chest.

Collin walked toward the kitchen door to leave. Jewell's father made no attempt to move from his position, leaning against the door frame. Collin looked at him, and turned sideways, carefully sidling out the door, keeping his eyes on Jewell's dad the whole time. He walked to the door and turned; seeing Jewell standing beside her father, his arm protectively around her. "Good afternoon, sir. Umm…I'll see you later Jewell."

"You hope." Her father answered. Jewell didn't say anything as Collin carefully closed the door behind himself.

CHAPTER 23

Jewell pulled up to Ashley's apartment about five minutes late. Ashley was outside pacing impatiently. As Jewell pulled up to the curb, Ashley grabbed the handle on the door before Jewell had time to come to a complete stop. Ashley jumped in and pulled the door shut behind her. "Tell me every…" Her words trailed off as she actually looked at Jewell. "What are you wearing?"

"Clothes. I prefer it to being naked, partially because it's more comfortable and partially because I believe I could be arrested for driving naked in the state of Louisiana."

"Ha ha. I mean, where did you get those clothes?"

"My closet."

"Yes, but it is quite obvious that *you* didn't choose those clothes to put in your closet. Your taste isn't that good."

"Gee, thanks for not pulling any punches there Mike Tyson."

"Oh, you know what I mean! Who bought those for you? Did *he* buy them?"

"Yes," Jewell answered demurely.

"Well, he definitely has good taste. These are designer too! Not knock-offs. I'm impressed!" Ashley was practically bouncing in her seat. "So tell me *everything.*"

"Well," Jewell started

"Did you kiss him?"

"Yeah…"

"Is he a good kisser?"

"Are you going to let me tell you, or are you going to just keep interrupting?"

Ashley pushed her lips shut and mimed locking them and throwing away the key. When Jewell was satisfied, she started again. "Yes, he's a good kisser. What did we do? Well, on Monday, he took me shopping…" She explained her three days with Collin, filling in as many details as she could. By the time she finished, they were near the end of the Lake Pontchartrain Causeway.

"Oh…my…God!" Ashley sighed. "He is so romantic. Just the fact that he always opens the door for you is so cool. I don't think I've ever met a guy besides my dad that still believes in opening a door for a woman." She sighed again, wistfully. "How good a kisser?"

"REALLY good! I mean, when he kisses me on the cheek or the hand…oh, he does this really cool thing. He brings my hand up and kisses right inside my wrist." She shuddered as she imagined the sensation of his lips on her wrist. "When he does that, it's like…well, you know how when your hands are really cold, and you put them around a warm cup of coffee?" Ashley nodded. "It's kind of like that. Just a really, pleasant warmth that gradually moves through me. You know that song…'it starts in my toes, makes me crinkle my nose…' It's like that. It's just a really good kind of tingly feeling all over. But when he kisses me on the lips…" Jewell's tone had totally changed. She could feel the heat radiating through her, and she almost choked on the words.

"What?" Ashley half shouted.

"It's like a forest fire when it hits an area of dry brush. It's entirely unstoppable. I don't even know how to describe it because it's so wonderful, but it's so scary all at the same time. It's like I'm afraid I can't stop. I mean, Ash, what am I going to do if this doesn't work out?"

"Why wouldn't it work out? It sounds like he likes you as much as you like him."

"Ash…did you forget about…well, about the fact that he was in a serious accident that killed him, quite literally, only three weeks ago, but he's taking me on field trips of New Orleans? You can't tell me that's normal."

"Well, no, but…well, so what? The fact is he *is* taking you on very romantic field trips."

"I just don't know Ash. Somehow, I know that something's not right. I know that I should be running away from this as fast as I can, but I can't make my feet move."

Ashley didn't know what to say to make Jewell feel better. The fact was that she had a point. Something was weird, and not in a good way, but Ashley didn't have the heart to tell Jewell what she thought. Collin was good for Jewell, she knew that too.

*　*　*

Jewell met Ashley for 'lunch' just after midnight. "You know," Jewell said to her, carrying on their conversation from earlier as if it had never stopped, "his uncle knows something too, and Collin thinks Dr. Babineaux is involved."

"Really?" Ashley was suddenly much more interested in Jewell's personal life than what was being served in the cafeteria. "Do you think it's related to the accident?"

"Either that, or maybe something they found out *because* of the accident. They were awfully quick to get him out of here. I think they knew something then."

"Have you looked at his file?"

"No," Jewell looked at Ashley. "Do you think you can help me with that?"

"Sure. Whatever you need Jewell, I'm here for you."

"You know I can't get to the file room. Do you think you could get in there?"

"Sure, they send me in there all the time."

"Can you copy the file?"

Ashley sighed. She took a long time to answer. "I'll be honest; people are in and out of there all the time. If the wrong person catches me…"

"Don't worry about it. It's cool. This isn't worth your job. I'll see what I can do."

"Give me tonight. I promise I won't take any chances." Ashley smiled at Jewell and reached across the table to give her hand a squeeze.

Jewell smiled. "Don't get yourself in trouble Ash. This is my deal; I'll take care of it. I just need to figure it out."

They finished their lunch talking about how each other's day was going. When they got up to leave, Ashley grabbed Jewell's arm, "don't try anything tonight. Promise me that."

Jewell looked into Ashley's face. Ashley was her best friend. Ashley would do anything for her, even risk getting fired. She couldn't let Ashley take the chance. "I promise, if you promise too."

"Sure, whatever." Ashley walked toward the elevators to go back to obstetrics, while Jewell turned the other way toward the ER.

Fortunately, Jewell didn't have a lot of time to think about anything other than work. The ER was crowded with everything from sniffles to strokes that kept her mind occupied. She also couldn't find any time to sneak away to the file room to investigate Collin. When she was finally released to go home, Ashley had already changed and was waiting for her in the locker room. Jewell walked in and changed as quickly as she could. As they walked out the doors to the hospital, Ashley reached into her bag and pulled out a folder which she handed to Jewell.

"What's this?" Jewell asked, her mind still on duty, thinking of procedures and dosages.

"What do you think it is – it's Collin's file. A photocopy of course, but everything's in there."

"Ashley – I told you not to." Jewell was thrilled, but also disappointed that Ashley had broken a promise.

"I didn't." Ashley smiled smugly. "I have a friend who's an intern. His name's Ray. He's way cute, and I think he likes me. I told him I needed a copy of a patient's file and when he asked me why, well, I sort of helped him think of something else."

Jewell turned to stare at her friend. "Ashley! What did you...never mind; I don't even want to know."

She opened the file and started looking through it when she suddenly walked right into something solid. Her mind registered his smell first. Then the warmth radiating from his body, and then his warm arms wrapped around her. She looked up and saw the most beautiful storm gray eyes laughing at her. "Interesting reading?"

"As a matter of fact, it is. It's your medical file."

All of a sudden, she saw Ashley's hand, open, palm up between them. Jewell looked at Ashley and then dug in her pocket for her car keys. As Jewell dropped her keys in Ashley's hand, Ashley commented to Collin, "Can you just drop her at my place. It's easier than doing the car swap, and she lives in the wrong direction for me to pick her up for work."

Collin nodded as he looked over Jewell's shoulder at the file. They heard Ashley's hasty retreat as they turned to walk towards Collin's car.

While Collin drove towards the French Quarter, Jewell read through the file. "Anything interesting?"

"Not really so far, just the usual. Wow, I had forgotten how bad it was when you came in. There are pictures in here." She kept flipping through the pages. "Notes about procedures, tests, I don't really see anything. I'll look at it more closely when we stop. I think I'm getting car sick."

"You do look a little green," he chuckled, pulling on to Decatur St. He found a place to park, and they walked to Café du Monde.

Sitting at a table, Jewell started looking through the file again, carefully reading all of the notes. She handed the pages with the pictures across to Collin. "Wow. Did I really look that bad?"

"Are you kidding, those pictures don't do you justice. I wrote you off the minute they brought you in."

"Gee, thanks for the vote of confidence."

"Well, you didn't look that great. And you did die, sort of."

He handed the pictures back. "Is there anything else?"

Jewell kept leafing through the file. "X-ray results, lab results. It looks like they did the standard tests for an MVA, drugs, alcohol…wait. Now this is interesting."

"What? What's interesting?"

"Somebody ordered a DNA profile. Why would they order a DNA profile for a trauma victim?" She started flipping through the pages, looking for more information.

"Is that unusual?"

"Well, that's definitely not standard…oh wait. Aha…you'll never guess who ordered the test."

"Babineaux." It was more of a statement than a question.

"You guessed it. It's got the name of the lab, but no number. I'll see what I can find out today." She downed the rest of her coffee and stood up.

"Do you want me to help?"

"No, you can drop me at Ashley's. She'll help. I've got to work tonight too. Meet me there at about five thirty and I'll tell you what I can before work." She gathered up all of the papers and shoved them back in the envelope.

"So, you think this DNA stuff is the answer?" Collin asked when they started back toward the car.

"I don't know, but it's the only thing in the file that doesn't make sense. Another thing I noticed, they took out the information regarding your death and…resurrection."

"For heaven's sake Jewell, I'm not Jesus."

"Oh really, then *what* are you?"

Collin didn't answer. "So, that's unusual that that information isn't in the file?"

"Very. *Everything* is documented and the hospital keeps *very* accurate records. There's something going on here." Jewell was already thinking about the ramifications of what she had found. Not only was this unusual, there was a cover up, and Dr. Babineaux and Collin's uncle were at the center of it.

When Collin dropped Jewell at Ashley's apartment, rather than just getting her keys and driving home, Jewell asked Ashley for help in her investigation.

"What do you need me for?" Ashley asked, flipping through the file on the table in front of her.

Jewell leaned over her shoulder and flipped up a couple of pages. When she found what she was looking for, she placed her finger on the questionable tests that were run on Collin while he was at the hospital.

Ashley looked up at Jewell. "A DNA test? Why would they run a DNA test?"

"That's what I'm saying!" Jewell was frustrated. She had been thinking about this for well over an hour and it wasn't making any sense.

"Well they sent it to Dyna Labs. Why don't you just call them?"

"And say what? Why were you running a DNA test on a trauma victim?" Jewell asked sarcastically.

"I can call. We send stuff to them all the time. Amnio samples and what not. All you need to do is give them the patient number. They don't know who the patient is, just what tests were run."

"Really? You can do that?" Jewell hadn't handled anything but drug and alcohol testing and that was all done in house.

"Sure. Give me a minute." She walked over to the phone and dialed. "Hey Abby. I've got a patient file here that says we sent some stuff over to you for some tests but I don't have any results, can you help me out?" She paused, listening to the person on the other end. "Sure, it's 1-8-3-Alpha, Delta, 4-4–Victor." She paused again. "Is there any way you can pull it now? I'm trying to close out this file and it should've been done yesterday. If my boss finds out I've been slacking…Thanks, Abby, I owe you big time!"

"What? What's going on?" Jewell whispered.

Ashley put her hand over the phone's mouthpiece and whispered, "She's going to pull the file. It'll probably take a minute." Ashley put the phone on speaker and set it on the table. While she was waiting, she idly leafed through the file. "Hey, didn't you say that doctor Sandstrom was the one that called it?"

"Yeah," Jewell answered. "So?"

"He's not listed in the file. It says that Dr. Armstrong called it."

"What?" Jewell grabbed the file from Ashley and started looking through it again. "Sandstrom's name isn't in here anywhere!"

"Didn't he just accept a job in New York or California or something too?"

"Yeah, Dr. Sandstrom was offered a job at Sinai in Baltimore. It was a step up so he took it. He left a little over a week ago."

"Interesting. Do you think it's just coincidence?" Just then, they heard Abby on the other end of the phone interrupting their conversation.

"Ashley, I have the file. It looks like the only test we ran was Dr. Babineaux's research profile."

Ashley flipped the phone off speaker and picked it up. "Thanks Abby. That explains why there are no results in the file." Another pause. "Nope. Thanks again Abby." She hung up the phone.

"Research profile?" Jewell asked.

"Yeah. Every now and then Dr. Babineaux asks us to run his research profile on a sample. We always get the results of the other tests, but the results from the research profile are sent directly to him."

"What type of research?"

"I don't know; I never paid much attention. We could look it up though." Ashley got up to walk into the office where she had her computer. "So do you think there's anything to this Sandstrom/Armstrong switch?"

"I don't know. I was there too, and there were two other nurses. None of us were offered great jobs or anything."

"Yeah, but none of your names are in the file either. Besides, wasn't someone in the next day talking to Sandstrom; someone from the press or something?"

"Yeah, now that you mention it, there was. He never had a chance to talk to Sandstrom though. Babineaux talked to him instead."

"Babineaux again. Curiouser and curiouser."

"Curiouser indeed." Jewell replied as Ashley typed Dr. Babineaux's name into Google. There were well over a thousand hits. Ashley clicked on one that looked promising.

"Here's one of his articles. 'The Effect of Telomerase on the Hayflick Limit in DNA Reproduction and Prolongation of Lifespan.'" Ashley clicked on the article. Jewell read over her shoulder as they scanned the information.

"Oh, I see." Jewell commented cynically. "So he thinks he's found the Fountain of Youth in this Telomerase enzyme."

"Awesome!" Ashley chimed in. "Of course, I'll probably be dead and buried before they figure out how to make this stuff work, but imagine it Jewell, immortality!"

"A German philosopher once said 'To desire immortality is to desire the eternal perpetuation of a great mistake'. I tend to agree with him."

"Oh yeah, I forgot that you're the eternal pessimist." Ashley snorted in disgust.

"Anyway, I still don't see why he would want a sample of Collin's DNA."

"Yeah, weird."

"Well, I know I need some sleep if I'm going to be able to work tonight and so will you. Pick you up at five?"

"Yup, sounds good. See ya." Ashley closed the door behind Jewell.

*   *   *

When Ashley and Jewell walked up to the door to the hospital at five thirty, Collin was waiting for them in the darkness beside it. Jewell thought about how creepy it was the way he could just appear and disappear in the shadows.

"Hey Honeysuckle," he said grabbing her around the waist.   "Hi Ashley. How are you tonight?"

"Good Collin. Thanks for noticing me. I'm surprised you actually know my name." She crossed her arms over her chest.

"Of course I know your name. Other than me, you're all Jewell talks about." He smiled as he put one hand on Ashley's shoulder. "I appreciate everything you've done for Jewell and I'm sorry I've been too occupied to speak to you before now."

Ashley grunted. "Whatever. Apology accepted I guess." Her tone was joking, she really liked Collin and it hadn't bothered her that Collin had ignored her on all of their previous encounters.

Collin took both girls by the hand and led them into the shadows of the parking garage so that they wouldn't draw attention. "So, what did you figure out?"

"Not much," Jewell said dejectedly.

Ashley wasn't so negative. "Not much?" She turned to look at Collin. "We only found out that there is some mass conspiracy at the hospital involving you, Dr. Babineaux and your uncle, and that some people have taken great pains to cover it up!"

"Give me a break Ash. Sandstrom could have just been a coincidence, and just because Babineaux took some of Collin's DNA for research doesn't mean there's a conspiracy."

"Wait." Collin interjected. "He took what? A sample of my DNA? Why would he do that?"

"Just research," said Jewell. "Apparently there's this enzyme called Telomerase that he thinks is the secret to immortality."

"So what does that have to do with me? And how is my uncle involved?"

"We don't know." Jewell said, shrugging her shoulders. "What we do know is that information has been removed from your file, and that some of the information has been changed."

"Well, you did your best." He bent over and gave Jewell a kiss on the forehead. "I appreciate your efforts." He turned to include Ashley in his gratitude. "You ladies need to go to work. I'll see you," he turned to Jewell, "in the morning." He picked up her hand and kissed the inside of her wrist. She shuddered. Ashley smiled. After he had turned to leave, Ashley held out her hand. "You might as well just give me your keys now. It'll save you time when we leave."

Jewell laughed and dropped her car keys into Ashley's upturned hand.

Collin was waiting at Jewell's car when she and Ashley left in the morning. He took her hand and started walking toward where he was parked. Jewell smiled and waved at Ashley with her other hand as she walked away. Over breakfast at Café du Monde, they discussed the file in more depth.

"So, what were you saying yesterday, about information being changed?" Collin asked, brushing powdered sugar from the front of his shirt.

"Well, here's what's interesting. The name of the attending doctor has been changed and has relocated to Baltimore."

"That doesn't seem like much. What else was changed?"

"Well," Jewell said, sipping on her coffee, "they had called your time of death. That should have been in the file. It's happened before, where a doctor makes a mistake and calls it, but it turns out that the patient actually survives. The fact that it was called always stays in the file; along with details of the resuscitation. Those details are extremely important if there are complications later, which, unlike with you, there usually are."

"So what does it say about the whole thing?"

"It just says that you were in cardiac arrest when you arrived, CPR was being administered by emergency personnel, and that they were able to restore a sinus rhythm after five minutes of continued CPR and oxygen."

"What's a sinus rhythm?" He pointed to himself, "history major, remember."

"Oh yeah. That just means that your heart started beating normally again."

"So then, there's nothing in there about me...well, dying?"

"Nope. Not a word. According to this, there was nothing abnormal at all. You were brought in, your injuries were documented – it looks like those are all accurate, all procedures performed during surgery and your follow up care until you were *transferred* to a private facility. Where did you go anyway?"

"What do you mean?"

"Well, I checked out Jaffa Continued Care Facility. It didn't check out."

"You were spying on me?"

Jewell blushed. "Well, um...I was following up on your transfer?"

"Yeah right. From the time I left the ER I was no business of yours. You were looking for me because you missed me." He grinned and poked her in the side.

"Oh, and this coming from the guy stalking me at my job every night!" Jewell countered.

"Okay, you got me. What can I say? I am totally, completely, and irrevocably in love with you."

Jewell pushed up from the table. "You'd probably better get me home. I have to work again tonight and I'm beat."

Collin got up and followed her as she walked towards his car. "What did I say?"

"Nothing. I'm just tired." She crossed her arms over her chest as Collin reached for her hand. He put his arm around her shoulders instead. She stiffened, but didn't protest.

Collin opened Jewell's door and then walked around to the driver's seat. He put the key in the ignition, but didn't start the car. Instead, he looked at Jewell. She was looking out the window. "Jewell," he whispered. "Jewell, what's wrong?"

"Collin, this is just getting stranger. Instead of finding answers, I'm just coming up with more questions. Your uncle knows something, how do I know that you don't know something you're not telling me. I don't know what to think."

He reached across the seat and put his hand on her shoulder. "Jewell, look at me." She turned and looked at him. "Look at my eyes. I'm not lying. I'm just as confused about this as you are. If I knew something else, I swear I would tell you. Can't you see that I'm telling you the truth? I'm scared too, and confused. Imagine how this feels to me, to find out that not only are secrets being kept from me and by my family no less, but secrets *about* me are being kept from everyone."

Jewell suddenly felt selfish. He was right. This wasn't about her at all, this was about him. She could just walk away, at least in theory. He couldn't walk away from his secrets. "You're right. I'm sorry. It's just so overwhelming."

"You know, I would understand if you didn't want anything more to do with me. I wouldn't try to stop you if you wanted to walk away." He looked down, as if he thought that might be what she wanted.

Jewell reached out and took his face gently in both her hands. She leaned over and kissed him lightly on the lips. "You know I can't leave you. Not even if I wanted to." She leaned back and laughed. "I mean really, I spent an entire day driving around Lake Charles looking for some imaginary place just so I could see you again. Where did your uncle take you anyway?"

"Honestly? Just back home. He is a doctor after all."

"Speaking of home…I checked out your home address, too. It appears you live at a florist in Lacombe."

"My, my; you sound a little obsessed. Are you stalking me?"

"Just a little."

*   *   *

That night she dreamed of Collin. In the dream, Collin was standing in the sunlight. She could see him, but it looked like he was looking for her. She was engulfed in shadow. She tried calling to him, but when she called his name her voice made no sound. She tried to walk forward, but couldn't move. It felt like she was tied down, her arms pinned to her sides. She kicked her legs, but could not escape her bindings. She started to panic. Her panic pulled her from sleep, breathing hard, her blankets twisted around her arms fixing them against her body.

CHAPTER 24

Ashley and Jewell walked together into the hospital. As they walked towards the hospital, they joined a crowd of other employees arriving for work. Collin had promised to help his uncle with some things tonight, so he didn't meet Jewell as usual. Suddenly, something caught Jewell's eye. She quickly moved to Ashley's other side, and pulled Ashley to the outside of the crowd.

"What's going on?" Ashley asked.

"Don't turn your head, but look over by the wall, in the corner."

"What, the guy?"

"Yes, does he look familiar to you?"

Ashley tried to look without looking as they moved towards the hospital doors. It was difficult to get a good look at him because he was in a shadow, and partially obscured by the wall. Also, the people in the crowd kept passing in front of her view. "No. Should he?"

"Ash, it's the same guy from the Burger King in Lake Charles. The same guy from the emergency room I told you about, the idiot with the coffee. Now do you remember?"

"Yeah, I remember you telling me about him. Are you sure that's him? How do you know?"

"Well, the brace on his leg for one thing. That guy broke his leg. Do you remember the guy in Lake Charles; he was having trouble getting out of his car because his leg was in a cast?"

"I don't know I wasn't paying attention."

Jewell huffed in exasperation. "Besides, there's something about him. Trust me, it's the same guy. I think he's following me."

"You're being paranoid. It's probably not the same guy, or maybe he's here for another reason or something."

"Just because you're paranoid doesn't mean the world isn't out to get you." Jewell quoted as she kept Ashley between her and the stranger while she passed through the doors into the hospital. The man was looking the opposite direction towards some other employees who were just arriving. Jewell shivered. "The hairs on the back of my neck are standing on end!" She reached up and rubbed the back of her neck. "I don't know, maybe you're right. Maybe I'm just being paranoid. I'm so tired I'm just not thinking straight."

Jewell tried not to think any more about the man she saw outside the hospital until she was checking some information on a patient with Lea, who works at the front desk. "Hey, Jewell; some guy came by, I think he might have been looking for you."

"Really?" Jewell's suspicions flared to the surface. "What did he look like?"

"I don't really remember I didn't look at him much. He was asking for a blonde nurse that usually wears a pony tail. Since you're the only blonde on night shift, I figured he was talking about you."

"What...what did you tell him?"

"I told him that I couldn't give out any information on employees of course." She turned to look at Jewell. "You look really pale. Do you feel alright?"

"I'm not sure. Did this man...did he have a brace on his right leg?"

Lea thought for a minute. "Actually, now that you mention it, I think he did. He was walking with a cane. Do you know him? He didn't seem to know your name."

Jewell leaned against the counter. Lea got up and moved her chair behind Jewell prompting her to sit down. "What's wrong? You do know him, don't you?"

"He came in about two weeks ago. It was a single car MVA; he had spilled coffee in his lap. I remember seeing him as they pushed him past me in the hall. When he looked at me, it was just...I don't know, creepy." Jewell rested her head in her hands for a minute, trying to slow her heart rate and her breathing. "I was in Lake Charles a couple days later, I saw him there. I didn't think too much about it at the time; I thought it was just a coincidence. He didn't seem to notice me. But then, him being here tonight...I saw him standing outside. I thought it was weird, but now that you said he was asking for me..."

"He was here tonight?" Lea sounded worried.

"Yeah, outside waiting by the employee entrance, why?"

"Because he was asking for you *last night*." Lea reached for the phone, quickly dialing the number for security. "I think we have a problem. There's somebody here that may be stalking one of our nurses." She waited for a minute, listening. "Jewell McKean. She's right here with me. She can probably give you a better description than I can." Lea handed the phone to Jewell.

"Hello?" Jewell described the man to security who told her that they would look into it. She turned to Lea, "Can you pull that file for me? I want to know who this guy is."

"I'm really not supposed to..."

"Please, this guy is stalking me. I should at least know who he is. Maybe I can go to the police and get a restraining order or something." She was on the verge of tears. The idea of this man following her was spine-chilling. She had heard of people being stalked before. All of the stories she read ended badly.

"Let me see what I can work out."

"Thanks Lea. Do you know where Nurse Yohanan is?" Jewell asked standing and looking towards the treatment area.

"The last time I saw her she was walking towards exam 3."

Jewell steadied herself. She felt extremely nauseous and a little dizzy. When she was certain that she could walk, she went to find Nurse Yohanan to ask if she could take a break. Even though she had just come on her shift, Nurse Yohanan was sympathetic and told her to take twenty minutes to compose herself. Jewell went straight upstairs to talk to Ashley.

Jewell and Ashley sat at the nurses' station as Jewell explained that the man she had seen tonight and in Lake Charles had also asked about her yesterday. "What do you think he wants?" Ashley asked Jewell when she had finished explaining everything.

"I don't know. That first night he was here though, the way he looked at me. I can't describe it. He didn't look at me like he thought I was attractive, or like he was just watching me because I was more interesting than the wall. I don't know, it was just sinister, you know?"

"Did security say what they were going to do?"

"No. Officer Garrett said that he was going to send a couple of guys to see if he was still lurking somewhere. He said that one of his officers had reported a suspicious man loitering near the ER yesterday. He fit the description of the guy that was there tonight. I asked Lea to see if she could find his file so I could find out who he is, maybe where he lives or something. What should I do? Ashley, this is really scaring me! What does he want?"

Ashley reached over to give Jewell a hug. "I don't know honey. I'll make sure I ride with you so at least you won't be coming and going alone. Our schedules are pretty much the same, but I'll talk to my supervisor and see if she'll work with me. You might want to talk to Nurse Yohanan too. Then, we should probably call security when we come in and leave. Tom is usually at the gate, I'm sure that if we let him know, he can radio security when we come in, and we can just call security when we get ready to leave. Plus, now that they know about this guy, they'll be watching for him and I'm sure they won't let him in the garage. It'll be okay, you'll see."

"I hope so." Jewell was feeling a bit better. Now that she had time to calm down a bit, and after everything Ashley had said, she felt reassured. She looked at her watch. "I've got to get back to work. I'll see you at lunch."

When she went back downstairs, Lea was talking to Officer Garrett, the head of security. She was handing him a patient file, she assumed it was the file for the man following her. When Lea saw her, she motioned to Jewell to come over. Jewell spoke to Officer Garrett for about an hour, explaining everything: the first time she saw him, the visit to Lake Charles, and coming in to work tonight. Officer Garrett told her that they didn't catch him, but had a description from the previous night, along with a description of his car and his license plate number. He also promised to notify the New Orleans police.

"If you see anything suspicious, make sure you let us know. And we suggest that you don't go in and out of the hospital alone. Call security for an escort if it makes you feel safer."

Jewell smiled and thanked the officer.

She ate lunch with Ashley, saying little. She did tell Ashley about her conversation with Officer Garrett. They agreed to meet in the locker room after work to walk to Jewell's car. When it was time to go, a security officer walked Ashley and Jewell to Jewell's car. As usual, Collin was waiting for her. Still out of hearing distance, Ashley leaned over and asked, "What are you going to tell Collin?"

"Oh no, I hadn't thought of that. What should I tell him?" The officer was walking behind the two girls and hadn't heard their conversation; he was looking for signs of danger. Jewell turned back to the officer, "can you give me a minute? I'll just be over there." She pointed toward where Collin was standing.

The security guard looked toward Collin, "You know him?"

"He's my boyfriend. I've got to go talk to him."

"I'll wait here." The security guard stood in a professional at ease position, legs slightly spread, his hands clasped loosely in the small of his back. Jewell briefly wondered if this officer had a military background. She walked over to Collin who looked confused.

"What's with the escort?" Collin asked.

"There've been some problems with some guy hanging around. It's just to ensure the security of the nurses until they're sure they have the situation under control."

Collin glared at her suspiciously, "problems related to you?"

Not wanting to upset him, Jewell quickly shook her head. "No, just in general."

"Then how come you two are the only ones with an escort?" Jewell was finding that it was going to be very difficult to lie to Collin, but she stuck to her story.

"We were just the last ones out."

Collin continued to eye her, clearly not convinced. "Well then, why don't we grab some coffee and beignets?" He reached for her hand.

Jewel shifted away from him, shrugging her shoulders. "Collin, I'm so tired. I really need to go home and get some sleep; tomorrow?"

"If you're sure." The concern was evident both on his face and in his voice.

"I'm sure. I'll see you later, okay?" She gave him a hug that, without realizing it, conveyed her fear clearly to Collin.

"I'll pick you up for work."

"No, I'm riding with Ashley. Her car's not working so I have to drive her." The lies were uncomfortable, but until she knew what was happening, she didn't want to tell Collin about it.

"I love you." He hugged her back.

"I love you too." She smiled, looking up at him. At least that had been an honest answer. He watched her as she walked back to Ashley and the security guard, and then followed her as they walked to the car.

"What did you tell him?" Ashley asked.

"I didn't tell him anything."

"Jewell, don't you think you should tell him?"

"No, the police and security have everything in control. It'll be okay." Her voice was shaking. Ashley looked at Jewell. It was obvious that she thought Jewell was making the wrong decision, but she wasn't going to tell her friend what was best for her.

CHAPTER 25

Collin walked into the front door and looked around. He heard voices coming from the kitchen so he walked down the hall in that direction. When he opened the door, everyone stopped talking and looked at him.

"What?" He looked at the group of people sitting around the table.

"Percy?" Gladys said, looking at Collin's uncle.

"Collin, you know how I feel about you getting too close to people. We won't be here forever. What are you going to do when we leave?"

"Maybe I won't do anything. Maybe I'll stay here." Collin responded defiantly.

"You can't Collin."

"Why? Because you're my legal guardian? Well, I have something to tell you Uncle Percy, I'm an adult now. What I do with my life from now on is my choice. Don't get me wrong, I love you, and I'm grateful for all you've done for me, but I love Jewell."

Percy sighed. He looked at Gladys who just shrugged. Kendryck got up to get a glass of water and Dot and Carl were engaged in their own personal conversation, too interested in each other to help Percy. Percy looked at Collin, clearly exasperated, but not knowing what to say.

"Is that it, then?" Collin asked, glaring at everyone sitting at the table. When no one said anything, he walked out, going to his quarters behind the house. He grabbed a fishing pole and wandered out to a pond, or more of a swamp, about two miles from the house. Living on such a large piece of land definitely had its advantages.

After he had been out for a few hours, he started feeling better and started walking back to the house. The worst part about all of this was Jewell. What was going on with her? He glanced at his watch. It was only noon; the middle of the night for Jewell. It would be rude to drive to her house just to make himself feel better. He didn't really feel like going to New Orleans. He wasn't sure what he wanted to do. After he put his pole away, he walked into the house and headed toward the kitchen. He wasn't really hungry, but he couldn't think of anything else to do. Walking into the house, he saw his uncle watching TV in the parlor. Collin walked in and sat down next to Percy.

"I'm sorry." Collin didn't look at his uncle.

Percy put his arm around his nephew. "I'm sorry too. I know that you really like this girl, but you know that you can't get too involved with people. We've already been here for a couple of years, we'll probably move on in another year or so."

"But why? Why can't I get close to someone? Why do I have to move?"

Percy, with his usual evasiveness said "I thought we'd go to Australia. I haven't been there in a while, and I miss vegemite. Have you ever had vegemite?

Collin sighed. He gave his uncle a quick hug and got up from the couch. "I'm going to see if I can find some lunch, do you want anything?"

When Collin arrived at the hospital before Jewell's shift, he parked his car and went to stand in his usual place, a place where he would be certain to see her as she walked into work. He had noticed that security seemed to be tighter. At the entrance to the garage the gate, which was usually up, was lowered and he had to stop to give the attendant his ID before entering the garage. He was also surprised that the attendant knew who he was. The man had laughed as he handed Collin's driver's license back to him. "So you're Collin. I've heard a lot about you." Then he lifted the gate so that Collin could enter the garage. Collin noticed a security guard discretely positioned so that he could see who was entering and leaving the garage. In the guard house, Collin noticed a piece of paper tacked to a bulletin board with a license plate number, the description of a car, and the physical characteristics of someone, apparently with a broken leg.

As he wound his way through the garage, Collin spotted two more security guards on foot with billy clubs out, and one sitting in his car near the exit to the garage. Maybe Jewell wasn't lying; maybe the person didn't have any interest in a particular person, but rather was just some sick freak with a nurse fetish. While he was waiting, he watched several nurses walk into the building. He noticed security guards walking past, but none of them took any particular interest in the nurses entering the hospital.

Collin didn't see Jewell's car as he wound through the garage which meant she probably wasn't there yet, but he knew that he would see her as she walked toward the hospital. He watched towards the parking area, waiting for her. When he finally saw her, he noticed a security guard, following behind her and Ashley as they made their way to the hospital. This only confirmed his fear that this was about her in particular and not about the nurses in general. When Jewell saw Collin, both Ashley and Jewell walked toward where he was standing. Collin smiled at Ashley and asked if he could have a minute alone with Jewell. Ashley winked at him and started toward the employee entrance. Collin watched the guard as Ashley left. He hadn't moved. He stood a discrete distance from them, but his attention was definitely focused on Jewell.

Jewell practically threw herself at Collin; out of excitement or fear, Collin wasn't certain. "Did you want to tell me the truth now?" He asked her gently.

She sighed and leaned the top of her head against his chest staring down at the pavement. "A couple of nights ago a guy came in looking for a blonde nurse with a ponytail. Since I'm the only nurse on night shift with blonde hair, they assume he meant me. He showed up again last night, but left before they could catch him."

"Catch him? Why were they trying to catch him? I'm up here every night looking for you and they've never tried to catch me."

"A couple of the nurses saw him and reported him. He just looked a little weird, that's all."

"Seems like pretty tight security for 'a little weird.' Maybe I should start driving you to work."

"No, it's fine. Security here has everything under control, and the guy hasn't come back. I'll be fine. Plus Ashley rides with me every day, so I'm never coming in alone. Tom at the guardhouse lets security know when I come in and I tell security when I leave, so it's fine, see?" Jewell looked up at Collin, trying to read his face. She didn't want a personal body guard.

"Do you know what this guy wants?"

"No. He's probably just some creep. He came into the ER a couple of days after you came in. I guess he saw me and just got obsessed or something."

"I can definitely understand how that can happen." He smiled and gave her a little squeeze. "Well, it does look like they're taking pretty good care of you." He waved at the security guard who waved back, but didn't smile. The security guard's eyes were constantly searching the shadows and the surrounding area for possible danger. "It's a good thing the guy at the guardhouse knew who I was too, or he wouldn't have let me in! Apparently, you've been telling stories about me."

She hugged him. "It's kind of unbelievable that you're mine. I can't help telling everyone how wonderful you are. I've got to get to work. Will you be here in the morning?"

"If they let me in."

"I'll make sure security knows who you are." She gave him a quick kiss and ran towards the hospital.

As Collin walked back to his car, he stopped to talk with the security guard. "What do you think about all this?"

He shrugged. "It's definitely worth taking seriously, but we've had incidents like this before, usually with ex-boyfriends," he eyed Collin, "but the group we've got here is pretty tight and none of our nurses have ever been hurt while they're on hospital property. We've also alerted the New Orleans police, although they can't do anything unless the guy tries something."

"Tries something?" Collin asked. "What does that mean?"

"Well, he actually has to try to attack her before they can arrest him. They have his name and description of his car. He doesn't have a criminal record if that makes you feel any better."

"Yeah, much." Collin said sarcastically. "Does Jewell know all of this too?"

"I know she knows what he looks like, and security told her what his car looks like, but I don't know if she knows his name or anything."

Collin gave the man a pat on the shoulder and nodded as he turned toward his car. He thought about the guard's words, *while on hospital property*. He wasn't convinced that this guy wasn't a real threat, and he definitely wasn't convinced that Jewell knew about the danger she could be in. His uncle didn't like his relationship with Jewell, but maybe he would have some ideas about what could be done to protect her.

*   *   *

When Collin got home, he found his uncle out walking in the garden. "Can I talk to you for a minute?"

"Sure kid. What's on your mind?" He smiled up at Collin as he pulled a weed out from between some oleander plants.

"Well, I know you don't approve of my relationship with Jewell, but I need some help with a situation she's involved in and I don't really know what to do."

Collin's uncle stood up and gestured to a bench that was on the side of the path. "It's not that I don't approve, it's just that there are circumstances that would make your relationship with her…complicated."

"Well, it's complicated now. Someone is stalking her."

His uncle was quiet for a minute, contemplative. "What do you mean, stalking her?"

Collin explained the situation at the hospital. "I'm not really concerned about her at work, I think that security is taking care of her, but I'm worried about her when she's not at work. I don't know anything about this guy, and she doesn't know very much. I'm scared something is going to happen to her, but she doesn't seem to take it seriously. The police can't do anything, I was wondering if you had any advice. Any ideas about what I can do to protect her?"

"Where does this guy know her from?"

"He was a patient in the hospital, about the same time I was there. For some reason he just keeps following her."

"Does anyone at the hospital know about your relationship with Jewell?" His uncle asked harshly, almost accusingly.

"Well, Ashley for sure. That's her best friend. The guy at the parking garage seemed to know. I would guess if he knows than it's not much of a secret. Why?"

"When did you start seeing her? When was the first time that you two were together?"

"I don't know Uncle Percy. I guess when I was in the ICU. What difference does it make?

Percy got up from the bench, mumbling to himself and walking toward the house leaving Collin sitting on the bench speechless and confused.

CHAPTER 26

When Jewell came out of the hospital in the morning, she was accompanied by Ashley and a security guard. Collin approached them, pulling Jewell aside. "I'm going to follow you to the house."

"What? Why?"

"I'm not worried when you're at work. They're doing a great job, but what about when you're not at work? What are you going to do if he shows up at your house or something? Have you even told your dad?" The concern in his voice was apparent.

"Well, no. I guess since the hospital is the only..." Jewell's voice caught.

"The hospital is the only what?"

"Um, never mind." Collin glared at her. She couldn't lie to him. "Well, I was going to say the hospital is the only place I've seen him..."

"But it's not." It was an accusation. "I'm following you home." He didn't even look back as he walked purposefully toward his car; his stride angry.

"What did he say?" Ashley was curious as Jewell rejoined her to walk to the car.

"He figured out that this guy hasn't just shown up at the hospital. He's worried. I think he's taking it upon himself to be my personal bodyguard."

Ashley sighed. "That's so romantic."

"Well, he's going to follow us home." Jewell got into the car and unlocked it for Ashley. They drove home without talking.

"So I guess you're going to stay with Collin for the next couple days?"

"Apparently, he's not going to leave me alone. Not that I really mind, of course." She smiled. "I'll call you and let you know if officer heartthrob is going to let me ride in to work with you on Saturday, or if he's going to insist on chauffeuring me around."

"Okay, have fun." Ashley winked and shut the door. She watched as Jewell backed out and noticed Collin's silver corvette near the end of the road, waiting for Jewell. She drove past, and he followed.

Jewell pulled into her driveway. Her father was home, so Collin parked on the street. Jewell waited by her car as Collin walked up the driveway. He put his arm around her shoulders protectively as they walked toward the house. Inside, it was apparent to her father that something was wrong. There was tension in both of their faces.

"What's wrong?" Jewell's dad asked as soon as they walked into the living room.

Collin walked to the chair, other than the couch and the table the TV sat on it was the only furniture in the room. He gestured for Jewell to sit down, and stood behind her, his hand resting on the back of the chair. Jewell looked up at him to see if he was going to explain to her father what was going on at work. It was clear that he wanted her to tell him.

"Well," Jewell started, "there's this guy at work who is kind of hanging around me."

"Hanging around you how?" Her father asked suspiciously.

Jewell shrugged. "He just showed up a couple of times at work, that's all. Security is taking care of it. They've also told the New Orleans police."

"And…" Collin prompted.

"What? What else is there?" Jewell asked.

Jewell's father looked at Collin for an explanation. "He hasn't only shown up at the hospital. Apparently, she saw him when she was in Lake Charles with Ashley."

Jewell's father got out of the chair and walked over to the phone. He punched in a number. "Alex? Tommy. I need some help. Would it be easier if I come down to the station or do you want to stop by after you get off work?" He waited. "Okay then. We'll see you in a few minutes." Tommy hung up the phone. "Alex is going to come to the house and take an official report."

Jewell sighed. "Dad, is this really necessary?"

"Yes," answered Collin and her father at the same time.

When Alex Stanley arrived at the house, Jewell told the story again with Collin filling in details that he felt were important. After asking questions and taking notes for about forty-five minutes, Alex stepped out to his squad car. Jewell watched him out the window, talking on his cell phone.

After several minutes, Alex came back inside. "I called the information into the station. He doesn't have any charges that we can pick him up on, not even a parking ticket. I have a couple of friends in New Orleans police department. We also let Andy Baraven with the St. Tammany Sheriff's department know what's going on. Now, you understand that we can't do anything unless he threatens Jewell, but we'll definitely be watching her."

Jewell's dad had stood up to stand by Alex. He clapped Alex on the back, "Thanks. That makes me feel a lot better."

"Anytime Tommy," Alex said, reaching for the handle on the door. "I need to get back to the station so that I can write this up before my shift ends. I'll call you if anything comes up." Alex opened the door and stepped out.

"Thanks Alex." He shut the door and sat back down on the couch. Jewell was pale, visibly shaken by having to recount everything that's been going on.

Jewell's father looked at her. "Jewell honey, you don't look good. I know you're tired. Why don't you go to bed?"

"Yeah dad, you're probably right. She turned to Collin and gave him a hug. He hugged her protectively then leaned down to kiss her cheek. "I promise I won't let anything happen to you," he whispered.

She just smiled at him. She gave her dad a hug and then disappeared into the hall heading towards her bedroom. Jewell's father turned toward Collin and looked at his watch. "She'll probably sleep until about six, especially since she got to bed so late."

"Yes sir. I'd like to stay here if that's okay with you. I told her I'd make sure nothing happened to her. I don't like to break my promises."

Jewell's father gestured to the chair. "Can I get you a book or something, or maybe you can find something on TV that you want to watch."

Collin looked at the shelf under the television. It was piled high with hot rod magazines. He walked over and started shuffling through the pile. He pulled out a magazine discussing the history of Mustangs and went back to the chair.

"Good choice." Jewell's dad smiled at him.

"I've always liked cars. I had a Mustang GT500 that was totaled in the accident."

"What a waste." They sat and talked about Mustangs, and then moved on to discussions of other cars. Even though Collin preferred the sports cars, he loved the old muscle cars as well so he was able to keep up his end of the conversation. They talked for a while, and then sat silent, each involved in their reading. Collin found several issues discussing the high end sports cars that he fancied.

Whenever a car passed, Tommy and Collin would both glance nervously out the window.

CHAPTER 27

When Alex had arrived back at the station, he immediately called Sheriff Payne in New Orleans. Although Jewell wasn't an Infinitas, she was dating an Infinitas, and regardless, the first duty of a Templar was protection. But this case had brought attention to the Templars because Collin was involved. Sheriff Payne had immediately called a meeting, and he had set about calling all of the New Orleans Templars to let them know that there would be a meeting at Dr. Babineaux's house on the North Side of the causeway in Mandeville. Dr. Babineaux lived in a large plantation style home on several acres. The house was set back from the road, and shrouded by massive oaks. This made it easier to gather all nine people without drawing attention.

The Templars were gathered for their second meeting in three weeks. Under normal circumstances, the group met once every three months to manage the accounts, and usually share a drink. Having two meetings so closely together, and outside the usual schedule did not bode well. While all knew what their commitment meant, most did not ever believe they would be called to duty. It was a dangerous job. The last time an Infinitas was identified; several Templar Knights were killed. Unfortunately, in that case, the Infinitas were killed as well.

Alex pulled onto the long driveway leading toward the house; he could see evidence of other cars recently passing. As he pulled onto the concrete parking pad, he saw that six others had already arrived in addition to Dr. Babineaux. They were waiting on only one other. He recognized all of the cars. Taking inventory, it appeared that Sheriff Payne was the only participant who had not yet arrived.

Alex rang the bell and was greeted by Dr. Babineaux. As he walked in the door, he saw Sheriff Payne's car pull into the driveway followed by an unfamiliar SUV. He stood inside the door and watched as Sheriff Payne exited his car and walked back to the SUV. An unfamiliar older man emerged and shook Sheriff Payne's hand. Together, they walked to the house.

Once everyone was inside, the nine Templar Knights and the single stranger settled at the massive table in Dr. Babineaux's dining room. Sheriff Payne sat at the head of the table, despite this being Dr. Babineaux's home, the unknown man sat to Sheriff Payne's right and Dr. Babineaux sat to his left. The other seven Templars arranged themselves around the table in no particular order. Sheriff Payne stood up and gestured to the man sitting to his right.

"Gentlemen, this is Percival Knighton. He is the uncle of the identified Infinitas, and an Infinitas himself. He has identified himself in secrecy to request our protection for him and his family while they reside within our territory. There are four others including the two previously identified." The other knights nodded in greeting at the newly introduced individual. "There have been some recent developments that require our attention. Most of us know Jewell McKean. She is currently in a relationship with Collin, Percy's nephew. She is neither aware of the Infinitas, nor what they are. Collin, though an Infinitas himself, is also unaware of his…uniqueness." He gestured to Dr. Babineaux "Will you call the meeting to order?"

After the meeting had been called to order, Sheriff Payne sat down and gestured to Alex. "Alex, please tell us what you know of the situation concerning Jewell."

Alex stood and told everyone about his conversation this afternoon with Tommy, Collin and Jewell, referring to his notes to ensure that he didn't leave anything out. When he was finished, he sat down.

Sheriff Payne rose again and gestured to Christian Johnson, who was an officer with the New Orleans police department. Christian stood up and explained the details of the situation as presented to him by Garrett Roes, head of security at the hospital. He told of the two incidents at the hospital, including the confrontation with Lea Coles. Finally, Sheriff Payne gestured to Dr. Babineaux and requested that he give his report.

"The individual's name is Edgar Durand. He's 28 years old. He has lived in the same apartment in Chinchuba for approximately six years. He has no criminal record. He was born and raised in New Orleans, but I searched the federal database. He has no record there either. He works at a private sanitation company in Madisonville as a bookkeeper. He's worked there for six years and hasn't missed a single day of work…until recently. I couldn't find any record of his having been previously treated for any illness." Dr. Babineaux paused to add emphasis to the oddity of recent events. "He was admitted to the hospital eight days following the admission of Collin Sykes. He was the victim of a single car MVA. The circumstances surrounding his accident are suspicious. A review of security tapes indicate that he tried on two prior occasions to get into the hospital, both after Collin was admitted. On one of these occasions, he tried to get into the hospital claiming to be a friend of Collin.

"After he was treated in the emergency room, he was moved to a room on the same floor with Collin. Shortly thereafter, Percival removed his nephew from the hospital for obvious reasons. I documented the move, indicating that Collin was being moved to a private facility in Lake Charles. After Edgar was discharged, this piece of paper was found in his room." He passed around a piece of paper almost completely colored in with pencil. "If you look closely, you will see the address of that private facility. This facility is nonexistent and was fabricated for the protection of Collin and his uncle. Two days later, Jewell saw Edgar in Lake Charles only blocks from this address. In the past month, Edgar has missed eight days of work, not including the two he missed as a result of his *accident.*

"Recently, he has been requesting information about Jewell at the hospital. We feel that the actual target is probably Collin. Percival has requested our assistance until they are able to relocate."

Sheriff Payne stood up. "Because Edgar has no criminal record, and has not made an overt threat toward either Jewell or Collin, we cannot authorize that he be questioned or held for any reason. However, his description and automobile information have been circulated throughout Orleans and St. Tammany Parrish law enforcement units. In addition, hospital security has been authorized to contact us if Edgar is seen at the hospital. Edgar has been ordered to stay off the property and told that if he is seen on the property he will be charged with criminal trespass. Although this is a misdemeanor, law enforcement officers have been given authorization to detain him." Dr. Babineaux sat down.

Sheriff Payne looked at Percy. "Dr. Knighton, do you have anything that you would like to add?"

"Thank you all for your efforts. I know that this is a difficult thing that I am asking of you and I know the dangers you face. Collin's parents were both Infinitas who were killed by the people like Mr. Durand. We thank you for pledging your lives to our protection.

"We have only just recently, within the past hours, learned of this development. Already, my *family* is taking steps so that we may leave this area, hopefully eliminating any threat to you, and any threat to us. We will communicate with either Sheriff Payne or Dr. Babineaux of our plans as soon as we can. We hope to leave within the week." He sat down, his head dropped in defeat.

"Does anyone here have anything to add?" Sheriff Payne looked at each man sitting at the table. When he determined that there were no additional comments, he thanked the men and dismissed them.

CHAPTER 28

Thirteen men sat in a non-descript warehouse just outside the New Orleans airport. Secrecy was crucial to their task. Very few people were even aware of their existence though their sect had existed for over one thousand years. It was not often that this group of men had been called upon to mete out justice. In their thousand years of existence, they had been called to duty fewer than fifty times. There were thousands of men in the Order. They came from different countries, different backgrounds, different values, but they all had the same purpose. That purpose was to retrieve the artifacts stolen from the Temple of Solomon by the Templar Knights, and to punish all those that had defiled these ancient relics. These relics included the Shroud of Turin, the Ark of the Covenant, and the most famous of relics, the Holy Grail.

The thirteen men sat on folding metal chairs in one of the office sections of the warehouse. The warehouse was obviously old, and Edgar questioned when the last time was that it had been used or cleaned. The carpet was a commercial loop in shades of orange and gold, reminiscent of the late 60s and early 70s. It was dirty and well-worn in some places, and stank heavily of dust and mildew. There was one office area located directly adjacent to a large warehouse with cement floors, and metal walls and ceilings. The noise from the airport was deafening when a plane took off or landed. It rattled the metal walls and echoed throughout the warehouse for several seconds after the plane had passed. It was slightly quieter in the offices, but conversation was still difficult.

Edgar stood inside the circle of men. "We know that infidels exist and walk among us. They look like us, they act like us, but they are not like us and must be punished for their crimes. We have been charged with the responsibility of identifying these people and meting out justice." He turned in the circle, looking at each person in the room. They looked at him with curiosity, excitement. This was the purpose that the group remained in existence for so many centuries. It was rare to find an infidel despite the numerous groups seeking them out, but it was even more unusual to verify one so quickly. Usually, once a person was suspected as an infidel, they were tracked for years before it could be ascertained that they deserved punishment. Edgar claimed to have identified one in less than a month. Naturally, there was some skepticism, so the group interrogated Edgar thoroughly.

Edgar did not let their scrutinizing stares or endless questioning dissuade him. He was certain of his information. He carefully explained everything he knew about Collins Sykes.

For three hours, Edgar was grilled by his brothers of the Obsidian Knights. These men were trained for this purpose. This was a fight between a sacrilegious, condemned, disbanded order and an order seeking to carry out the original sentence upon that order, and to prevent the continuing corruption resulting from their existence.

CHAPTER 29

Jewell woke up earlier than she expected. Her dreams had been plagued by shadows and danger. She was always alone, but she could sense Collin, reaching out to her, trying to find her before it was too late. She put on a robe and wandered into the living room. Collin was dozing on the couch but she couldn't find her father. She walked into the kitchen to find something for her and Collin to eat, and glanced at the calendar as she walked by. It revealed that her father had started a forty-eight hour shift at the firehouse. Due to recent events, she expected that her father would probably try to come home if he could. She knew that he would at least call. She glanced at her watch. It was five-thirty. Her father would probably call in a couple of hours when he was certain that she was awake. She was glad that he had let Collin stay.

As she sniffed at a container she heard Collin behind her. "What are you doing?"

"I thought I'd find us something to eat."

"How about going out for dinner? What do you want? The sky's the limit."

"I don't know..." she tried to think of what she was in the mood for.

"How about Outback? I'll call in an order and go pick it up."

She shrugged. "I suppose, but I'm going with you. I don't want to be left here alone." She hadn't realized how truly scared the incident at the hospital had left her. She could feel the tension in her shoulders and tried to relax.

Collin went into the office and brought back Jewell's pink laptop computer. He plopped down on the couch and started it up. Navigating to the restaurants web site, he turned the computer so that Jewell could see the menu. "Just a salad I guess." Collin looked at her.

"That's it? A salad? Fine, but I'm going to pick which one." He carried the computer into the kitchen to the phone and called the restaurant. When he came back into the living room he looked at Jewell who looked a bit peaked. "You okay?"

"I'm just worn out. Too, I'm worried about that..." she didn't want to say stalker, but couldn't think of any better term. Instead, she let the sentence trail off. "I'm just really tired."

Collin put his arm around her and pulled her so that her head was resting on his shoulder. "We'll get you fed, and then you can go back to sleep. Your dad pulled out the bed in the office and gave me some sheets and a blanket. I guess he figured that leaving me in the house with you was safer than leaving you alone." He grinned. They sat and watched the TV until it was time to leave.

The drive to the restaurant was uneventful. When they got to the restaurant they sat at Curbside delivery and listened to the radio. Jewell's eyes wandered to the Wendy's across the street; something had caught her attention. She sat up, leaning toward the window so that she could see the man getting out of the car parked at the Wendy's.

Collin was startled by Jewell's sudden movement. She had paled visibly and was shaking. He looked at her face and tried to follow the direction that she was looking. In the Wendy's parking lot, he saw a man with a black leg brace and a cane walking towards the door. His car had been parked facing the restaurant, away from where Collin and Jewell were sitting and his back was to them. Collin's gaze alternated between Jewell and the man across the street, but Jewell's eyes never wavered until the man had disappeared inside the restaurant. When the man had disappeared from view, Collin heard his own breath whoosh out in a relieved sigh. Jewell had leaned forward in her seat, her head between her knees.

"Was that him?" Collin asked rubbing her back, trying to calm her down.

"Yes." Her voice was barely a whisper.

"You're sure? You only saw him from the back. It would be pretty weird if he were here at the same time you were."

She had calmed down a little bit; her breathing was a little easier. "Maybe. Do you think he followed us here?"

Collin looked out the window at the Wendy's as he thought about Jewell's question. "I don't think so. He didn't act like he knew we were here. When we leave, we can watch to see if he follows. At least we know what his car looks like." He reached over into the glove compartment and pulled out a small pad of paper and a pen. He looked at the car, then scribbled some information on the sheet of paper and handed it back to Jewell. She looked at it.

"His license plate number?" She looked up and squinted, trying to make out the characters on the plate. "How can you see that far?"

"I've always been pretty good at stuff. I can see better than most people, hear better, I was always first in track. I never really studied either. I could read a page in my book and just remember everything it said." He shrugged. She stared at him for a minute, and then ripped the top piece of paper off the pad, and put the pad, with the pen, back in the glove compartment. Just as she finished, their food arrived. Collin thanked the waitress and handed her some cash. He handed the bag to Jewell and started the car. When he backed out of the space, he stopped his car in the aisle, ready to leave. He watched the door to the Wendy's. When the door opened, they both held their breath, but it was a mother and her daughter.

Collin drove through the parking lot to the main road. He drove slowly, watching the Wendy's in his rear view mirror. Jewell had turned to look. The side windows were tinted so it was unlikely that he could see into Collin's car. They both watched the restaurant as they drove towards 190. Collin turned right while Jewell continued to watch the restaurant. Neither of them had seen any indication that there was an attempt to follow them.

"He probably didn't see us. I think it was a coincidence. Of course, that probably means he lives around here somewhere."

"Great. So I might just run into this weirdo while I'm out grocery shopping or something?" Her voice shook on the edge of terror.

"Well, we don't know for sure. Is there some way to find out where he lives?"

"Maybe. My dad knows some of the police officers in Covington; he might be able to find something out."

"Good. We'll call him when we get back to the house."

They drove home without any additional incident. Jewell's father assured her that he would try to find out some information about him. He could call Andy with the sheriff. He would be able to let him know if Edgar lived anywhere in St. Tammany Parrish. Jewell felt a little better, but was still unable to eat. Her stomach was twisted in knots.

Collin sat on the couch. Jewell lay down with her head in his lap. He rubbed her back trying to help her relax. At the same time, he tried to send her happy thoughts. He didn't know if it would work, but he figured it wouldn't hurt. He tried to think of the most beautiful things had ever seen in his life. He thought of the glades with daffodils in Tagla Mountains in Romania, the sunset at Cinque Terre in Italy, Winchester Cathedral in England, the Piana rocky inlet and the Girolata gulf in France, Aeroe island in Denmark, and of course, Jewell McKean in Louisiana. As he thought of these beautiful places, he imagined he could feel Jewell's thoughts moving from the darkness, as if his thoughts were affecting hers. She relaxed, and was soon asleep.

As Jewell slept, she dreamt of beautiful beaches, stained glass windows, interesting doors on beautiful cottages, and a valley in the most beautiful mountains she had ever seen, dotted with thousands of white daffodils.

CHAPTER 30

On Saturday, Collin took Jewell to work, even though Ashley offered to drive. He dropped her off, and went home. He needed some sleep. He thought about Jewell having to work all night and sighed. It wouldn't do anyone any good for him to stay awake all night just because she was.

When Collin arrived home, he went into the house to let his uncle know that he was home. His uncle didn't approve of his relationship with Jewell, but seemed to be tolerating it. When he walked into the parlor, everyone stopped talking. They sat, staring at him with somber looks on their faces.

"What? Did someone die?" Collin laughed. No one laughed with him.

"Collin, we're leaving." His uncle said with little emotion. Collin knew that when his uncle said it this way, it meant they were leaving soon. He looked around and noticed for the first time the boxes stacked in the corner.

"When?"

"Tonight." Collin looked at his uncle, and then glanced around the room at the rest of the sober group. A few of them nodded, Gladys was the only one who looked like she cared about what this news would mean to Collin.

"Fine. Have a safe trip." Collin turned and started walking toward the door. His uncle caught up with him and gently grabbed him by the arm.

"Collin, you need to leave too." His tone was gentle, but the authority in his tone was unmistakable.

"Why?"

"It's…complicated."

Collin moved to a chair and sat down, with his arms crossed over his chest defiantly. "Fine, explain it then."

Collin's uncle glanced at the others in the room. *Why does he always do that*? Collin thought. Every time he asks his uncle to explain what's going on, he looks at everyone else. Apparently, everyone was in on the secret but Collin.

"I can't." His uncle replied, defeated.

"Well it's settled then. I'm staying. If I can't stay in the house, I'll find an apartment. I'll get a job, I'll keep in touch." He stood, waiting for his uncle to try to stop him.

"I'm sorry you feel that way." His uncle sighed. "Your aunt Gladys made spaghetti and her huge meatballs. We were just getting ready to eat. At least sit down and have dinner with us."

Collin looked at his uncle, suspicious. He knew that this was just going to be one more attempt to convince him to leave with them, but as he started to tell his uncle that he didn't want dinner, Collin felt his stomach rumble. He could smell the garlic and spices drifting down the hall. "Fine. But I want you to know now; I'm not leaving with you."

"I understand."

They all moved into the dining room and sat down. Gladys and Percy went into the kitchen to fix plates for everyone. Percy brought in Collin's plate last, with his own, and sat down next to him. Collin glared at him before taking a bite of his food. His uncle sat and watched him eat. All of a sudden, Collin started to feel lightheaded. As he looked across the table toward his aunt the room started to spin and he fell sideways in his chair. Kendryck, on his other side, caught him and laid him gently on the floor.

He heard his aunt Gladys moving around the table. "What's wrong with him?" Her voice was filled with fear and worry.

His Uncle Percy's voice seemed to come from far away. "He'll be fine."

As he slipped into unconsciousness, he heard Gladys' voice, "You drugged him?" It was more an accusation than a question.

*   *   *

"You know, you're going to have to tell him," Gladys called to Percy who was in the back of the van monitoring Collin who had been switched to an inhaled anesthesia for the duration of the trip. "You should have told him years ago when you first figured it out."

"I wasn't sure. I didn't want to tell him something like that and then have it turn out wrong."

"Oh baloney. There've been plenty of signs. You just didn't want to admit it was true. After the accident though. You should have told him then. There was no doubt after that."

"Well, he was...fragile. I didn't want to upset him." Percy replied from the back.

"That's crazy and you know it. I don't know why you don't want to tell the boy."

"Because if I don't tell him, maybe it won't be true." Percy mumbled under his breath.

"I heard that. Percy, admit it. If you had just told him from the beginning, maybe he wouldn't be in this position. It's not your duty to live his life. He has a right to make his own decisions, right or wrong. But it's not fair to let him make those decisions without having all of the facts. Haven't you noticed that ever since the accident he knows you're keeping something from him? Do you think that prolonging the inevitable will make it any easier for him to understand, or to accept? The longer you wait, the worse it gets. He knows and he's going to find out, one way or another. It would be better if he heard it from you. If he has to figure it out by himself, he'll just resent you when he finds out you've known all along." Impassioned, Gladys didn't realize that she was going faster. The van hit a bump.

"Hey! Slow down, will you! It's bad enough that I need to do this while we're moving, I don't need you making it worse!"

Gladys eased up on the accelerator, "Well, maybe if you'd told him the truth, both of you could be sitting in seats like normal people, rather than drugging and kidnapping your own nephew!"

"I did not kidnap him. It was for his own good and whether he knows it or not, it's better for Jewell this way. When those people find out we're gone, they'll leave Jewell alone and go back to being lunatics! Besides, I haven't known all along. You know as well as I do that he should have been a *skip*."

Percy laid his hand lovingly on Collin's arm. "He should have been a *skip*." He mumbled, wishing for something he knew would never be true.

"Shoulda, woulda, coulda!" She retorted. "Have you tested him for telepathy?"

"No." Percy replied like a child being scolded for forgetting his homework.

"If you had tested him, you could have had Kendryck help him to develop it. Now it'll take years longer, and he'll never be as talented."

"I know. I just wanted to do what was best for him. I don't want him to end up like his parents. I've made so many mistakes in my life. I don't know how I could have lived this long and still be so ignorant! I just couldn't hurt him like that," Percy was nearly frustrated to tears. Gladys let the matter drop, nothing more could be done about it until they reached the House.

The drive was long. Kendryck drove Collin's car, Dot and Carl were in Percy's SUV with John and Ann. Percy was in the back of a rented van with Collin and what medical equipment he could squeeze into the van comfortably, while Gladys drove. Every four hours or so, they stopped for gas, stretched, and swapped drivers. The only two that never took a turn at driving were Collin, who was in an induced coma, and Percy, who was the only one qualified to monitor Collin's condition while under anesthesia.

When they finally reached the House, nearly twenty four hours later, everyone was tired. The House hadn't been opened in several years and the air inside was thick with time. While Ann and Dot went around the house opening windows, Kendryck and John carried Collin upstairs to one of the bedrooms. Gladys ran ahead, carrying a set of clean linens and pulling protective covers off of furniture, trying not to stir up too much dust. In Collin's room, she made the bed quickly so that John and Kendryck could lay Collin in the bed.

Carl and Percy followed behind, carrying a portable pulse oximeter so that Percy could keep an eye on Collin's pulse rate and oxygen levels. Percy pulled a chair up next to the bed and sat down.

"You can't stay up with him. You've already been up for almost twenty four hours. How much longer do you think you can keep this up?" Gladys looked at him with weary eyes.

"I have to. I did this to him; I need to make sure he's okay before I leave him alone."

"Can I bring you a cup of coffee?" Gladys understood what Percy felt. She was worried about Collin too. Not only about his condition now, but what he would face when he woke up. Already Collin was beginning to stir, showing signs that the anesthesia was wearing off.

"Please." Percy said, rubbing his face with his hands. He took up one of Collins hands, measuring the pulse rate with his fingers. Then he touched his own cheek with the back of Collin's hand. "I wish that things were different, boy. I really do." He carefully ran a hand over Collins peach fuzz hair, shaved to reveal the cut from the accident. The scar, which should still be an angry red, was nearly impossible to see, looking as if the injury were years old.

By the time Gladys returned, Collin was moaning and starting to move his head from side to side. She had two cups of coffee, one she handed to Percy, the other she set on the dresser while she pulled a chair up to the other side of Collin's bed. She took her cup of coffee, and sat down.

"Gladys, you can go to bed. I can handle this." Percy said as he watched Gladys settle in next to Collin.

"I don't trust you." She responded succinctly. Percy shrugged. If Gladys wanted to stay, so be it.

*   *   *

Collin tried to open his eyes. His eyelids felt like they were made of lead. His head hurt. He felt like the battle of Thermopylae had been fought in his head, and his brain was King Leonidas. He moaned, moving his hands. He tried to think about what had happened. He thought back to his car accident. Was he still in the hospital? Had anything over the last three weeks actually happened? He carefully moved both arms, and then flexed his knees. No, not the accident. His thoughts were a fog. He searched for the last clear memory he had. Jewell. He had driven Jewell to work and dropped her off. What had happened after that? Suddenly, he remembered dinner. Maybe he got sick, it could be food poisoning. His stomach was upset, and felt empty. His mouth was also dry and felt like he had been sucking on cotton balls. He licked his lips and felt a glass of water touch them. He tried to gulp the water, but it just trickled in slowly. He wanted to grab the glass from whoever was holding it and pour it down his parched throat, but he couldn't lift his hands. Too soon, the glass was taken from his mouth.

"Collin? Can you hear me boy?" Percy cautiously asked. Collin tried to speak. He could move his lips, but the only sound that escaped them was a slight moan.

"Collin? If you can hear me, squeeze my hand." His uncle gave a slight squeeze to the hand he was holding. Collin realized then that the reason he couldn't raise his hand was because his uncle was holding it. Collin gave his uncle's hand a light squeeze.

"Can he hear you?" Collin heard Gladys' voice on his other side.

"He's coming around. Sevoflurane wears off relatively quickly. He should be okay before too long."

Sevoflurane. Collin searched his memories. He had heard his uncle speak of this before. What was it? It was...the memory escaped him, just like all of the memories following dinner. His uncle brought the glass to his lips again. This time, his uncle allowed Collin to drink a bit more. When his uncle pulled the glass away again, Collin relaxed back into the pillow, trying to find sleep.

Jewell! The thought suddenly hit him. He could almost feel Jewell turning to face him, stopping as she rushed through her day at the hospital. His uncle had wanted him to leave Louisiana, but Collin didn't want to go. His uncle hadn't argued. Collin winced. He should have known. His uncle didn't put up a fight because he knew that Collin was leaving, one way or another. Collin forced his eyes open and worked to focus them so he could see the room surrounding him. He could sense the air was different; no longer the humid Louisiana heat, but a dry desert heat. His eyes focused enough for him to see the color of the room. It was a sage green. There were no rooms this color in the Louisiana plantation home.

"Where…" Collin's voice was hoarse, barely a whisper.

"Shhhhh." His uncle answered him. "Just rest."

"Jewell." He choked out.

"We'll talk about that later, when you're feeling better." His uncle's voice was irritatingly soothing. Collin wanted to jump up and scream, but thanks to his uncle's drugs, he could barely think, let alone move.

"Feel…fine."

"You just get some rest. I'll come back and check on you later." His uncle stood, brushing Collin's head before bending down to kiss Collin's forehead. "I love you. This is for the best." Collin didn't hear him walking out. Carpet, he thought; not the hardwood he had grown used to in the past couple of years. He heard the latch on the door snick as it closed.

CHAPTER 31

Jewell walked out of the hospital and glanced to the spot where Collin always waited for her. She was dumbfounded that he wasn't there, leaning across the wall, looking like the romantic lead in an old film noir. Ashley noticed too.

"Didn't he say he would be here to pick you up?"

"Yeah. Even when he doesn't take me home, he's here. Especially with everything that's going on, I know he should be here." Jewell's voice was worried.

"Well, maybe he ran into traffic," Ashley joked. Jewell didn't laugh. "C'mon. Maybe he saw the car and decided to meet us there."

Jewell knew that Collin wouldn't be there. She could feel it. She suddenly realized that she felt an empty spot inside her chest. It was the same empty feeling she had felt when Collin had disappeared from the hospital. Collin was gone. He wasn't coming back. She fought to hold the tears back. Jewell scanned the cars in the garage, looking for Collin's familiar silver corvette knowing she wouldn't find it. When they reached the car, Collin wasn't there.

"I'm sure he's on his way. Do you want me to wait with you?"

"No, he's not coming. Will you drive me home?" Jewell's voice was dead, devoid of all emotion. Ashley recognized the voice.

"Hang on…I…I forgot something. Wait here, I'll be right back." Ashley turned and started walking swiftly toward the hospital. Once she had disappeared behind the door, she pulled out her cell phone. "Tommy? Hey. We've got a problem. Collin's gone again." She listened for a minute. "I don't know, but he wasn't here this morning like he usually is. I just wanted to let you know. I'll keep her at my place until you get home."

She hung up the phone. She walked quickly back to the car, not wanting to leave Jewell alone for too long. Jewell was standing in the same place she had left her, her tote on the ground next to her feet. Ashley couldn't tell if Jewell had set it down, or it had simply slipped off her arm. She stood next to her bag in front of the car staring at nothing.

"Not good, not good, not good." Ashley muttered to herself as she walked back to the car. "Okay, are you ready?" Ashley asked in a cheerful voice. Jewell didn't say anything. Ashley walked over to the passenger side of the car and opened the door for Jewell. She watched Jewell get in the car, without retrieving her bag. Jewell sat in the car, staring forward. Ashley bent down and picked up Jewell's bag. She walked around to the driver's side of the car and got in, throwing both bags in the back seat. When she looked at Jewell, she was sitting in the same position staring out the window at emptiness. Jewell hadn't fastened her seatbelt so, sighing, Ashley reached over Jewell and grabbed the seatbelt. Jewell didn't move. Ashley started the car, and they drove silently home. When Ashley pulled up to her apartment, Jewell didn't ask why Ashley didn't take her home. She just walked in, following Ashley into the living room.

Ashley went into the kitchen to grab two Cokes from the fridge. She opened Jewell's and set it down on the table in front of her. "I'm sure he'll be back. Something must have happened; he probably had a flat tire or something." Ashley tried to sound cheerful.

"No, he won't." Suddenly Jewell sighed and reached for the Coke that Ashley had brought her. Her stomach hurt, but the Coke tasted good. "No, he won't be back. "

"Why don't you call him?" Ashley handed Jewell her cell phone.

"Can't." The answer was short, pronounced as a resolute fact.

"Why?"

"I don't know his number. I don't even know where he lives. Well...lived. He's not there anymore. He's left."

"You mean you dated this guy for like a month and you don't know his phone number or where he lives?" Ashley was incredulous. Getting a guy's phone number was always the first thing she did when she was dating someone.

"Never needed it. He was always there when I wanted him to be there. It's like he always knew what I needed. I thought..." Her voice trailed off.

"You thought what?"

"It's stupid. You know how you always tell me that you can't change a guy, you need to accept him for who he is, and if you can't, then he's not the right guy for you?" Jewell's voice was starting to show a little emotion.

"Yeah..." Ashley answered, unsure of where Jewell was going with this. She couldn't imagine what needed to be changed about Collin. As far as she could tell, he was the perfect guy.

"Well, I guess I never told you this, but he never stays in one place. He lives someplace for a couple of years, and then he moves on. He used to tell me that his uncle didn't approve of our relationship because he thought Collin was growing too attached...I guess Collin finally agreed with him and decided it was time to move on."

"But without saying anything? Without at least talking to you? Oh, that is so rude!" Ashley was starting to see some faults with Collin.

When Tommy called, Ashley drove Jewell home. Jewell sat quietly, looking out the window. She didn't say anything for the whole ten minutes they were in the car. When they arrived at the house Tommy walked down the path towards the car. Ashley rolled down the window as he approached.

"How is she?" he talked quietly so Jewell wouldn't overhear him.

"I don't know. She's hurt. She's acting like she accepts it, like she knew it was coming. She's putting up a good front, but I don't buy it." Ashley shrugged.

"Thanks." Tommy stood up and tapped the top of the car as he moved away so that Ashley could leave. He watched Ashley pull out of the drive then turned to go into the house. By the time he got inside, Jewell was already in her room, sitting on her bed.

"Hey. Can I come in?" Jewell's dad rapped gently on the doorframe, looking in at her through the open door.

"Sure dad."

Tommy came in and sat on the bed next to his daughter. "You okay?"

"Yeah dad, I'm fine. He told me in the beginning that he didn't like to get too close to people. I guess it was too much, too fast. I mean, it really was crazy, wasn't it?" She forced out a laugh.

"Do you want to talk about it?"

"Talk about what? It's no big deal, really." She could hear the tremor in her own voice; she couldn't talk about this now; maybe not ever. "I'm really tired dad. Can we save this for tomorrow?"

Tommy stared at his daughter, trying to judge Jewell's true feelings. Finally, he leaned forward and gave her a hug. I'll see you later then."

"Night dad."

"Good night Jewell. I love you." He shut the door quietly behind him when he left.

That evening, Ashley came to pick Jewell up. She arrived early so that Jewell wouldn't leave on her own. Both Tommy and Ashley were still apprehensive with Jewell's apparent acceptance of Collin's disappearance. Jewell grabbed a package of Pop Tarts out of the box in the cupboard. She kissed her father on the head, as she left to meet Ashley.

Jewell sat down in the car and opened her breakfast. She handed one to Ashley who set it on her leg until she had pulled out of the driveway onto the main road.

"So, did you do anything after I dropped you off?" Ashley was trying to keep the conversation going.

"I just went to bed."

Ashley tried to think of something else to say. "Do you want to do something tomorrow? Maybe go see a movie or something?"

"I don't know. I think I'm just going to hang out at the house."

"Cool, I'll rent a movie and come over. What do you want to see?"

"I don't care. Whatever."

"K. I'll pick up a couple, that way we can choose." Jewell turned to look out the window at Lake Pontchartrain as they drove across the Causeway.

Jewell threw herself into the cases that came in, trying to stay busy. Everything was pretty normal; at least it had been busy enough to keep her mind off of Collin.

"Jewell!" It was Collin. He sounded scared? Startled? Worried? Jewell turned to look before she realized that she hadn't heard the sound coming from behind her, but from inside her head. It was like she was hearing Collin calling her, but only in her mind. She stood for a moment, surprised. The sound had been so real, not like the voice she often imagined when she thought of him. She could hear his muddled European accent that she thought was sexy along with the emotions in his voice. She glanced at her watch, four forty-five, still an hour and fifteen minutes of work. She felt tears falling from the corners of her eyes. She wiped them away with the back of her hand as she continued what she was doing.

CHAPTER 32

As the sedative wore off, Collin started to remember things. Sevoflurane was an anesthetic gas. No wonder he felt so out of it. He looked around. He didn't recognize the room; he hadn't been here before. He tried to sit up so that he could get a better look at where he was, but when he sat up the room started to spin. He glanced toward the windows. The curtains were closed. It was dark outside; he wouldn't be able to see anything anyway. The last thing he remembered was Aunt Gladys' spaghetti. That made sense; the acid in the tomatoes and the garlic would cover the taste of whatever Mickey Finn his uncle had slipped him. He couldn't believe it. His uncle had drugged him! No wonder Uncle Percy had been so disposed to let him stay. Uncle Percy figured it would be easier to drug him than to argue.

He closed his eyes. His head hurt and his stomach was queasy. When he started to feel better, he opened his eyes and looked around as much as he could without sitting up. The room was large. There was a tall chest of drawers next to the bed and a mahogany wardrobe opposite the bed. The walls were painted a sage green, with a parchment colored carpet. He pushed the covers down to see that he was still dressed in the same clothes as he had been wearing the other evening. He pulled his wrist to his face to see if he was still wearing his watch; he was. He stared, trying to focus on the tiny numbers on the face. It was six o'clock. Based on the faint glow starting to seep through the curtains, it was six o'clock in the morning, but what day? He couldn't read the tiny numbers of the date at the three position on the watch. He tried for several minutes until his head started to hurt, before giving up. He picked up the glass of water on the nightstand and took a long drink before realizing what he was doing. He set it down and eyed it suspiciously. It seemed he couldn't trust anyone anymore. He tried again to sit up. The room tilted and swayed, but at least it didn't spin. He waited until the room stopped moving, and then put his legs over the side of the bed.

"Oh good, you're up." Uncle Percy came through the door, smiling.

Collin scowled at his uncle. "You drugged me, and then you kidnapped me!"

"I did not drug you. I sedated you." Percy sat down on the bed next to Collin. Collin tried to stand up to move away from his uncle, but immediately collapsed back onto the bed.

"Still a little woozy? Well, that's normal." He picked up Collin's wrist between his thumb and first two fingers to check Collin's pulse. Collin jerked his hand away. The gesture was weak, but he had made his point. "I'm sorry, but there just wasn't time to explain. We were in danger, all of us. I thought it would be easier this way. I want you to understand, I couldn't leave you there alone."

"I wasn't alone. I had Jewell!" Collin said through clenched teeth.

Percy sighed. "I know, and that was the problem. Your relationship with Jewell was putting her in danger."

"What? How?"

"The man that was stalking Jewell was after you, not her."

"What are you talking about? Why?"

"Because of what you are." Percy sighed as he realized it was time to tell Collin the truth.

Collin stood up. This time he was able to hold his feet, but needed to lean against the nightstand next to the bed to maintain his balance. "And you left her there? She's in danger, and you left her? How could you?" Collin was incensed.

"Now that you're gone, she'll be safe. Sheriff Payne and his faction will see to it.

"Sheriff Payne and his *faction?* What's that supposed to mean?" Collin was getting more agitated. He needed to get back to Jewell and his uncle was talking in riddles.

"Sit down boy," Percy said simply, patting the bed next to him. "You are in no condition to leave right now. I think that it's time we had that talk you've wanted to have."

Collin glared at his uncle suspiciously before sitting back down on the bed. "Go on then. I'm listening."

"Because of what you are, of what I am, of what your parents were; we are hunted." Percy sighed.

"The longer we stay in one place, the greater the risk of discovery. Because of your accident, we were discovered. We had allies who tried to help us, but apparently their attempts were unsuccessful. We should've left when we took you from the hospital, but I got careless. I didn't want to move you when you were still injured. And then, there was Jewell. I never wanted to deny you love, but I should've told you before you became so…attached." Percy hung his head. "It wasn't fair to you, and it wasn't fair to Jewell. And for that, I'm sorry. You can't imagine how much this hurts me."

Collin looked at his uncle. As usual, his uncle was evading the subject. "So who's hunting us?"

"Most governments, scientists, religious groups…Anyone who finds out what we are."

"And what exactly are we?"

Percy turned to his nephew. "Collin, I am eight hundred and ninety four years old."

"Excuse me?"

"Collin, we are immortal. Well, not exactly immortal…"

Collin didn't let his uncle finish his thought. He jumped up from the bed and barely caught himself as a wave of dizziness and nausea washed over him like a tidal wave; an effect of both the medicine, and the insanity that his uncle was telling him. "I always thought you were a little crazy, but I just thought of it as eccentricity. I didn't know you were certifiable!"

"Collin, sit down before you pass out."

Collin didn't sit down. "So let's pretend for a moment that you are immortal. So what if they find us?"

"Collin, Area 51; that was because of us. Vlad the Impaler, the original Count Dracula, the Salem Witch trials, that was because of us too."

"Oh my God! You're telling me you're a vampire or something? You really are nuts." Collin tried to stumble to the door, but was short of reaching it as he fell hard to the floor. "We've been running from myths and fairytales my whole life!" He pushed himself up into a kneeling position.

Percy walked over to Collin and bent down, gently trying to help his nephew off the floor and back to the bed. Collin jerked away, crawling toward the door, trying to escape this man that he now realized he didn't really know. Just as he escaped his uncle's grasp, the door opened. Gladys came in followed by Kendryck, Carl, Dot, Ann, and John. He shrunk away from them, pushing himself protectively into a corner.

"Collin," Gladys said gently.

"It's okay Collin." Kendryck added.

"So you're all in on this? You all think you're some sort of immortal vampire freaks or something? What, do you drink your blood in private? Do you shop at the local blood bank?"

Percy held his hand up, signaling the others to let him handle it. "Collin, you are one of us, as were your parents."

"So what, I'm supposed to go out and make my first kill to complete the change? Or do I just need to drink your blood?" Collin had calmed down a little, his initial fear replaced by anger.

Percy sat on the floor, keeping several feet between him and Collin so he would be less threatening.

"I was born in 1114 in what was then Normandy. My family name was Kilkenny, and my given name was Peredur. When I was 16, I joined the Templar Knights.

"While serving, I had an accident where I should have died, but did not. I served the knights for nearly 200 years. When King Philip accused the Templars of heresy in the early 1300s, I was brought before the accusers as proof that the Templars had found the Holy Grail and had used it to grant me everlasting life, thus condemning me a heretic and accusing me of defiling the Grail. I was imprisoned, awaiting execution when I was rescued by a group of fleeing Templar Knights who took an oath to protect me, and those like me. I changed my name to Percival Knighton, after the knight of King Arthur's court and escaped to Scotland. Sheriff Payne, as you may have guessed, is a Templar, as is Dr. Babineaux. They and their order are duty bound to protect us which is why they will protect Jewell.

"When I met my wife in 1331, she was mortal, like Jewell, but chose to live her life with me. We moved often, as we do now, so as not to raise suspicion. Our flight brought us to London in 1347." He looked at Collin. "As a history major, I would assume you know how I lost my wife."

Collin stared at his uncle, unable to speak. He swallowed, hard. "1348, the Black Death swept London, killing millions," he whispered.

Percy nodded slowly. "It was December, 1348. Avelyn was one of its early victims. She was only twenty seven." Percy was crying, the pain as fresh as if she had died yesterday instead of nearly 700 years ago.

"What did you do?" Collin had forgotten his earlier incredulity.

"Well, I tried to kill myself. I started working with the priests, visiting plague victims in hopes of catching the plague myself. I wasn't so lucky. When that didn't work I threw myself from the cliffs, knowing that my Avelyn was waiting for me on the other side."

"What happened?" Collin asked.

"It hurt," Percy answered acerbically. "I was encouraged as the tide came in and I found myself completely submerged, but in a wretched twist of fate, the tide receded before I died of suffocation. I laid there for three days before a local fisherman found me, and took me back to his home where I stayed until I had recovered enough to escape his hospitality. Like I said, we are, for the most part, immortal, as my suicide attempt, and your most recent escapade has displayed."

"What do you mean, for the most part?"

"Well, we do age, just more slowly than everyone else. It's different for each of us, but on average we age about one year for every twenty. Eventually, just like everyone else, we die of old age. We can drown, though as I discovered, it takes an unreasonably long time; fire will eventually kill us but as with anyone else, if we don't die from the burns, the pain is excruciating. Decapitation is the quickest way to ensure a premature death. That's about it."

Collin's hand involuntarily rubbed at his throat as he thought back to his parents. They had been decapitated, and then the house was burned. Someone hadn't been taking any chances. "But, I'm 23 and I look my age, well, maybe a little young, but I don't look like I'm only a year old."

"The Lazarus Gene, the key to this...disease, lies dormant until after puberty, though there are other signs that are present before that. The rapid healing, a photographic or near photographic memory, we tend to be stronger and faster than everyone else. Not excessively, but enough to make it noticeable. And some of us have other..." he paused, searching for the right word, "talents. The aging doesn't begin to slow until after the Lazarus Gene becomes active, usually between the ages of sixteen and twenty-five."

"What kinds of talents?" Collin asked, curious.

"Well, telepathy is common, but there are other unusual traits as well; traits that most people would refer to as ESP."

"So, because both of my parents were, well...were like this, I am too? Why didn't you tell me before? Why keep it a secret?" Collin's anger had been replaced with curiosity.

"Because most children born to our kind, even those exhibiting the trait, are considered *skips*. In other words, one or more of the factors is missing. In some, the Lazarus Gene is never triggered, but lies dormant throughout their lives. These people live abnormally long lives, super centenarians who live to be over one-hundred years old." Collin's uncle paused for a minute. "Even though both of your parents were carriers of the disease, there was only a slim chance, perhaps one in ten million that you would exhibit all of the traits as well, *and* the Lazarus Gene would activate. You should have been a *skip*."

"But I wasn't." Collin replied succinctly.

"No." His uncle's response was short, poignant.

Collin's uncle slowly stood. His face was weary and filled with pain. He walked slowly to where Collin sat, still huddled in the corner, and reached his hand down to his nephew. Collin took his uncle's hand and allowed his uncle to help him stand. His uncle put his arm around Collin's waist to support him as they walked slowly to the bed.

"You still need some rest, and I haven't slept in..." Collin's uncle thought for a moment, "nearly forty-eight hours." He looked at the rest of the people still standing in the room, watching the exchange between uncle and nephew. "Gladys, you need some sleep too. Dot, can you bring him some breakfast? Nothing heavy. Some fruit and toast. Maybe some scrambled eggs." Dot nodded and hurried from the room, followed by the others. "I'll let that sink in a little. You'll have questions I'm sure. We'll talk more later." He leaned over and gently kissed Collin on the forehead before walking slowly from the room, his head hung dejectedly, a beaten man.

Collin lay in bed thinking about what his uncle had told him. It couldn't be true. There was no such thing as immortality; well, not physical immortality. Of course there was religious immortality, the idea of life after death, and hypothetical immortality, living on through one's fame, but humans had been yearning for immortality since the dawn of man. There were stories of immortality in every culture. The Iliad, Gilgamesh, Ponce de Leon, the Holy Grail; maybe these weren't just stories; maybe they had some basis in fact.

What else had his uncle said? Other traits? He had always been better at sports than all of his friends. And telepathy; he thought that having telepathic powers would be really cool. It just seemed so unbelievable. Everyone knew that physical immortality was not achievable, at least not yet. He remembered the movie Highlander. "There can be only one," he said to himself with a small laugh. Then he thought about what Ramirez had told McLeod about McLeod's mortal wife, "You must leave her, brother... When Shakiko died I was shattered. I would save you that pain. Please, let Heather go." Wasn't that exactly what his uncle had been trying to tell him? Collin jumped when Dot opened the door, bringing him his breakfast.

"How are you feeling honey?" Dot asked, carefully placing the bed tray over his legs. Collin hadn't realized how hungry he was. Well, he thought irritably, of course he was hungry; he hadn't eaten in over twenty four hours thanks to his uncle.

"A little better, I guess. A little hungry, actually." Dot smiled and started to leave. "Wait. Can you sit with me while I eat?"

"Sure." She pulled up the chair that Percy had been sitting in earlier and placed it next to the bed. She sat quietly, watching Collin pick at his food. "Did you want to talk about something, or did you just want the company?" She smiled warmly.

Collin ate a strawberry and then took a bite of scrambled eggs before answering. "I think...I want to talk." Dot waited patiently while Collin ate a few more bites of his breakfast. "Is my uncle crazy? Is that what's really going on here? You all wanted me to know that Uncle Percy is delusional?"

Dot looked into Collin's eyes as she laid her hand gently on his leg. "No, honey. Your Uncle isn't crazy. We've all wanted to tell you for years, but your uncle was just so sure that you would be a *skip*. He wanted so badly for it to be true. You don't know how hard it was for him to admit that you were afflicted."

Collin nodded. "You? Are you immortal, or whatever, too?"

Dot nodded. "We all are. Everyone in the *Family*."

"So then, if this is genetic, are we all really related?"

"No. It's like any other genetic disease. Many people can have it, but that doesn't necessarily mean that they're related."

Collin sat quietly for a moment, thinking about what Dot had told him. "Why...why do you all talk about it like it's a disease? I mean, isn't immortality what everyone wants? Isn't it humanity's ultimate desire; to achieve immortality in some form or another? Isn't that why we have religion?"

"Maybe some people want it. The grass is always greener..." Dot shrugged. "But that's what it is Collin. It's a genetic mutation, like a cancer. It's not normal. And it's not..." Dot trailed off.

"It's not as wonderful as you thought it would be?" Collin finished for her.

Dot shook her head and started to get up.

"Wait." Dot paused as Collin called her back. "How many are there? How many of you...of us?"

"In the *Family* there are not quite two hundred. We tend to stick together. That's enough for now. Finish up." She walked quietly from the room, closing the door behind her.

Collin carefully set the tray on the other side of the bed and got up. He didn't feel too bad. He walked to the window and pulled the curtains back. The view was breathtaking. He stared across a desert landscape, beautiful in its bareness, against a backdrop of majestic mountain peaks. He turned when he heard the door open.

"Do you feel well enough to come downstairs?" His uncle was standing in the doorway.

"Yeah, sure. I guess." Collin walked into a hallway painted in light earth tones. He followed his uncle through a large kitchen and into a sitting room with a large fireplace on the far end. The window shades were open displaying a yard with a pool, landscaped to look as if it was a natural oasis in the desert surrounding it. Everyone was waiting, an impromptu meeting. He sat down in an overstuffed suede chair and looked around the room.

"Well, what do you want to know?" Kendryck started the conversation.

"Where are we?"

"Just outside of Tucson." Carl answered. Collin nodded, surveying the group surrounding him.

"And you all feel the same? That coming here was necessary?" Everyone nodded. "When can I leave?"

"What?" His uncle was clearly surprised by this question.

"When can I leave? I need to get back to Jewell."

His uncle was momentarily speechless. "Didn't you listen to anything we told you? You can't go back. You need to forget about Jewell."

"I don't see how that's your decision."

"It's not yours either Collin! If I hadn't been selfish, Avelyn wouldn't have died. You have no right to do to Jewell what I did to Avelyn. If you truly love her, you'll let her go now, before it's too late."

"That's between me and her Uncle Percy. I think she has a right to know the truth and make her decision based on that."

"That's not all. You're putting her in danger by being with her. We think the man stalking her is one of the Obsidian Knights, the same group that killed your parents."

"Excuse me? The who?" Collin was getting exasperated. He needed to get back to Jewell.

"The Obsidian Knights. They were formed in the 1300's by order of King Phillip IV with the specific task of obtaining evidence to prove the accusations of heresy brought by the King and supported by the Catholic Church. The Obsidian Knights continue to look for people like us. We…" he gestured around the room, "are summarily executed for drinking from the Holy Grail to obtain everlasting life."

"Great. So you're saying that my girlfriend, because of me, is being stalked by some religious fanatics that think I drank from a mythical cup? How do they know I didn't just go swimming in the Fountain of Youth?" The more Collin heard, the more he knew that he had to get back to Jewell, at least to warn her. "So what about these Templar Knights? Where are they?"

"Sheriff Payne is overseeing Jewell's protection. The Obsidian Knights will probably lose interest in a week or two when they don't find you."

"Probably?" Collin looked at his uncle unconvinced.

His uncle shrugged. "The point is we need to think of the *Family* first."

Collin had had enough. He got up from the chair and started walking around the house looking for his keys. He was in an unfamiliar place so he quickly became frustrated. Gladys found Collin sitting in the dining room with his head in his hands. She walked up to him and put her hand on his back. He looked up at her, his eyes glistening with tears. She placed a set of car keys on the table in front of him and walked away.

Collin slipped the keys into his pocket and went back into the bedroom where he had been when he first regained consciousness. He looked in the drawers of the bureau and found his clothes, neatly arranged. He pulled out a clean set of clothes, and wandered down the hall looking for a bathroom. After he had showered, he felt a little better. He pulled the keys out of the jeans he had been wearing and slipped them into his pocket. He looked around the room and found a small suitcase in the closet. He placed it on the bed and packed it with as many clothes as he could fit in the bag. He set the bag inside the closet, and walked back into the living room where his family was watching television. The TV was on the far wall, facing away from the doorway, but the living room was adjacent to the front door. He wandered around the house until he found a side door, leading into a huge garage on the opposite side of the house.

He went back to his room and picked up the suitcase. He walked back to the garage and slipped out of the house. His car was parked in the driveway behind the other cars. He got into his car, and started it, wincing at the sound as the engine revved. He sat for a moment, watching the front door. When no one came out, he shifted his car into reverse, and backed out of the driveway.

Once on the road, he didn't know which way to go. He turned right, driving until he found a service station where he purchased a map of Tucson and asked directions to the nearest airport. He was back in New Orleans by eight. He rented a car, opting for something nondescript rather than his usual choice. He had noticed that he still had a key to the New Orleans House on his keychain so he drove there. He half expected someone to be waiting for him, whether his uncle, or one of the mysterious Obsidian Knights. But when he arrived, the house was empty, looking just as it had when he had last been there two days ago.

He went to the back of the house, to the servants' quarters where he stayed before. He set his alarm for five, planning to drive to the hospital in the morning to wait for Jewell. If she wasn't there, he would drive to her house. He lay down on the bed and closed his eyes.

Collin fell asleep quickly, despite having been asleep for over twenty-four hours the day before. Collin dreamed of Jewell. Initially, his dreams were pleasant. He dreamt of the two of them together. They were happy, they were both young. Soon however, he began to sleep more fitfully, his dreams unpleasant. They were running, huge black shadows chasing them. As fast as they ran, the shadows moved faster, always gaining on them. When the shadows reached them, they were plunged into blackness so deep that he couldn't see his hand in front of his face. He called for Jewell, there was no answer. Abruptly, the scene changed. He was sitting in front of an old woman. She was crying, apologizing over and over again. He held her hand, trying to soothe her. When she looked up, he saw that it was Jewell; she was apologizing for growing old, leaving him behind.

As he drove to the hospital the next morning, he thought about his dreams. Then he thought about the story his uncle had shared with him. If he stayed with Jewell, would he put her in danger? Would he put her family in danger? Would he put his *Family* in danger? As he drove into the garage at the hospital, he no longer had the resolve of this morning. Instead, he realized that his uncle was right; he had to leave her, to let her live a normal life. But first, he told himself, he would make sure she was safe. Just look at her one more time, but without letting her know he was there.

He parked his car near the employee entrance and watched as employees filed out the doors. Jewell was not among them. She must not have worked last night. He was a bit disturbed that no one had asked him why he was there, but he thought that perhaps it was because Jewell wasn't working, and since she was the target, security was not as careful. He left the garage, turning towards the Causeway leading to Jewell's house.

CHAPTER 33

"He's only been gone for three days. What do you mean 'get over it'?" Jewell was irritated that her best friend wasn't even supporting her.

"C'mon Jewell; you know that's not what I meant. I just meant…you need to keep going. It's not going to do you any good to stay in bed all day. I want to go to the Aquarium and I don't want to go by myself. Neither of us has been there since Katrina. Let's go." Ashley gave Jewell her most pathetic, needy, pleading look. "I let you stay in bed all day yesterday feeling sorry for yourself. You need to get out and do something."

Jewell didn't want to go to the aquarium; she didn't want to do anything. But looking at Ashley standing there, she knew that if she didn't go, Ashley would stand there all day; it wasn't going to change the fact that Collin was gone, but Ashley was right, lying in bed feeling sorry for herself wasn't going to make anything better. "Fine. It might be good to get out. At least the aquarium is one thing we didn't do together. Maybe it'll take my mind off of him for a while. Let me take a quick shower."

Ashley put down the magazine she had been leafing through when Jewell came back into the bedroom. "That's my girl!" Ashley handed Jewell a white sleeveless Polo top and a pair of floral shorts.

"Where'd these come from?" Jewell asked pulling on the shorts.

"I'm getting fat. They don't fit me anymore." She shrugged.

Ashley put the shirt on and buttoned it up. "Let me brush my teeth and blow-dry my hair." Jewell walked slowly back to the bathroom.

Ashley pulled open Jewell's closet and started sorting through her shoes. She sighed at the collection of shoes that looked like they belonged to a twelve year old. Finally she found a pair of cute white strappy sandals. She pulled them out of the closet and waited for Jewell to come back. When Jewell came back to her room, Ashley handed her the sandals, "here, put these on and we'll go."

Jewell stared at the shoes for a minute. "No, not these," she said quietly. She put them back in the closet and pulled out her white Keds.

"What was wrong with those, they would've looked cute…" Ashley looked at Jewell's face. "Oh, you're right, the Keds are more practical. I don't know what I was thinking." Ashley silently scolded herself. She should have known that Jewell would have never bought those shoes for herself, they were too stylish. They must have been one of the pairs that Collin had bought for her.

Jewell pulled on her shoes and they walked out to the driveway. Ashley had parked her Corolla on the street so they could take Jewell's car. "So when are you going to get a car as stylish as your clothes?" Jewell asked, opening the driver's side door to get in.

"As soon as I can afford a Nissan Z convertible." Ashley answered bluntly, pulling her door closed. Jewell carefully backed out of the driveway and drove to the end of the street. Neither of them noticed the silver Mazda sedan pulling into traffic behind them.

Collin followed Jewell's car as she turned right onto West 21st Avenue. He tried to keep a couple of cars between them so that the girls wouldn't notice they were being followed. He was happy to see that she was getting out. He had been concerned about how his leaving would affect her. He had sat in front of her house all day yesterday and hadn't seen her at all. He knew she wasn't at work, and that she wasn't with Ashley. The fact that she hadn't left the house had worried him. He saw Ashley pull up this morning. When Jewell's dad opened the door, he looked tired and anxious. He spoke with Ashley at the door for a minute before nodding and letting her in.

Collin followed Jewell and Ashley to the Aquarium of the Americas. He tried to stay far enough behind them that they wouldn't notice him if they turned around as he followed. He knew that if Jewell saw him, she would recognize him immediately.

He hadn't intended to stay once he determined that Jewell was alright, but somehow, he just couldn't leave. Part of him knew that it was best for Jewell if he would turn around and walk away now, but part of him couldn't live without her. He justified following her by telling himself that he was just making sure that she wasn't be followed by anyone, well…anyone undesirable.

He didn't have any trouble keeping an eye on the two women. Jewell's hair practically glowed, sending out its own light, a beacon guiding him home. He looked around the crowd surrounding the shark tank. His eye was caught by two middle aged men staring at Jewell and Ashley. He tensed as the men walked up to them. He watched as the girls listened to the men, then Jewell and Ashley looked at each other, smiling. She saw Ashley shake her head, and gesture between her and Jewell, taking Jewell's hand. The two men looked at the two girls holding hands and stepped away, holding their hands up as if in apology. When they had dissolved into the crowd, Jewell and Ashley looked at each other and laughed. They moved in the opposite direction as the two men, moving towards the stairs to the second floor.

He watched them as they moved through the exhibits slowly, pointing to the different animals as they looked into the tanks; they even went to the stingray touch pool.

When Ashley and Jewell turned to leave the stingray pool and head to the food court for some lunch Jewell stopped, staring. "Did you see that?" Jewell asked Ashley pointing towards the sea otter exhibit.

"See what?" Ashley asked as Jewell grabbed her hand and pulled her in that direction.

"I saw Collin." Jewell said excitedly.

"What?" Ashley pulled her hand free of Jewell's and stopped, crossing her arms across her chest.

"Ashley, c'mon. I'm serious. It was Collin, I'd know him anywhere." She started walking, not checking to see if Ashley was following. She searched the area where she had seen him standing and saw him as he turned the corner heading towards the Frogs exhibit. Moving as fast as she could through the crowd, she searched for the figure she had seen watching her. As she came to the corner, she stopped, searching.

Ashley walked up beside her. "Jewell, it was probably just someone who looked a little like him. I know how much you miss him, but you need to let him go."

Jewell was still searching the crowd. She walked forward into the Frog Exhibit, straining her head to see if she could catch sight of him again. Not seeing him, she turned, walking toward the seahorse gallery. Ashley sighed and followed. Finally, they had made a full circuit of the second floor. "I know it was him." She said, depressed and frustrated.

Ashley put her arm around Jewell's shoulders and led her into the food court. They bought a couple of hamburgers with some French fries and Cokes. Finding an empty table, they sat down to eat. Jewell sat, facing the aquarium, watching the people as they passed. She didn't even touch the hamburger sitting on the tray in front of her. Ashley sighed. She was trying not to worry, but if Jewell was going to see Collin in strangers…She worried about the possibilities if she followed the wrong person.

When they finished eating, they cleared their table and started toward the stairs leading to the ground floor. "You think I'm crazy." Jewell said, suddenly a hint of anger in her voice.

"No." Ashley responded. "I think you really loved him, and you miss him, and it's going to take time before you can accept that he's gone."

Jewell nodded, looking at her feet. After a few minutes, she looked up. "Thanks. For being here, I mean; for understanding."

Ashley reached around and squeezed Jewell's shoulders. They walked like that, Ashley's arm around Jewell's shoulder as they left the aquarium.

Collin sat on the ground near the parking lot waiting for Jewell and Ashley to leave the aquarium. He had managed to slip into a bathroom, and then leave the aquarium after Jewell had passed. When Collin spotted the girls, he followed them to the French Market in the French Quarter, a sort of large flea market, where they wandered slowly between the displays, picking up an item here and there, putting it back and moving on to the next display.

On their way back to the car Ashley and Jewell walked past Jackson Square where Jewell stopped. Collin could see Jewell gesturing toward St. Louis Cathedral as if she was explaining something. After a minute, she stopped, and he saw Ashley pull her into an embrace. Although he wasn't close enough to hear or see what was happening, he could tell that Jewell was crying. He took several steps towards the two girls before realizing what he was doing. He yearned to take her in his arms, to comfort her, to tell her he loved her and they would be together forever. He felt guilt wrench at his insides, knowing that he was the one that caused her pain, knowing that he was the one that could end it.

But then he thought of what his uncle told him about Avelyn. How her choice, in his uncle's mind, had caused her more misery than she would have suffered had she stayed in Bishop's Lynn with her family. Collin's uncle also blamed himself for Avelyn's death; and even though Collin knew that Avelyn would have probably suffered the same fate at home in Bishop's Lynn, he couldn't help but think that in those last moments, her thoughts were probably of her family. He also thought about the pain her decision must have caused her family, never knowing of her fate.

Could Collin do that to Jewell? He thought of her father, the only family she had left. She was the only family he had left. Taking her away from him would not be fair to either of them; and if he did take her away, what then? Could he subject her to the life he led? Even though he had been unaware of the dangers that followed him up until a couple of days ago, moving every few years was a hard life. He had always hated when his uncle moved them. Though now he understood the necessity, when they moved to a new town, he had to make new friends, and he found it difficult to leave those relationships that he had formed behind. Could he ask her to do the same? And what about her father? How much contact could she have with him? Would his enemies go after her father to get to him?

He slowly retreated across the street, trying not to draw attention to himself. He watched her as she cried. "I am so sorry I did this to you Jewell. If I had known, I would have never hurt you this way," he whispered, as if somehow, she would hear his words. A tear trickled down his cheek. "I love you." He saw Jewell look up, and watched as Ashley turned to look behind her.

Finally, Jewell seemed to calm down. Ashley pushed her away a little bit and reached up to wipe Jewell's tears away with her thumbs. He could see Ashley talking to Jewell and Jewell nod in response. Finally, Ashley gave Jewell another quick hug, and they started walking back toward the car. Collin wished he could see Jewell's face. He hoped that this small gesture of friendship had made Jewell feel better. He silently thanked Ashley for seeing Jewell through this.

It wasn't until they had turned onto Iberville Street, walking back to the car that Collin noticed that he wasn't the only one following the two girls. The two middle aged men from the aquarium were also following Ashley and Jewell. While he wasn't completely certain of this, he found it interesting that they were walking back towards the aquarium from Jackson Square at the same time as Ashley and Jewell.

Collin followed the girls toward Covington. It was easy to follow them back since it was rush hour. Besides, on the Causeway, the cars around you don't change much, so it would be difficult to determine whether you were being followed, even if you were looking. As Collin cruised two cars behind Jewell and Ashley, listening to the radio, he noticed a black sedan moving quickly towards them, weaving in and out of traffic. It wasn't unusual, but for some reason, this car caught Collin's notice. As he watched it move past him, he noticed the two men sitting in the front seat. It was the same two men from the aquarium.

At first, Collin tried not to be concerned, though the hairs on the back of his neck were standing up. After all, this was the only way back across Lake Pontchartrain; but as he watched the car pull into the lane right behind the girls' car, he tensed, his hands gripping the steering wheel. He pulled around the car in front of him so he could be right behind the car with the two men. It was a long uneventful drive, but when they exited the Causeway, Collin became alert, watching the car in front of him.

As they exited the causeway, Jewell turned towards Ashley's house. When they turned into the apartment complex, the car with the two men kept driving. Collin debated whether to follow them, or follow Jewell. He chose to follow the sedan. They pulled into a restaurant a couple of miles away. Collin pulled into a parking lot across the street, and sat watching the restaurant. After three hours, Collin was getting tired. Nothing had happened, and though several people had gone into the restaurant, he didn't know if any of them had anything to do with the men at the aquarium. He thought about going inside, but was concerned that if the two men were Obsidian Knights they may recognize him.

After waiting for three hours for the men to leave the restaurant, Collin started thinking that it may have just been a coincidence that the two men were here. After all, the Causeway was one of only two ways out of New Orleans, and the only one that went north, and they hadn't actually followed Jewell into the apartment complex. Collin started up his car and drove back towards Ashley's apartment. He cruised through the parking lot, but when he didn't see Jewell's car, he drove back to Jewell's house. Ashley's car was parked out front, and Ashley and Jewell were sitting on the porch swing drinking Cokes. He drove past, going the speed limit so as not to draw attention. As he passed, he glanced in the rearview mirror and saw Jewell staring at the car. He continued around the curve in the street until he was out of view. He toyed with the idea of driving back around so he could watch the house, but discounted the idea. Ashley was there, so Jewell wasn't alone. He didn't know if her father would be home, but he assumed that because they had stopped at Ashley's house before coming here, Ashley would probably spend the night. He decided to go get something to eat and come back later to make sure Jewell wasn't alone.

CHAPTER 34

Jewell waited for Ashley as she picked out some pajamas and clothes for the next day. Tommy wouldn't be home tonight, and Ashley had convinced Jewell that a sleepover would be fun. Ashley stuffed everything in a bag, and they drove back to Jewell's house.

"Do you want a Coke?" Jewell asked, opening the fridge.

"Sure. Let's go sit out on the porch. It's not too hot with the sun going down."

They took their Cokes to the porch and sat on the swing, watching cars drive by. One, a silver Mazda, caught Jewell's attention.

"What?" Ashley asked, looking at the car.

"I don't know. Something about that car…It's weird, like, I don't know. Like I wish it would stop at the house."

"Do you know who it is?"

"No, that's what makes it so weird." She watched as the car disappeared out of view. She shrugged, and both girls went back to their Cokes, and talking about their favorite fish at the aquarium.

When Ashley left the next morning, she didn't notice the silver Mazda that passed her as she turned onto the main road.

Collin kept his face turned toward the road but watched the Corolla as it passed. Ashley was the only one in the car, and she didn't seem to notice him as she watched for oncoming traffic before turning onto West 21st St. Collin moved slowly past the blue ranch house where Jewell lived. He didn't see any lights on in the house, but that wasn't surprising, because the morning sun was so bright. He pulled to the end of the street, and turned around parking at the corner where East Saint Mary met West Saint Mary, partially concealed by the landscaping on the corner. He watched as Jewell walked to the end of the driveway to collect the newspaper. She was wearing an old pair of sweatpants, and the collar on her t-shirt was so stretched out that it fell off one shoulder. Collin's heart raced as he watched her. When she turned, looking in the direction of where Collin was parked, he could almost see the sun reflecting off the clear blue of her eyes, just as the light bounces off a mountain lake. For a moment, he thought that she could see him, but after too brief a moment, she turned and walked back into the house.

Jewell shrugged as she turned back to the house. She felt like someone was watching her, but instead of feeling worried, it made her feel safe. She put the paper on the couch, then went into her room and saw the book Twilight that she had started reading before she met Collin. She had never finished, somehow she had lost interest after Collin entered her life. She picked it up and flipped to where she had left off.

"But I'm not saying goodbye," I pointed out.

"Don't you see? That's what proves me right. I care the most, because if I can do it" - he shook his head, seeming to struggle with the thought – "if leaving is the right thing to do, then I'll hurt myself to keep from hurting you, to keep you safe."

Jewell slammed the book shut and dropped it on the floor. Absolute drivel, she thought kicking the book under her bed. Or maybe he'd leave because she was cramping his style. She crossed her arms over her chest and glared at the wall before grabbing a load of clothes to wash.

"You look like you're feeling better." Her father remarked when he she walked through the living room.

"What do you mean?"

"Well, the way you acted with Collin, and well, the way he acted with you. I really thought..." His voice trailed off. Jewell knew what he thought. He had met her mother when he was eighteen and she was seventeen. He always said that it was love at first sight. He told her that everyone has one true soul mate, and when you meet each other, your hearts sing and there is perfect harmony between you. *Yeah*, she thought, *my heart was singing alright, but apparently I was off key!*

"Yeah, well," she shrugged, swallowing the lump in her throat. "I guess he wasn't the one." She finished in a choked whisper.

Her father reached out and patted her leg. "Sometimes honey, it seems right, but the puzzle pieces don't quite fit, and no matter how hard you try to make them fit, the picture is never complete."

"Thanks for the Zen wisdom there dad."

"Anytime kiddo." Her father smiled at her. It made her think. There were so many people around her that really truly cared; why couldn't she stop thinking about this guy who was obviously too good to hang around?

"I'm going to bed, Dad. I've got to work tonight."

"Sweet dreams."

Not likely, she thought bitterly as she turned toward her room.

CHAPTER 35

"Hey Jewell," Ashley called as they walked toward the locker room. Ashley ran to catch up as Jewell waited by the door. "A bunch of the nurses and some of the interns are going to IHOP for breakfast. Can we go?"

"You can, I don't really want to." Jewell responded.

"But no one's going that lives on the other side of the pond to take me home. Doug's going," Ashley commented suggestively. Douglas Haim was one of the interns. He had always shown an interest in Jewell, and until Collin had come along, she had certainly shown an interest in him; tall, dark, and handsome; definitely an interest.

Jewell's heart hurt. She never thought that having your heart broken would physically hurt. She tried to smile through the pain, but couldn't feel anything but the ache in her chest. "Fine, but only because you want to go, not because anyone else is going."

"Cool!" Ashley sounded excitedly. "Ray Baskin is going too." Ashley was practically jumping up and down; Ashley had her eyes set on Ray the first time she saw him. He was another example of tall, dark and handsome but in a rugged way. Ashley and Jewell changed quickly and walked out to the car. Security was starting to loosen up a little since that weirdo hadn't shown up in almost two weeks. Jewell was glad that people weren't watching her the way they had been.

Jewell didn't really know where IHOP was so she let Ashley drive. Jewell was pretty tired anyway; she had had a really rough night. She leaned her head against the window. In the rear view mirror, she saw a silver Mazda in the lane a few cars back. She sat up in her seat and turned around. As she did, the car slowed, letting several cars move in front of it. There was something about it; she had the same feeling that she had when she saw a similar car drive past her house, and the same feeling of being watched that she had felt this morning when she went to get the paper. Of course, there had been no Mazda this morning...or maybe there was and she just hadn't seen it.

"What's wrong?" Ashley was looking at Jewell out of the corner of her eye.

"Nothing. I guess I'm just hungry."

"Give me a break Jewell. Who do you think you're talking to?" Ashley responded indignantly.

"Okay fine. It's just that, lately I feel like I'm being watched."

"What, you mean like that weird guy with the leg brace?" Ashley sounded worried.

"No, this is different. It doesn't feel bad. It's sort of like..." She paused for a moment, trying to think of how she could explain it. "Well, have you ever been sleeping, and in your dream you feel like someone's watching you, so you wake up but it's just your mom watching you sleep?" Jewell paused again "And, you know, that safe, warm fuzzy feeling you have as you close your eyes and drift back to sleep, knowing she's watching you?"

"Yeah, I guess I kind of know what you mean." Ashley shrugged.

"That's what it feels like. It kind of frightens me, that feeling of being followed, but at the same time, I feel really safe. I keep wondering if it's Collin."

"Jewell, Collin is gone; you need to face that fact. Maybe we should just go home." Ashley started to slow the car, taking her foot off the accelerator.

"No, it's fine." She tried to give Ashley a smile. It was so hard not to let Ashley just take her home, but Jewell knew how much Ashley liked Ray so she let Ashley drive her to the IHOP.

* * *

Collin could barely see Jewell in the passenger seat of the Focus. He saw her lean her head against the window, but when she suddenly sat up and turned back to look toward his car, he quickly took his foot off the accelerator and slowed down so that he was several cars back. Had she seen him? Did she know it was him? Probably not, she definitely wouldn't recognize the car, and he didn't think she would've recognized him so far back. He had much better eyesight than she did, but he really only knew it was Jewell in the passenger seat because he knew the car, and the passenger was blonde, while the driver was brunette; probably Ashley.

Then Collin started to think about what his uncle had told him. Someone had been stalking Jewell to get to him. Was he scaring her? Did she think that he was the stalker? He watched as the Focus pulled off onto the service road at the Bullard Avenue exit. If he knew Jewell, they were probably heading to IHOP. Rather than following them, he drove past the exit. If she had seen him, when he didn't follow, maybe she would feel better. He exited at Paris road instead, and took the service road back towards Bullard Avenue. He pulled past the IHOP and saw Jewell's car parked in front. Pulling around back, he parked his car near the dumpster where it couldn't be seen from inside the restaurant.

He got out of his car and pulled up the hood on the short sleeved cotton hoodie he was wearing. He knew that he wasn't exactly inconspicuous, but he hoped that if Jewell saw him, she wouldn't recognize him. Walking into the restaurant, he saw a large group of doctors and nurses sitting in the rear of the restaurant in a separate area. He asked to sit near the kitchen where he could watch, but would not likely be noticed.

Collin sat in the seat that was most obscured from the group in the back, but with a clear view of the exit. He asked for pancakes and coffee when the waitress came for his order then sat with his head down as if inspecting the menu. He occasionally raised his head to look toward the group. Jewell was sitting with her back to him, but each time he saw her, his heart started to pound and his hands began to shake. Watching her with her friends made him long to join her; to sit next to her, holding her hand, smelling the subtle scent of honeysuckle. He wondered if anyone else noticed it. He wanted to look into her blue eyes; he wanted so badly to tell her how much he loves her.

Jewell leaned closer to Ashley "Someone's watching," was all she said. She didn't need to say any more. Ashley understood exactly what Jewell was talking about. She stood up and started to leave the table.

"Where are you going?" Ray, who had been staring at Ashley ever since she arrived, asked curiously.

"I have to go powder my nose. It's important for a woman to keep herself beautiful." She flashed her most dazzling smile at him.

Although she knew exactly where the bathroom was Ashley made a circuit of the restaurant so she could survey the other people. She walked slowly to the hostess at the front of the restaurant, casually surveying the other diners. "Excuse me," she asked the hostess, "can you tell me where the restroom is?" She looked at the people waiting to be seated.

"It's right over there, dear." Ashley looked to where the hostess was pointing.

"Thank you." Ashley turned, again surveying the people in the restaurant. She went to the restroom, and then walked back to the table, passing the kitchen instead of walking along the front of the restaurant. She tried to look, without looking, at each diner as she walked past. As she approached the kitchen, she had to turn to squeeze past a waitress who was placing a plate of pancakes in front of a single diner. She tried to look around the waitress, but saw only that it was a man; based on the well-defined muscles on those very perfectly sculpted arms.

When she came back to the table, she flashed Ray her smile as she slid into her seat next to Jewell. Ashley leaned toward Jewell, placing her hand in front of their mouths to keep her voice from carrying. "I didn't see anyone that looked familiar. Weirdo isn't here, at least."

"Thanks Ash. It's probably just one of Sheriff Payne's deputies still following me around."

"You sure you don't want to leave?" It was obvious that Ashley didn't want to.

"No," said Jewell, almost too quickly as she glanced between Ashley and Ray. "I mean, it's like I said. I can feel it, but it's not creepy or anything. I just wish I knew who it was. I'll call Sheriff Payne later and ask him about it."

The group stayed for another thirty minutes or so before they started to disperse. Everyone was tired from a long night, and most of them had to be back at work later that day. Ray and Doug lingered along with Ashley and Jewell. As they turned toward the door, Jewell saw a man wearing a hoodie with the hood pulled up hurrying out the door. Immediately, her heart beat quickened and her skin tingled. She grabbed Ashley's arm.

"What?" Ashley asked, looking at Jewell's face worriedly.

"He's here, that was Collin. Come on." She started dragging Ashley toward the door.

"Jewell, not again. I don't want to sound negative, but it's been a week. And besides, don't you think that if he wanted to see you he would just come up and talk to you? Why would he be stalking around and hiding from you?" By the time she finished, she was practically yelling at Jewell across the restaurant as Jewell ran out the door after the stranger.

Ashley handed their receipt and her money to Ray and ran after Jewell seeing her just as she disappeared around the back of the building. "Jewell!" She shouted picking up her pace to catch up.

When Ashley caught up to Jewell, she was standing in the middle of the parking lot by the dumpster, looking confused. Jewell turned as Ashley walked up behind her. "I saw him Ashley, I really did." Her voice sounded like she was on the verge of tears. Ashley put her arm around Jewell and Jewell turned her head into Ashley's shoulder.

"It was just a guy that looked kind of like him."

"I don't know Ashley. Maybe I am losing it. I swear I saw him. I watched him come around this corner, but when I got here, there was...nothing. Was there even anybody there? Am I imagining things?"

"No sweetie. I saw him too."

"You did? Really?"

"I can see how you could mistake him for Collin. He had a similar height and build, but Jewell, it wasn't him." Jewell nodded. "Come on. Let's go home."

CHAPTER 36

"Idiota!" Collin cursed as he pounded the steering wheel with his fist, accenting each word. "Stupido! Imbecile!" His slip today had almost revealed him to Jewell. It was time to make a choice; he either had to leave her, allow her to live her life, or he had to confront her with the truth and let her make the choice.

He exited on the 310 South, heading towards home. He had to think and he couldn't do it while he was following Jewell. Besides, she would be going home to sleep for her shift tonight. As he drove down the long drive toward the house, he started to feel uneasy. Something here was not right. As he approached the house, he saw his uncle's SUV sitting in the driveway. "Great," Collin said to himself. "Just what I need now; an unbiased viewpoint." He had wanted time alone to think, he didn't want to listen to his uncle yammering on about the choices he had made.

He pulled into the drive and parked his rented car next to his uncle's. His uncle was sitting on the porch, waiting for him to show up. "Fancy meeting you here," his uncle called from the porch sarcastically.

"I was wondering how long it would take you to get here." Collin walked up the porch steps and sat down next to his uncle. "Did you come alone?"

"Of course not." His uncle smiled brightly. "I brought Gladys and Kendryck."

"Kendryck? Why Kendryck?" Gladys had become a given. Collin knew that wherever he was involved, she would be his defender, which made him feel a little better, but what did Kendryck have to do with all this?

"Well…I thought he might be able to help you out with some things. You haven't been back in touch with Jewell yet, have you?"

"Not…not exactly." Collin stood up and turned towards the door to go inside.

"What do you mean 'not exactly'," his uncle asked, grabbing his arm gently and pulling Collin to sit back down next to him.

"I've sort of been following her. I think maybe…well, I think maybe she saw me a couple of times, but I left before she could find out that it actually was me."

"Oh, now that's nice. My nephew has turned into a stalker." His uncle got up and Collin followed him inside.

"I am not a stalker," Collin said irritably to his uncle's back. "Besides, you're a kidnapper."

"Let's see…you follow her around without her knowing, I'm willing to bet you've hung out outside her work, waiting for her. Have you sat outside her house waiting to see what she does and with whom?" His uncle turned around to see Collin's reaction. Collin nodded resentfully. "Sounds like you're a stalker boy. I think we need to get you some help." But he winked at Collin to let him know that he understood.

"We need to return that rental car as soon as possible too," Percy told Collin as they walked into the parlor.

"Why? What am I going to drive?"

"Because, I am quite certain that that car has a GPS locator in it which is something that could cause trouble – especially if you rented the car in your own name." He glanced at Collin who hung his head indicating that he had. "As for what you're going to drive, you can drive my car...*when* I give you permission. You need to leave Jewell alone."

"Fine!" Collin was not happy, but wasn't going to argue with his uncle. Especially when he knew his uncle was right.

Inside, Kendryck was sitting in the parlor. He had set up two chairs facing each other about five feet apart. He gestured to the other chair, inviting Collin to sit down. Collin glanced at his uncle, who nodded, and sat in the proffered seat.

"As your uncle may have told you," Kendryck began, "in addition to our pseudo-immortal state, we also possess some additional abilities. Photographic memory is common to us all, as is empathy. But some of us have talents unusual to the rest. The most common is telepathy, although cases of telekinesis, divination, precognition, astral projection, and clairvoyance have also been documented."

"What do you mean by 'most common'?"

"Well, probably one in ten." He glanced at Percy for confirmation. Percy nodded.

"So, what does this have to do with me?"

"Well, because it's more common than the other talents I'd like to test you. I would have liked to test you earlier, but your uncle is a bullheaded, stubborn, ass." Percy shrugged.

"So...what?" Collin looked between Percy and Kendryck. "Are you saying I'm telepathic or something?"

"Well, I'm saying you need to be tested," Kendryck responded. "That's why I'm here."

"What do I need to do?"

"Just relax, don't try to block me."

"Block you?" Collin was confused.

"Just don't, well you'll probably understand once I start." Kendryck relaxed, looking intently at Collin.

Collin sat in his chair watching Kendryck, waiting for something to happen. After what seemed to be several minutes, he felt something touching his forehead. He moved his head reflexively feeling for whatever was poking him. It was then that he realized, something wasn't poking at the *outside* of his head, the probing was on the inside. The more he thought about it, the more he thought it felt like someone was kneading his brain; looking for a way in.

"You're blocking," he heard Kendryck say quietly into the empty space between them. "You're actually doing a really good job. I may be able to teach you something yet. Right now though, I need you to relax. Stop trying to keep me out."

Collin hadn't realized that he was doing anything; he had just been concentrating on the strange feeling in his head. He tried to relax as Kendryck instructed.

"I've never..." Kendryck just sat there shaking his head. "Among our *Family*, I am one of the strongest. I've never met anyone who could resist me so easily. You actually pushed me out!" He sat there, shaking his head. He looked at Percy, his voice cold. "I can train him, but you did Collin a great disservice keeping him from his talents for so long." Kendryck stood up and left the room.

"You deserved better. I shouldn't have been so selfish. If I would've listened..."

"What are you talking about?" Collin looked at his uncle.

"I've known almost since the day you were first put into my care that you were one of us. I should've raised you to understand what you are. I should've had you tested, had you trained from the beginning."

"You did what you thought was best," Collin said trying to comfort his uncle.

"No, I didn't. I treated you like I wanted you to be. I've failed you." Percy moved to stand up, Collin held him, forced him to stay seated on the couch.

"You treated me like a son. You loved me, you cared for me, and you taught me right from wrong. I couldn't have asked for anyone better to have raised me." Percy looked at Collin, his face still masked in misery. Collin smiled, and gave his uncle a hug. "So what if I'm never some great telepath? It hasn't hurt me so far. What would I do with it anyway? You can't do it; you seem to be just fine. It's not the end of the world."

"I guess you're right. For a kid, you talk like you've been alive for centuries. Now, what are we going to do about Jewell?"

CHAPTER 37

Edgar sat in the musty, moldy office of the warehouse, as he listened to the arguing around him. His nose itched, and his eyes were watering. The room had some boxes pushed in a corner, obviously soaked and then dried; grim reminders of the hurricane that had swept through here and devastated most of the Gulf Coast. He studied the mildew patterns on the bottom of the box, wondering at what these meetings were doing to his lungs.

"I can't believe you lost him!" Art was pacing irritably back and forth across the room, stirring the dust and mold that had settled into the stale 1970's gold carpeting. "After two weeks of watching the girl, we finally see him and you let him get away?" Art stopped, pushing his hands through what was left of the graying hair surrounding his balding pate. The long strand that normally covered his shiny head, pushed out of place, fell to the side, hanging almost to his shoulder; a stark contrast to the short, well groomed cut of the rest of his hair.

"We couldn't exactly run, what good would that have done, leading the police back here? It's bad enough that the cop has our names and license plate; if we had run from him, then what?" Angry at having his judgment questioned, Elliot pushed himself up from his chair, bowing his body toward the older man who had assumed the position of leader. Elliot was not a large man, but when he wanted to, he had an imposing presence about him. It wasn't enough to defer Art's frustration at the loss.

"If you had used better judgment, you might have figured out who he was before you had to fly out of the parking lot to follow him. Did you stop to consider that maybe *she* was going the same place he was, maybe in a different car?"

Elliot didn't like having his judgment questioned. He was an influential person in the academic community and most of his colleagues accepted his theories without question or dispute. He had an Irish temper, as hot as his red hair, inherited from his mother, and he was doing his best to control it now. Taking a deep breath, he turned from his accuser. "I don't think so," Alan chimed in. He was young, the youngest member ever accepted into the Obsidian Knights, and a new recruit having very little influence with the group. Art spun to look at him, angry at being addressed by the young man. "He was hiding his face, running from her. He left the restaurant ahead of her and ran to his car. He left before she was able to get a good look at him. There's definitely a connection between them. He's watching her, for whatever reason. I think she suspects it, but doesn't actually know."

Art sat down. They had been rotating surveillance over the past week, working in groups of two, always following the girl in different cars. Two days before the incident at IHOP, Kevin and Norman had seen the girl with one of her friends at the aquarium. While finding the girl was not as direct an approach as catching *him*, the general consensus among the group was that they could ransom her to great effect.

Kevin and Norman had taken the initiative, approaching the two young women, attempting to lure them away from the crowds, but the girls made it clear that they were not interested. The men had followed the women to an apartment complex in Mandeville, confirming Edgar's suspicion that she lived on the North side of Lake Pontchartrain, but discovering little else. They had not seen Collin during that surveillance either, which had been typical of late.

When the group first convened a little over a week ago, Edgar had described his observations at the hospital and had shared the name of the man, Collin Sykes. He thought that the woman's name might be Jill, and he knew that she worked the night shift in the ER at University Hospital, but had discovered little else. Shortly after the group had arrived, security had been tight at the hospital due to Edgar's bungled attempts to locate Collin, but over the past week security had diminished. The security efforts of the hospital however, had provided important information. The security was much tighter on the nights that the woman worked, allowing the Obsidian Knights to determine her work schedule. Her schedule consisted of two or three days on followed by two or three days off. Over two weeks, the faction had identified the pattern of her schedule. As the week wore on with apparently no further threat, the guard at the gatehouse had stopped carding people entering the garage, and the number of guards on duty each night had gone from six to two. However, the number of guards doubled to four on the nights that *she* worked.

The biggest problem was finding Collin. Up until today, no one had even seen him. In fact, the group was beginning to think that he had left the area, as their type often do, but this recent sighting had confirmed that he was still in town. The relationship between him and the nurse was difficult to determine, though it was apparent that he was interested in her regardless of her feelings toward him.

The gathered group was formidable. They had been hand chosen for their abilities in detecting, hunting, and killing the infidels. All had training in the use of a sword; many having chosen to pursue training in traditional Japanese sword arts such as Laido, Kenjutsu, and Kendo, while others had trained in traditional European sword fighting techniques. This was important because the infidels could be killed in only three ways: decapitation, burning, or drowning. Decapitation was the only sure method however as burning and drowning were less than reliable, and often difficult. Decapitation was often more difficult and more gruesome, but in the end, it was more reliable.

Of the thirteen gathered, Daniel, Matthew and Alan were all active in mixed martial arts. Alan had been specifically recruited because he was the youngest UFC champion at twenty-one and continued to hold the title. Art had been in the FBI for nearly two decades before going into partial retirement recently and still had high level security clearance with the government. Kevin was a private detective and Elliot held two PhDs, one in European History, the other in Religion. Although Edgar only had a bachelor's degree, he had an extensive knowledge of the Templar Knights and the histories of the Holy Grail. Other similar groups existed around the world, but it usually took only one faction to dispatch an infidel. In most cases, only a single infidel was identified at a time, though even that was rare. Only those that drank from the Chalice had the gift of eternal life. Only those had the ability to rise from the dead. The secrets of the Grail were closely guarded and very few had been able to steal its gifts.

As the group discussed strategy, Edgar daydreamed about the opportunity to hold in his hands the cup that had been held by Christ. Perhaps, if the Holy Grail was found, the Shroud of Turin and the Arc of the Covenant would also be revealed. Simply knowing that he was working to preserve those holy relics filled him with a sense of pride. He had not made his mark on the world yet, but he would. Oh yes, he would.

CHAPTER 38

"I just don't know what to do." Collin dropped his head into his hands, sighing despairingly.

"I can't tell you what to do kid. It'll rip your heart out, whichever way you choose. Either way, you'll break her heart. There are no easy answers." Percy looked at his nephew sympathetically. "What you need to ask yourself when you make your decision is whether you're you doing it for you, or doing it for her?"

Collin lifted his head and looked at his uncle. "What do you mean, doing it for me or doing it for her?"

"Well, it makes a difference. If you're doing it for her, then it's an easier choice. If you are doing it for you, you'll always wonder if you did the right thing. When I asked Avelyn if she wanted to come with me, I told myself that I was doing it for her. I wasn't though. I was doing it for me. By the time she realized she had made the wrong choice, it was too late."

"But, how do you know the decision you're making is for her, and not for yourself? What if it had been the right choice? What if you hadn't given her a choice but left, thinking that you were giving her a chance at a normal life? But after you left, she killed herself because she couldn't live without you?" Collin shook his head. "How do you know what the outcome is going to be, either way?" Collin went on, his voice becoming agitated. "Either way, I'm doing it for myself. Either way, I'm trying to do what's best for her, to mollify my own conscience."

"That's why you can't make the choice today. You need to give yourself time, give her time. And most of all, you need to stop stalking her. That's just going to make it harder, both for you and for her."

"I know, but I can't just leave. I *need* her."

Percy stood up, patting Collin's leg comfortingly as he did. "I know. I needed Avelyn too." Percy left the room, leaving Collin alone with his thoughts.

Collin could have been sitting there for five minutes or five hours, he couldn't tell. Nothing was clearer for his efforts when Kendryck walked in.

"Shall we start training then?" Kendryck pulled a chair up in front of Collin so that when he sat down, his knees were only inches from Collin's.

"I assume you're speaking of my training in telepathy?" Collin turned serious, but his voice was weary. Too much had happened today.

"Of course. You're already years behind thanks to your uncle. The sooner we start the better."

Collin sighed. "I suppose we ought to start then."

CHAPTER 39

After nearly a month of surveillance of the woman and no more sightings of the infidel, the group had split into two distinct camps. The first, led by Elliot felt that the hunt should be abandoned. It was clear that their only link to the infidel was no longer viable. In addition, it appeared that the infidel was no longer in the vicinity, taking it from their responsibility. The second camp, led by Art, was more determined to find and punish the infidel and believed that enough of a link still existed between him and the woman that she could be useful. Both groups agreed that continued surveillance would not bring them results.

Days of arguing and debate was beginning to wear on Edgar. He was with Art. He felt like something needed to be done. He was among the most zealous of the group, having studied the histories more intensely than the others. Edgar was often brought in by other groups of the Obsidian Knights to lecture and educate the other affiliates; not only for his knowledge, but for his persuasive abilities. He sometimes thought that he would have made a great televangelist.

Finally, the debate became too much for Edgar to tolerate. He stood up and spoke to the group, "We have two primary responsibilities as Obsidian Knights. First, we are to seek out the relics stolen by the Templar Knights from the Temple of Solomon, and to return them to the Church. Second, we are to identify, and punish those who have either secreted these items, or stolen their gifts. To identify an infidel, and to simply let him escape because we 'lost track' of him," he said these words with disdain, "would be to abandon our duty. If we were to do that, we would be no better than the infidel."

Edgar paused, looking around the room. "Many of you have daughters. If a man had raped your daughter, and you knew who this man was but 'lost track' of him, would you give up? Would you deny your daughter's justice? Or would you hunt him down by whatever means possible and make sure that he was punished?" He paused. Angry whispers between the men indicated that the actions these men would take would include everything from turning the rapist in to the police, to punishing him in ways that would help him to understand the pain he had put his victim through. "Is this different? The Holy Grail, one of the most holy of relics has been defiled, and we are going to simply give up because it's too hard to find this man who stole from the innocent?

"We have ways of finding him. We have the woman."

The men in the room nodded. Soon, excited conversation broke out as plans were made for finding any information they could on this man.

Within days, the group of thirteen men gathered around a table studying maps, photographs, and information relating to Jewell McKean. Because there was no information on Collin Sykes, the group's only connection to the infidel was through her. She would lead them to the infidel.

CHAPTER 40

Collin sat on his bed, the book he was reading lay open on his lap. He could almost feel his lips touching Jewell's. He could feel the fire, the electricity, the need that he always felt when he touched her. He remembered her warm, soft lips. The smell of honeysuckle drifted in through his open window, nearly completing the image. He missed her. As each day passed, it was getting more and more difficult to resist going to find her.

His telepathy lessons were helpful in distracting him but he could only practice for an hour or two at a time. It helped that his uncle had thoroughly hidden the keys to his car. In fact, he had hidden them so well that even Gladys couldn't find them. This at least kept Collin close to home, but it didn't stop his thoughts of Jewell.

Collin's uncle was aware of Collin's angst and worked to keep him occupied. While Percy usually wouldn't let Collin go anywhere on his own, they made frequent trips into New Orleans. Spending a night on the town with Percy wasn't exactly Collin's idea of a good time, though it was better than sitting at home thinking about Jewell.

"This isn't fair!" Collin shouted at one point when his uncle had refused yet again to give him the keys to the car. "If you hadn't dragged me away, if you hadn't interfered, everything would have been different! You ruined everything for me!"

"For you." Percy said succinctly. "What about Jewell?"

"But she's not happy. Not like when she was with me. I can feel it. While I've been practicing, sometimes I can sense what she's feeling."

"Are you sure that you're sensing her feelings, and not imagining what you want her to feel?" Percy reached a hand over and touched Collin's leg. "Let her go kid. It may be difficult now, but losing her gets harder the longer you're with her, and you *will* lose her. Spare yourself that pain, if you aren't willing to spare her. You have to let her be happy, even if that means she finds that happiness without you; *especially* if she can find it without you."

Collin sighed. Maybe his uncle was right. "I suppose then, maybe we should think about leaving. I don't care where we go, just as long as it's away from here."

Percy thought about telling him that that's exactly what he had done before, but gloating wasn't going to help Collin. "I think that's a good idea. We don't need to make a decision immediately, though the sooner the decision is made, the better, I think."

Collin only nodded. He couldn't speak through the lump in his throat, but if this is what he had to do for Jewell, he would. He finally realized that he loved her so much, he was willing to let her go for her happiness, even if it cost him everything.

CHAPTER 41

"We don't have to work tomorrow," Ashley said, leaning in the passenger side window of Jewell's car. "Did you want to do something tonight?"

"Yeah, that sounds good. My dad won't be home until tomorrow morning at the earliest. Maybe you can spend the night."

"At your house? Yeah right! I need cable girl! How about you stay over here?"

Jewell smiled. "Good point. I'll swing by here about six. We'll grab a bite to eat and then decide what we want to do."

"Sounds perfect." Ashley replied. "Right now though, I've really got to get some sleep. We had eight babies born last night! Unreal!" She stood up and waved as she walked towards her apartment.

Jewell went through the drive-through at McDonald's on the way home. When she pulled into her driveway, she didn't notice the black Chevy Tahoe pull up behind her and park in front of the house across the street. Not that she would have thought anything about it if she had. She reached into the back seat to grab her bag of scrub clothes and her shoes; then she grabbed her McDonald's bag and opened the door. She stood; bumping the door shut with her rear-end and started walking toward the house.

If it hadn't been for the twig snapping, she would have never seen the man sneaking up behind her. As Jewell turned towards the sound, a second man grabbed her from behind, pushing a rag against her mouth to stifle any sound she could have made. As she struggled against the second man's hold, the first man stepped up to her and wrapped his arms around her in a bear hug, pinning her arms to her side. Though she struggled and kicked, the second man was able to deftly wrap a piece of duct tape around her mouth, holding the rag in place. He grabbed her upper arms roughly, pulling them behind her back until they hurt. Her hands were secured with E-Z Cuffs before the man moved around to her feet. She was able kick him squarely in the nose before he grabbed her legs and secured her ankles with another set of E-Z Cuffs. He tightened them until they felt like they were biting into her flesh. Kicking the man in the nose wasn't much, but it gave her some satisfaction as she watched the blood dripping off his chin and the awkward angle of his nose indicating that it was probably broken. He quickly retaliated with a hard slap across Jewell's mouth before he reached down and pulled her legs from under her. Her eyes started to water with pain, but she choked back the sob trying to escape. She refused to give either of them the satisfaction of knowing how much they had hurt her.

The two men quickly carried her to the waiting Tahoe and pushed her into the back seat. The car smelled like leather and a mixture of different colognes that didn't blend well. Slowly, as if nothing was wrong, the Tahoe pulled away from the side of the street and toward the main road. Lying across the seat as she was, Jewell was unable to gain enough purchase to either sit up, or cause any damage to the man sitting next to her.

When they finally stopped, the man at her head opened the door and dragged her unceremoniously from the car dropping her on the damp ground. She heard other doors opening and closing, and several voices. She heard the zipper on her tote open, and someone rifling through it. Then she heard the distinctive tone of her cell phone being turned off.

Great, she thought. For the next twelve hours, anyone who tried to reach her would assume she had turned her phone off while she was sleeping. It would be at least six o'clock before anyone knew she was even missing. Ashley would get worried, at least Jewell had that hope to hold on to. Jewell was patted down, but other than her bag with her clothes and cell phone, her keys, and her breakfast, she didn't have anything with her.

Eventually, she was shoved brusquely into the back seat of another car. The car reeked of cigarette smoke and old fast food. The smell made her gag. After what seemed like an eternity, she heard planes; they were low and loud indicating that they were probably near the airport. Her first thought was that they were going to take her somewhere by plane, but then she realized that they couldn't get her through the airport unnoticed without her cooperation.

Finally the car came to a stop. She heard the driver get out and she heard what sounded like an industrial garage door opening. The driver returned, climbed back in the car and drove forward, finally stopping. She heard the garage close with a very final sound, shutting out any idea she had of escape or discovery.

CHAPTER 42

"Jewell!" Collin sat up in bed, looking around as if trying to find her. He dropped his head into his hands and tried to concentrate, the way Kendryck had taught him to. There were so many emotions washing over him, that he felt as if he would suffocate. His head was pounding and his eyes were blurred. He stood up, and the power of the feelings caused him to fall against the bed. He forced himself to stand and start moving toward the door. He was wearing only his boxers, but he didn't stop to pull on pants or a shirt. As he ran to the main house, he screamed his uncle's name, "Uncle Percy, help! Oh God, please, help me! Uncle Percy!" He stumbled as he ran, dizzy, his head pounding, he couldn't see anything in front of him. He was running blind. As he tripped over the first step his uncle caught him.

"What is it? Collin?"

"Jewell," Collin whispered as he passed out in his uncle's arms.

Percy gathered Collin up into his arms. It was almost comical, this frail old man carrying his strapping young nephew into the house. By the time Percy got into the house, the others had come downstairs and were waiting. Gladys ran over to Collin, touching him gently on the face. "What happened?" she asked?

"I don't know. He was screaming and just before he passed out, he said 'Jewell'."

Kendryck's face went white. "Who is Jewell? Is this someone he's close to?"

"He loves her," Gladys answered, tenderly brushing her hand along Collin's cheek. She was sitting on the couch next to where Percy had laid him.

"Something's happened to her. When someone emotionally close to a telepath has a strong emotional response to something, it can cause a sort of…overload. If the telepath isn't trained to block the inrush of information, to protect the telepath's mind, it shuts down. It's a defense mechanism."

"What kind of emotional response? What do you think happened?" Percy was worried, his brow was creased, and he was holding Collin's hand.

"Well, it's hard to say," Kendryck responded. "It could be something as simple as losing a pet to being involved in a car accident. There's really no way to tell. Can we call her, find out what might be going on?"

Percy stood up, placing Collin's hand gently on Collin's chest. "I can make a few phone calls."

Percy called Sheriff Payne first. "It happened just after 7:30 a.m. Kendryck isn't sure what could have triggered it, but I thought it would be a good idea to check." Percy listened then thanked the Sheriff before hanging up.

"What did he say?" Kendryck asked, glancing at Collin's still unconscious body.

"He's going to call Alex. He's one of the Templars on the police force in Covington. He'll have Alex drive by the house and check on her. He's going to call me back when he finds something out."

"So what do we do now?" Gladys asked wringing her hands.

Percy glanced at Collin. "We wait."

As Alex drove slowly by the McKean house, everything seemed to be in order. Jewell's car was parked in the front driveway, the house was closed. He parked the squad car in the driveway behind Jewell's car and walked to the door. He knew that Jewell worked nights at the hospital in New Orleans and he hated to wake her, but Sheriff Payne had said that it was very important that he ensure that Jewell is safe. Alex walked up to the door and rang the bell. He waited for a few minutes then knocked when there was no answer. When no one responded to his knock, he radioed the station. Nothing seemed amiss, but something didn't feel right. He walked around the house while he waited for the station to call Tommy to come home.

Tommy's car had barely come to a stop before he had jumped out of the car and was running for the door to his house. Mike Forester, another fireman, and Templar was in the passenger seat. He got out of the car and looked at Alex. Alex shrugged as they both followed Tommy into the house. Mike heard doors opening and closing as Tommy yelled Jewell's name.

"Tommy, is there anyone else that she might be with? A friend maybe?"

"Of course! Ashley!" Tommy jumped off the couch and ran to the phone in the kitchen. "Ashley! Do you know where Jewell is?" Tommy was silent for a time before he hung up the phone without saying anything else. He walked dejectedly into the room. "She dropped Ashley off at six forty five this morning and then came home. Ashley hasn't heard from her."

"Well, does she have a cell phone?" Alex asked Tommy.

Tommy slapped his forehead with the palm of his hand. "Of course she does." He walked back to the kitchen and quickly dialed the phone. He listened for a second before hanging up without saying anything. "It went straight to her voicemail. Her phone is turned off."

"I'll call Luke at the firehouse and let him know what's going on and we'll open a missing person report." Tommy sat on the couch shaking. Alex felt for him. Tommy had lost his wife, and now his only daughter was missing as well.

When Alex left the house, he called Hugh Payne. Jewell was under the protection of the Templar Knights. The police would do their part, but the Templars would do their part as well.

CHAPTER 43

Edgar watched as they unloaded the woman from the car. Her wrists and ankles were bound. She had a gag across her mouth and a cloth was tied around her eyes. Matt easily pulled the woman from the car by her shoulders, then balanced her as he picked her up and cradled her against his body to carry her across the warehouse. She looked so small and fragile held against Matt's large, muscular frame. For a moment, Edgar thought that she was unconscious, but when she shifted in Matt's arms, trying to get more comfortable, Edgar realized that she was more resigned.

While the commando team did their part, the remaining six members decided how to contain her. There was an office area in the warehouse. Within that area there was a large conference room, eight offices, a reception area, a lunch room, and a supply closet. Four of the offices were interior offices, two with windows looking toward the inside of the warehouse. It was determined that she would be held in an interior office. Behind the chosen office was the conference room, there was a hallway to one side, and another office on the other. In front of it, there was a hallway with two additional offices. The consensus among the group was that this office would be the easiest to secure to prevent either rescue or escape.

There were two goals; first, to find Collin. To do this, they had chosen to use the woman as bait. The second, several felt that because she was involved with Collin, it was likely she was an infidel as well. As soon as Collin was located, some wanted the woman killed as well. Others wanted to know that she was an infidel before she was executed.

Matt, following Elliot's lead, carried the woman into the chosen office. Two chairs were inside the room. One of them was one of the solid wood chairs that had decorated the reception area of the warehouse. The second chair had been pulled from the conference room. It was padded, and therefore more comfortable than the folding chairs that most of the Obsidian Knights had to sit on.

Matt carried the woman into the room, placing her on the wooden chair. Her hands were released first from the E Z Cuffs then placed, one on either arm of the chair, and secured again using new sets of the disposable E Z Cuffs. Likewise, her legs were released, and then secured on to each of the front legs on the chair. The position was uncomfortable.

As Jewell sat, she heard arguing outside the door but couldn't make sense of the argument. It had to do with some sort of test. After several minutes, the door opened and she heard someone enter the room. "Are you one of them?" A gruff voice asked, close to her ear. She could smell a combination of cigarette smoke and coffee on his breath. She shook her head and shrugged, not being able to answer because of the gag, and not knowing how to answer even if she was able to speak.

He slapped her, hard. "An infidel!"

She paused, not knowing what he meant or how she was supposed to answer. Suddenly, she felt a sharp pain as a knife sliced from her shoulder to her elbow; a deep cut, one she was certain would require stitches. "We'll find out soon enough." She heard him slam the door as he left. She could feel the blood dripping off the end of her hand when she heard the door open. The door immediately slammed and she heard a voice beyond the door swearing at, she assumed, the man that had cut her.

"Just what the hell do you think you were doing?" The voice seethed with anger. "This was *not* part of the plan!"

"She could be one of them! You know that as much as I do. We have a duty to find out at least!" This was from the man that had cut her.

"Those decisions are made by *me!*" He emphasized the last word indicating that he was the one in charge. Those were the last words Jewell heard until someone came quietly into the room, closing the door. She heard the squeak of a chair as he sat down.

Jewell sat in silence. The chair was hard against her back, and her legs were too far apart to be comfortable. She had an itch where the rag over her mouth was tickling the end of her nose. She couldn't smell very much beyond the rag, which smelled faintly of fabric softener, but what smells she was able to identify were musty and moldy. The air inside the room wasn't damp, but it smelled like it should be. The acrid smell irritated her nose. She could hear the person in the room with her leafing through a magazine or newspaper. She waited for him to say something; he didn't. The only sounds she heard were the muted conversations of those outside the office, and the periodic turning of a page in the magazine.

Her stomach rumbled; she hadn't eaten anything since midnight. It had been near seven when she was taken, and it had to have been at least an hour since then, probably closer to two. She strained to hear the conversations going on outside of the room. She could catch a word here and there, but not enough information that she could piece together the reason for her kidnapping. The organization of the kidnapping, the planning, seemed to indicate that she was not a random victim. They wanted something, and they wanted it from her. The man who had sliced her arm seemed to think that it would give them some information about her as well; something to do with infidels. She didn't attend church regularly, but her job made that prohibitive for the most part. She believed in God. What did the man think slicing her arm would prove?

The tape securing the rag to her mouth was starting to irritate the sides of her face where it stuck to her cheeks causing them to itch and burn. It also pulled at her hair when she turned her head. The cuffs around her wrists and ankles were starting to chafe her skin, and the blood on her arm was caking where it had collected near her elbow. The cut stung terribly. As she waited for something to happen, she tried to remain calm; to try to gather as much information as she could while she sat imprisoned in this room. Other than that, her only option was to wait and hope that someone noticed she was gone before she was supposed to meet Ashley at six. The longer it took them to start a search, the less likely they were to find her.

As she breathed the dirtied air in the room, her eyes started to water from the pervasive mildew smell in the air and her nose began to get congested.

Before long, she was working to suck air through her blocked nose; she realized that if she did not get the gag off her mouth, she was going to suffocate. She started sucking breaths through her nose, harder and harder, but despite her efforts, she began to feel dizzy as her oxygen levels began to drop. Her lungs burned for lack of air. Finally, she heard her captor put his magazine down and walk toward her, casually. She felt his big hands picking at the tape on the side of her face while he held her head against his chest with his other hand. When he had a hold of the corner of the tape, he ripped it from her mouth causing a scream to escape her lips though she tried to hold it in. It wasn't much of a scream, she had no air behind it, but having the duct tape ripped from her face, pulling out clumps of hair around her ears and at the base of her neck caused excruciating pain.

She sucked in deep breaths of the dank, polluted air, trying to fill her lungs and bring her breathing back to normal. She felt a tickle running down the back of her neck, something wet, soaking the neckline of her shirt; blood, she realized, where a clump of hair had been torn from her scalp. "Thank you" she said when she was finally able to breathe again. She heard her captor grunt what might have been an acknowledgement as he sat down and picked up his magazine again. "Why am I here?" She asked, hoping to gain as much information as she could now that she could talk. He didn't answer. "What are you reading?" Her voice was shaking as she spoke. She tried to stay calm; if an opportunity for escape presented itself, she may be able to take advantage of it but only if she could think clearly, though she doubted an opportunity would present itself. "What's your name?"

Her captor continued his silent treatment, refusing to answer any of her questions. She sighed. At least she didn't have the gag over her mouth any more. She didn't try to scream. The kidnapping seemed to be too well planned. She was certain that they had chosen a location where no one would be near enough to hear her scream, and the constant drone of airplane engines would drown out almost any sound. Besides that, she strongly doubted that anyone who might hear would be willing to come to her rescue.

She wasn't sure how long she sat in that room. She tried to think about things that would make her feel better. Thoughts of Ashley, Collin, and her father flitted through her head. She felt a tear escape her eyes as she thought about the fact that she may never see any of them again. Suddenly, she caught her breath. She heard Collin's voice, his muddled European accent, filled with worry. "Where are you Honeysuckle? Please hold on, we're coming for you." She wanted so much to believe it was true, that Collin knew what had happened and was looking for her, but Collin was gone, her father wasn't home, and no one expected her to be anyplace but her bed until sometime around six this afternoon. Then it would take time before they could organize a search. Since her car was at home, and everything looked normal, she didn't even know where they would begin. She sniffed back a sob; she couldn't give up, no matter what, she knew she could survive this, if she could just remain strong.

CHAPTER 44

By the time Collin finally regained consciousness, a search effort was in full effect. The Templars were doing what they could, but it didn't hurt that Jewell was known and loved by most of the public servants in St. Tammany Parrish. Andy Baraven, a deputy sheriff in St. Tammany Parrish and Templar Knight had brought in a forensics team to work with the Covington police force. They were scouring Jewell's car, yard, and house for clues. Andy didn't have any doubts about his team, or the team with the Covington police department. Their personal relationship with Jewell and her father would not affect the quality of their search. In fact, he thought, it would probably make them even more meticulous than they usually were.

At nine thirty, Andy received a call from Alex. Even though Alex was not chief of police, because of the Templar relationship, they remained in constant contact. Apparently, Tommy, Jewell's father, had determined that everything in the house was intact. There was no sign of a forced entry, and no sign of a struggle within; nothing was missing except of course, Jewell. Outside the house, the car also lacked any sign of a struggle. However, the grass around the walkway leading from the car to the house was muddied and damaged. Because of the mud, it was difficult to determine how many people had been in the area.

There were at least two shoe prints that they were able to decipher, one being Jewell's, the other was larger, a man's. It was unlikely they had taken her anywhere on foot, but there were no distinctive tire marks anywhere on the road to indicate what type car she may have been taken in. The neighbors, those that had been home, had neither seen nor heard anything.

Sheriff Payne had chosen a different lead to follow; the man, Edgar Durand, who had been watching her so closely in past months. The Sheriff called Andy and told him that Edgar had an apartment in Chinchuba, in St. Tammany Parrish and would therefore be in Sheriff Baraven's jurisdiction. The sheriff had already sent three officers to the apartment. When it was ascertained that Edgar was not at home, he sent one of his officers to get a judge to sign a search warrant. Depending on which judge was making the decision that could take a while. The truth was they did not have a lot of evidence to show that a search warrant was necessary. All they had was the circumstantial evidence showing Edgar following Jewell and asking about her over a month ago, and the fact that Jewell was now missing. Because she was over 18, that would pose additional problems as she had only been missing for a couple of hours. Sheriff Baraven hoped that the testimony of several civil servants regarding the likelihood of Jewell's disappearance as involuntary, and the evidence at the scene would help convince the judge that a search warrant for Edgar Durand's apartment was justified.

After nearly an hour, Sheriff Baraven left the judge's chambers with his two officers...without a search warrant. While the judge was sympathetic, she told the sheriff that without just cause, she couldn't allow them in to search. She needed some solid evidence, some proof to indicate not only that Edgar had something to do with Jewell's kidnapping, but she also needed to know what they were looking for.

Sheriff Payne seemed to think that Jewell wasn't in any mortal danger as long as Collin didn't do anything stupid, so Sheriff Braven posted plain clothed officers outside of Edgar's apartment, and at either end of the hallway. He hoped that eventually Edgar would have to come home. Until then, there was little he could do. The area outside Jewell's house had been thoroughly searched. A receipt for an Egg McMuffin bought at McDonald's just after seven that morning, but other than that, they had found nothing. The shoe print had been from a pair of Nike Dunks, size ten. Not only one of the most popular brands of shoes, but also one of the most popular sizes. Jewell's fingerprints were the only prints on the car and there were no tire prints or eye witnesses. They had nothing.

CHAPTER 45

Collin finally woke up about two hours after he had his vision of Jewell. Kendryck told his uncle that it was important that they not wake him if at all possible, because the unconsciousness was his body's way of protecting what he could not control. He awoke violently, lashing out at those around him. Percy and Kendryck were able to grab his arms and hold him against the couch until they could calm him down. When Collin was finally fully awake and aware of his surroundings, Percy let go of him, and Kendryck pulled a chair up to face him. If Kendryck could help Collin understand what he was seeing, strengthen the telepathic link, they might be able to get some information that could help in the search.

Kendryck gently laid his hands on Collin's shoulder. "Collin," he said gently, "I need you to look at me." Collin moved his face so that it was more or less facing Kendryck's, but his eyes still held a haunted look. "Collin." Kendryck said his name again with a little more force. Collin's eyes moved slightly. "I need you to look *at* me. Look at my eyes." Collin slowly moved his eyes, trying to focus on Kendryck's face. It was difficult, as if he was trying to see someone through a window coated with years of dust and filth. Finally, Collin's eyes found Kendryck's. "Something has happened to Jewell." Collin's eyes went wide with shock and he struggled to stand, but Kendryck's hands on his shoulders kept him seated.

"What? What's happened? Is she all right?" Collin was frantic, looking to his family for answers.

"We don't know. She's missing. We think she's been kidnapped. Sheriff Payne is heading the search effort. The Templars are involved as are pretty much every police officer and Sheriff in both Orleans and Covington Parishes. They are doing all that they can do."

"I have to go. I have to help find her!" He tried to stand again. Kendryck placed his hands on Collin's thighs.

"You will help. But right now, the best help you can give her is to help us to understand what happened this morning. It seems your vision happened at the same time that she disappeared. We," he gestured to the people gathered in the parlor, "believe that this was no coincidence. We need to find out what you know, to see if there's any information that can be useful. Can you do that?"

Collin nodded his head numbly. "I'll do whatever I need to. If this is what will help the most, then let's get started." He focused his attention back on Kendryck.

"Now…I need you to tell me what you felt."

Collin took a deep breath, trying to settle his nerves. He was trembling violently; so much so that he needed to grip his thighs to keep his hands from flopping like a fish on the bottom of a boat. "It was Jewell," he started. "I smelled honeysuckle." He struggled to put his thoughts into words.

"Good," said Kendryck. "I want you to remember the details like that. It's important that you try to express every feeling you had."

"Well, okay I guess. Let's see..." Collin's eyes drifted to the ceiling as he tried to remember everything that had occurred. "I was lying in bed. I had just woken up and had looked at the clock. It was a little past seven. I was thinking that Jewell would probably be getting home from work and..." he blushed a little as he voiced his next thought, "I was imagining her coming through the door of the house, you know, like she was coming home...to me."

"That may be why you were able to feel what happened so strongly. In a sense, you had already created a connection without knowing it. If you hadn't been thinking about her when it happened...." Kendryck's thought trailed off.

"I might not have felt anything." Collin finished, resentfully. Had he been trained, he might be able to provide more than daydreams and fantasies. "It was really weird, because I suddenly felt like there were people around me and my heart started beating faster. I was scared, not for Jewell, but for me. It felt like it was happening to me. It only took me a second to realize that there was no one in the room with me and that's when it occurred to me that it was something Jewell was experiencing." He paused, looking at Kendryck. "I tried to focus, like you've been teaching me. I put all my energy into feeling what she felt." A tear trickled down his face. "He grabbed her. I don't know how I knew that, but I knew she was restrained somehow. She was really scared. That's the last thing I remember." After Collin finished explaining everything, everyone was silent; it was as if someone had hit the mute button. Collin sat and looked at everyone in the room. "What?" His concern was growing as the silence stretched on.

Finally, Kendryck broke the silence. "Okay, we need to see if we can establish a connection now. We need to see if we can figure out anything that might give us a clue to where she is, or who she's with."

"Well, it doesn't take a genius to realize that that weirdo from the hospital took her. What did you say he was; a Black Knight or something?" Collin asked.

"Obsidian Knight." Percy mumbled.

Gladys came over to sit next to Collin. She put her arm around him and gave him a hug. "It's okay honey, we'll find her." Collin just nodded his head against Gladys's shoulder.

"Okay." Kendryck pulled Collin's attention back to him. "Now, just like we practiced. Try to focus your thoughts on Jewell. Try to feel her thoughts." His voice was low, hypnotic. Collin could feel himself drifting and his thoughts start to focus on what Jewell was feeling. As he started understanding what she was feeling, he tried to tell those sitting with him what he...what she, felt.

"She's terrified." He started. "She's...hungry?" He was having trouble sorting through all of the emotions that were flooding his mind. "She's hostile or maybe defiant. Anxious, but she's also hopeful. Pain, exhaustion, resistance." He stopped for a minute, frustrated. "I don't know; there's just so much!"

"That's understandable. Let's try to focus on one emotion at a time." Kendryck tried to sort through what Collin had said so that he could help Collin focus. "The hunger is easy. They found a receipt from McDonald's. They must not have given her a chance to eat. That's not really important right now." He looked at a notepad where he had been jotting down notes as Collin spoke. "I guess we should probably focus on the pain first. Can you tell whether it's a physical pain, or an emotional one?"

Collin closed his eyes and tried to focus, attempting to block out all of the memories other than the pain. "It's both, but...more physical I think."

"Where? Can you tell where she's feeling the pain?"

"Ummm...here," Collin pointed to the back of his neck. "That pain is different than the rest. It's like...it's more of a burning pain, like a cut or a scrape. Her arm, it stings like a cut. Her back. That's ummm...like it's cramped maybe? Her wrists." He thought for a second. "And her ankles too. It's like something is wrapped around them." Collin opened his eyes and looked at Kendryck.

"Maybe they've her tied up?" Percy supposed.

"That would make sense, if they've got her as a hostage." Gladys added.

"Well, they're not exactly known for their gentle treatment of their victims."

Gladys glared at Kendryck as Percy answered Collin's worried look. "She's not dead. That's the important part. If they thought she was one of us, she would be dead. They decapitate infidels. They must want her for something else."

"What else would they want her for?" Collin asked.

"You." Percy answered succinctly.

Collin frowned and tried to make a connection with Jewell. "Where are you Honeysuckle? Please hold on, we're coming for you."

CHAPTER 46

Jewell didn't know how often her guard had changed while she was sitting in the room. She had no way to guess the time between changes, but she thought that it was probably every hour or so. There had been four different guards which meant it could be just after noon. Jewell heard the rhythmic knock on the door indicating that someone new was coming to take over. She knew there were at least three men based on the different sounds they made as they moved.

"Tell the others that they can take a break, go home and get some rest. It's hard to say how long this is going to last." The voice was that of an older man, one that had reached full maturity. It carried with it an air of influence as if he was used to delegating authority or giving out orders. "Tell them not to get any ideas. I'm in charge right now, and as far as I'm concerned, unless we learn she's one of them, she *will* leave here alive."

Gee, she thought, that made her feel a whole lot better; and one of whom? Who did they think she was?

"Do we know if he knows yet?" The man sounded younger than the first.

"Not yet. We were hoping he would show up on his own. We certainly didn't take any steps to avoid him. It may be that he's just waiting for an opportunity."

"Thanks Gary. She's not much trouble, but then what's she going to do?" The younger man laughed at himself. "Take it easy."

Jewell heard the door closing and then she heard the familiar scraping of the outside lock.

Maybe because he seemed to want to make sure she left her ordeal alive, Jewell felt a connection to her newest guard. "I'm Jewell," she started.

"Gary." He responded. He was curt, but not exactly rude.

"Why am I here?" She didn't know how much information she was going to get, but she felt like she deserved to know why she had been kidnapped and was now being held hostage.

"Bait, for the infidel. We're going to ransom you for him."

"Infidels?"

"A violator of the grail."

"The grail?" She asked, confused. "What do you mean the grail? Like the Holy Grail?"

"Yes, the Holy Grail; violated by those that seek immortality. The infidels must be killed."

"Wait, are you saying that I'm being used as bait to lure someone who's immortal because he drank from the Holy Grail? Are you serious?" Surely this man was joking with her. The Holy Grail was a myth, and immortals didn't exist. "So who is this immortal?" But even as the question escaped her lips, she knew. They were looking for Collin. Suddenly everything fell into place. His miraculous survival, Dr. Babineaux's interest, Dr. Babineaux's research in longevity, Collin's uncle not wanting Collin to get too attached, his family constantly moving from place to place; but certainly he wasn't immortal, that was crazy. "So, you think that…," she didn't say his name, just in case she was wrong, "that this infidel drank from the Holy Grail and so is immortal? If he's immortal, how do you expect to kill him?" Her captor didn't say anything. She heard him pick up the magazine; the conversation was over.

Great, Jewell thought, I'm being held captive by a bunch of religious fanatics who believe in fairy tales. That wasn't a refreshing thought. She wasn't a fan of extremists of anything, and these people seemed to have taken religious fanaticism to new heights.

Jewell drifted in and out of sleep. As far as she knew, she had been awake for over twenty hours. Her thoughts were getting muddled from her lack of sleep and persistent hunger and she was having trouble remembering where she was and what was happening. Once in a while, the guard on duty would feel the need to assert his authority, generally through some form of physical assault; a slap to the face or a kick if she tried to say something. Before long, she stopped trying to talk to her captors.

Eventually, nature's call caught up with her. At first, it wasn't too bothersome, but as her bladder began to expand, the pressure began to become unbearable. She was afraid to ask to use the restroom, afraid of what the circumstances would be, though she was afraid of what the circumstances would be if she wasn't taken to the toilet. Other than being uncomfortable, with these men, she could be punished as well. Sitting in an enclosed space with someone who had urinated on herself would become very unpleasant, very quickly.

She decided to risk a slap or a kick. She cleared her throat quietly and heard the sound of a paper being moved. "I need to use the restroom," she whispered.

"What?" The voice was gruff, irritated. Whether from her speaking, or having to sit in the room with her, she didn't know.

"I need to use the restroom," she repeated, a little louder. This time, she heard the chair squeak and the man rapped on the door, signaling whoever was outside that he needed the door opened. After a few short seconds, she heard the rasp of the key in the lock and the door opened.

"She says she has to go to the bathroom." The door closed again. Jewell's head dropped to her chest in defeat. She would hold it as long as she could. However, she heard the door open again within a few minutes. Someone walked over to her. "You had better not try anything." It was the voice of the man that had asserted his authority when she had been cut. She nodded. Then she felt a piece of metal slide between her wrist and her chair, and the E Z Cuff fell away. She sat submissively as the other cuffs were removed.

The man took her hand and pulled her from the chair. She stumbled as she tried to stand up, the man steadied her. When she was stable, he led her from the room. She held her hand in front of her, trying not to walk into a wall. After a few turns the man put her hand on the top of the cold porcelain toilet. She stood, waiting for the man to leave. When it was obvious he didn't intend to leave her alone, she untied her scrub pants, and pulled them down, letting them fall to her ankles. She felt for the seat of the toilet and sat down. When she finished, she pulled her pants back up and was led back to the room. She was secured again to the chair where she was left with a guard.

Every once in a while, she would hear Collin, whispering to her to hold on; but when she opened her eyes, there would be nothing to see, the blindfold was still firmly affixed to her eyes and her arms and legs securely bound to the chair. Though the duct tape gag had been removed, it didn't help make anything easier.

Sometimes, when her captors changed, the door remained open long enough to hear sounds from outside. Some of the sounds were hard to identify; if she had to put a name to the sounds, she would have said it sounded like sword fights. She heard snippets of conversations, but most of the topics were mundane, not offering any information about her captors, or their quarry. She wanted to tell them that Collin was gone, that he had left her and didn't care about her any more, but she knew that they would never believe her. After all, why believe the truth, when they had so many more interesting stories to believe.

At this point, she was certain of three things. Her captors were hunting Collin, she was the bait, and they were all crazy. Not a winning combination.

CHAPTER 47

Both police officers stood up as they watched the man with the brace on his leg slip his key into the door of Edgar Durand's apartment. As the man slipped into the apartment the officers followed behind, one of them gently pushing on the door to keep it from closing. "Excuse me." the second officer said as she pulled the badge from under her shirt. "My name is Elizabeth Thomason; I work with the St. Tammany Parrish Sheriff's department. This is my partner, Kory Doucet. Are you Edgar Durand?"

Edgar looked at the badges held out by the two officers. "Is something wrong?" Edgar winced inwardly as he said that. By asking if something was wrong, they would obviously know that he knew something was wrong.

"May we come in Mr. Durand? We have a couple of questions we want to ask you."

Edgar swallowed and forced a smile. "Of course. You'll have to pardon the mess; I'm not much of a housekeeper." He walked in ahead of them clearing several papers off a couch and moving them to the coffee table. "Can I get you officers anything?"

"Yes, thank you. Do you have some sweet tea? It's so hot outside." Elizabeth glanced at her partner.

"That sounds wonderful Mr. Durand. Thank you."

Edgar nodded curtly and grudgingly walked into the kitchen to fix the two drinks. "If you have some lemon Mr. Durand; that would be wonderful." Elizabeth called into the kitchen as she leaned forward to glance at the papers on the table looking for any clues. Technically, she couldn't sort through the paper, but whatever was in plain sight was fair game. Most of the papers seemed to be old bills; there were a couple of final notices. She saw a to-do list with mundane tasks: grocery shopping call the cable guy; get the oil changed on the car. Under the list was a handwritten address in New Orleans. The street name was obscured, but the number was clear. Elizabeth pulled out her cell phone and snapped a picture, putting her phone away just as Edgar walked into the room, carrying two tall glasses of iced tea, each with a lemon wedge perched on the side, and the handle of a spoon protruding from the top of the glass.

Edgar sat on a chair opposite the couch upon which Sheriffs Elizabeth and Kory sat, perching on the edge of the chair expectantly. Elizabeth and Kory accepted the glasses and each took a sip before setting their glasses on the glass table top.

"That's an interesting cross you're wearing Mr. Durand." Elizabeth remarked when Edgar sat down.

Edgar pulled the simple black cross from his shirt. "It's just a cross, a symbol of my faith and love for God."

"It's beautiful. What's it made of? Onyx?" Elizabeth admired the plain black cross on the silver chain knowing exactly what it was. This was the symbol worn by all Obsidian Knights, given to them upon entry into the order; a plain black cross of obsidian on a silver chain.

"Ummm...I'm not really sure. It was a gift." It wasn't a complete lie; the cross had been a gift. "I think it's obsidian."

"Do you know Jewell McKean," Kory started abruptly.

"I'm sorry," Edgar lied smoothly, "I'm not familiar with the name."

Kory fished a photograph out of his notebook and handed it to Edgar. "She's a nurse at University Hospital in New Orleans. I believe you were a patient there."

Edgar took the picture and stared at it before handing it back. "She looks familiar, but I'm not sure I know who she is."

"We have reason to believe that you were stalking her about six weeks ago." Elizabeth interjected coldly.

Edgar gave a brief, but forced laugh. "Yes, now I remember. She was a nurse in the trauma unit. I was in an accident a while back." He gestured to his leg. "She was working in the trauma center when I was taken in, and she was so pretty. Honestly, I was hoping to catch her after work, I wanted to ask her out." He smiled, trying to look embarrassed. "I don't understand. That was several weeks ago

"She's missing." Elizabeth replied coldly. "She was taken this morning. We wanted to know if you knew anything about her disappearance."

Edgar feigned shock. "My goodness. How horrible. I wish I knew something officers, but I really haven't seen her since...well; it's been several weeks now."

"Would you be willing to come down to the station and make a statement Mr. Durand?" Tyler asked.

"Well, if you think it would help, I'd be happy to. If you can just give me a minute? I need to feed my cat and call my mother." He smiled apologetically. "She's expecting me for dinner."

Both officers nodded and Edgar got up to leave the room. They heard an electric can opener and a small gray tabby darted from the back rooms into the kitchen. They heard Edgar talking baby talk to his cat before they heard him pick up the phone in the kitchen. "Hi mom." There was a pause. "I'm sorry that I can't make dinner. The police need me to answer some questions about a girl from the hospital. I'll try to come by as soon as I'm finished there." The officers heard the phone settle back on the hook.

"He didn't say 'I love you.'" Kory whispered.

"What?"

"Don't you always tell your mother that you love her when you call? I do."

"So? Maybe he doesn't love her."

Kory hesitated, "Or maybe he wasn't calling his mother, but someone else to let them know that we were questioning him."

Elizabeth let out a low whistle.

Edgar walked into the room, placing his cell phone in his pocket. "Okay, I guess that's everything. Do I ride with you, or should I take my own car?"

"If you don't mind, we'll have you ride with us. We'll bring you back here when they're done."

Edgar gestured to the door. "After you," he said politely as he followed them out the door, locking it behind him.

At the warehouse, Art Lewis considered the phone call he had received from Edgar. The police were now involved. This would complicate things.

Andy Baraven walked into the police station, glancing at the notes Elizabeth had given him from her interview with Edgar Durand. He found the obsidian cross Edgar wore to be particularly interesting.

"What do you have for me?" He asked Melissa St. Johns, a special deputy, as he walked into her office. She was beautiful, even at nearly sixty. Andy could imagine that she must have been courted by every man who saw her when she was young. Her once auburn hair had turned almost completely silver, but it didn't make her look any older. She handed him a Yahoo map. "This is a map to the address that Elizabeth and Kory found on the table at Mr. Durand's apartment. It's a warehouse. It was rented a little over a month ago by a company called Vex Lexicon, Inc. They are incorporated in Delaware, and have offices all over the world. It seems to be an umbrella company with…well, hundreds of subsidiaries. It's a very profitable company though. Here's their corporate info sheet. Don't know if it'll be much help."

"Thanks beautiful," Andy flashed Melissa his most brilliant smile. In fact, it gave him a lot of information. For one, Vex Lexicon was a very interesting name for a company. If the letters were reordered, it spelled *Vox in Excelso,* the order disbanding the Templar Knights. It was the corporation used by the Obsidian Knights to maintain and fund their organization. The Templars had similar corporations, designed to help them protect innocents, but also to help fund the order. Much of the original money for the corporation came from the Templar fortune, but through the purchase of several successful companies, they were well funded, to say the least.

The fact that Edgar was a member of the Order coupled with this information gave him a very promising lead into the whereabouts of Jewell McKean. As much as he wanted to go after her immediately, he knew that without careful planning, they could be putting Jewell into jeopardy. The first thing he needed to do however was call Sheriff Payne.

CHAPTER 48

"There must be something we can do!" Collin protested, looking at Percy. When Percy didn't respond, Collin resumed his pacing. "They know where she is! Why won't they do anything? Why won't they let us do anything?"

Percy gestured for Collin to sit down. Collin crossed his arms across his chest defiantly, staring down his uncle, before finally submitting and slumping into one of the velvet covered chairs facing the chaise where Percy sat. "These people have two roles Collin. They are public servants. As public servants, their jobs are to protect the people. They have taken a vow before the city, or the state, 'to serve and protect'," he quoted. "Some of them are also Templar Knights. They have taken a vow before God. They have pledged their lives to protect those that are in need of their protection. We happen to be high on their list." Percy sighed dramatically. "Believe me, I understand your frustration, but we're special Collin. That entitles us to certain...benefits."

"I would hardly call this a benefit!" Collin jumped up and resumed his pacing. "Because I entangled her in this mess, isn't it my duty to help get her out?"

"Sheriff Payne assures me they'll do everything they can to get Jewell back to her dad." He didn't add dead or alive. Percy wasn't sure if the kidnappers thought Jewell was one of them and using her to root out any others in the area, or if they knew that she wasn't. If they knew she wasn't one of the *family*, they had a better chance of bringing her home alive. As misguided as the Obsidian Knights were, they had honor, such as it was. They didn't kill innocents without reason.

Collin sat in the chair again. "But not back to me. They won't bring her back to me." He rested his elbows on his knees and cradled his face in his hands.

"That's her choice Collin, but you have to understand; I gave Avelyn a choice. She chose wrong."

"So her only choice is to leave me? Or for me to leave her?"

Percy didn't answer Collin's question. Instead, he left the room, calling for the others. They were all going to Dr. Babineaux's house where they would be safe.

The Templar Knights sat in Dr. Babineaux's living room. Percy, Kendryck, Gladys, and Collin sat with them. Nine Templar Knights and four Infinitas, thirteen people in all. Although the gathered group believed that Jewell had been kidnapped to get to Collin, no ransom demands had yet been made, and no one was even certain that Jewell was still alive. If the Obsidian Knights thought she was immortal, she would have been summarily executed.

Sheriff Payne gave a brief explanation of the rescue plan. Because the warehouse where Jewell was probably being held was in Orleans Parrish, Orleans Sheriff had priority on the case, despite the fact that Jewell was from Covington. The Templars that would be involved in the rescue would be Christian Johnson and Eric Wilder, both New Orleans police officers, and Hugh

Payne, Sheriff of the Orleans Parrish Sheriff's department. Dr. Babineaux would also be within a short distance in case Jewell required medical attention. He'd also called in his best staff to work the trauma center during the rescue. Herb Ilkay, a Templar and New Orleans fireman would be on duty if the fire department was needed.

Andy Baraven, a Templar and officer in the St. Tammany Parrish Sheriff's department would remain with the Infinitas at Dr. Babineaux's house on the North side of the lake. Luke Jefferson, and Mike Forester, both Templars and firemen in Covington would stay with Jewell's father and Jewell's best friend Ashley at the McKean house along with Alex Stanley, also a Templar and a Covington police officer.

As Sheriff Payne was briefing the Templars and Infinitas, one of the Louisiana S.W.A.T. teams was being briefed along with a crisis negotiation team. Surveillance teams were starting to set up in the area to gather information.

Outside the warehouse, two of the kidnappers were patrolling. They were armed; each carried a firearm and a sword. A third individual, also carrying a firearm and a sword was located at the main entrance to the warehouse offices. The windows were tinted making it difficult to see inside, but sometimes men could be seen as they passed close to the windows. Initial observation indicated seven men; three outside, and an additional four inside. A blueprint of the warehouse showed several offices inside which could hide additional individuals. The team couldn't get a visual on Jewell, if she was there.

There was no active phone line to the warehouse, so communication at this point was impossible. The team radioed back what information they had. A law enforcement command center was set up at one of the nearby office buildings where Sheriff Payne met the S.W.A.T. team and the other law enforcement officials that had been assembled.

Shortly after three a.m., Tommy McKean received a phone call. It was short, and to the point. "Bring the immortal and we will release the girl." Immediately after the call was complete, Alex called the station to begin a trace on the call. Unlike in the movies, tracing a phone call was much easier than they would have you believe. Within an hour, the police had identified the phone call as having been made from a prepaid cell phone purchased from a Wal-Mart in San Diego, California. It had been purchased and activated only hours prior to the call and the information on the phone's owner was invalid. Triangulation of the cell phone's signal placed the call as being made from somewhere in the San Diego area. Calls made to the number went unanswered.

"What is the immortal?" Ashley asked Alex after hearing that the cell phone lead was a dead end. Tommy looked at Alex after Ashley asked the question that had probably been on his mind, but worry for his daughter had left it unasked.

Alex looked at Ashley, and then at Tommy. How much could he tell her? How much *should* he tell her? Alex had known Tommy a long time. Alex's wife had been best friends with Tommy's wife. He had known Jewell for most of Jewell's life and loved her as he did his own children. What would he expect Tommy to do in the same situation? He knew something that could potentially save Tommy's daughter's life, but he was also sworn to protect the Infinitas – the immortals.

Alex finally decided that a partial truth would suffice…for now. "There's a group of religious fanatics who believe that the Templars stole the Holy Grail during their time on the Temple Mount." He looked at Tommy. "Do you know the history of the Templar Knights?"

"A little," Tommy replied. "I know that they were headquartered in Solomon's Temple and some thought that they found certain holy relics there, the Grail being one of them. But the Templar's haven't been around for thousands of years."

"Well, for the most part, yes." Alex thought for a minute. "Well, these religious fanatics, the Obsidian Knights, believe that they have discovered people who are immortal because they have defiled the Grail by drinking from it. When they find someone whom they think is one of these immortals, they're summarily executed as infidels."

"Summarily executed?" Tommy's voice was shaking with fear for his daughter.

"They're beheaded." Alex looked at Tommy sympathetically. "But since they're ransoming your daughter for the immortal, Jewell is probably alive."

"But there's no such thing as immortals, right? Who is it they want?" Ashley asked.

"There are no people that have drunk from the Holy Grail and become immortal." Alex explained. The Infinitas may seem immortal, but they aged and died as did all people and their immortality was genetic, not the result of drinking from a mythical cup. "They want Collin. They believe him to be an infidel."

"But why?" Ashley looked at Alex, clearly upset and confused. Even though he had left Jewell without so much as a good-bye, she still liked him enough not to want him killed. "Because he survived that accident? Have these people heard of modern medicine?"

"Precisely because he survived that accident. And yes, they've heard of modern medicine, but the only miracle they believe in is the gift of the Grail, and Collin should *not* have survived that accident. You know that as well as I do; as well as they do."

"Collin left." Tommy hung his head dejectedly. "Even if we wanted to hand him over to these people, we wouldn't know where to find him." Alex looked at Tommy. Sympathy filled his eyes. He was torn between his duty as a Templar, and his duty as a friend. "The NOLA team will get her out," was all Alex could say to reassure his friend.

"I hope so," said Ashley.

Tommy just buried his head in his hands and wept for his daughter.

CHAPTER 49

"I'm not just going to sit here and wait!" Collin said angrily, pulling against his uncle's surprisingly strong grip. "Not when I know where they are and what they want! It's my fault she's in this mess; I'm going to get her out!"

"Collin, they'll kill you!" Gladys pleaded.

"I don't care! Better me than her. If something happens to her, if she dies…" He gave his arm a sharp tug, escaping his uncle's strong grasp only to fall into Andy's arms. Although Andy wasn't as strong as Collin, he slowed Collin enough for Percy and Kendryck to grab hold of him and force him back into one of the plush chairs in Dr. Babineaux's sitting room. "So what? Are you planning on sitting on me until she dies? Or are you actually going to do something to try to help me?"

Collin was angry. First he was kidnapped, taken away from Jewell and told he could never be with her because he had some rare genetic disorder that made him, for all intents and purposes, immortal. Then he finds out that, because of his disease, his true love has been kidnapped by a bunch of seriously deranged religious fanatics who are holding her hostage and may kill her, so that they can kill him. He was determined to do what he could to save her, regardless of the cost to him. The people with him could help him, or get out of his way.

Andy looked at Collin as he was held down by his uncle and Kendryck. If nothing else, he could understand Collin's frustration. He quietly left the room to make a phone call. When Andy returned, Collin was still seated in the chair, but Percy and Kendryck had reverted to guard positions, no longer physically holding him in the chair. Andy could see the calculation in Collin's eyes; he intended to find a way to save Jewell. Fortunately, Sheriff Payne had offered a suggestion. Andy cleared his throat to get everyone's attention. "I just got off the phone with Hugh." He waited to make sure everyone, especially Collin, was listening. "He thinks it would be best if I took Collin down to the command center." Andy noticed Percy's eyes narrow. "He would be safe there," Andy quickly added to calm Percy and interrupt any repudiation he might offer. "Hugh feels Collin could be useful in the hostage negotiations."

Collin practically jumped out of his seat; this was exactly what he had been hoping for, an opportunity to help. Kendryck and Percy looked uneasy, but they didn't make any attempt to push Collin back into the chair. Percy looked at Collin sternly, the way he had when Collin was a child, just before he did something by himself for the first time, like crossing the street, or walking to school on his own. "You will do *everything* they tell you. You will not make any attempt to rescue Jewell on your own. Do you understand?"

"Yes sir," Collin responded contritely trying to suppress his eagerness. Percy stepped out of the way and Collin walked toward Andy.

* * *

At the command center, the crisis negotiation team had been patched into the line at the McKean house and two negotiators had been sent to the McKean house as well. Because a demand had been made, they hoped that they could negotiate Jewell out of the situation which would be a lot safer for everyone.

After Collin and Andy arrived, they were briefed on the situation. While the S.W.A.T. team had prepared a rescue plan, they intended to wait for a couple more hours to see if another call was made. Then the crisis negotiation team would take over.

It was almost eight that evening before another call came. It was from the same number as the previous call. Tommy McKean picked up the phone. "Hello?" Kade Lee, one of the crisis negotiators at the McKean house listened in on the phone.

"We want the immortal. The girl will be released unharmed if we have the immortal within twenty four hours." Kade hastily scribbled some notes on a pad next to Tommy.

"What immortal?" Tommy asked, reading the notes.

"Collin Sykes, the infidel." The voice on the other end of the phone responded curtly.

Tommy looked at Kade's notes again before responding. "How can we be certain that the hostage is alive?" Tommy's voice shook as he asked this question.

"We know about your surveillance. We'll show you the girl. Be assured though, that she will die should any attempt be made at that time to remove her from our...care."

"What time?" Tommy asked, glancing at the pad again.

"Eight forty-five." The voice was cold, sinister. "You will have twenty four hours from that time to produce the infidel. If we don't have him by eight forty-five tomorrow night, she will suffer the same fate he would have. We will then hunt him relentlessly and mete out God's justice to those who oppose us." There was an emptiness on the other end of the line indicating that the caller had ended the call. Triangulation of the caller's location placed him near Reno. He was moving to avoid being caught.

*   *   *

Someone eventually brought Jewell some water. She didn't know if she had been there for over a day, or not yet a day. At one point, she smelled syrup and she could hear plastic scraping on Styrofoam as one of her captors ate what she presumed was breakfast. If that was true, she had been there for at least twenty four hours.

When she heard the knock, and the scrape of the lock at the door, she was relieved to know that she would have a new guard. Some of them were actually nice. They were concerned with her comfort and did what they could to make her more comfortable, despite not being able to untie her. She had been to the restroom three times. She looked forward to that, because it gave her an opportunity to stretch and rub the pain from her wrists. She was bound more loosely by the first man that had taken her to the restroom, so the chafing had eased a bit, though she was never bound loosely enough to escape.

When her next captor released her wrists and ankles, binding her wrists in front of her, she had assumed that it was so that she could be taken to the restroom again. Though she didn't have to go, she welcomed the opportunity to stretch, so she didn't argue; but when they left this time, rather than going right, and then right again, she went right, and then left. She was taken through another door onto a tile floor, led a short distance, and then another door was opened. This one brought with it the smell of the outdoors. The air was fresher, not musty, and smelled of pavement and exhaust. The sound of the airplanes passing overhead was deafening. She heard the door close silently behind her, and she and her captor stood silently in front of the door. What were they waiting for? They stood like that, silently for several minutes before her captor turned and led her back inside, securing her once again to the hard wooden chair in the empty, musty smelling room.

At eight forty-five that night, Tommy McKean sat in his daughter's room, looking at the screen on her computer. A secure internet link sent a live image video back to him of his daughter, standing handcuffed and blindfolded in front of a warehouse. She had bruises on her face and arms. A long, deep cut went from her shoulder to her elbow.

Andy confirmed that the video he was viewing was live. Jewell had walked from the warehouse on her own. She walked stiffly, as if she had been held in a position that allowed little movement. The look on her face was one of mixed terror, and relief though why her father thought that he could see relief in his daughter's face was beyond him. Could it be that she thought they were going to let her go? He knew that wasn't the plan, not until they had Collin. Not until they believed they had carried out God's justice.

Collin backed away from the screen that everyone had gathered around and screamed. The rage he felt at the pain Jewell had suffered at the hands of those monsters, at his expense, infuriated him. "Why aren't we doing anything?" He paced furiously across the room to where Sheriff Payne was sitting. He leaned down, placing his hands on either arm of the chair lowering his face to within inches of the focus of his fury. "We know what they want, why don't we give it to them?" he hissed through clenched teeth. Though his voice was barely louder than a whisper it carried across the suddenly silent room. "She's suffering what was meant for me."

Hugh Payne sighed and rubbed his face with his hands. "What she's suffering was not meant for you," he stated in a matter of fact tone. "What's meant for you is far worse. The men gathered in this room," he scanned the gathered forces with his eyes, "are experts at what they do. Let them do their job."

Collin lowered his hands to his sides, making fists that shook with his combined desperation and fury. He scanned the room finding the captain of the S.W.A.T. team and holding the Team Leader's eyes with his own. "What are you waiting for?" His fury had not diminished, though it had found a new focus. None of the men in the room would be intimidated by Collin, but all understood his pain.

"We're waiting for information." Jeff Wagner, the platoon's Team Leader responded calmly, returning Collin's glare with one filled with sympathy. "We need more information before we move." One problem they had was that the interior of the warehouse was almost completely concealed, and getting close to the warehouse was nearly impossible.

Currently, lack of information was their biggest enemy. They didn't know how many captors there were, or where Jewell was being held, or the types or quantities of weapons the captors had. Those on perimeter duty had guns and swords. If the team chose to take an aggressive approach, they weren't comfortable that they would be able to locate and secure Jewell before she was killed.

They had tried to establish communication with the kidnappers, but all attempts had been rebuffed. In addition, attempts to gain surveillance through gifts of food had been refused. At this point, waiting was their best option.

Hugh's phone rang. He looked around the room and stepped into a corner to separate himself from the group. He spoke into the phone in low tones. After a few minutes, he turned and walked to Collin holding the phone out to him. "It's Kendryck," he said as Collin looked at him questioningly, holding out his hand to accept the phone.

"Hello?" He asked into the phone. "Yes sir." Collin was silent for several minutes. "Yes sir, I understand. I'll do what I can." Collin hung up the phone and handed it to Sheriff Payne. He looked at the S.W.A.T. leader. "I need someplace where I can be alone, away from all of this activity. I need some time to be by myself."

Jeff was quiet for a moment as he thought. "I reckon the best place for you to get some quiet would be that office next to the bathroom. It's furthest from the entrance, and it might be far enough away from this room to give you some peace." His voice was full of sympathy.

"Thanks," Collin replied, grabbing a chair by its back and dragging it towards the office. As long as people weren't going in and out of the bathroom, it should be quiet enough for him to concentrate. He didn't know if he could do what Kendryck had suggested, but he had to try. He placed the chair in the center of the empty room and started thinking about Jewell. He tried to think about every detail until he could see her in his mind, and then he tried to speak to her. "Jewell, I need your help. Can you hear me?"

*   *   *

Jewell sat tied back in her chair. Her guard sat beside the door. He had fastened the E Z Cuffs loosely; for which she was grateful. Her wrists were chafed and she could feel the sores that had formed on both her arms and legs. She tried to concentrate on rearranging herself so that she was as comfortable as she could make herself. As she shifted from side to side trying to get comfortable, she heard Collin's voice, "Jewell, I need your help. Can you hear me?" She looked up, not that she could see anything through the blindfold. "Excuse me?" she said out loud.

"Excuse you for what?" her captor asked.

"I'm sorry; I thought I heard you say something." Her captor just grunted. Jewell shook her head, as if something had crawled inside her head and she was trying to shake it free. She thought she had heard something but wasn't sure what she was hearing, or if she was actually hearing anything.

Collin felt the shift in Jewell's emotions from desolation to confusion when he made contact. He had to try harder.

"Jewell. Honeysuckle. It's Collin. You're hearing me. Listen, I'm sorry I left. I love you. I can't help you though unless you help me. Please Jewell; I can't help you unless you can talk to me." Collin focused all his energy into his thought.

"Collin?" Jewell whispered.

She heard the guard shift in his chair. How could she answer him without drawing attention? Did she need to talk out loud, or could she think what she wanted to say.

She heard him! He couldn't hear or understand her words, but her feeling of relief washed over him in response to his pleas. He didn't know if she could understand his words either, or just his feelings, but as he thought the words, he tried to convey what he needed with his feelings as well. "Oh God, Honeysuckle! God, I love you. Don't give up. I need you to give me some information about where you are and the people who are holding you." He tried to organize his thoughts so he could get as much information as he could.

"We know you're in the warehouse. Where are you in the warehouse? We have a map. Just think about where you are, don't say anything out loud, and just think it."

She knew she was probably hallucinating, but at least it was better than sitting in silence waiting for someone to attack her, or worse, kill her. Where was she? Now how was she supposed to answer that? She was blindfolded and being led everywhere they went. Wait, they had just gone outside. From the front door, they had gone left, then right, and then left through a door. After the door, they had gone right, walked down the hall a little ways, and taken a right into the room. She concentrated, how had they got to that room from the warehouse? Through a door, then right, then right again into the room. And the bathroom, out the door, then right and the bathroom was just down the hall on the left. Those were the only places she had been.

Collin could almost feel her movements as she traced the paths through the warehouse. He could feel her captors' hands tight around her arm, controlling her, pulling her through the office. He tried to suppress his anger and the overpowering fear that Jewell was feeling as it washed through him, and tried to focus on how she was moving. He could feel her movements as they came in from outside, as they came in from the warehouse, and as she went to the bathroom. He didn't have the building blueprint with him so he wrote down the directions. "Good love. Now tell me, how many people are there with you?"

How many people, she thought? She tried to think through the guards. Some of them she recognized as being different, but some, she didn't know if they were people that had already been there before, or new. If they hadn't left, the original four were there, plus the two in the car. One of them had guarded her at one point. She pressed her fingers into the arm of the chair to keep track; that was six. She thought the first guy with the hamburger may have been one of the people there when she transferred cars; his voice had a distinctive

Southern drawl, if she had to describe it, she would say Redneck. One of her guards wore Fahrenheit cologne; it smelled like he bathed in it. The only reason she knew the smell was that Mike Forester at the firehouse wore it. He said he wore it as a joke, Fahrenheit because he was a fireman. She smiled a little thinking about Mike. As far as she could count, there were at least nine, but she didn't think there were more than twenty.

At least nine, but no more than twenty he thought. The emotions were flooding his mind quickly. He was trying to make sense of what she was thinking. There was too much. The terror in her thoughts was overwhelming.

"Hold tight Honeysuckle. I'm close by. We *will* get you out love, and I will never leave you again."

He was close, he was close. Relief washed over her as she realized people were looking for her.

CHAPTER 50

Collin stood up from the chair. His muscles were tight and his shoulders hurt. He must have been sitting in that chair longer than he had thought. He looked at his notes as he moved his head from side to side trying to get the kinks out of his neck and walked to main room. The pandemonium in the room assaulted his senses like a tidal wave. He stopped at the entrance, watching what appeared to be complete disarray, soon realizing that the room was controlled chaos, each person working on their task, attempting to bring about Jewell's release.

He scanned the room until he saw Sheriff Payne on the other side of the room. He carefully maneuvered his way around and through the confusion toward where the Sheriff was standing. Sheriff Payne gave Collin a smile as he moved to one of the tables that had a blueprint of the warehouse. The S.W.A.T. platoon member smiled at him as he handed the sheriff a rolled up copy before turning back to his work. The sheriff walked back to where Collin was standing and took him gently by the arm, leading him outside.

"Were you able to learn anything?" Sheriff Payne resisted the urge to ask Collin what he had been doing in the other room.

"Yeah, I think so." Collin took the map from the sheriff and unrolled it on the sidewalk. He studied it for a minute, pulling his notes out of his pocket and compared them with the map. "I'm not entirely sure, but I think that she's here." He pointed to an interior room on the map. Collin showed the sheriff his notes and explained how he had reached his conclusion.

"Did you get any other information?" Sheriff Payne asked after they had finished with the map.

"Well, I think that they keep a guard in the room. And there are about nine people, maybe more." He looked at Sheriff Payne, and then down at his hands. "They want me."

"Well we already know what they want!" Sheriff Payne responded. "But that other information… Let me see what I can do." Sheriff Payne held the door for Collin. Collin hesitated before going inside, his gaze lingering at the end of the street in the direction of the warehouse. They wanted him. If they had him, they would let her go. "I know what you're thinking." Sheriff Payne interrupted his thoughts. "We don't know if surrendering you to them would help Jewell. Don't get any crazy ideas. Let these guys do their job and stay where I can keep an eye on you." Collin sighed and walked inside.

The sheriff walked straight to Jeff Wagner, the sea of chaos parting before him. As he reached the table where Wagner sat, he laid out the blueprint and pointed to the room that Collin had shown him. "Here, this is the room where they're holding her."

Wagner looked up from the documents he had been studying to Sheriff Payne. Wagner's eyes studied the sheriff's for several seconds before he looked down at the blueprint lying on the table. The room the sheriff had indicated was one of the key locations the S.W.A.T. team had been considering. "Are you sure?"

"Relatively," the sheriff responded.

"May I ask how you know this and where your information comes from?" Jeff was looking at the sheriff, not so much with suspicion, but doubt. Wagner had been a S.W.A.T. officer for over a decade and information like this didn't usually fall into lap.

"I have a source that has some inside information. For safety reasons, I can't tell you anything else."

Jeff nodded his head once in acknowledgement. "Do you have any other information?" The sheriff sat and explained everything that Collin had told him.

After he was finished speaking with Sheriff Payne, Wagner called his team together to discuss their plan. The three guards patrolling outside would be taken with non-lethal force, subdued, and placed into custody. That would leave at least six captors inside, one in the room with Jewell. If the S.W.A.T. team rescued Jewell rather than negotiating her release, it would have to be well planned and swift. There was a risk that the captors would kill Jewell if an alarm was raised.

Another concern was access to the building. A master key to all locks in the building had been provided by the building's owner, but they would need to eliminate the outside guards. There had been nine individuals rotated through outside guard duties. They changed individually on three hour shifts, one guard being changed every hour. But it was impossible to determine how many remained inside the building. It was assumed that all captors were armed at a minimum with a gun and a sword.

Collin sat quietly in the corner, listening as the S.W.A.T. team made plans. He also tried to figure out how he would escape Sheriff Payne to go with the team when they left to rescue Jewell.

Finally, after more than two hours of discussing details, they decided they would move at four o'clock that morning. By planning the rescue early in the morning, it was more likely that fewer of the captors would be awake. It was just after one a.m. so the team laid down for a few hours rest. While everyone was resting, Collin slipped silently out a rear door and headed down to the warehouse where he planned to wait until the S.W.A.T. team arrived.

At three thirty, the S.W.A.T. team donned night vision goggles, loaded non-lethal weapons, and checked their handguns as well. The plan was to cause as little death as possible.

*   *   *

Collin sat near some landscaping that decorated the perimeter of the warehouse. From where he sat, he could see the S.W.A.T. team assembling just outside the range of the warehouse lights. Their dark uniforms made them difficult to see in the black night. Collin's gaze shifted between the S.W.A.T. members and the guards circling the building's perimeter.

As Collin watched, the S.W.A.T. team formed into a single file line, moving to the corner of the warehouse where they wouldn't be seen until the first guard turned the corner. Collin could see both sides of the corner, the side along which the guard would walk, and the side along which the S.W.A.T. team waited.

Benjamin Lindgren was thirty-two years old. He had been a full member of the Obsidian Knights for almost six years. His specialty was weapon design. His father was a bladesmith, a skill that had been passed down in his family for generations. Benjamin had been helping his father to craft swords since he was old enough to pull himself up using the anvil. Lindgren blades were some of the finest blades in the world. Many of the Obsidian Knights, not just in his Order, but from around the world, owned Lindgren Swords. Of course, a sword was the quickest and easiest way to kill an infidel. A properly sharpened sword could easily slice through bone and flesh, severing a person's head from his body

This was the third time Benjamin had been outside, endlessly circling the building. As he walked, he practiced his sword formations. The sword that he carried was not a replica. This was a real, high carbon steel, heat treated and tempered blade with a double edge sharpened until it could split a single hair. He also carried a Glock 21 45 mm pistol. He was well armed. He sighed and slid his sword home into its hand tooled leather scabbard and continued his relentless circling.

Benjamin paused before he rounded the corner that would take him to the street side of the warehouse. He glanced up at the landscaping that separated the warehouse from the buildings on the other side; he thought he saw something move. He pulled out his PolyTac Xenon flashlight and held it at shoulder height, pointed towards the trees. With his other hand, he released the clasp on his holster, pulling his pistol out slightly and letting it drop home, just to make sure it was clear of the holster. After carefully scanning the trees and bushes for several minutes, he decided that it was probably just a dog that he had seen. He put his flashlight back in the flashlight loop on his belt, and secured his gun in the holster. Laughing at himself, he rounded the corner of the warehouse.

There was a pop, and something hit his chest, hard. Benjamin was wearing a bullet proof vest so he wasn't concerned that he had received a mortal wound and he quickly realized that there hadn't been enough force behind the pellet that hit his chest to have been a bullet. These thoughts went through his head instantaneously as he reflexively looked down to where he had been shot, moving his hand to his chest. That's when the gas hit him. He recognized it immediately as CS; pepper spray. Turning his head to the side, he tried to inhale to warn his partner on the other side of the building, but as he took a breath of the poisoned air, the burn in his throat and chest caused him to choke and start coughing, forcing him to his knees. He could feel the gas as it invaded his nose and mouth, penetrating and saturating his sinus cavities.

In the next moment, he felt rough hands securing his wrists behind his back and he was jerked roughly to his feet. He tried to get a look at his captors, but the chemicals made it impossible to open his eyes. He was dragged some distance from the warehouse before he was shoved into the back of a car. The door slammed and the car immediately pulled away. Benjamin didn't believe in

Karma as such. He was a devout Christian, a warrior and servant for the Lord, but in those few moments, he had his first thought that maybe kidnapping the girl to get to the infidel was not such a good idea after all.

* * *

Shawn "Kountree" Robins had known that he wanted to be S.W.A.T. ever since he was a little boy. He was point man because he never missed. This occasion was no different. Squatting silently against the wall, Kountree could hear the snap of a gun holster being secured, and a flashlight slipping into its holster. The muted footsteps in the grass let Kountree know exactly where his target was, even though Kountree couldn't see him. At the moment that his target was visible, Kountree fired the tear gas pellet, hitting the startled guard square in the chest. As Kountree's target clawed at his face, the arrest team, wearing gas masks, secured the man and carried him to a waiting NOPD squad car stationed a few blocks away.

The second and third guards were also taken down without incident, succumbing to the gas before they were able to sound an alarm.

On schedule, the door to the warehouse opened to let out the next guard. Kountree expertly placed his shot directly in the exiting guard's chest, while Jayce Miles fired a CS gas shell inside the open door. Within seconds, the five member team had moved in to secure the gas infested room. Even though they were wearing masks, the gas made the team's eyes water and noses burn. From here, they would avoid using gas to shelter Jewell as much as possible. While it was non-lethal, the affects would traumatize and frighten her, making rescue that much more difficult.

Kountree entered first, quickly scanning the room with his night vision goggles. The rest of the team followed closely behind in single file. The reception office was dark and empty; the door leading to the other offices was securely closed. The team moved quickly to their areas of responsibility, securing the room and stood silently, waiting for their next command.

After ensuring that the area was clear, Kountree opened the door to the main office scanning for captors. The hallway outside the office was clear. Kountree used hand signals to silently move the team into the hallway. The team quickly moved through offices other than the one holding Jewell to make sure they were clear.

When the conference room was the only room that remained Kountree slowly reached for the door handle, signaling his men to be ready. As he began to pull the handle down, he heard movement inside the room. He slowly released the handle and moved his men to the far end of the hall. He whispered into his headset, letting the command center know that the office area had been secured with the exception of the conference room, which was occupied. He waited for several minutes while the tactics unit worked to make a plan.

Outside, Christopher Mills, a member of the S.W.A.T. team scanned the surrounding area. It was little more than ten minutes after the infiltration team entered the building when he saw the lone man running alongside the building. He quickly turned his rifle toward the target and sighted. As he carefully took aim, he realized that the young man running alongside the building attempting not to be seen was Collin Sykes. Christopher sighed and lowered his weapon. He should probably shoot him with the pepper pellet just to teach him a lesson, and keep him out of harm's way, but while the pellets were classified as non-lethal, they still had the potential to kill. Christopher quickly communicated to the rest of the team that Collin was entering through the front entryway.

Kountree cursed under his breath when he heard Christopher's message through his headset. If he made it into the building, there could potentially be two hostages instead of one. Kountree pointed at Ryan, and then pointed at the door to the reception area, signaling him to intercept Collin and escort him to safety. With Logan guarding the warehouse door, and Ryan moving to intercept Collin, his team was down to three; three men against at least six.

Kountree watched as Ryan stood up and started moving towards the reception area's door. Ryan hadn't had time to take two steps when the door to the conference room opened and a man stepped out. His eyes immediately found the S.W.A.T. team hunched at the end of the hall, and turned to signal the alarm. As he did, the man pulled a pistol from a holster on his hip. Ryan instinctively raised his rifle and fired an OC pellet at the man standing in the doorway. The man stumbled backward two steps and then, despite being incapacitated by the painful gas, fired off six shots blindly. It was then that Collin opened the door leading into the hallway.

When Collin entered the building, he was immediately struck by an overwhelming smell. His eyes immediately started watering and he blinked heavily pulling the collar of his shirt up over his mouth and nose to help filter the gas. As he staggered across the dark room, he heard gunshots from hallway beyond the door. Without thinking, Collin burst through the door to the hallway. He could barely see through the tears in his eyes, but he quickly took in the situation, seeing the S.W.A.T. team to his left and the now incapacitated man to his right.

Between where he stood, and the fallen man was the door to the room where Jewell was. He didn't think; he simply turned and started running towards the door. Behind him, he could hear the S.W.A.T. team chasing him. Before he had taken two steps, the door to the room imprisoning Jewell opened and a man stepped out holding a gun. His eyes fixed on Collin as he fired two shots. At the same moment, Collin dove towards the man's ankles. One shot hit Collin's left shoulder, but he barely noticed the pain. As Collin hit the man he heard Jewell scream his name. He quickly pushed the downed man out the door, closing and locking it behind him. The S.W.A.T. team would have to deal with the guard.

Collin sat on the floor, catching his breath and listening to the sounds of the S.W.A.T. engaging in full battle outside the door. He could feel the door shake as bodies were thrown or fell against it, but all he could do was sit and stare. In seconds, he took in all of the details. Each of Jewell's ankles was fastened to a leg of the chair, which were too far apart for her small frame. Blood had soaked through the pants of her scrubs in random spots. The rope that held her to the back of the chair had caused her scrub top to creep up, baring her belly which showed hints of bruising. Her wrists were bound to the arms of the chair with plastic ties. The ties did not look tight, but nonetheless, they had abraded deep wounds on her arms that dripped blood steadily down each side of the chair marking the light wood with its crimson path. She was blindfolded, and she held her body stiffly against the chair pushing away from the unknown danger that had just entered the room. Her face and neck were covered with new bruises. There was a dried trickle of blood running down the back of her neck turning the collar of her lavender scrub top a rusty brown.

Suddenly, he realized that as he entered the room she had called his name. Through the terror, he could see a sliver of hope. He stood up quickly, crossing the room in two steps. He laid his hand gently against her face, afraid to hurt her. There was no place that he could touch her that did not show some evidence of injury. He worried about the wounds that her clothes must be hiding. As he touched her, he felt the sudden warmth, the shock of passion that he always felt when he touched her. His breathing quickened, both in response to touching her, and in anger for what they…what he, had done to her. He whispered her name. "Jewell. Honeysuckle." He choked back a sob as he carefully untied the blindfold, lowering it from her eyes.

Jewell knew she was hallucinating. She was hungry, she hadn't slept in days. She looked to the corner where her guard had been sitting reading his book; the chair was empty, his book placed face down on the floor to hold his place.

When she felt the electricity from his touch, the pain left and her hope swelled. "Are you really here? Or am I just imagining your voice again?" She winced in pain as she formed the words.

"Shhhh. I'm here. You're going to be safe." He started to speak more quickly as he explained everything that had happened, how what she had heard was really him and how her information had helped the S.W.A.T. team. He tenderly moved his hands over her wrists, afraid to touch them. He quickly scanned the room for something he could use to cut the bindings from her wrists and ankles. Except for the chair in the corner, the book sitting next to it, and the chair to which Jewell was secured, the room was empty. He looked at the cuffs, trying to determine if there was a release mechanism. "How do they take these off?"

"They cut them." He gave her a curt nod of acknowledgment and stood, moving toward the door. "Don't…" He turned and saw tears streaming down her face. "Don't leave me again."

Again. Her words tore at his heart. He moved back to her side and placed his hand gently on her shoulder, hoping that he wouldn't hurt her.

Collin sat on the floor next to her resting his hand on the edge of the chair where he could touch the ends of her fingers. While they sat, listening to the muffled sounds of the battle raging outside their room, they heard a loud crash against the door. It came again before Jewell heard the familiar sound of the key in the lock. She glanced at Collin, terror in her eyes. The door burst open, and two men dressed in jeans and t-shirts burst in, each carrying a sword.

*   *   *

Edgar pushed the man out of the way. "Idiot" he thought. He was never going to break through this door by slamming his shoulder against it; that only worked in the movies. Both men carried a sword in his right hand. If Collin Sykes was in this room, they would deal with him. Edgar didn't have his gun anymore. He had used all of his ammunition in the fight that was raging in the warehouse. He fumbled with the key before he felt it slide home. He moved into the room, Daniel close behind. Daniel had a gun, but Edgar wasn't certain how much ammunition he had. Daniel's strength was hand to hand combat, but a gun would take the infidel down long enough for them to do their job with the sword.

As Edgar moved into the room, he heard a gun discharge next to his ear. He looked at Daniel and called him an idiot. Daniel was the same age as Edgar, but he definitely lacked the common sense that comes with age. Then Edgar saw the hole in the wall across the room. Daniel had missed.

The infidel had moved between them and the hostage. "Well now isn't that sweet," Edgar crooned. "Trying to protect your girlfriend. Why bother? By killing you, we spare you an eternity of pain. If we kill her first well," he shrugged impassively, "she would have died long before you anyway. Either way, God's will is fulfilled."

"You don't know anything about God's will," Collin replied, watching both swords carefully. When one of the men moved around the chair, Collin noticed that he had a brace on one leg. As he watched for vulnerabilities, he hadn't realized right away that the man he faced was the same man that had been stalking Jewell at the hospital. Keeping one eye on the man with the gun, he watched the man with the brace limp to circle around behind Jewell's chair. Collin carefully repositioned his body as the swordsmen moved, trying to stay between them and Jewell, but still avoid getting killed. Both men were well trained and Collin was tiring quickly. He had caught a couple of hours of sleep while he waited in the bushes the night before, but he hadn't slept much over the last three days.

As Collin moved backwards, he saw the man with the gun take aim at his chest. Collin dodged, but the bullet still caught him in the side. It would have hit him in the heart had he not moved. The fact that he was nearly immortal gave Collin little consolation. Collin stumbled backward with the force of the bullet, tripping over the corner of Jewell's chair and falling on his back. The man with the gun aimed again pulling the trigger, but the only sound was the click of the hammer hitting the firing pin. Collin let out a rush of breath he hadn't realized he was holding and rolled to his knees. The man threw his gun to the ground and advanced on Collin with his sword. Collin was able to get one foot planted, and as the man expertly swung his sword in a cutting blow aimed at Collin's neck, Collin launched himself under the sword knocking him to the floor.

Edgar watched as Daniel swung his sword in an attempt to decapitate the infidel. The speed with which the infidel was able to move to avoid the blow while advancing his own attack was astonishing. Edgar marveled at the grace with which the infidel was able to move. Despite Daniel's size, which was at least as much as the infidel plus half, and Daniel's experience in the MMA, the infidel was still able to knock Daniel from his feet. As Daniel fell to his back, Edgar moved in for his own attack. With Daniel underneath the infidel, it was nearly impossible to use a cutting swing, but if he was careful and pulled his thrust, he would be able to injure the infidel allowing Daniel to recover. Although, Daniel shouldn't have any difficulty handling the young man atop him, they still had to work together as a team. The other knights were battling with the S.W.A.T. team in the warehouse leaving dispatching the infidel to Edgar and Daniel.

Edgar moved in and tried to catch the infidel in the leg with his sword, but missed as Daniel threw the infidel to the side. As Daniel stood, he looked quickly to the floor. He had lost his sword when he fell, a rookie mistake. When he didn't immediately see it where he had fallen, he looked to the side where he saw the infidel, holding the sword pointed at his throat. Daniel quickly moved backward throwing a head kick. With nimble dexterity, the infidel dropped his stance, thrusting the sword into Daniel's thigh. As Daniel pulled his kick, the sword sliced a long deep gash in Daniel's leg. Daniel had been careful to maintain a sharp blade, now he wished he hadn't been so diligent. Daniel moved to the side, allowing Edgar to assume the advance, as he attempted to staunch the quickening flow of blood. He pulled off his belt and wrapped it around his leg creating a tourniquet.

As Edgar quickly moved in to take up the offense against the infidel, he tried to take quick glances at Daniel who had crawled into the corner. Daniel had slowed the flow of blood, but still looked extremely pale. Despite his expert sword skills, Edgar was having difficulty penetrating the infidel's defenses. It was clear that the infidel had training in swordsmanship, though Edgar was able to note several faults in his form. Attempting to use these faults against his assailant, Edgar lunged, and retreated expertly, forcing the infidel to remain on the defensive.

Collin realized quickly that he was outmatched. The large man, the one with the gun, had been a lucky thrust. Collin had thrown the sword up to protect himself and was lucky to hit a vulnerable area. The other man though, the one with the limp, was an expert swordsman and Collin found himself unable to find an opening to take up the offensive. As he parried his enemy's expert thrusts, he found that he was quickly losing strength. Blood soaked his shirt where he had been shot in the shoulder. The blood from the injury was starting to dry and he could feel the sticky blood fusing his shirt to his arm. His left side had also been injured when he was shot a second time by the man now dying in the corner.

With each movement, Collin felt a shooting pain in his side that caught his breath. As Collin became more fatigued, he began to stumble, allowing the limping man to catch him with glancing cuts to the arms and legs. Though not deep, they added to the pain. Finally, the man was able to breach Collin's defense and slice a deep gash across his right upper arm. Collin stumbled and fell against the wall, dropping the sword when the pain of bearing its weight became excruciating. As he fell to the floor, his head hit with enough force to cause his vision to swim. He fought against the encroaching darkness.

As the man watched Collin fall, rather than advance on him as Collin expected, he walked over to Jewell. Collin struggled, dizzy, and finally pushed himself into a sitting position. As he stared uncomprehending, the man knelt and picked up the discarded blindfold, placing it carefully over Jewell's eyes. "You shouldn't have to see this," he whispered as he carefully secured the scarf in place, checking his work to ensure that she was unable to see.

Jewell screamed through her tears, her words incoherent except for Collin's name which she interjected over and over again. Collin watched as the man moved across the room to where his partner lay. The man with the cut on his leg was either dead, or unconscious, Collin was unsure and he couldn't tell from the limping man's reaction. The man with the limp gently laid the injured man on the floor, checking the wound and the tourniquet that had stemmed the flow of blood. He carefully folded the man's arms over his chest, touched him on the cheek lightly, and got up.

Daniel was not dead, yet. Edgar knew that Daniel needed medical attention soon. Daniel's heart rate had increased exponentially. He was pale, and cold to the touch, but still breathing. Edgar turned his attention to the incapacitated man on the other side of the room. Almost regretfully, he moved slowly across the room knowing what he must do. All infidels must be executed for their sins. He watched as the infidel tried without success to grab the sword. With the man in a sitting position with the wall behind him, it would be difficult to make a clean cut. He moved closer and used his foot to push the man over onto his side. The infidel struggled to remain upright, but in the end, his injuries prevented him from maintaining his balance. He fell over, his head hitting the ground with a thud.

The infidel lay on the ground, staring up at Edgar insolently. Edgar's concentration was so intense that he barely heard the sobbing girl behind him. As he tried to determine the best way to sever the infidel's head cleanly and in one stroke, the infidel defiantly held his head back to give Edgar a clean cut. Edgar raised the sword over his head and stood like that, staring down at the body below him. He had never killed a man before. Remorsefully, he lowered the sword and took a step back wiping sweat from his forehead with his sleeve. He swallowed hard against the bile that was trying to rise in his throat at the thought of what he was about to do. Gathering his resolve, he stepped forward and raised his sword.

*   *   *

Collin lay on the floor, his eyes closed and his neck bared to the sword's killing blow. He thought of Jewell, and in his head, told her over and over again how much he loved her. He could feel her pain through his own. He felt her tears tickling her cheeks as he waited. When the expected cut didn't come, he opened his eyes and looked at the man who no longer had his sword raised. He looked tired, and a little sick. The green pallor of his skin made him look less like a killer, and more like someone who belonged in bed. Suddenly, the man lifted his head and looked Collin in the eye. There was no remorse, only resolve. As he took two steps forward, he raised the sword over his head again. Just as the man shifted his weight, preparing for the killing blow, Collin heard a loud blast and saw a blinding flash of light. Then he heard only silence. He couldn't see or hear anything. He found it interesting, the effect of decapitation, and wondered how long he would be able to continue his thoughts before he died. He briefly wondered if his body was still moving. He tried to move his left arm and felt a searing pain through his side. He wondered that he could still feel his body, but he had heard of phantom limbs, maybe he had a phantom body.

Slowly, as his hearing and sight returned, he saw two men in body armor wrestling with the limping man. Another man in body armor was carefully cutting Jewell's restraints. In the corner, another man wearing a dark blue pair of pants and light blue shirt was inserting an IV into the man on the ground. A woman, dressed like the man in dark blue pants and a light blue shirt, was carefully examining Jewell's injuries. Before he could take it all in, including the fact that he was not yet dead, he passed out.

*   *   *

As Jewell struggled against her restraints, screaming Collin's name, his muddled European accent cut through her distress with the only words she wanted to hear. "I love you," over and over again. She tried to think the thoughts back to him, letting his love wash away the hate she felt. As she listened to his words and let them calm her and take away the pain of her injuries, she heard a loud blast, and through the blindfold, she could see a bright light. She couldn't hear anything, but within seconds, her blindfold was removed and she saw a man in full body armor with gentle eyes carefully examining the restraints, looking for the areas where he could insert the cutters to release her.

As she realized that these people were here to help her, she glanced quickly around the room, seeking out Collin. She couldn't hear him in her thoughts anymore, and the possibility that he was dead frightened her more than the possibility of her own death ever had. Finally, she saw him against the wall, his eyes wandering blankly around the room, looking, but not really seeing anything that was going on. In front of him, two more men in black body armor were putting E Z Cuffs on the man with the leg brace.

The next several hours went by in a blur. Collin was carried out on a stretcher while another stretcher was brought in for Jewell. As they carefully lifted her out of the chair and gently laid her on the stretcher, she marveled at how good it felt to lay down and stretch out despite the pain it caused. Regardless of her pain, and the people hovering around her, cleaning her injuries, checking her vital signs and inserting IVs, she felt herself slipping toward sleep. She struggled to keep her eyes open, to see if she could catch a glimpse of Collin, but she only saw the multitude of police cars, S.W.A.T. vehicles, and a single ambulance. Apparently, she had been the last victim taken from the scene. As the ambulance started up and pulled away from the warehouse, the gentle hum of the engine, and the rocking of the ambulance as it moved down the road lulled her into a deep sleep. Of course, the morphine may have had something to do with that too.

CHAPTER 51

Jewell licked her dry lips as she started to wake from her drug induced sleep. Above her she could see the soft glow of hospital lights reflecting off of yellow walls. There was a vase with flowers on the table next to her bed along with a cup filled with water and a pitcher. She started to reach for it, but as she did, a moan escaped her lips as she worked her bruised muscles. She heard a noise, and saw someone stirring in the corner. As she watched, the shadowy shape got up and moved toward the bed. Her eyes were out of focus, and it took several minutes to recognize who was standing vigil in her room.

Ashley smiled down at Jewell. "How are you feeling?"

"Like I just did a triple shift in the ER." Jewell laughed lightly invoking a cough from her damaged body.

"Shhhh." Ashley sat carefully on the bed and brushed Jewell gently across her forehead. "Your dad is downstairs getting us some food. I offered to go, but he's been here since they brought you in, and I think he wanted to stretch his legs. He should be back in a minute. I came in this morning."

"How long have I been out?" Jewell felt disoriented and dizzy from the medicine. The fact that she was in a hospital bed in a room she faintly recognized helped a bit, but she had lost all sense of time since she had been abducted.

Ashley laughed. "You've been sleeping for almost twenty-two hours lazy bones!"

"What day is it?"

"Sunday." There was a hint of strain in her voice. Jewell had been abducted on Thursday morning. Only three days, she marveled. It had seemed so much longer than that.

"Collin?"

"He'll be fine," Ashley assured her. "He's in intensive care…again. He's unconscious, but it's not a coma. He's only in there for another couple of hours. They just wanted to make sure that his injuries weren't life threatening. If that boy continues to get himself into messes like this, it's a good thing he's dating a nurse. He's going to need you! I mean really, what sort of guy gets hacked up by a sword? Don't most people around here just use guns? What was up with those people anyway?"

"Well, they didn't tell me a whole lot," Jewell sighed. "For the most part, they said that they kidnapped me to get to Collin because he drank from the Holy Grail and was immortal or something." Jewell shrugged but the idea brought up some interesting, unanswered questions. Why was Dr. Babineaux so interested in Collin? How did Collin survive that first night in the ER? Why did he move around so much? Why was his uncle so unhappy with their relationship? All these questions were pieces to a puzzle with a picture that didn't make any sense. Immortality was impossible. The science just wouldn't allow it to work. Of course, there were examples of immortality in nature. There was a jellyfish that was immortal, hydras, bacteria, some plants. Was it possible that science had tapped into that capability? And if they had, was

Collin a part of an experiment? Did Collin know? Jewell's mind was spinning, partially from the morphine and partially from her thoughts, when her father came in.

"Oh!" Tommy McKean walked into the room and set a couple of sandwiches and drinks down next to the flowers. "It lives," he said in his best imitation of Dr. Frankenstein as he leaned over to kiss her forehead, one of the only places that showed no evidence of her recent ordeal.

"Nice flowers." Jewell said, seeing her father looking at them smugly.

"You like those? I bought 'em." He smiled and pointed toward the window. "But I sure didn't buy all of those." Jewell carefully turned her head to look in the direction her father was pointing. Any movement was painful, so she hadn't really examined her surroundings. Beside the window were rows of flowers, piles of stuffed animals, and enough balloons to carry her away. She smiled. "I think every public servant in both Covington and Orleans Parrish bought you something, and that big one in the back is from your friends down in the ER."

As Jewell marveled at this outpouring of compassion, Dr. Babineaux walked in. "Well, look at that, she finally woke up." He was dressed in a pair of khaki pants and a white Polo button down shirt. "How are you feeling?"

"Hey, Doc. I know you're not my doctor, and I can see by the way you're dressed that you're off duty. You don't have to play doctor with me."

"She's still acting like she knows everything, and has a bit of a sharp wit too. I reckon that's a good sign. Just humor me for a minute, would you? The x-rays and the MRI came out clean. I'm surprised considering the amount of bruising and swelling. You have several deep tissue bruises that will hurt for a while, and those cuts on your wrist aren't going away anytime soon. I'm a bit concerned about the cut on your arm though. It did some nerve and muscle damage. Fortunately, whatever you were cut with was as sharp as a scalpel so the cut is clean. We poked around in there to make sure and then put in some stitches. You may feel some tingling or loss of sensation in your hand, but I don't think that'll be permanent. We'll keep an eye on it anyway. So, besides all that, how are you feeling?"

Jewell was surprised at how superficial her injuries really were considering how much pain she was feeling. "I guess I hurt a little."

"I'll let Dr. Wilson make the decision, but I think that we can take you off that morphine drip. She'll probably agree with me. You should be up and around in no time."

"What about Collin?" Jewell choked on his name. He had survived a life threatening injury once, she was afraid that he wouldn't survive again.

"Collin? He's a trooper, that one. He lost a lot of blood, and he had a concussion with minor hemorrhaging. He had several cuts that needed to be repaired, along with a shattered collarbone, three broken ribs and a collapsed lung." Dr. Babineaux stopped talking when he realized that all of the blood had drained from Jewell's face, and a tear was marking its path from her eye to her chin. "He's going to be alright though, don't worry!" Dr. Babineaux smiled. "It's going to take a lot more than a little bleeding and a few broken bones to kill that one." His voice had become distant. He looked down at Jewell. "Don't worry. I'm taking care of him personally."

"Why are you so interested in him?"

Dr. Babineaux caught his breath. Jewell was observant. He carefully considered his words. "As you may know, much of my research is dedicated to healing injuries faster. Collin, well, I'm sure you noticed that Collin heals faster than the average person. This is due to a rare genetic anomaly. I suspected it when he was with us the last time."

"Can he die?"

Dr. Babineaux laughed. "Of course he can die. Everyone dies eventually Jewell. It's a part of life." He smiled and patted her hand. "I'd better get going. I have a golf game scheduled in forty-five minutes." He touched his forehead reminiscent of when men would tip their hats, and walked briskly from the room.

After Dr. Babineaux had left, Ashley turned and looked at Jewell. "Can he die? What kind of question was that? That morphine must really be making you loopy!" Jewell smiled weakly. "I'm afraid I need to get going. Work you know." She leaned down and gave Jewell a loose hug trying not to hurt her, and then she gave Tommy a hug too. "I know you'll take care of her." She whispered. Tommy just nodded.

When Jewell woke up, the room was empty. There was a cot against the wall that looked as if it had been slept in. Before Jewell was able to sit up and look around her father came striding in pushing a wheelchair. "Collin's awake. He was asking about you. Are you up to a wheel chair ride across the hall?"

Jewell thought about it for a few seconds. She really wasn't, but she wanted to see Collin so badly that she couldn't resist the offer. She nodded and her dad helped her as she moved slowly from the bed to the chair. Her legs supported her, that was a welcome surprise, and she found that moving actually helped to loosen some of the muscles and made some of her injuries feel better. Once she was settled, her father stepped behind and pushed her around the nurses' station to the other side of the hall where Collin was resting.

As her father pushed her through the door, she braced herself for what she was going to see. She briefly flashed back to the first time he came into the hospital, reliving the moment of what she had thought was his death. His face had been so distorted by his injuries. As she approached the bed, he was facing away from her, just like the first time she entered his room. His right arm was bandaged, and he had a square of gauze taped onto his left shoulder where the doctors had inserted the pins to repair his collarbone. His torso was taped tightly. The sheet on his bed was pulled up to his waist so she couldn't see his legs. The scene was so familiar to her that she almost wondered if she had imagined the past few months.

When she reached the side of his bed, he turned to look at her. Her breath caught. His face was unmarred and more beautiful than she remembered. She wanted so badly to reach out and touch his cheek, to kiss his lips but as she started to reach her hand toward his face, she was brought up short. At first, she didn't recognize the emotion in his face. It wasn't joy, or even relief. It was guilt. "Collin?" Jewell moved her arm uncertainly to touch him lightly on the hand. He turned back to look at her. "What's wrong?"

"If it hadn't been for me, this would've never happened to you. I tried, but I couldn't save you." A tear trickled down his cheek and soaked into his pillow. "I'm so sorry."

"What are you talking about? This isn't your fault. How can you blame yourself for something that you had no control over? How were you supposed to know?"

"I didn't. I couldn't. But I should have. I should've known that something was..." his voice trailed off.

"Something was what?" Jewell asked, coaxing him to talk to her. She waited for several minutes before trying again. "Why did you leave?" She wanted answers, but more than answers, she wanted Collin to talk to her. She just wanted to hear his voice again.

"I didn't leave. Well, not exactly. It's more like I was taken." A trickle of anger seeped into his voice.

"What? What do you mean taken?"

"It's a long story. My uncle thought you would be better off without me and so...well, he drugged me and drove me across the country."

"Why? Why didn't your uncle..." her thought trailed off as she realized that everything that had happened to her, the kidnapping, the beatings; it was all because those lunatics wanted Collin. Collin's uncle must have known. He must've known that something was going to happen and so he tried to save her, to keep her away from Collin. "Why did they want you?" she finally asked.

"I didn't know!" He let the anger loose. The anger he felt toward his uncle, the Obsidian Knights, at what they had done to Jewell. Jewell cringed, pushing her back into the chair and looking behind her for her father. He wasn't there. She hadn't heard him leave, but she suspected that he understood that she and Collin needed to work things out. As he shook with anger, Collin realized that he was directing it at the wrong person. He tried to relax, in his mind apologizing for yelling at her, searching for the words to tell her what she needed to know.

Jewell sat up, looking at Collin as he stared intently into her eyes. "How do you do that?"

"Do what?"

"I can hear you, talking to me, you're not. It's like you're inside my head. It happened while I was..." she choked on the words, not wanting to say out loud what had happened over the last few days. As if not talking about it would mean it never happened.

"What did you hear?" Collin asked cautiously.

"You said that you were sorry, that it wasn't me you were angry at."

Collin considered for a minute. He looked at the bruises, at the bandages on her arms, the swelling on her face. She deserved to know; she had suffered for what he was. She had to know why he couldn't stay.

Jewell waited patiently, watching his eyes as he considered. She tried to hear what he was thinking, but she couldn't. She couldn't hear anything but the beeping of the machines in the room.

"I want you to know...I need you to know how much I love you," he started.

"I love you too, Collin...." She stopped and swallowed the lump that was forming in her throat.

"I'm so sorry if my leaving hurt you, but now I know that my uncle was right. I can't stay with you. As much as I love you, as much as I need to be with you, I love you too much to put you in danger again. If something were to happen to you, I don't think I could survive without you."

"Collin, you're not making sense. What do you mean? You can't leave me again." She choked on a sob. "Please Collin, you can't."

"I don't want to. Please believe me that leaving you will be the hardest thing I'll ever do in my life. But if I leave, I know you'll be safe. If that's what I need to do to keep you safe..." He shook his head.

"Is it because of what happened? That wasn't your fault. All those men, they were arrested. That won't happen again."

"It will! Don't you see? Because of what I am it will happen again and again and again! You will never be safe!"

"What those men said, about you being..." She couldn't say the word. It wasn't true; it wasn't possible. "Are you immortal?" Collin barely nodded. Jewell started shaking her head, staring at him. "What are you?"

"Jewell, please." He was crying. "I didn't know, I swear. My uncle told me. He told me that was how I survived the accident; that I couldn't die. He told me that he fell in love once, that she wasn't like him, that his love was what killed her. I didn't want to come back, but I couldn't stay away. I couldn't even save you." The words came out in a rush, almost incoherently.

"It really was you, following me; wasn't it?" Collin nodded. "Dr. Babineaux knows too. That's why he's so interested in you. He knows what you are." Collin nodded again. Jewell sat silently for several minutes, trying to understand, to believe. "And the telepathy? Is that part of it to?" Collin nodded. Jewell sat silently for a long time while Collin watched waves of emotion wash over her battered face. She didn't look directly at him, her eyes staring past him, out the window on the other side of the bed. Finally, her head dropped slightly, her eyes looking to the ground. "I love you," she whispered.

She reached up and pressed the nurse call button on the side of his bed without looking at him. Kelly Wills was on duty. When she came in all Jewell said was, "I'm ready to leave now."

As the door to Collin's room closed, she heard him whisper in her head, "I love you, too."

In her room, Jewell tried to think about what Collin had told her. She wasn't thinking about him telling her that he *was* immortal, but that he loved her. She knew she loved him, but what kind of a relationship could she have with him. Even if they stayed together, she would cause him so much pain. She knew the pain of watching someone you love die, she had experience it.

She must have fallen asleep because it was dark outside her window when the door opened and Dr. Babineaux strode in. He smiled, picked up her chart and pulled a chair up to the side of the bed so he could sit down. This time he was dressed in his work clothes. His white jacket had his name embroidered in italic letters across the left breast and hung down to the middle of his thigh. It hung open to reveal a pair of perfectly pressed, tailored, probably custom, gray dress slacks, a light blue button down oxford, also perfectly pressed, and a silk jacquard tie. His classic black oxfords looked like they had been spit-shined. This was obviously not a social visit.

As he sat down, he opened Jewell's medical chart and started scanning the notes made by her other doctors. When he was finished, he looked up and asked, "How are you feeling?"

"I don't hurt as much as I did yesterday. As long as I don't touch any of the really sore parts like my face, or my wrist, it's not so bad."

Dr. Babineaux glanced at the IV drip still attached to her arm. "You haven't been using the morphine for pain." It was more of a statement than a question. Jewell shook her head. "I'll have Sarah take that IV out then and prescribe some Tylenol with Codeine instead and we'll see how you do. If you aren't hurting too bad tomorrow, we can probably let you go home." He wrote a few notes in her chart and signed his name with a flourish. When he looked up, he watched as a tear trickled down Jewell's face. He reached out and gently wiped it away with his thumb. "Now, do you want to tell me how you're *really* feeling?"

Jewell turned her head to look at him. He sat silently, watching her, his eyes filled with compassion. "Have you talked to Collin?" she asked. He nodded sympathetically. "So you know that he told me".

"I do. I'm here to answer any questions you might have."

"You told me everyone dies. If he's immortal, he won't die, will he?"

"Well, he won't die in the same time frame as you or I. Eventually, he'll die from old age; but it won't be for a very long time."

"How long?"

"Well, I've been involved in this research for about twenty years, and the oldest Infinitas I've met was almost a millennium old."

"A thousand years?" Jewell asked incredulously.

"Well, just like us, they all have different life spans. I think the average is somewhere around eleven hundred years."

"Does Dr. Knighton know? I mean, does he know his nephew is like this?" Dr. Babineaux nodded in response. "And does he help you with your research?"

"Actually, Dr. Knighton is trying to find a cure. He views this as a disease, similar to cancer or leukemia. The difference is, while cancer tends to shorten life, what Collin has will extend his."

Jewell nodded her head. "It is."

"It is what?" Dr. Babineaux asked.

"A disease. It's not something that people should see as a gift, but as a curse, a burden."

"You don't dream of immortality?"

Jewell gave him a dismayed look. "No, death is essential to continued life. We shouldn't try to cheat it." She thought for a moment. "Why is he like this? What makes him different?"

"Without getting into too much detail, it's a genetic anomaly that's triggered sometime after puberty. Some people carry the anomaly, but it's never triggered."

"What triggers it?"

Dr. Babineaux shrugged. "We don't know."

"How many people have the anomaly?"

"More than you would think. About one in every ten thousand people has the anomaly, but it's only triggered in about one in every fifteen thousand who carry the anomaly. There are fewer than five hundred people in the world like Collin."

Jewell nodded once. "So, then it's sort of like cancer in reverse?"

"Well, at a very basic level I guess you could say that. Do you have any other questions?" Jewell shook her head.

Dr. Babineaux stood to leave. As he started to walk away, Jewell reached out and grabbed his hand. "Thank you." Dr. Babineaux nodded a serious look on his face. He knew all that she wanted to say with those two simple words.

CHAPTER 52

It was early in the morning when Dr. Wilson came in to sign Jewell's release papers. Jewell waited for Dr. Wilson to leave and then carefully got up and walked over to the duffle bag that Ashley had brought for her. She took out a hairbrush and ran it through her hair, then pulled it back in a high ponytail like she usually wore to work. She dug through the bag for some clean clothes and found a pair of light weight pants, a shirt with long sleeves, obviously designed for summer wear, and a pair of shoes, all with tags still on them with the price carefully marked out. A note was stuffed in one of the shoes. "I left the tags on in case they didn't fit. Ash."

Jewell pulled on the new clothes and looked at herself in the mirror. Her face, except for a little swelling, looked like her face. She smiled at Ashley's thoughtfulness in choosing clothes that would cover her bruised and battered body. She grabbed her toothbrush and toothpaste and went into the bathroom to brush her teeth.

Finally, she took a deep breath, opened the door and stepped out into the hallway. Jewell looked over at Collin's room. When Jewell pushed open the door, she heard the television. Collin turned his head and smiled. When he smiled, Jewell's heart started racing. "Wow! You look like an angel."

Collin reached his hand out to her. She took his hand and felt the familiar lightening of his touch shoot through her. He pulled her around so she was sitting on the bed next to him.

"How are you feeling?" She asked, and then laughed. "Never mind; I'm sure you're tired of answering that question. I know I am."

He flashed his most brilliant smile at her. "With you sitting beside me, I feel like I'm in heaven."

"I can't stay. My dad is waiting for me downstairs," she sighed.

"Would it hurt too much to give me a kiss before you leave?"

Jewell leaned down and gently brushed his lips with hers. Before she could sit up, his arm tightened around her shoulders, pulling her closer. She pressed against him when all of a sudden she felt a shooting pain run through her lip and up into her head. She sat up, her hand moving to her mouth.

"I'm sorry," Collin whispered. "I forgot for a minute. I just…wanted you so badly."

"I know. Me too." She brushed her fingers over his lips. "I'll talk to you later?" Collin just nodded silently as he watched her leave.

Collin watched Jewell leave. Even though he knew that he would see her again, it still hurt every time he had to say good-bye. He wondered what would happen if they decided it would be best to say goodbye forever. He tried to change the direction of his thoughts. Something would happen. Something would make it work out. He thought about what his Uncle Percy had said about Avelyn. He had let Avelyn make her own choice, and Percy believed that his selfishness let her make the wrong one. He believed that Avelyn would have been better off if she had stayed with her family.

All Jewell had was her father. Would it be right to let her choose him over her father? Could he take her away from him knowing that there was a chance that she would never see him again? And if she made that choice, if she chose to leave everything behind for him, could he let her do it? Could he tell her that she had made the wrong choice? Could he tell her goodbye? Should he tell her goodbye? The questions were pouring over him like a waterfall. The morphine was making him dizzy and his circling thoughts weren't helping. What he knew now was that he *would* see her again.

As he lay there thinking about all of the ramifications of maintaining a relationship with Jewell; his Uncle Percy walked in. "Well kid, we're going to keep you in this prison for another week or so. That'll give your bones time to set so that it doesn't hurt when you breathe. It's a good thing that you have a hard head too. I've never seen the effect of brain damage on one of our kind and frankly, the thought of feeding you baby food for the next thousand years is not pleasant." He sat down on the edge of Collin's bed. "What's with the face? You look like you've been pondering the meaning of life."

"Jewell left today. She wants to talk to me. She wants to talk about us. I don't know what I'm going to do." Collin slowly blinked, the effects of the morphine pushing him toward sleep again.

Percy gave Collin a grim smile. "All I can do is tell you what I think is best, but in the end, it's your decision…and Jewell's. Before either of you make a decision, both of you should sit down with the *family*. I think that she needs to know everything. It wouldn't be fair of you to let her make an uninformed decision."

Collin nodded. "Good. Well, you look like your healing well, which isn't much of a surprise, and that morphine seems to be sending you off to la la land. I'll stop by tomorrow and check on you." Percy stood up and patted Collin's cheek affectionately before leaving Collin with his thoughts.

Ashley brought Jewell to the hospital a couple of days after she checked out so that she could visit with Collin. Ashley had some things that she needed to do because she had been out for so many days. Other than that one visit, Jewell didn't get the opportunity to talk to or visit Collin during the week that he remained in the hospital. Ashley told Jewell when Collin's uncle checked him out, but other than that, Jewell was in the dark. She had nothing to do but wait until Collin was ready to talk.

Three weeks after she left the hospital, she was sitting in her living room, reading. Her thoughts often strayed to Collin, but she tried to divert those thoughts to other things. She spent time reading, cleaning, and cooking. She finished Twilight and wondered at the end. Edward had asked Bella if she was ready to give up everything for him. Was she ready to give up everything for Collin? Would the heartache she would cause him be worse if she left now, or if she lived for another fifty years and died of old age?

Her thoughts were interrupted when there was a knock at the door. She looked at her watch and walked to the door thinking that it was probably Ashley stopping by to check on her before going on to work. Frankly, Jewell was tired of being "checked up on" and coddled. She felt fine; most of the bruising had faded to a light yellow that was barely noticeable except in a few spots where the injury had been more severe. The cut on her arm was healing nicely. The surgeon had done a beautiful job on the stitches so although there would be a scar, it would not be noticeable to the casual observer. Her legs still hurt, there was some deep bone bruising on her thighs which still bothered her when she walked.

Jewell reached for the doorknob and opened the door. Rather than Ashley, Percy was standing in the doorway. Jewell stood there for a moment, gaping, before she remembered her manners and invited him in. The fact that Percy was there and not Collin made her nervous. She gestured to a chair so that Percy could sit down and offered him a Coke. Percy declined. "How are you feeling," he asked compassionately.

Jewell sighed. She had lost count of how many times people had asked her that question. Sometimes she wanted to reach out and choke the person asking, but she always managed to remember her manners and respond politely. "I'm healing well. Thank you for asking. How's Collin?"

"Collin is great." Percy scrutinized her. "Actually, I think he looks at least as well as you do." He paused and reached for Jewell's hands. Holding her hands in his he looked into her eyes. "I can understand what my nephew sees in you; I just wish it didn't have to be so hard." He paused. Jewell waited quietly to see where Percy was going with the conversation. "Collin would like to bring you to the house. He would like to discuss your relationship with the *Family.*"

The way that he emphasized the word "family," Jewell knew that Percy wasn't talking about mom and dad. Percy was talking about the others that were like Collin. "Are you a part of the F*amily."*

Percy sat straighter in his chair, as if that were possible. "I, my dear child," he began, "am nearly one thousand years old. I was once a Templar Knight. I've met Florence Nightingale, I've fought in…well, a lot of wars. I have lived the history that most people only have the chance to study." Jewell stared at Percy, her mouth gaping. She couldn't find a response to his words so she just continued to stare. Percy finally spoke again. "If you would like, I can take you to Collin now. We can talk with the *Family* or you can just visit if you prefer. There's no rush right now, but I wouldn't want to wait too long."

She glanced at Percy, "do I need to drive?"

Percy smiled and shook his head, "I'll be happy to bring you home if you would prefer."

Jewell glanced at the car keys she held in her hand. If she rode with Percy, she was trapped in whatever situation she was getting into. If she drove herself, she had a quick and easy escape. She briefly weighed the keys in her hand before setting them gently on the table. "I'll let you drive." She smiled weakly looking around the living room. "I guess I have everything I need. Shall we go?"

Percy smiled and gestured Jewell in front of him. When they reached the door, he opened it for her. He waited politely on the porch while she locked the door, before offering her his elbow like the princes did in the movies. She looked at it briefly and placed her hand gently on top of his proffered arm. Percy reached over with his other hand and patted her hand gently. "It will all work out my dear." Jewell just nodded. When they reached the car, Percy opened the passenger side door for her, gently closing it after she had pulled her feet in and settled into the seat.

When Percy had settled himself into the driver's seat and started the car, Jewell looked at him a little nervously. "Aren't you going to blindfold me or something?"

Percy laughed, "Why would I do that?"

"I don't know. Collin was always kind of secretive about where he lived. He wouldn't even give me a phone number to call him."

"I'm afraid that's partially my fault." Percy frowned slightly. "Because of what we are, we need to keep our houses private. As you know, there are some people who would sacrifice much to kill us."

"Then why do you trust me?"

"Because Collin trusts you," Percy answered with a hint of admiration in his voice.

Jewell just nodded, wondering at what she had gotten herself into. She leaned her elbow on the door handle and cradled her chin in her hand as she watched out the window. She watched the water shimmering on the lake as they drove across the causeway. The water sparkled, drawing her eye towards its rippling surface. She must have fallen asleep because she didn't remember anything until they turned onto a gravel road. She blinked, clearing the sleep from her eyes and yawned. The huge oak trees were dripping with Spanish moss, completely blocking the sun that fought desperately to shed its light on the winding road before them. Every once in a while the sun would win the fight creating mottled patterns with strange shadows.

Jewell sat silently as they drove, turning occasionally onto smaller and smaller roads until they finally turned onto what looked like a driveway. It wound around some old oaks and Cyprus trees before opening on a beautifully landscaped yard. When Jewell saw it, she sat forward to admire the artistic beauty. She assumed it must have been planned to carefully keep the surrounding trees at bay, but what made it so beautiful was that it could very easily just be a clearing where someone decided to build a house.

The house was something else entirely. While its white majesty was a sharp contrast to the surrounding trees, it still seemed to fit into the environment, as if it had grown there; a rare and unique flower. It had clearly been there for some time. The style harkened back to the large plantations of the eighteenth and nineteenth centuries. Jewell remembered that Collin had once mentioned that he lived in Houma. She knew that the area had once held some of the largest sugar cane plantations in the world.

The beautiful white house was surrounded by porches on both the first and second floors. Large balconies decorated the third floor of the house. It had been immaculately kept, or restored, in its original beauty. The large magnolia trees decorating the front of the house, and the random dogwoods dotting the yard, would provide a brilliant array of white flowers to accent the house each spring.

Percy pulled to the front of the house and parked right next to Collin's silver corvette. Somehow, just seeing his car made her feel better. Percy walked around to the passenger side and opened the door, offering his hand to help her from the car. As she stood up, the faint smell of honeysuckle wafted past her on the breeze. She took a deep breath inhaling its spicy sweet fragrance. Percy led her around the car and up onto the porch. Several white rocking chairs and a porch swing moved lazily in the breeze. Percy held open one of the huge wooden doors and ushered her in.

Inside the home, the massive foyer was lit with a beautiful chandelier that was large, yet didn't seem ostentatious in this beautiful old home. To her left and right were identical French doors inset with leaded glass panels. Percy ushered her towards the doors on the right. "Are you ready?" Percy asked; breaking her silent reverie that she was certain must be a dream.

Jewell took a deep breath, not knowing what she would see on the other side of the doors. Percy grasped the handle on each door and pulled to reveal the interior of the room. Jewell's breath caught, and her knees weakened. Before she was aware of what was happening, she found herself sitting on the floor, trying to remember how to breathe. The room, along with its occupants, was exactly the same as her dream.

CHAPTER 53

When Jewell realized that she was sitting on the floor, she moved to get up but was gently pushed back to the floor. She glanced up and saw Percy's gentle eyes. She looked around her and saw Sheriff Payne and Dr. Babineaux. "What happened?"

"Oh, get out of the way boys! Let the girl get some air!" A woman with a firm voice but gentle eyes was approaching. The men standing around her parted like the Red Sea before Moses. She knelt next to Jewell and held a glass of cold, freshly squeezed lemonade to Jewell's lips. Jewell took two long swallows of the cold, sweet-tart liquid. After a minute or two, the woman commented, "there now, that's better. Can you stand up?" Jewell nodded as the woman helped her to stand. "See. She just swooned a little. I'm sure that all of this is a bit overwhelming." She put her arm around Jewell's shoulders and led her to a loveseat where Collin was sitting. Collin stood with a little effort and helped Jewell to sit on the seat next to him.

His tender touch and the warmth that radiated from his fingers through her entire body calmed her as she looked at the people that were sitting in seats arranged in a semicircle in front them. Before sitting down, Collin began introducing each of them. He started with the woman that had helped her when she "swooned." The thought of her swooning seemed almost silly. Southern Belles living on plantations with names like Tara, swooned; not girls living in tract houses in Covington.

"This is Gladys." Collin started introducing the people sitting in the room. The woman smiled warmly. "I lived with her until I was five." He gestured to the man sitting next to her. "This is Kendryck, a friend of my uncle's." Kendryck studied her, but didn't smile. "You know Sheriff Payne and Dr. Babineaux."

Jewell nodded. "Why are they here?"

Percy motioned to Collin to sit down. "Hugh Payne is a Templar Knight. He's the Grand Master in this region. Dr. Babineaux is his second." Percy paused to let Jewell absorb the information.

"But, the Templar Knights were disbanded," she looked at Collin for confirmation, "almost a thousand years ago."

Collin nodded. "*Officially* disbanded. In fact, there are Templar Knights around the world continuing their duty to protect those requiring, and deserving of their assistance. The *Infinitas*, what we are," he gestured around the room, "are a…special undertaking, thanks to Percy."

Jewell looked at Sheriff Payne and Dr. Babineaux. "Are you like them too? Are you immortal?"

"No," Dr. Babineaux responded. "Sheriff Payne and I are just like you. And just to clarify, they aren't immortal. They will age and die just as the rest of us do," he glanced at Percy who was clearly the oldest immortal in the room, "they just do so at a much slower rate."

Jewell started to feel dizzy again. She leaned forward, letting her forehead rest on her knees so she wouldn't "swoon" again. Collin placed his hand on her protectively. She stayed in the same position, letting his strength wash through her.

When she could breathe again, and her head stopped spinning, she sat up and looked at Dr. Babineaux. "And this is your research? You're trying to figure out how to extend peoples' lifespan so that they'll live as long as," she gestured to the others sitting in the room, "as long as they will?"

Dr. Babineaux smiled indulgently. "That's part of it Jewell. Immortality, or at least the ability to live an extended time, has been an interest of humans for thousands of years. Every generation we get a little bit better, but the progress is slow. If we could determine the cause of their longevity, we might be able to extend life to thousands of years instead of a mere hundred. Two hundred years ago, thirty five was considered old age. Now, many people are really just beginning their lives at thirty five." He looked at Jewell's horror struck face. "There are other benefits as well." He looked at Collin. "Consider their rapid healing abilities for instance. Imagine if we could harness that; if we could give someone a shot, or an ointment that would heal their injuries in a fraction of the time that it takes now. These people are the equivalent of superheroes. Their genes have the ability to save the human race."

Jewell considered. The idea of giving everyone immortality made her feel ill. Despite the loss of her mother when Jewell was young, she had never wished that people could live forever. There were so many negative ramifications. And yet, she had to admit that if they could use it to help in the healing process... She looked at Percy. "And you're helping him with this?"

Percy smiled, but his eyes were sad. "My research is very similar to Dr. Babineaux's. I too seek the reason for our longevity, but I'm seeking a cure." Jewell looked at him, her eyes questioning. "Not all of us consider this to be a gift. Many of us think of it as a disease. Something we've been struck with that prevents us from living a normal life." He looked at Collin and Jewell sitting on the couch, Collin's arm was wrapped protectively around Jewell. "In more ways than one, I'm afraid."

Jewell looked at Collin. "What does he mean by that? Does it have something to do with us?"

Collin squeezed Jewell's shoulders. "Not as far as I'm concerned." Jewell noticed Gladys smiling.

Kendryck shifted in his chair and cleared his throat. When he spoke, his words stung, but he didn't speak them in malice, but in pain. "We cannot have relationships with...normal people."

"What? Why?" Jewell looked at Collin but it was Kendryck who answered.

"As our normal companion ages, we don't. It creates...problems."

"What kind of problems?" Collin was suspicious.

"Don't you see Collin? When she's eighty, you'll look like you're thirty. It draws attention. You know that we must be very careful about who we reveal our secrets to. As the world continues to shrink due to more advanced transportation, and the ability to communicate easily with anyone around the world, it becomes more and more difficult to remain concealed. Look at how quickly you were identified due to a simple accident. The more chances we take, the more risk there is of exposure." He looked at Collin with hard eyes. "And exposure doesn't just threaten the individual, it threatens the *Family*. Sometimes, we need to make difficult choices because our choices affect others as well."

"Selfishness is not an option for us," Kendryck added quietly.

"So what you're saying," Collin spoke the words Jewell was thinking before she could process all of the information and form coherent thoughts, "is that because I'm like you, Jewell and I can't have a relationship." It was a statement, not a question.

Collin and Jewell both looked around the room. Everyone except for Gladys was nodding in agreement, even Dr. Babineaux and Sheriff Payne. Percy spoke. "I've explained to you why this relationship is impossible. I tried to make it easy for you, but you refused to listen. I thought that if Jewell was aware of the ramifications, she could help you to make the right decision. She's not like us; her memory isn't as long." He turned to Jewell, "don't misunderstand me Jewell. You're a beautiful, wonderful person. I could easily love you as a daughter; but we cannot allow this relationship to continue. You're young. This is your first love. You'll remember Collin fondly, but the pain will fade, you'll meet a nice young man, get married, and have children. You'll grow old, and you'll watch your children and your grandchildren grow. Collin will become nothing more than a fond memory."

Kendryck spoke again. "We don't like having to tell this to either of you. I haven't had the opportunity to get to know you Jewell, but I truly regret any pain that this may cause you."

Jewell barely heard Kendryck's words. They were empty, meaningless. She could tell that none of them was concerned about her. Their concern was the *Family*. She could feel Collin's arm pulling her in tighter, no longer protective, but possessive. She looked over at Gladys who had not contributed to the conversation. Her face was pulled tight into a forced neutral expression. Jewell thought that the expression conveyed a disagreement with the overall sentiment of the conversation. Perhaps she and Collin could find an ally in Gladys.

Jewell looked around at the expressionless faces surrounding her, "so that's it then?" As she looked at each person, they gave her a curt nod as they cast their eyes downward, not willing to meet Jewell's eyes as she looked at them. She swallowed once and took a deep breath. "I see. Will you be kidnapping Collin again, or will you actually give him the chance to say good-bye properly?"

Percy looked at Collin but answered Jewell. "That depends on Collin. We would all prefer a proper good-bye. Of course, we will do what we have to." He let the last sentence hang in the air between him and Collin.

Jewell nodded again. "Can I have a minute with Collin?" No one moved. "Alone?" She emphasized the last word.

Gladys was the first to move. She took Kendryck and Percy by the hand and started leading them out. "Percy, Hugh, Nicky." Nicky? Jewell suppressed a laugh at how this apparently young woman addressed her superior.

When they had all left the room, Jewell gently pushed herself away from Collin so that she could look at him. "What now?"

"I don't know. I'll try to think of something, but…" he looked around as if he was trying to ascertain whether someone was listening. "Kendryck, is a telepath. Kendryck is very talented. I'm not entirely sure that my thoughts will be as private as I want them to be." He kissed her, gently on the forehead and pulled her head to his chest. "I can't live without you, I won't. I'll find a solution. I love you Honeysuckle." Jewell just nodded against his chest. He pushed her back a little bit so that he could kiss her lips.

Jewell savored the touch of Collin's soft, warm lips, savored the taste of honey and almond on his breath, breathed in his unique smell of cedar, rain and laurel. She tried to think of what life would be like without him, but she couldn't. Her thoughts reeled as she thought about everything she had been told, but primarily about the very likely possibility that she would never see Collin again.

They were still kissing when they heard a knock on the door. Collin and Jewell looked up in time to see Percy opening the doors to the parlor. "Jewell, honey, it's time to get you home." Jewell looked at Collin and tightened her grip on his hand. "You'll see him again. I will promise you that."

"Do you swear on the Templar Cross that I will see him again?" Jewell didn't completely trust Percy's word, but she did know a little about the Templar Knights. If he made that swear, he would do whatever possible to ensure that she saw him again.

Percy looked startled for a moment as he stood in the doorway. He sucked in a deep breath and whispered quietly, "I swear on the Templar Cross that you will see Collin again."

Jewell nodded curtly and stood, still holding Collin's hand. She leaned down and kissed him again on the mouth, passionately and not caring that Percy was watching. "I love you Collin Sykes. I will always love you no matter what happens. Please always remember that. I will *always* love you."

"And I will always love you." He reached for a cane leaning on the edge of the couch. Jewell helped him as he struggled to stand. By the time he was standing and leaning on his cane, his breath was coming in sharp pulls. She waited until his breathing returned to normal, and walked with him slowly across the room. Percy preceded them down the hallway and out the front door. When Collin and Jewell reached the stairs leading down from the porch, Collin stopped. Jewell looked at Percy standing next to the passenger side of the door. Collin dropped the cane and pulled her close, holding her as if he was willing them to become one person. Finally, she pushed herself away and started down the stairs toward the car.

Jewell didn't see Collin again for another week. She had started back to work which helped to alleviate some of the boredom she was experiencing at home. It also gave her less time to think about everything she had learned in the past couple of weeks.

Jewell had very strong feelings about the idea of immortality. She definitely did not think that it was a trait that should be explored and exploited. The fact that people were now living longer thanks to better medicine and nutrition, and the number of live births has increased, the world population is exploding. Without new sources of nutrition and additional space to house these individuals, immortality would lead to ultimate suffering. Another problem was that despite scientific research, progress is usually generated by new people. If people don't die, then there will be no progress, because new people are necessary to create new ideas.

But she loved Collin. The fact that he represented something that she found objectionable didn't change her feelings for him any more than finding out he had cancer would change her feelings for him. And the thought of living without him was almost unbearable.

As she worked, she mulled over the arguments presented by Collin's *Family*, Dr. Babineaux, and Sheriff Payne. She understood their position. She was a threat to their existence, not just Collin's, but everyone like him. She also understood that as she grew older, he wouldn't age. Would he still love her when she looked twice his age? Three times his age? When she appeared old enough to be his grandmother? If he continued to love her, could she stand to let him watch her die? Could she inflict that pain on him? A pain that he wouldn't carry with him for decades, but for centuries to come?

"Jewell!" She glanced up to see Nurse Yohanan standing above her. "Honey, you've been sitting there for over half an hour without doing anything. I think that's enough for tonight. Why don't you go ahead and go home and get some rest. You're still healing and it's going to be difficult to get back into your usual routine."

Jewell rubbed her hands over her face. She looked at the patient chart sitting on the desk next to her. She had filled in the name on the computer screen but had not gone beyond that. She glanced at the stack of charts sitting on the desk waiting to be entered into the computer. "I don't know," she gestured to the charts sitting in her in box. "I'm fine. I just got distracted for a while. I just want to get these entered before I leave."

"Nonsense! I'll get an intern to do it on the day shift. You go home and I'll see you tomorrow night."

Jewell nodded and glanced at her watch. It was only midnight. She hadn't even finished half her shift. She had driven herself to work since she hadn't been working regular shifts. It seemed that these first few nights back had been more difficult than she had expected them to be and she found herself leaving early every night. She hated to leave work unfinished, but Nurse Yohanan was right. She wasn't very useful if she couldn't finish her work. She called Ashley upstairs to let her know she was leaving. She walked slowly to the locker room to gather her things before heading home.

Ashley met her in the locker room as Jewell was gathering her things. "Not feeling well?" she asked as she waited for Jewell to change.

"That's not it. It's Collin. I don't know, maybe because I'm not one hundred percent I'm having trouble concentrating on work. I've just got to focus."

"I thought everything was cool between you, now that he's back and all."

"It's hard to explain Ash. I want so bad to talk to you about it, but I just don't know what to say. It's really hard to put into words."

"That's okay, I understand. I'll be here whenever you're ready." She reached over and gave Jewell a quick hug as Jewell picked up her bag.

As Jewell walked to her car, she noticed someone standing next to her car, waiting. She picked up her pace, anxious now to meet the man waiting for her. "I needed to see you so badly." As she reached him, she fell into his arms, soaking in the electricity that his touch generated. "Collin, I missed you so much. I can't work, I can't sleep. I just keep thinking about you."

Collin pulled her closer, breathing in the honeysuckle scent he missed so much. "I knew you needed me, I could feel it. That's why I'm here. My uncle has been...reluctant to let me see you. He thinks that if I let you have your space, both of us will realize that we don't need each other as much as we think we do." He kissed her forehead. "I don't think it's working." He grinned sadly. "Jewell, can we talk?" he asked, suddenly serious.

"Yeah. Of course. Do you want to go somewhere, or you can come to my place, or we can go to yours?"

"I want to go back to my place. I know everyone will be there, but I need you to know where I live. I want you to be able to find me...in case."

"In case of what?"

"I don't know, just in case. The house isn't just used by my uncle and me. It belongs to the *Family*. I don't want what happened before to happen again. I want to be certain that if something happens, you can always find me." He left unsaid that if they were ever separated, someone in the *Family* could probably find him.

He opened the driver's door for Jewell and then went to sit in the passenger's seat. He directed her to the house while she tried to remember each turn as he pointed it out. He showed her landmarks to help her remember the way. Finally, she was driving down the long driveway that led to the house. He took her into the servant's quarters rather than the main house. "This is where I've been staying. I think that I'm the only person who really uses this part of the house. When we moved here, it was being used for storage. I fixed it up so that I could have a little more privacy." He laughed. "It seems like no matter where we are there are always at least five people living in the same place. Even though the houses are big, and there are plenty of rooms, I still feel crowded."

He motioned towards a comfortable looking, well-worn leather chair. As she sat, she asked, "What do you want to talk about?"

He pulled an ottoman that didn't match the chair closer to her and sat down so that he could rest his hands on her legs. "I've been thinking, about us. I mean, about what us would mean to you."

"What do you mean?"

"My uncle was right. If you and I were to stay together you would have to give so much up. I don't know if I could take that away from you."

"What do you mean?"

He sighed, tiredly as if he had been thinking about this for days. "Jewell, if you were to stay with me, you would need to give up everything. You couldn't stay here. You couldn't keep your job, your friends; even your dad. I don't know how often you would be able to see him, or even talk to him on the phone. It's my way of life. It's how I've always lived so I never really thought about it, but lately…" he shook his head. "I can't give you what you deserve. I can't be what I want to be."

Jewell sat quietly for several minutes. "So, this is it? You're leaving?"

"My uncle won't let me stay with you, and he won't let me take you with us. But it's your decision. In the end, I can't decide for you because if I do, I will take away from you the last thing that I can offer; your right to choose."

"Do I have to make a decision now?"

"No. Right now, we don't have any definite plans to leave, but we won't stay long; maybe a couple of months at the most."

"Right now then, I just want to spend time with you." She looked around. "It's really late. I don't want to drive an hour and a half home. Do you mind if I just crash here for a couple of hours?"

Collin looked startled at the sudden shift in the conversation. "No, not at all. You can take the bed," he started to walk toward a door on the other side of the room that Jewell hadn't noticed earlier. "I'll just sleep in one of the rooms inside. Or you can sleep in the main house if you feel more comfortable; there are plenty of rooms." Collin was babbling. He was nervous because for the first time in his life, he really wanted something. He had never wanted anything before in his life, but now he wanted, needed, something and whether he got it or not was no longer his decision.

"No, the bed is fine, but I don't want to sleep here by myself."

"Of course not." Collin answered. "I wasn't even thinking. The couch in here pulls out. I'll sleep in here so if you need anything…"

"I'm really tired. I just want to sleep, but right now, I don't want to be alone." She took his hand and pulled him toward the bedroom. She pulled down the covers, and crawled in on one side of the bed. Collin pulled the sheet over her, and lay on the bed next to her, cradling her head on his arm, and wrapping his other arm around her waist. "Thank you." She whispered as she dropped off into a peaceful slumber.

Jewell woke up with the sun sneaking in between the slits on the window blinds. She was in the bed alone. She got out of bed and walked to the door, where she saw Collin sitting in the old leather chair. When he heard her he looked up from the book he was reading. "Good morning Honeysuckle. Did you sleep well?"

"Wonderful. I would love to wake up like this every morning." She smiled as he stood up.

"I'm sure Gladys has breakfast. She makes the best biscuits and serves them with cane syrup." He took her hand and led her into the main house and down the long hallway to the kitchen in the back. True to his word, Gladys was taking a pan of biscuits out of the oven.

"Hey kids. Everyone else has already eaten. Sit down and have some biscuits. There's sausage on the table, and cane syrup is in the pitcher." Gladys smiled as she shuffled around the kitchen, pouring glasses of juice, getting plates and silverware, and making sure Collin and Jewell had everything they needed. When she was satisfied that all was in order she sat down.

Gladys sat at the table, watching them eat. "I want to talk to you two." She sat studying their faces. Reaching across the table, she took one of each of their hands and placed them together on the table, with hers covering theirs protectively. "Don't let anyone tell you what to do." She looked at them seriously, making sure that they were listening to what she said. "The *Family* can take care of itself. And the *Family* can and will take care of you too. No matter what you are told, *Family* protects *Family* and if you decide to bring Jewell into your life, then she's *Family* too. It won't be easy, but if you love each other," she paused, smiling, "it'll work itself out. If you need anything, you come to me and I'll take care of it." She stood up and left the room before either Collin or Jewell had time to process what she had said and formulate a response.

Jewell and Collin sat together quietly in the kitchen without saying anything for several minutes before Jewell finally broke the silence. "I really need to get home." Collin nodded and taking her hand, he led her back to the servants' quarters to collect her things.

Jewell drove Collin back to the hospital so he could pick up his car. As he started to get out of the car, he grabbed her hand. "It *will* work out." Jewell nodded without saying anything and watched him as he walked to his car.

CHAPTER 54

Jewell sat alone in her house. It was her day off, her father was at work, and Ashley was on a date with Ray. Jewell heard Collin's car when it drove into the driveway and she met him at the door. She didn't move to the side to let him in; instead, she stood blocking the doorway. What she had to tell him had to be short. If she let him in, if he sat down, she would lose her nerve.

Collin leaned forward to kiss her and she turned her head so he kissed her on the cheek. She suppressed a shudder as the electricity of his touch shot through her. She knew she would never find that again; she knew that she would never love anyone again. She was going to die an old spinster; a crazy cat lady. Her lips curved into a tight, painful smile at the thought.

"You're not going to come with me." It was a statement. Somehow, he knew all along that this was the choice she would make. It was almost a relief that she had made the decision; that he didn't have to tell her that it would be better for her to stay with her family. He didn't have the strength to leave her on his own, but he didn't have the heart to subject her to a life on the run, to take her away from everything she had everything she had ever known. He nodded, and started to turn to leave.

As he turned, she reached out, grabbing his arm to stop him. "Wait. It's not what you think. I can't bear the thought of you having to watch me grow old. Percy...well, the longer we're together the harder it will be for you when I..." she swallowed the tears that were trying to push through to the surface. She couldn't bring herself to say die. "...when I can't be with you anymore. I can't bear the thought of you suffering for centuries like your uncle. This way, you can remember me as I am and that way, I'll always be alive in your memories. I don't want your last thought of me to be of holding me when I die." She stepped back to close the door. "I just wanted you to know my reasons."

As she started to close the door, Collin put out his hand to stop it from closing. "I'll wait for you until the end of time. If you ever change your mind, I *will* be there. You will always be mine, Honeysuckle. I'll never love anyone else." He stepped back, dropping his hand to his side and turned to leave not wanting to see the door close.

As she watched him leave, she heard a single word echo through her mind, "forever."

www.ingramcontent.com/pod-product-compliance
Lightning Source LLC
Chambersburg PA
CBHW060804120626
46557CB00001B/86